Cherokee Joe and Jerusalem Camp

Two Full Length Western Novels

Cameron Judd

WOLFPACK PUBLISHING
EST 2013

Cherokee Joe and Jerusalem Camp: Two Full Length Western Novels
Paperback Edition

Wolfpack Publishing
5130 S. Fort Apache Rd. 215-380
Las Vegas, NV 89148

wolfpackpublishing.com

This book is a work of fiction. Any references to historical events, real people or real places are used fictitiously. Other names, characters, places and events are products of the author's imagination, and any resemblance to actual events, places or persons, living or dead, is entirely coincidental.

Paperback ISBN 978-1-63977-510-1
eBook ISBN 978-1-63977-311-4

Cherokee Joe and Jerusalem Camp

Cherokee Joe

For Denise, sister and supporter

CHAPTER 1

The hog charged and rammed its victim for the ninth time just as another .44 slug ripped through the shed wall. Joe Wolfkiller, a swarthy young man with long black hair and broad, high cheekbones sculpted by the Cherokee half of his ancestry, grimaced and thrust his face down into the mucky straw in which he lay. Splinters and grit from the punctured wall rained down around him. The hog retreated, squealed, charged a tenth time, then withdrew to the rear of the bullet-riddled shed, grunting and slobbering.

Slowly Joe Wolfkiller lifted his head, his face dappled with mud and manure and whiskered with straw. He lay behind a heavy foundation beam about ten inches high, the only piece of wood in the shed thick enough to protect him from the bullets sporadically spat toward him from the tiny house across the clearing. Cautiously he peered through a knothole toward that house.

Smoke drifted around a north-facing window. He saw movement behind the broken glass and thought of rolling closer to the shed door so that he could return fire from it, but the impulse was fleeting. Joe Wolfkiller, for once in his life, didn't want to fight, just get away. His antagonist, a usually harmless potbellied no-account named Hambone Coltrane, was not a man he wished to harm. In fact, Joe was used to thinking of Coltrane as a friend, or at least one of the closest facsimiles he had known in a largely friendless experience. Only when Coltrane was drunk and dejected, as now, did he turn sour and threatening, though never before had he tried to gun down his companion.

Behind Joe, the hog grunted loudly and sank into the reeking moist straw. Joe glanced back; tiny bloodshot eyes glared at him, full of fear and an animalistic approximation of hate.

Coltrane's voice came from the house. "You dead yet, Joe? You dead yet?"

Joe Wolfkiller put his mouth close to the knothole and shouted back. "Not dead—but this hog will be if you keep shooting!"

No answer. Silence hung heavy. Some instinct warned Joe, and he buried his face in the filth again, digging deep as another shot blasted the knothole into a ragged gash and passed through the shed to nick the hog's left ear.

The beast rose, squealing in pain, and charged Joe again. This time it bit him on the calf, jerking its head from side to side like a wolf trying to rip meat from a fresh kill. Joe let out a yell as he tugged free.

"Got ya that time, Joe—got ya!" Coltrane shouted triumphantly, misinterpreting the meaning of Joe's yell.

Joe had no time to answer, for the hog was on him again, ramming and grunting porcine threats. Joe could take no more. He rolled onto his back, aimed his mud-grimed Colt, and squeezed the trigger. The bullet took instant effect. The hog's pink eyes widened and dulled. It fell heavily to the side, a little rivulet of blood flowing from the bullet hole between and slightly above its eyes.

Joe rolled to the left and lay staring at the animal. Maybe he shouldn't have killed it, he thought. Now

Hambone really would be furious. He had always loved that hog.

"Joe?" Coltrane sounded uncertain. He had heard Joe's shot. "What'd you do just then, Joe?"

Joe wiped his pistol on his denim trousers. "Killed your hog, Hambone," he yelled through the wall.

A pause. "What'd you say, Joe?"

"I said I killed your hog."

In a moment a great muffled wail of grief reached Joe's ears. He dug himself into the mud floor again, knowing what would follow.

This time Coltrane fired three shots in quick succession, puncturing a wallboard with the first two and knocking it clean out with the third. Still vibrating, it fell back on the dead hog. As the noise of the gunfire echoed away, Joe heard Coltrane cursing in a voice hoarse with weeping.

Joe rolled back to the right, then heaved up and over the dead hog, using its warm mass for cover. Peering over its side, he eyed Coltrane's tiny house through the gap where the wall plank had been. He looked for Coltrane behind his window and did not see him.

A moment later the house's single door opened, and Coltrane came dashing out, carrying his smoking rifle, his ample belly jiggling as he ran toward the roughly built stable diagonally across the clearing. Coltrane wore galluses but no shirt. His greasy trousers rode so low that the upper part of his buttocks pooched above the baggy seat.

Joe recognized his opportunity to shoot his foe but did not take it. He still had no desire to harm Coltrane, and he felt guilty about killing Coltrane's beloved hog. It was a novel feeling. Joe Wolfkiller seldom felt guilty about anything.

"I'm sorry about the hog!" Joe yelled at the running man. "It was trying to eat my leg off."

By now, Coltrane had reached the stable. Joe wondered if

Coltrane planned to go around the stable and approach the hog shed from the side or rear. That theory was shattered by a shot from inside the stable. A terrible trumpeting whinny followed, then a dead thud.

With a burst of horror, Joe realized what Coltrane had just done. "You shot my horse, Hambone!" Joe yelled.

"It was fair—you kilt my hog!" Coltrane yelled back. "You had no call to kill my hog!"

Joe, fiercely angry, raised his pistol and impulsively fired a shot through the stable. Immediately he wished he hadn't. "Hambone! You all right?"

Hambone Coltrane, obviously unscathed, emerged from the stable and pounded heavily back to the house. Joe lowered himself behind the dead hog, wondering how long this foolish standoff would continue.

For a long time there was no sound except the wind and wails from the house as Hambone grieved over his hog. Joe thought about Coltrane's slaughter of his horse and became more philosophical about it. The horse hadn't been hard to come by, after all. He had stolen it, and its saddle too, a month before. His biggest regret was that now the horse was dead, he had no good means of escape. There was always Hambone's mount, of course, but that was nothing but a balky mule whose fastest clip was a weary lope.

Joe thought about kicking out a rear-wall plank, squeezing through to freedom, and making a run on foot, but he feared Coltrane would come after him, which could only result in his having to shoot Hambone, or vice versa.

So he just lay there, hiding behind the dead hog. Minutes passed. The day waned, and the March air began to cool, the hog cooling along with it. Joe watched shadows outside stretch east toward Missouri, growing longer and darker as the sun traveled westward and down. A gopher skittered across the clearing. Joe began to feel tired.

Hambone Coltrane's curses and moans became softer

and less frequent. Joe watched the window carefully for signs of Coltrane repositioning himself to shoot again. Every now and then he would see Coltrane's face look out, but no shooting followed. Finally, as dusk came, Joe concluded that Coltrane had gotten over his anger, or maybe had drunk himself into a stupor.

Standing inside the shed, keeping his eye on the house, Joe stretched his stiff legs and moved his body from side to side. All the filth that covered him had now dried to a thick crust that stiffened his pants and long dark coat and scabbed his skin. He longed for a good wash.

Softly, Joe walked to the door of the shed. Still watching the house, he stepped into the dusty clearing. Noiseless and light as cattail fluff in the wind, he crossed to the stable. His horse was dead, as Coltrane had said. Joe looked at it regretfully. At least he still had the saddle, which lay on its side in the corner of the stable. He picked up the saddle and heaved it onto his shoulder.

Joe was sure now that Coltrane was asleep or passed out, so he grew less cautious. He was surprised when the door opened and Hambone Coltrane came staggering out. Joe dropped the saddle and drew his pistol. Coltrane came right on toward him, carrying something. Joe saw it was his saddlebags, which he had taken into the house prior to the card game that had led to this altercation in the first place.

"I seen you leaving, Joe," Coltrane slurred, sounding meek as a puppy now. "I knew you'd want these here bags." Coltrane's face, from what Joe could see in the early evening darkness, was puffy and red, his eyes swollen from drinking and crying about the hog. Coltrane glanced down at the pistol in Joe's hand. "You don't need that, Joe. I don't want no more trouble with you."

"You wanted plenty of it before," said Joe, keeping the pistol right where it was.

"I know, and I'm mighty sorry." Coltrane had put on a

shirt sometime before and swiped the crusty sleeve of the left arm under his rheumy nose. "I didn't never want to hurt you. Not really."

"Drop the saddlebags and move over yonder," Joe said. "And keep where I can see you."

"Joe, don't treat me so. You got nothing to worry over from me."

"You gave me plenty to worry over in that hog shed. And you killed my horse."

Coltrane sniffed again. "I was wrong to do it. I admit it." A tear rolled down his face.

Joe was repulsed. He disliked drunks and trusted them less, and Coltrane was proving to be that particularly unstable kind who swing from mean to maudlin. Joe figured he could just as easily swing back to mean again. The last thought made Joe realize how unwise it would be to set out on foot, leaving Coltrane with a mount. The man might turn on him again and try to chase him down in the dark. "I'm taking your mule," Joe announced.

Coltrane nodded as if he had expected nothing else. "It's fair payment for what I done, I reckon."

"Payment, but not fair payment. The horse you shot was worth a lot more than that mule," Joe replied sourly. He felt wronged; it was his way to take bitter note of wrongs done him, overlooking those wrongs he did to others. At the moment he had all but forgotten that the slain horse was never honestly his to begin with.

"I'm a sorry old soul, Joe. I've always knowed I was," Hambone blubbered, almost ready to cry again. "You was right to shoot my hog, just to punish me for the way I done you."

"I shot it to keep it from taking a bite out of me, that's all. You can get some meat off it at least." Joe holstered his pistol and went to the stable. He led out the mule and began saddling it.

"Can't bring myself to eat that hog," Coltrane said. "My Maudie loved it since it was just a little pink thing. Treated it like a house pup that winter she died. Ever since I laid her away, that hog's always put me in mind of Maudie " He choked as a sob welled up.

Joe Wolfkiller had no time to listen to a grown man crying over a dead hog or a dead wife. He finished his saddling and mounted. The mule, not used to so light a rider, moved its ears and seemed bewildered. After some goading, the mule began to step forward. Joe kept Coltrane in the corner of his eye, just in case he had a pistol hidden on him and had done all this to get an opportunity to shoot on the sneak.

He didn't. His fleshy figure looked rather pitiful there in the darkening clearing. "Goodbye, Cherokee Joe," Coltrane said as Joe went out of sight in the dark.

Joe Wolfkiller made no reply. The mule plodded along through the thickening Kansas night as the wind grew more chilly.

It was by the name Cherokee Joe that the twenty-two-year-old halfbreed named Joe Wolfkiller was best known in the Indian Territory and up into Kansas. He had never been particularly fond of the nickname, but he was proud of the growing infamy attached to it.

Joe had known from childhood that a life of trouble lay before him. He had been able to smell it coming, as a good hunter could smell a deer or buffalo. His father, a full-blood Cherokee named Sam Wolfkiller who raised Joe alone after his white mother died giving him birth, had also foreseen his son's destiny and worried over it. Sometimes young Joe had been able to see his father's concerns reflected like the fire-light in the deep black of his eyes. Such visions had never disturbed Joe. If strife was to be his lot, let it be. He would not run from it. He would drink deeply of it, slake his greatest thirsts on it, thrive from it.

Such an attitude, predictably, had made Joe's anticipations and Sam Wolfkiller's worries self-fulfilling. Before he was into his teens, Joe Wolfkiller was known as a fighter and troublemaker among his peers in the Cherokee Nation of the Indian Territory. Before he was twenty, he was suspected in a string of thefts and beatings. One of the latter had proved nearly fatal to the victim. To the chagrin of the law and many of the Cherokees there was never enough evidence to prove Joe's guilt, though no one doubted it.

The authorities had thereafter kept a close eye on the halfbreed whom the soldiers at Fort Gibson began calling Cherokee Joe. The fact that he was neither fully Indian nor fully white was enough to make many distrust him. That he was prone to violence made him unlikable as well. The older he grew, the more Cherokee Joe found himself at odds with the world around him. Gradually he grew bitter and in an odd, paradoxical way, found his bitterness sweet. It gave him a rationale for breaking any rules he wanted to break and a justification for coddling the hatred and anger that drove him.

Joe had been on the run for many months now, living by his wits on the grasslands of Kansas, making or taking a living however he could. It had been a new accusation of crime that drove him from his home near Tahlequah. The charge was attempted murder, the victim a troublesome roughneck who had tangled with Joe several times. Now the roughneck would do nothing for the rest of his days but sit silently in a chair, staring and drooling.

But this time Joe was innocent. The man who had administered the beating was the outlaw Caul Slidell, whose gang Joe had ridden with on occasion. Slidell, like many of his ilk, frequently hid out along the rivers and ravines of the

Indian Territory. He had never liked Cherokee Joe enough to let him affiliate fully with his select band of hellriders, as he called them. Joe suspected that Slidell had deliberately set him up to look guilty.

The mule plodded through the darkness. Joe's belly was empty and grumbling, but he had no food. He swore at himself for not having thought to take food from Coltrane.

At last a distant sparkle of light off to the west caught Joe's eye. He knew the source. It was the lantern hanging out front of Shadrah Camp's Boardinghouse and Restaurant, which, along with a handful of houses, stood beside a livery stable and mercantile store where two dirt roads crossed. Joe was tempted to make for the light. It meant food, a bath, shelter, maybe a game of cards. Countering the temptation was the fact that he had little money and could easily run in to the law or some other trouble at a public stop like Camp's.

He halted the mule, weighed his options, and temptation overruled prudence. He justified the decision with the thought that maybe at the little community he could find a way to replace Coltrane's mule, by trade or theft, with a more worthy mount. He called the mule a foul name and goaded it forward. The flicker of light grew brighter and closer, and when Joe was near enough to catch a whiff of beef stew wafting out of the cafe, he was as trapped as a sailor hearing the song of Sirens.

Joe hitched the mule, then paused at the window of the cafe and examined its occupants before going to the door. He recognized no one. The door was homemade of rough lumber but beautified somewhat by a pane of red-and-white-checkered glass. Joe paused to gather his long hair in his hand and tuck it up under his wide-brimmed hat. In his youth, the teachers at the Indian Agency school had made him cut his hair short. Now he wore it long in defiance of them and their world. But when a man's belly is empty, Joe had learned, sometimes it's best to put defiance aside long enough to find a meal.

The door creaked as it opened, and everyone inside turned to watch Joe enter. From the lifting of brows and the subtle movements of the corners of mouths, Joe knew he was rousing interest. Proprietor Shadrah Camp, a beefy man in armbands and an apron, wiped his fingers on a towel and stepped up to him, lowering heavy brows, the only hair on him from the neck up.

Camp's flyspeck eyes looked Joe up and down. "You can't come in here all filthied up like that, boy," Camp said. "Take you a wash at that trough yonder if you want in here."

Joe held Camp's gaze a few seconds, then turned so abruptly that Camp was startled into a backstep. Joe heard the patrons inside give a titter of laughter at Camp's reaction.

Ignoring the cool air, Joe stripped off his jacket and shirt at the trough and washed his skin in the dirty water. He washed his hair out, too, and let the wind dry it partially before he tucked it beneath the hat again. By now, the muck on his pants and shirt was dry enough to flake off; what remained he was able to remove partially by dabbing the dirtiest spots with trough water. When he was as clean as he could get, Joe dressed again and returned to the cafe.

This time Camp did not try to stop him, though he did glance down at Joe's hip, clearly wondering if there was a pistol under the long coat. He opted not to ask.

The meal, which cost Joe almost all his money, was salted ham, potatoes, biscuits, and coffee. Joe was halfway through with it when the glass-paned door opened again. When he saw the man who walked through it, he set his coffee cup down and reached for his pistol.

The newcomer was Tom Pease, and Joe knew him well.

Chapter 2

When he noticed Cherokee Joe, Pease gave no other reaction than a fleeting look of surprise, followed at once by a slight grin. Pease glanced at the row of pegs on the wall to his right; five gunbelts hung there, but there were six patrons in the room. Joe figured that Pease would have no problem deciding which of the six had not given up his weapon.

Pease took off his hat, revealing a closely cropped head of stiff brown hair. His eyes flickered to Joe another moment; then he looked away and walked to a corner table.

Joe Wolfkiller returned to his meal, but kept Pease in the corner of his eye. He watched as Pease sat down, laid his hat on the table before him, and placed his order with Shadrah Camp. While he waited for his coffee, Pease fiddled with the crow feather stuck into the band of the battered tan hat. When his coffee arrived, Pease turned slightly in his chair so that he faced Joe Wolfkiller more squarely. His eyes lifted and looked at those of the half-breed while he took his first sip. When the cup was lowered, Pease nodded slightly, his first open acknowledgment of Joe.

Joe did not return the gesture. His right hand was still

under the table. Pease grinned again as he noted Joe's coolness, then shifted, looking away. Shortly after, Camp came in with a plate of eggs and bread.

As Camp turned away, Pease said, "Just a minute, friend," and stood, scooting back his chair.

Joe Wolfkiller watched cautiously now. Pease made a deliberate show of pulling back his coat and unbuckling the fine leather holster belt around his waist. He handed the belt, bearing a Remington pistol, to Shadrah Camp. "Hang it on them pegs for me until I go," he said. "That's the house rule, ain't it?"

"Yes, sir, it is," Camp replied. As he walked away with the gunbelt, he fired a quick glance toward Joe.

Pease sat down again and looked back at Joe, smiling openly and lifting his coffee cup in salute. Joe relaxed somewhat; he recognized Pease's relinquishing his pistol as an obvious message of nonaggression. Still he did not let his hand drift far from his sidearm, for he knew from experience that Tom Pease was not to be trusted.

Pease gulped down his meal like a hungry dog, then wiped a checked napkin over his mouth. Joe remained at his table even though his meal was finished; he wanted to keep his eye on Pease. Something in Pease's manner suggested that this chance encounter would not pass without words, and Joe had to admit some curiosity about what Pease would have to say.

Pease stood, fished coins from his pocket, and laid them beside his plate. He picked up his hat and coffee and walked over to Joe's table.

Joe stared up at the tall, gangly man dressed in woolen trousers, a faded blue collarless shirt, checkered vest, and a long-tailed overjacket. Pease's soft leather boots reached up almost to his knees, the trousers tucked down into them.

"Howdy, Joe," Pease said quietly. "Mind if I have a seat?"

Joe's stare gave no permission, but no denial either. That

was good enough for Pease. He pulled back the chair across from Joe's and sat. "Didn't expect to walk in here and find Cherokee Joe filling his gullet," Pease said.

"What do you want?" Joe Wolfkiller was always forthright.

"Just to talk to you," Pease said. "I'm glad to run into you—there's something you ought to know."

"Say what you've got to say."

"All right. It's about your father."

Joe Wolfkiller felt a prickle on the back of his neck. He had not been in contact with Sam Wolfkiller in months. A deep-rooted fear was that his father would come to harm, or the end of his life, with him far away.

Pease took another swallow of coffee and looked solemn. "Sam's in a poor way, Joe. He's bad sick, real bad."

Dread settled over Joe Wolfkiller. "How long?"

"Three weeks, maybe a month. He ain't long for this world, from what I hear. He's been calling for you to come back."

Joe's heart sped in his chest, though he presented no change of expression. He studied Pease's face, his eyes, looking for signs of deception. He found none. "I can't go back," Joe said. "There's trouble waiting for me in the Territory."

"It's your choice. Look, Joe, you and me have had our differences. I could have walked out of here and not told you about your father, and what little conscience I got left wouldn't have hurt me enough to make me scratch. I don't figure I owe you nothing. But I figure a man has a right to know when his father's calling for him."

"If I return to the Territory, I'll end up in Parker's jail."

"Not if you don't get caught, you won't."

Joe thought it over. A surge of uncomfortable heat was rising in his gut. He did not like to admit fear, even to himself, but the cold truth was that the prospect of returning to the Indian Territory frightened him. If it was common knowledge that Sam Wolfkiller was ill and calling for him, the law would be lying in wait for the son's return. Joe was ever mindful of the attempted murder charge pending against him across the Territory border.

Pease resettled himself and gave Joe a sincere look. "Listen, Joe, I know it ain't my business, and you probably don't want me nowhere around, but by Satan's granny, if you want me to go with you, I will. I'll do whatever I can to let you see Sam and then get you safe out of the Territory again."

Now Joe Wolfkiller seemed to withdraw. A hard, impenetrable coldness frosted his small eyes. "Why should I trust you?" he said. "I know the man you are."

Pease fidgeted uncomfortably. "You got cause to feel that way, I admit. There ain't nothing I can tell you but I'm a better man now than I was when all that other happened. Besides, you paid me back fair and square. I hated you for it, but I know I got what I deserved."

Through Joe's mind played the memory of Pease's treachery. Two years ago it had been. He, Pease, and two others had broken into a reservation store by night and forced open its strongbox. They had been detected. Men had come, bearing badges and guns. There had been shooting. Pease deserted Joe in a narrow graveled wash, forcing him to shoot his way out only to find his horse gone. Pease had taken it to replace his own, which had thrown a shoe. Joe fled on foot, the darkness his only ally. Amazingly, he came through the encounter alive and uncaptured, swearing vengeance upon Tom Pease. He had achieved that vengeance shortly afterward, knifing Pease so badly he had almost died. Glancing down now at Pease's left hand, Joe noted the long scar across his palm, a vestige of a slash received as Pease tried to push away Joe's blade.

"I'm ready to put all our trouble behind, Joe," Pease said. "A man can't carry his grudges forever."

That was a novel notion for Joe Wolfkiller, who had never let a grudge go in his life. He wondered if Pease might be sincere.

Still faced by Joe's silent stare, Pease exhaled loudly. "Well, Joe, I can see this is over and done. I've done the right thing by telling you about Sam, and I'm ready to help you if you're willing. And if you're not, I'll just walk out of here and ride away."

Joe lowered his head a moment, then raised it again. "I'll go with you," he said. "But if you turn on me, Pease, this time my knife will cut out your heart."

"I won't turn on you. You'll see what I mean when I say I'm a better man. We'll ride out tomorrow."

"Tomorrow," said Joe Wolfkiller.

Joe had known little good fortune in his life and was surprised when some came his way the next morning. Pease eyed the recalcitrant mule Joe had been riding and declared it unsuitable for the long ride back to Joe's home in the Cherokee Nation. Shadrah Camp ran a few horses for trade in a lot a hundred yards behind the boarding house, and there Pease haggled, threw in a little cash, and replaced the mule with a quarter horse that was old but somewhat better.

"It's yours, Joe," Pease said.

Camp, meanwhile, was taking a closer look at the mule he had just accepted as partial payment for the horse. "This looks like Hambone Coltrane's mule," he said.

"It was, until I won it on a fair wager," Joe replied.

Camp, still maintaining a cautious tread around the grim halfbreed, cast a suspicious glance but wisely said nothing.

"He's thinking you stole it," Pease side whispered.

"Let him say it to my face," Joe replied coldly. "He'll regret it for the rest of a short life."

Pease wondered why Joe Wolfkiller was so offended at being thought a thief when he truly had been a thief so many times. Joe had always been hard for Pease to decipher.

They mounted and rode southeast. "I want to know why you were willing to give money to get me a horse," Joe said.

"Because I want you to know I mean it about making up for what's been wrong between us," Pease replied. "You can pay me back later, I figure."

Joe thought about it, feeling suspicious. Why was Pease here in Kansas to begin with? He had always stayed in Arkansas or around the railroad stations in the Indian Territory. Despite his doubts, Joe continued riding beside his sometime partner and sometime foe, carrying distrust like an unseen mantle over his shoulders.

By the time Joe and Pease were deep into the wide bluestem grasslands of the Flint Hills, Joe knew that Pease really had changed in one way, from taciturn to talkative.

As the miles dropped away behind them, Pease kept up a continual droning chatter, talking in his Arkansas brogue of the changes that were coming to the world Joe had known all his life. "Mark my words, the Indian Territory like we know it ain't long to be," Pease said. "Them Washington gents is getting ready to open the district up for settlers, and when they do, look out and stand aside! Satan's granny, Joe, when I rode up a week ago, there was already wagonloads of folk setting up camps all along the south Kansas border, just waiting for word to start their run. Give it a few more weeks, and you'll see thousands more joining them, snorting steam and ready to race."

"Those lands were promised by the United States to the Indians for as long as the rivers run," Joe commented. His words carried no passion. Joe had learned the futility of raging at the broken promises of the whites. Rage achieved nothing. Careful vengeance did.

"What the government gives, the government takes

away." Pease had no more affection for the government than Joe. The son of an embittered Arkansas ex-Confederate, Pease kept alive his father's dark viewpoint on the conflict of the 1860s. "The Five Civilized Tribes ain't been forgave yet for siding with the South against the Yankee aggression."

Even so politically apathetic a fellow as Joe Wolfkiller understood the situation Pease referred to. The Five Civilized Tribes, consisting of the Choctaws, Cherokees, Creeks, Seminoles, and Chickasaws, had signed individual agreements after the outbreak of the Civil War to support the Confederacy. The Cherokees had been divided on the issue, but because many prominent Cherokees owned slaves, the Southern cause won the Cherokee Nation's official allegiance. When the war ended, the triumphant U.S. government had used a predictable means to punish the Civilized Tribes for their part in the rebellion. They forced the Tribes to cede portions of their western Territory lands to serve as homes for the Kiowa, Osage, Comanche, Arapaho, and others.

In the midst of the ceded portion, however, sprawled the "unassigned lands," or "Oklahoma," the "district" Pease had referred to. This section was held by no tribe, and for years land-hungry whites called Boomers had advocated the view that the district was not properly a part of the Indian Territory and should be opened for settlement.

Some of the most radical Boomers, led by a Kansan named David L. Payne, had attempted to establish settlements within the Indian Territory but had been driven out by Fort Reno troops assigned to protect the Territory. The Boomer movement now concentrated mostly on influencing Congress, and the conventional wisdom was that soon the Boomers would prevail in Washington.

Joe didn't doubt it. When government and Indian faced off, the Indian always lost. It was an old story for Joe. As a child, he had watched the white man maintain a political grip on the Indians of the Territory, even though those Indians were in theory supposed to be largely independent. Early on, cattlemen had trespassed on Territory grazing lands and had carved major cattle trails right through Indian lands to the Kansas cowtowns. To their credit, many cattlemen faithfully paid the per head trail tolls charged by the tribes and enforced in the Cherokee Nation by the police organization called the Cherokee Light Horse. But many other cattlemen were defiant.

The worst part to young Joe had been seeing Indian men degrade themselves before white cattlemen hoping for a handout. Even Sam Wolfkiller had done it from time to time, much to Joe's shame. It had always been heartbreaking to see Sam Wolfkiller grinning as he led away a scrawny longhorn already on its last legs, happy to have received a pittance from a Texas trail boss. Sam Wolfkiller had always said such placations were gifts. Joe had not agreed. Nothing bought at the price of a man's dignity was a gift in his book.

The railroad boom had changed the cattle business since those earlier cattle drive days and changed the landscape in the process. Now smoking locomotives dragged long lines of freight and passenger cars across the Territory plains. Early in the previous decade, the Missouri, Kansas, and Texas Railroad had built a route southward through the heart of the Cherokee Nation, passing through Fort Gibson and providing a direct connection between Texas to the south and Kansas on the north. The Atchison, Topeka, and Santa Fe also ran a line through the enticing unassigned lands. There was talk that the tiny railroad stations along the Santa Fe would become instant cities once the government opened the district for settlement.

Pease rattled on about such changes until Joe was weary of it. As night fell and the riders prepared to make camp along an old cattle trail, Joe turned to Pease as the latter built a fire. "Why are you really riding with me?" he asked.

Pease seemed surprised. "I done told you. Because I want to make up for all them bad things before." He paused. "Don't you believe me, Joe?"

Joe didn't answer.

"There—see them?"

Pease was crouched alongside Joe Wolfkiller in a cluster of brush growing around the base of a cottonwood on the north bank of a little rivulet beside which they had stopped for water and rest. Far down a shallow grassland slope beyond them were two riders, slowly approaching.

"They saw us," Pease said.

"No," Joe replied. "I don't believe they did."

"They saw us," Pease reaffirmed. "I don't reckon it matters though."

"It can matter to me. I'm wanted here."

They were in the Cherokee Nation now, near the Neosho Paver and about twenty-five miles north of Fort Gibson. Since crossing the Territory border, Joe had been even more tense and distrustful of Pease than before. He had several reasons. For one thing, Pease was unwilling to discuss Sam Wolfkiller's purported illness at any length. Further, Pease had grown noticeably more nervous the farther they had gone. Nevertheless, Joe had continued riding with Pease, wondering if he were foolish for it.

"I'll go down and meet them, talk to them, just to keep everything friendly," Pease said abruptly.

"No!" said Joe.

It was too late. Pease was already standing and waving. He shouted a halloo and splashed across the rivulet. Joe swore and ducked lower in the brush.

Pease walked energetically down the slope toward the riders, who put their hands on their rifles as soon as they saw him. Pease reached them and talked with big gestures. The riders never unbooted their rifles. Finally Pease pointed back up the slope toward Joe.

When he started back up the slope again, the riders came with him.

Chapter 3

Joe Wolfkiller looked back at the dark eyes glittering at him from the other side of the campfire and thought the thoughts of a mouse surrounded by cats. The two riders Pease had greeted on the plain sat drinking coffee, talking to Pease about this and that, and casting discomforting glances at Joe. Their names, they said, were John Berg and Arasmus Little, and they were railroad men working for the Santa Fe line. Why they were out riding these parts alone they did not say.

Joe did not believe their story, nor did he even remotely trust Pease anymore. There was something unseen at work here, something hiding behind a facade of small talk and forced casualness. Joe determined that he would remain with Pease no longer, but he could not simply rise and leave, not with those two men watching him so closely. Berg's eyes reminded Joe of the pink orbs of the hog he had killed back in Hambone Coltrane's shed. Beyond that, there was something uncomfortably familiar about Berg.

Pease seemed different now that the others had joined them. He was jovial, almost giddy, cracking silly jokes and laughing at them, even when nobody else did. He walked around a lot, mouth running on, legs and arms in constant nervous motion. Joe chided himself for having ridden this far with him. True, Pease had introduced Joe to the newcomers by the false name of Henry Feather and said they were riding to seek jobs as deputies of Judge Parker over in Arkansas, but Joe did not feel the story was believed. The stares were too continual and suspicious.

"Mr. Feather, would you like a cup of coffee?" Berg asked.

"No. I don't drink coffee much."

"Smart Indian, smart Indian. The stuff keeps me from sleeping, but I can't bring myself to get shut of it. You're a sound sleeper, I'll bet, Mr. Feather."

"I sleep well."

"I'll bet you do, yes, sir." Berg stood and poured the remnants of his own coffee on the ground. "Well, I'm ready to turn in. Like as not, I'll lay awake two hours before I can get my eyes to stay shut. Then I'll have to wake up for a squirt. Too much coffee, that's what it is."

Joe felt his hackles rise. Berg's purposeless commentary was too artificial. Joe's hand, hidden beneath a blanket he had thrown over himself, slipped to the butt of his pistol.

But nothing happened. Berg spread his bedroll and crawled in, yawning broadly and snoring within five minutes despite his prediction of sleeplessness. The others spread their bedrolls as well.

Pease walked up to Joe and looked down at him questioningly. "Why you looking that way, Joe?" he whispered. "There ain't nothing wrong with them two."

Joe looked into Pease's eyes. "If I find you have lied to me, Pease, I'll see you repaid double for it."

Pease responded with only a vague grunt. "I'm turning in," he said, and headed for his bedroll.

———

It all came to a head exactly an hour and fourteen minutes later.

Joe Wolfkiller was huddled beneath his blankets, and though his body was weary, his mind was alive and racing. He had kept silent, feigning sleep, for more than an hour. He was still trying to fetch out the memory of whom Berg reminded him of, but mostly he was just waiting until he was sure the others were not awake, so he could make his run.

At last he decided to try. Making no noise, he sat up. The fire was a feeble flame on red embers, smoking up into the darkness. Snores rose from three bedrolls. Joe laid his blanket aside and began to stand. He was fully clothed, and his pistol was still holstered at his hip.

Berg rolled over and began to sit up just as Joe was on the verge of creeping toward the horses. Joe saw it, turned to the side, and pretended to beat something out of his blanket.

"What's wrong, Mr. Feather?" Berg asked softly.

"Spark from the fire," Joe replied. Inwardly he fumed. Now he would have to wait even longer.

"That right, Mr. Feather?" Berg asked—and right then Joe Wolfkiller knew him.

John Berg was a deputy of Judge Parker's court. Joe had seen him the very night Tom Pease had run out on him after the robbery that went sour. It made sense now. Pease had betrayed him. Probably his story of Sam Wolfkiller's illness was a lie designed to lure him across the Indian Territory border. No wonder Pease had been willing to help him buy a horse. For all Joe knew, Pease might have turned deputy himself.

The scene that followed was eerie and muted in the dim light of the fire and the dimmer light of the moon. Joe Wolfkiller tossed his blanket aside and rose, drawing his pistol at the same moment.

John Berg simultaneously threw his blanket aside to expose a sawed-off Greener shotgun to the red glow of the fire. "That's enough stirring around, right there, Cherokee Joe," Berg said. "You ain't going nowhere but to Arkansas."

At the same time, Little and Pease also came awake, if they had really been asleep at all, and threw aside their blankets to reveal drawn weapons. Pease had a pistol, Little a shotgun that was twin to Berg's.

"Well, Joe, looks like it's time for taking off masks, huh?" Pease said, laughing his giddy laugh.

"I'll kill you, Pease." Joe had not let go of his pistol.

"You're threatening a soon-to-be-reinstated deputy of the Arkansas court," Pease replied. "Bringing in Cherokee Joe ought to be enough to put me back in the judge's good graces."

"Drop that pistol, halfbreed," Berg ordered.

"That's right, Joe, drop it." Pease chortled. "Drop it and come in alive, and let Judge Parker see that the very deputy he fired for worthless is good enough to bring in Cherokee Joe."

Joe did not drop his pistol. "My father?" he asked Pease.

"Dead, Joe. Gunned down he was by Caul Slidell himself in a robbery down at the Guthrie rail station. He and a bunch of his redskin friends had hired out to freight something to the station for somebody or other. Picked a bad time to go—Slidell shot down three of them just for the fun of seeing a little Cherokee blood. Sam, he coughed up aplenty of it before he kicked off." Pease chortled.

"Drop the pistol, halfbreed," Berg commanded again.

Joe looked from face to face, all featureless in the fading red fire-glow. He sighed loudly, then let his pistol fall to the ground.

Pease chuckled and stepped forward. Berg and Little lowered their shotguns and did the same, all eager to be the first to lay hand officially on the much-wanted Cherokee Joe, now a prisoner of Parker's court.

Joe Wolfkiller dropped with the speed of a stone. He

landed flat on his stomach, sweeping up the pistol he had let fall. Little raised his shotgun and fired, but the shot passed a good two feet above Cherokee Joe's head. Joe's aim, not as hurried, was better. Little took the bullet in the stomach and buckled. Berg swore and fired off his Greener. Joe felt pellets fan past and plow the ground beside him. His responding shot passed through Berg's skull, killing him before he could fall.

Pease fired next, but he was scared and might as well have aimed at the sky. Joe rolled and fired three quick blasts that caught Pease in the chest so firmly that his feet kicked off the ground. He fell back, took one rattling breath, and died.

Little was still alive. Joe walked over to him and looked down. Little had lost his shotgun when he fell and now scrambled toward it. Joe kicked it away, then with a swing of the same foot kicked Little backward and down.

He raised his pistol and aimed it at Little's face. The deputy closed his eyes.

Joe diverted the pistol as he squeezed the trigger, sending the slug into the dirt beside Little's ear. He holstered the empty pistol, walked over to Little's shotgun, and picked it up. "If you live, you spread word," he said to Little, who was gasping for breath like a man pulled from a lake. "Tell it that Cherokee Joe is going to find Caul Slidell and kill him, and that he will take Slidell's scalp in return for the life of Sam Wolfkiller. You understand, Deputy?"

"Yes, yes." Little's voice sounded high-pitched with pain and fear. "Thank you, thank you for letting me live."

"Slidell—where can I find him?"

"Kansas, somewhere north of Great Bend. That's the best we've heard."

Joe turned and collected the guns from the fallen men, pausing long enough to spit in the face of Tom Pease as he reloaded his pistol. He considered taking Pease's scalp, but he had never scalped anyone before and was not sure how, so he didn't. There was another reason: He didn't want Little to see how badly he was shaking.

Joe Wolfkiller had always wondered what it would feel like to kill another man. Now he knew. It made him feel sick and scared.

The implications of what had happened were clear. This would mean the gallows for him if he was caught, and the thought scared him terribly, for he had a particular horror of hanging, having once witnessed such an execution during a visit with Sam Wolfkiller to Fort Smith.

Joe selected the best two horses from those hobbled nearby and saddled them with the best saddles. He would ride one as hard as he could, then switch to the other and ride hard some more. He took the saddlebags too, loaded with trail food and shells for the Greeners. Little still lay on the ground, moaning and watching Joe in silence. When Joe was done with his preparations, he mounted and rode off. He stopped shortly after he was out of sight of the camp, pausing only long enough to be sick. Then he rode on.

He rode as if the devil were nipping his tail. A murky moon sailed above, and cold air numbed his ears and nose. Hunger and thirst raged within, but he ignored them. He fancied he heard horsemen closing in upon him in the darkness, though he knew this was all but impossible. Not enough time had passed.

Joe rode for many hours before he stopped. Both mounts were dripping and exhausted by then, and Joe's head was reeling. He had grown too weary for the pretense of fearlessness that fooled most others and usually himself. He wished he had not told Little to spread word of his plans to kill Caul Slidell. Such talk would only make him seem all the more dangerous and murderous, and make capture and death on the gallows come all the sooner.

Joe hobbled the horses. He still felt sick in his stomach and tight in his groin, and every time he thought of his father's death, he suffered great waves of grief. Though Pease had proved untruthful, Joe did not doubt that he spoke truly about the shooting of Sam Wolfkiller, for Pease no longer had a motive to lie when he told him of that.

Joe wrapped himself in a blanket and lay down in a little ravine where he shivered and fought back the urge to weep. Soon it would be dawn. He desperately needed rest before continuing.

Dreams came with sleep. At first they were dreams of Parker's court, his jail, his gallows built to accommodate as many as a dozen doomed men. He dreamed of the somber face of George Maledon, Parker's efficient hangman. Joe had heard Maledon discussing his craft that day he had seen the hanging in Fort Smith. In his restless imaginings Joe now stood on the gallows, the twelve-by-twelve beam above his head, as Maledon slipped the noose over his head, placing its nine coils carefully in the empty place behind his left jawbone. He smelled the oily pitch Maledon coated his ropes with and heard Maledon's matter-of-fact voice in his ear: "Don't worry, Cherokee Joe, it'll be a quick passing for you. The secret of a clean hanging is an old pre-stretched rope and a good size knot. You're a light fellow, so I'm dropping you eight feet and eight inches to make sure it's a good snap. You won't feel it, at least not much."

Then, shortly before they dropped the trap from under him, Joe twisted his head and saw Parker standing in his window, watching as he always watched the hangings he mandated.

Joe jerked awake. Maledon and the gallows vanished. Nothing now but the dark sky above and the wind through the grass. He fell asleep again, and again he dreamed.

But this time the dream was very different—and confusing, even in his sleep. He was no longer in the Indian Territory but in some mountainous green region, wearing the sparse clothing of a Cherokee hunter from long past days. A rocky stream gushed down a lush hillside before him. A hazy, cloud muted daylight permeated the scene. Joe felt a gnawing dread as his eyes were drawn to a deep pool in the midst of the stream. The pool began to move.

A great coiling glistening thing rose from the water, a horned and scaly beast with a body thick as the trunk of a large tree, ringed with brilliant colors that caught and amplified the light. The boulder-size head rose, reaching up nearly to the treetops, and then it looked at him, just as the sun pierced the clouds and struck it.

A lightning bolt flash of reflected light emanated from a shining crystalline crest on the beast's forehead, struck Joe squarely in the face, and he fell back, covering his blinded eyes with his hands as the massive head came down upon him, the mouth open and dripping.

Joe yelled when he awoke and for a terrible moment thought his dream was not a dream, for a bright light still flashed in his eyes. He sat up and saw he was still in the ravine, damp with dew and shaking from cold and fear, and knew it had all been a vivid nightmare, for the light in his eyes was that of the rising sun.

He stood, relieved but still shaking, and wrapped his arms around himself. A shudder racked him from head to toe, and he took deep breaths until he was calm.

The horses grazed about fifty feet away, their legs still firmly hobbled. Joe had not taken the saddles off them. They lifted their heads and looked at him, standing side by side. And then Joe blinked in surprise, for he saw a third horse there.

He turned and saw a Cherokee man kneeling on a blanket not twenty feet from him. He was ancient and thin, wearing a pair of store bought wool trousers, tall boots, and an oversized threadbare coat of faded blue, a coat like those the Union troops had worn more than two decades ago in the Civil War. The old man was staring deeply into his cupped hands and seemed as oblivious to Joe's presence as the morning sun.

Chapter 4

In the span of two breaths Joe Wolfkiller's pistol was leveled on the old man. "Who are you?" Joe demanded.

The old man drew his cupped hands closer to his face and frowned as if Joe's threatening voice were no more than an irritating distraction.

"I asked you who you are!" Joe said. The pistol was heavy and cold in his hand, and his muscles hurt from his tense sleep on hard earth in cold air. He was embarrassed to note that he was shaking.

The old man lowered his hands, sighed, and shook his head. He dug his left hand into a pocket of the coat, causing Joe a moment of uncertainty, but all he drew out was a little hide pouch. Whatever had been in his hands he enclosed carefully in the hide and thrust into his pocket. Only now did he look at Joe, a mildly exasperated expression on his face. "Hello, Joe Wolfkiller," he said. "I can tell you this much: There are riders coming from the southeast, and they will reach you soon if you do not run very fast and turn westward. If you had kept your mouth shut, I might have been able to tell you how many they are and how many guns they carry."

"Tell me who you are, or I will kill you," Joe said.

"I am the wind, the sun, the earth, the voice of the toad, and the eye of the eagle." After that grandiose pronouncement, the ancient man gave Joe a polite little tea party smile like an old woman's, his black eyes crinkling until they almost vanished in the double handfuls of weathered wrinkles surrounding them.

"You are a fool, that I can see," Joe replied. He was wary of this strange old fellow. "What is your name?"

The silver-haired Indian shrugged. "What difference does a name make? But call me Bunyan if you wish. It is as good a name as any."

Joe thought that a peculiar name for an Indian. He lowered his pistol a little. "How do you know my name, Bunyan?"

"I know what the eagle knows. I fly across the earth and see all things. My skills as a magician have told me that before me stands the young man named Joe Wolfkiller, a great brave warrior feared and wanted by the white man."

Joe was beginning to wonder if this was real or just a continuation of his dreams. "What do you mean, a magician?"

The old man looked at the sky and shook his head again. His white hair was stiff as broom straw and all but rustled with each movement of his head. "How little do our young remember of the old ways!" he said, mostly to himself. "Now the young know only the ways of the white men and the white doctors, whose ways work well enough for their own but are often poison to the Cherokees." He looked squarely at Joe now. "I am a magician, a conjurer. I am wise in the old lore, and nothing escapes my knowledge."

"You know, then, that I'm thinking about killing you."

"Of course I know this, Joe Wolfkiller. But you would not be wise to slay me because I want to help you escape the great evil coming upon you."

"How can you help me, old babbler?"

The old fellow reached into his pocket again and with a broad grin pulled out the little pouch he had placed there earlier. "With this," he answered. "It tells me all I need to know. It is this crystal that told me your name and warned me of the danger coming."

"Crystal?" Now Joe understood. "A divining crystal?"

"The best divining crystal of them all."

"I don't believe in divining crystals. I believe in this." Joe shook the pistol.

"I had one of those too, and also believed in it very much, but now I've got it no longer," the old man said. "I sold it to help me get money enough to buy that horse yonder and begin my journey."

"I have a journey of my own and no time to hear of yours, you old Raven Mocker." Joe holstered his pistol, now sure his unexpected companion was senile and harmless.

Until now, the old man's face had been lighted with a friendly expression. Now the lines of his face straightened and narrowed and he looked deeply offended. "I am no Raven Mocker," he said. "The Raven Mocker takes life—I seek to give it. I eat no man's heart. If you are wise, you will let me ride with you and listen to my counsel. Otherwise those who pursue you will kill you, Joe Wolfkiller. But first you must eat."

It was the food that finally led Joe Wolfkiller to accept the company of the old man who called himself Bunyan. From a large pocket stitched inside the oversized Union coat the old fellow pulled half a loaf of stale bread, some dried meat, and a small flour sack nearly filled with parched corn. Joe ate hungrily, feeling the food give him new strength. When it came time to ride again, Joe grumpily agreed to let the old man come along. "But if you get in my way, old babbler, or slow me down, I will leave you," Joe warned.

"We must ride straight west," the old man said.

"No. It's north for me, so I can reach the Territory border sooner."

"Very well, Joe Wolfkiller," the other replied. "North is the best direction for me, even if you should avoid it. But if you insist upon riding this direction, I must tell you that when we see the riders who are chasing you, I will be forced to leave you, for my quest is too important to be interrupted by death."

And so they rode north, the old man twenty paces behind Joe. Joe felt less panicked today than the day before. He did not push his horses as hard, feeling he had a good lead on any pursuers. Even so, he looked back repeatedly. All he saw was the slumped, almost comical figure of the old Cherokee astride his bone-bag horse. Joe wondered which was more thin and decrepit—horse or rider.

The sun rose higher and brightened the land, though a rising cloudbank scudding from the west raised the prospect of a murky midday and a rainy afternoon.

After a while the old Indian began a chanting refrain that he repeated endlessly: *"Ha tciye-hyuwe, Ha wiye-hyuwe, Ye we-yuwehe, Ha wiyehyu-uwe..."*

As the sky darkened at the end of the day, Joe felt fear rising again. Against that background the old man's song became irksome. At last he turned in his saddle. "Old babbler, close your mouth. You are as bothersome as a cricket in a corner."

"It is only the first lines of a song sung by mothers to babies," the old man replied. "Did not your mother sing the old songs to you, Joe?"

"My mother died giving me birth. And she was white. She would not have known the old songs."

"Ah, ah yes, I had forgotten that."

"You had not forgotten. You never knew. Crystal stones do not whisper words to old babblers, else they would have told our fathers long ago how to defeat the whites."

"If the crystal is powerless, then how, Joe Wolfkiller, did I know your name?" the old man asked.

Joe did not answer him. He was twisted in his saddle, looking at the southern horizon behind the older rider. The sun had met the cloudbank long before, but its rays still shone behind the clearer sky to the south, and in the glow Joe clearly saw a little line of riders approaching.

The old Indian also looked back. After gazing a few moments, he turned a wry look back to the halfbreed. "I told you," he said. "You should always listen when a wise conjurer speaks."

"Shut up," Joe said. "Ride down that way—there's a ravine. If we make the horses lie down in it and hide with them, they will go past us."

By the time Joe Wolfkiller and the old man crossed into Kansas, the halfbreed's attitude about the old man had changed. Of the three riders who had swept past the ravine, Joe had recognized two as deputies of Parker's court. He was surprised to have been pursued so closely so quickly. It could only have meant that the pursuing deputies had been close when he had the shootout with Pease and the others. Why there were so many deputies in that area Joe could only guess. Maybe they had hints that Caul Slidell or some other desperado was in the region.

Whatever the case, they had come far more quickly than Joe had expected, and the old self-proclaimed conjurer had been completely accurate in his prediction of the route by which pursuit would come. Joe wasn't ready to put his trust in divining crystals just yet, but he was impressed and interested in this Bunyan. Joe had come to believe that Bunyan wasn't his real name. It hardly sounded appropriate for a Cherokee conjurer, and from the way the old man smiled whenever the name called, Joe suspected that *Bunyan* was just a word the man had chosen because its ring was pleasant to his ear.

Crossing the Territory border had calmed Joe, though it hardly marked the end of his danger. He could be arrested in Kansas just as easily as in the Territory. Little, he figured, must have lived, at least long enough to find the other deputies and tell them the direction his assailant had fled. Joe told himself that he hoped Little was as dead as the others now, but he knew it wasn't true. The killing of Pease and Berg still left a bad taste in Joe's mouth, though he would never have admitted it to anyone else.

It shouldn't be that way. Vengeance and the appreciation of battle was an ancient part of the Cherokee tradition that Joe saw as his heritage. Yet every time he thought about the gun battle, he felt as if snakes were swimming in his stomach.

Supper was more dried meat and parched corn. They built no fire.

"Tell me more about your quest," Joe asked his companion. "Where are you bound?"

"I'm bound for Hays City," the old man said. His voice was creamy with age, worn smooth as a century-old doorstep. "There I will find the one I seek—or so my crystal tells me."

"Where did you get your crystal?"

"From my father, who died on the Trail of Tears and was a greater conjurer even than me until he became a Baptist preacher and had to give it up. The crystal came to him from my grandfather, and it had come to my grandfather from his mother's brother, back in the days of his youth when he lived in the town of Kanuga in the land that used to be our people's. Where it came from before that I will not tell, for it is a great secret."

"Is who you are going to find a secret, too?"

"No secret. I am going to find my daughter and give to her a great treasure." He smiled the old lady smile again and glanced around slyly.

"A treasure? What kind of treasure?"

"I will speak no more of it," he said.

"Tell me, Bunyan. I want to know what this treasure is."

The old man still refused to talk. Joe pressed a new question. "Why is your daughter in Hays City?" he asked.

"I will sleep now," the old man said abruptly. He spread his blankets, lay down, and quickly began snoring.

He truly is crazy, Joe thought as he watched the old man sleep. As crazy as a mad dog. But his talk of treasure may not be crazy. Maybe it is a treasure he will be willing to share... or perhaps he will find himself sharing it whether he wills it or not.

Such thoughts made Joe feel strong and dangerous, and he enjoyed them as he drifted off to sleep.

When Joe woke up, the old man was sitting alone in the dawn light looking into his hands again, but this time he wasn't consulting his divining stone. He was reading from a book covered with a homemade binder of fringed leather. When he looked up and saw Joe blearily watching him, the old man smiled. "A quest is a wonderful thing," he said. "I have told you of mine. What is yours, that put the riders onto your trail?"

He doesn't know about the killings, Joe thought. *Divining stone or not, he doesn't know.*

"My quest is to go north of Great Bend, find a man named Caul Slidell, and kill him," Joe replied.

"I have heard of this Slidell," the old man said. "He is a bad white man. Is that why you wish to kill him?"

"He killed my father, Sam Wolfkiller, at the railroad station in Guthrie."

"Yes. I heard that Sam Wolfkiller was dead, but I did not know it was Caul Slidell who killed him."

"You knew my father?"

"I know all men. Most of them, at least."

They rode, side by side this time. "You still have not told me why you were chased by these riders that my crystal foresaw," the old man said.

"I had trouble in the Territory. I was forced to flee."

"Did this trouble involve killing?"

"Why should I tell you? Tell me about this treasure instead."

"It is a treasure for my daughter alone. When she has it, I can be at peace."

"If you won't talk about the treasure, talk about your daughter. Is she pretty?"

The old man's answer was less ready this time. "She was pretty when last I saw her. She was pretty like a tiny flower held in my arms."

Joe took a moment to understand. "You haven't seen her since she was a baby?"

"No."

"Who raised her?"

"A family that is now in Hays City."

"A white family?"

A pause. "There was no other way. My wife died giving her birth, just like your mother did. I could not care for her well enough alone. The white man and his wife, they said they would raise her like she was their child, and I gave her up to them."

"Your crystal could find no better way, eh?"

"Don't scoff at powerful things, Joe Wolfkiller. The crystal told me your name. It told me of your danger, and of the riders' coming. It saved your life."

"Then why couldn't it tell you what trouble I was in?" The awe that Joe had experienced after seeing the riders pass as predicted was falling away as his usual cynical skepticism regained ground.

"I told you: Do not scoff at the crystal. It is a dangerous thing to do."

Joe looked darkly at the old man. "Are you threatening me, old babbler?"

"It is no threat to give a warning to one who is in danger."

"Am I in danger, old man?"

"Cherokee Joe, they say, is always in danger. And any near him, they are in danger too."

"Then why are you riding with me?"

"Because our paths lie over the same ground. Besides, I like you. Me and my crystal, maybe we can keep you alive."

"So I can grow old and silver-haired and babble like you? That doesn't sound good to me. Once Caul Slidell is dead, I don't care what happens to me. I ride a death road, old man."

"Then you do need me," the other said. "I have been riding that same road for many days now."

"What does that mean?"

"My crystal. It has told me that soon I am going to die."

Chapter 5

When they entered the southeastern corner of Sedgwick County, the old Indian pulled his scrawny horse to a halt, took a deep breath, slid out of the saddle, and collapsed on the ground.

Joe, riding slightly in the lead again, was a hundred yards ahead before he heard the man's feeble cry for help. Joe reined in, turned, and saw him rolling from side to side on the ground, moaning and gripping his middle. By the time Joe galloped back to him, he had emptied the meager contents of his stomach onto the ground beside him.

Joe leaped down from his saddle and ran to his side. "Old babbler, what's wrong with you?" he said, kneeling.

"I am dying," the old man moaned.

"Dying? You can't die here."

"It seems as good a place to die as any."

Joe had no idea what to do. "Come on, you white-headed fool. Get up and get on your ugly horse."

"No, no. I can't." He hacked and spat up a little more, making a sour face afterward. "Joe Wolfkiller, can you read?" he asked.

"Yes, some."

"Good. In my saddle pouch, the old book. .."

Joe rose, disturbed by all this and wishing he had never taken up with the old man. He opened the saddlebag and found it stuffed with bottles and bags of unidentifiable concoctions, assorted clay and corncob pipes, and tobacco in a tin. The leather-covered book was in the midst of it all. He retrieved it and went to the old man's side.

"Read to me as I die."

"Which part?"

"Just open it and read."

Joe opened the book and squinted at the title page. The book was *Pilgrim's Progress,* written by someone named John Bunyan. Joe immediately knew from where the old man had borrowed his name.

Joe thought back to his days in the Indian Agency school. "Isn't this a book of the white man's religion?" he asked.

"Yes. A grand book, the story of a quest."

"What use does a Cherokee conjurer have with such a book?"

"I am not only a Cherokee conjurer," the old man said. "I am also a Methodist."

"I didn't think a good Methodist was supposed to be a conjurer too."

"I said I was a Methodist. I did not say I was a good one." The old man writhed and gripped his stomach more tightly. "Read, Joe. Read before I die!"

Joe flipped open the book, picked a place at random, and began to read. He was a poor reader and stumbled through the old fashioned text in a jerky monotone. "About the midst of this valley I perceived the mouth of hell to be, and it stood also hard by the wayside. Now, thought Christian, what shall I do? And ever and anon the flame and smoke would come out in such abundance, with sparks and hideous noises.

"No, no. Do not read the fearsome parts," the old man

directed. "Go to the end. Read of the end of the quest at the Celestial City."

Joe flipped farther, to the final pages. He found many of the words difficult to decipher. Sometimes the old man would give him the right ones from memory. " 'Now I saw in my dream that these two men went in at the gate: and lo, as they entered, they were transfigured and they had raiment put on that shone like gold. There was also one that met them with harps and crowns, and gave them to them—the harps to praise withal, and the crowns in token of honor. Then I heard in my dream that all the bells in the city rang again for joy, and that it was said unto them, "Enter yet into the joy of your Lord." I also heard the men themselves, that they sang with a loud voice, saying, "Blessing, honor, glory, and power be to him that sitteth upon the throne, and to the Lamb, for ever and ever."'"

"Yes, that is the part," the old man said, relaxing now and smiling with his eyes closed. "Read more to me, Joe Wolfkiller."

Joe read for several more minutes with wearying difficulty. "And after that, they shut up the gates, which when I had seen, I wished myself among them.'"

Joe paused and glanced down at the old man. His eyes were closed, and he was breathing deeply, asleep with a look of calm and peace on his face. Joe closed the book, laid it on the ground, then gathered wood and built a fire to keep the old man warm. It was foolish and dangerous for Joe to stay long in one place, so he thought about remounting his horse and leaving his companion alone. But thinking about it was as far as it went.

Two hours later, near dusk, the old man opened his eyes and sat up. Joe was crouched nearby by the fire, roasting a rabbit he had snared.

"Am I alive?" the Cherokee asked, looking around. "This does not look like the Celestial City."

"Ask your divining crystal, Will Ax," Joe said sharply.

The old man blinked. "How did you learn my name?"

"From your book. It told me a lot more than your old stone ever could. I picked it up again while you slept. Your name was written inside the cover." Joe glared at his companion. "I've called you a fool, but it's me who was the biggest fool, taking up with a man everyone in the Cherokee Nation knows is insane. My father told me about you long ago, Will Ax. He said you were crazy and that no one with sense came near you. He said you called yourself a conjurer but really were nothing but a fool whose chants could not even quiet a sleepless baby. I remember how he ran you away from our house one time when you came to steal. I should have recognized you."

Will Ax looked sheepish. "Your father sometimes spoke words too harsh," he said. "I did not come to steal that day. I came to borrow."

"With you there is no difference. You have never repaid anything you owe. That's another thing everyone knows." Joe chuckled mirthlessly. "When you told me my name without being told it, I thought that maybe you really were a magician. Now I know that you knew me because you had seen me before."

"I admit that I knew you. .. but the crystal reminded me of your name."

"I do not believe in your crystal, babbler. Tell me— the men who chased me. . . you had seen them coming?"

Will Ax sighed and seemed to wither even more. "Very well, Joe. I admit that I saw them. I warned you for your father's sake. I knew you were the son of Sam Wolfkiller, who I have always thought of as my friend, even if he did not think of me as his."

"And I thank you for the warning. But I don't thank you for lying to me and keeping your real name from me, or for trying to make me believe you are something you aren't."

Will Ax's eyes were like those of a beaten pup. He rubbed his stomach gingerly.

"I still feel the death within me," he said.

"What you feel is the air in your gut, or the worms that keep you so scrawny," Joe returned. "I have wasted enough time with you, Will Ax. Starting tomorrow, I ride alone."

Will Ax made a pitiful and lonely sight the next morning when Joe Wolfkiller rode out. The old Cherokee, who had moaned and tossed all night, stood looking wistfully after Joe as he rode away. Joe topped a rise and glanced back at the camp, and suffered a pang of doubt. Maybe Will Ax really was sick. As angry as Joe still felt and as inconvenient, cumbersome, and dangerous a piece of baggage as Will Ax was, Joe didn't feel quite right about abandoning an old man in bad circumstances.

He rode over the rise, out of Will Ax's sight, and stopped to weigh the situation. Like Will Ax, he had a quest to fulfill. Somewhere to the northwest beyond the town of Great Bend he expected to find Caul Slidell, murderer of his father. The blood of Sam Wolfkiller cried out for vengeance. There was no place or time in Joe's life right now for a sick old man who would only be in the way. Joe spurred his horse and went on.

An hour later, he was glad of his decision. With Will Ax far behind, he felt free and purposeful. Let Will Ax deal with his own problems and fulfill his own quest. Likely as not, the whole thing—daughter, treasure, and all—was just some delusion anyway. If Will Ax had a treasure on him, Joe certainly hadn't seen it. Probably the old man's notion of treasure was his old book and that useless divining crystal.

Joe had known many older Cherokee men who were much like Will Ax, clinging to old notions but freely mixing in the white man's beliefs. Sam Wolfkiller had been a little like that, living in two worlds at the same time, fluctuating between them as Will Ax fluctuated between his self-styled Cherokee mysticism and the Christianity allegorized in his leather-bound Bunyan volume. Even Joe was somewhat the same way, though he usually didn't recognize it. Consciously he regarded the white half of his heritage with contempt, but there were times when a contradictory attitude buried deeper in his mind crept through, and he found himself despising his swarthy skin, his dark eyes, his shining black hair, his high cheekbones. He was embarrassed sometimes at the traditions and superstitions of his people and had refused to learn the old formulas and legends that men like Will Ax put such stock in. Only one part of his Indian heritage did he hold to dearly, though in a personalized and distorted form—the law of revenge.

The Cherokees and other Indians of old, his father had explained to him, had lived by a clear cut code of revenge, a law of blood. This was no anarchistic, unbridled vengeance but a controlled, governed system of retribution, following strict guidelines of tribe, clan, kinship. It regulated Cherokee society and interaction in much the same way the white men's laws, courts, jails, and gallows regulated theirs. As time passed and the white men's ways had taken over, the Cherokees substantially abandoned their law of blood. Perhaps, Sam Wolfkiller had said, that was for the best. Perhaps the old system could no longer work in a world far less simple than it once had been.

As Joe had grown, he had often thought about the old law of blood, and as his life had become more troubled, had redefined that law to himself in his own simplified fashion. Joe's law was this: Any who strike me and my kin will be struck in turn, no matter what the cost. Violence for violence, blood for blood. There was no sophistication to the law of blood as Joe had rewritten it. It was simple, direct, uncompromising, and most of all, personal.

That was why Caul Slidell had to die, no matter what effort it took.

Joe rode until the darkness was thick, then made camp. His horse grazed the brown winter-dried grass. Joe dug out a handful of Will Ax's parched corn and ate, then lay down to sleep, his stomach still grumbling. He had taken only a little food from his former companion; soon he would have to find more.

When Joe awakened the next morning, Will Ax was with him again, sitting looking at his divining crystal as he had the first morning. Joe sat up and swore.

Will Ax looked at him, grinned, and put away his crystal. "I have bread," he said. "Good bread, baked by a white woman. A wagon came by after you left our camp, carrying a family toward the Territory border. I put on a mean face and asked food from them. They gave it to me very fast because they were afraid of me; the children begged me not to take their scalps. When I had the bread, I thought my friend Joe might want some too, so I came to bring you some."

Joe, still seated, drew his knees up and put his head between them. Will Ax, it seemed, was like a shadow. He could not get rid of him. At least he had brought good food. Joe accepted half a loaf of bread and ate hungrily.

Will Ax ate more slowly, seated on his haunches, then stood, grasped his stomach again, and fell to one side. "I think, Joe, that you need to take me to Wichita."

"Why? You wish to die there?"

"No. My crystal told me I would not die. . . but only if I will see a white doctor."

"Your crystal is as crazy as you are, old man."

The doctor's name was Lansford, and he had taken it in his head a month before that he had missed his calling and should have been a novelist instead of a physician. Lately he had begun closing his office two days a week to devote himself to his first epic, *Bernard DuBrendle: Army Scout and Slayer of Savages,* subtitled A *Narrative of a Hero of the American Western Plains.* He was in the midst of a particularly bloody passage in which his hero was wiping out yet another dozen heathens with remarkably simple minds and easily crushed skulls.

He was preparing to face DuBrendle off with the most savage and heathen of them all, Scalpyanker, the narrative's brutal villain of unspecified tribe and background, when a knock on his door interrupted him. Swearing beneath his breath at illiterate fools who can't read posted hours on a closed door, he shouted, "I'm closed! Come back tomorrow!"

Another vigorous knock threatened to rattle the door off its hinges. This time Lansford did not bother to keep his oath beneath his breath. He tossed his script-covered pad on the desktop, rose, and stomped to the door.

His plan was to pull open the door and give a vigorous lecture to whoever was on the other side, but when the door opened, his plan immediately changed. Looking back at him was a living personification of his fictional Scalpyanker, a lean but muscled fire-eyed Indian with shocks of long black hair spilling out from under both sides of his hat. Dr. Lansford drew in his breath and felt faint.

"Open the door," Scalpyanker said softly but authoritatively.

Dr. Lansford, beginning to tremble, obeyed. The Indian

led in another, this one old and frail, his face as innocuous and pleasant as the first's was fierce and frightening.

"Listen, I'm not open for business today." Lansford cleared his throat. "Besides that, I don't treat. .."

"Yes, you do treat Indians, starting today," Joe Wolfkiller said. "And you are open for business."

Dr. Lansford swallowed. "Yes. It seems I am." His eyes flickered to Will Ax. "Him or you?"

"Him."

"All right. You can wait outside."

"I'll wait here."

"Of course. Of course."

Lansford had Will Ax sit in a straightback chair. "And just who are you, old fellow?" he asked.

"I am the wind, the sun, the earth, the voice of the toad, and the eye of the eagle," Will Ax said.

"Never mind who he is," Joe said. "Just fix him."

"What's wrong with you?" Lansford asked Will Ax.

"There is a sharp stick inside of me, or perhaps a gnawing bug is eating my entrails."

"He means his stomach is bad," Joe said.

"I see."

"The old formulas have failed to drive out the affliction."

" 'Old formulas'? Old heathen superstitions, you mean. You people are your own worst enemies, the nonsense you go by. Take off that coat and shirt so I can feel your belly."

Joe took the coat and hung it on a wall peg behind a partition on the other side of the office. The doctor, growing more used to his unusual visitors, probed and poked Will Ax, examined his tongue and eyes, and asked questions. Finally he pulled the partition over and behind it conducted a closer examination.

At last he came back around it to Joe. "He's full of worms, head to toe," he said. "Worst case I've seen, but no more than I'd expect in an—" His discretion stopped him just in time. "Anyway, I've got something over here that ought to scour them right out of him. You might want to take some yourself. If you've been much around him, you've probably got them too."

The doctor went to his shelf and selected a dark bottle. He poured some of its contents into a smaller bottle and corked it. Handing it to Joe, he gave directions for its use.

"How much money?" Joe asked.

The doctor, wanting only to have the Indians out of his office, waved his hand. "Free. Take it. Another gift from the white man to the red."

The comment was not well taken. "I can pay as well as any white man. I don't want gifts," Joe said coldly.

The doctor knew he had blundered and quickly named a price. Joe thrust his hand into his pocket to get the meager wad of money remaining.

It was gone.

Joe was stunned. He couldn't guess what had happened to the money. More than likely, he had simply dropped it sometime during his ordeals and flights.

The doctor stood looking at him with barely concealed contempt; obviously he figured Joe was about to tell him he had nothing and take the medicine for nothing after all. "You have no money?" the doctor ventured.

"No, but I can pay." Joe turned and walked over to Will Ax's coat on the wall. Will Ax was still behind the partition, slowly putting his smelly clothing back on. Joe reached into the pocket of Will's coat and withdrew the hide bundle containing the divining crystal.

"Here," he said, handing it to the doctor.

"What is it?"

Joe whispered, not wanting Will Ax to hear. "It is a Cherokee divining crystal. Very valuable."

Dr. Lansford took the bundle, opened it, and peered at the crystal. This was the first time Joe had seen it—a bullet-shaped clear stone with a red streak up the middle. It was a beautiful quartzlike object, not quite like anything Joe had seen.

"It's remarkable," Lansford said, holding it up. "Absolutely remarkable. I'll consider it fair payment."

He pocketed the stone as Will Ax came around the partition. "I think I won't die now, Joe," Will said.

"Good for you," Joe mumbled.

"Don't let anyone see you leaving," Lansford said. "I don't want it out that I've taken to treating Indians."

Chapter 6

Joe Wolfkiller slept little that night, not solely because of the violent storm that rolled in as the sun set or the hardness of the packed floor of the woodshed in which he and Will Ax had taken shelter. It was primarily dreams that kept Joe restless.

He and the old man were just north of Wichita, still in sight of the town. Joe would have liked to go farther, but Will Ax remained sick all day and could not travel well. The horses had also seemed weary and hungry, so north of town Joe had set up dry camp in a well hidden dry gully, sneaked to the nearest barn and stolen grain for the horses, and sat stewing in dissatisfaction, smoking one of Will Ax's pipes to pass the time as the old man took his rest and medicine.

By evening, the storm was beginning to well up, and Joe put them on the move again, looking for night shelter. Near a three-story clapboard house with gables and four chimneys they had found this substantial woodshed and moved in, Joe figuring that whoever was in the house would certainly be unlikely to come poking around in the shed during a storm. He tethered the horses at a stream-side grove nearby, out of sight of the house.

Will Ax, who seemed to be feeling much better, had begun talking as soon as they settled down in the woodshed, his voice a steady low monotone. The old man had been somber all evening, talking about his long lost daughter and hoping he would be able to find her before he died.

"How do you know you will die?" Joe asked. "That crystal is just a piece of rock." He at once regretted having mentioned the divining stone, for Will Ax did not yet know it had gone as payment for his medicine. Joe was not eager for the moment Will discovered he no longer had the stone.

"The crystal is not an ordinary stone. It's like no other crystal still in this world, and there will be no others like it to come."

"Maybe so. But it would take more than a piece of stone to make me believe I was going to die."

"The crystal is never wrong," Will Ax said. After a few moments, though, he added, "Well, that is not really true, not anymore. In the old days the crystal always spoke truly. Now sometimes it doesn't speak at all—" Will Ax leaned forward and whispered, "and sometimes it speaks lies. I think it is like me. It is getting old and hard to get along with."

They slept, and Joe's dreams started afresh. At first he relived the shooting of the deputies down in the Cherokee Nation, and dreamed of flight and pursuit, but this gave way to the same bizarre dream that had awakened Joe that first morning Will Ax joined him. Once again Joe saw himself garbed as an ancient Cherokee, standing beside the same deep mountain pool. The dark water stirred, and from its surface emerged the great serpentine head with horns and a crescent-shaped light that shone from its forehead, a light glancing off of, perhaps out of, a crystalline stone that was mystifyingly familiar. The light flashed into Joe's eyes, blinding him. Great fear overwhelmed him. He tossed and rolled and tried to wake up, for in the dream his legs would not move even though the Uktena was coming at him to kill him....

Uktena. Even as Joe awoke, he realized what the dream beast was. Memory raced back to childhood and dark nights in the cabin near Tahlequah. He recalled sitting at the feet of Sam Wolfkiller and hearing stories of the former days of his people. Several of those stories had dealt with the great Uktena, a serpentine water dragon that haunted the dark pools and gaps of the eastern mountains along the bounds of the Cherokee ancient world. The Uktena, beautiful yet terrible to behold, was the most dangerous of the monster beasts of Cherokee folklore, for to see it was enough to bring suffering and tragedy, and the stench of its breath carried death.

Joe sat up. The storm was raging outside, wind driven rain pounding the shed roof and sprinkling in through the gaps and knotholes of the walls. As Joe peered out the largest hole, a brilliant lightning flash struck him in the eyes. He remembered how upon awakening from the dream that first time, he had been looking into the sun. This time it must have been the lightning that accounted for the light from the Uktena's brow...but why had he twice dreamed of a legendary beast he had not thought of since childhood?

Joe turned and was surprised to see a figure standing in the darkness facing him. Half a moment later he knew it was only Will Ax, but during the brief span of confusion and lingering fear from the nightmare, the old Cherokee's presence was startling. More lightning flashed and illuminated the weathered old face. Joe was surprised to see water trailing from Will's eyes.

Will Ax's voice was slightly broken when he spoke. "You shouted just now," he said. "You shouted of an Uktena."

"I dreamed of one," Joe said. "How loud did I shout?"

Will Ax ignored Joe's question and asked his own. "Do you know why you have dreamed of the Uktena?"

"No, no. Listen to me—did I shout so loud, someone could have heard me from the house?"

"I can tell you why," Will Ax aid. "It is because you have been in the presence of the *ulunsuti* stone."

"What are you talking about, old man?"

"My divining crystal." Will Ax paused. Another lightning flash ripped the sky; the wind that came through the knotholes was cold. "I will tell you my secret now—why the divining crystal is so great a thing. It is not just a crystal like most of the magicians have. It is an *ulunsuti*, the last *ulunsuti* there ever will be, taken many years ago from the brow of the last Uktena."

Joe remembered more of the lore he had heard at his father's knee long ago—how the stone on the brow of the Uktena, the *ulunsuti* stone, was the greatest divining crystal any Cherokee seer could hope to possess. From it he could learn of things past, present, and future. He could predict the outcome of illness, good or bad. With it he could make rain, win the love of women, become a great hunter, and foretell the fate of warriors going to battle.

"But there cannot really be an *ulunsuti* stone," Joe said. "Such things are nothing but old stories. Uktenas, *ulunsutis* —they are lies."

Will Ax sat down wearily. "It does not matter now, I guess. The *ulunsuti is* gone anyway."

Joe's stomach knotted. "I know," he confessed. "I gave your crystal to the doctor to pay for the medicine."

Will Ax took the news quietly. "Forgive my tears, unfitting for a man," he said after a while. "I can't help but cry. The *ulunsuti* was the treasure I was carrying to my daughter. Now I have nothing to give her at all." He sighed. "Perhaps it was no longer a treasure anyway. I've not kept the *ulunsuti* the way it should be kept, and I believe that's what made it sick. It doesn't do what it is supposed to. White men, they are supposed to die when they see the *ulunsuti.*

But the white doctor—he did not die when you gave it to him?"

"He did not die."

"I thought so. The *ulunsuti's* strength is fading. It is old and sick and ready to die, like me."

At that moment the shed door burst open. In the doorway stood a man in a hat, longjohns, and a slicker. He held a shotgun with one arm; a lighted lantern swung from the other. He looked the surprised pair over. "Up nice and slow, you trespassing redskins," he said. "I thought I heard somebody squall out here. Now, which ort I to do—shoot you down, or take you in to see Mr. Christmas?"

Will Ax lifted his hands above his head, shrugged, and said, "If it's up to us to choose, I think maybe we'd rather go meet Mr. Christmas."

After disarming his prisoners, the man hustled them through the rain into a back door of the house and immediately to the left into a small windowless room. He closed the door and locked it from the outside. Joe fumbled in the darkness until he found a lamp with a box of matches beside it. He lighted the lamp. Will Ax's face was gaunt with fright.

The wall was papered with old newspapers and covered with framed pictures, documents, and the like. The only furniture in the room was a desk, lamp table, and three chairs. Will Ax sat down, but Joe paced about the room like a caged cougar. Neither man spoke. Both knew that bad luck had just come their way.

Time passed, and no one came to the room. Joe kept pacing and finally began studying the pictures and documents on the wall. He had the impression this was some sort of makeshift and generally unused office. At length he came to one framed portrait hanging near a corner and stopped in his tracks.

Looking back at him was the photographed face of Judge Isaac Parker. Scrawled across the base of the picture were the words *To my good friend and supporter, James R. Christmas. Isaac Parker, United States Judge, Western District of Arkansas, 1886. Best wishes to you, Jim.*

Joe Wolfkiller swore aloud.

The door rattled and opened. In walked the man who had caught them in the woodshed. He still had his shotgun. With him was another man, very tall and slender with bushy red hair and wiry sideburns that met the ends of a broad orange mustache.

"There they be, Mr. Christmas."

The red-haired man strode in and examined the prisoners as if they were statues on display in a gallery. He looked at Joe Wolfkiller a long time, then walked over to the desk, opened it, and removed a wooden box from which he took a long cigar. He made a slow and deliberate show of biting off the end and lighting up, his wide-spaced eyes on Joe all the time.

When the cigar was burning to his satisfaction, he exhaled a thick cloud and sat on the corner of the desk. "Mr. Miller," he said to the armed man, "do you realize that you have just captured Cherokee Joe?"

Miller's eyes bugged. "No! You don't mean it!"

"Indeed I do. Judge Parker only today wired me that Cherokee Joe was thought to be heading into Kansas. Seems he gunned down some deputies in the Cherokee Nation. He asked me to keep my eyes and ears open. I wager he'd be surprised to find that the subject himself has shown up, literally on my doorstep."

Joe felt a cold dread that left him struggling not to tremble. He let nothing show on his swarthy face.

Christmas smiled coldly at Joe. "You've gone one up on

your own reputation in the last little stretch, Cherokee Joe. You've suddenly become quite a talked-about villain in these parts."

Joe stared back at him, saying nothing.

"Perhaps you're surprised that I'm so well informed about such recent events in the Indian Territory," Christmas said to Joe, puffing his cigar languidly. "The reason is simple. I and Judge Parker—you know the famed 'Hanging Judge," I'm sure—enjoy a longtime association. I've helped him out several times in locating Indian Territory criminals who've fled this way, and he has shown his appreciation by regularly sending me wires, fliers, and the like concerning those he suspects might come over the border. Several months ago he sent me a sketch of 'Cherokee Joe' Wolfkiller, even before your most recent violent exploit. It's a good likeness." Christmas turned to Will Ax. "But this old fellow, I confess, I don't recognize."

Joe expected Will Ax to launch into his usual self-identification with wind, sun, earth, and so on, but this time Will answered in a lifeless tone, "My name is Will Ax." Joe noted how different Will Ax was, no spark in his eye, no joviality. It's because of the *ulunsuti,* Joe thought. It's gone, and it took his spirit with it.

Will Ax gave Joe a tired but searching look. Tonight was the first time the old man had heard the nature of the crime that had Joe on the run. Joe wondered if the knowledge would alter Will's apparent affection for him.

"Will Ax!" Christmas declared. "I've heard of you, after all, old fellow. Crazed Cherokee eccentric from the Territory. And crazed you must be to ride with the likes of this murderous young heathen." He waved his cigar toward Joe.

"Let him go," Joe said. "He has done nothing."

"Well, I wouldn't say that. He's trespassed on my property, far outside the reserved Cherokee grounds. And he's fraternizing with a known killer."

Will Ax, still seated, looked like a dried up sad old sack of bones. He raised no protest at his detention or any plea for release.

Christmas spoke to Miller. "Take the old one out. Lock him upstairs. I want to talk to Cherokee Joe alone."

Miller obeyed. Joe stood where he was, looking contemptuously at Christmas.

"Don't think of attempting to escape," Christmas said, taking a small pistol from his pocket. "I'll not hesitate to use this if you try anything."

"You intend to turn me over to Parker?"

"Not necessarily. There's something you can do for me. You can earn your freedom—if you will cooperate."

Joe had not expected to hear anything like this. "What do you mean, 'cooperate'?"

Christmas smiled. "Cherokee Joe, your arrival here is fortuitous—for both of us, whether you can believe that or not. I have a strong suspicion that I know what you're up to. I heard about Caul Slidell's murder of your father. Knowing the attitude you are reported to have about such things, I suspect you are on your way to get your revenge on Caul Slidell for gunning down your father."

"And if I am?"

"Well, then, Joe, if you are, you and I are in a position to strike a deal that will let you avenge yourself against Slidell and let me do a great favor for my good friend Judge Parker."

Joe's expression remained the same, but in his narrow eyes Christmas saw a spark of cautious interest.

"If there is a man Judge Parker is eager to see captured at the moment, it's Slidell. Parker wants him even more than he wants you. Slidell and his hellriders have been a thorn in the side of the Arkansas court too long. I'm in the position of owing Judge Parker a few favors, and I'd like to even the balance by being the man to deliver Caul Slidell to his doorstep."

"What does that have to do with me?"

"Simple. I want you to go out and capture Slidell for me. Bring him back here. I have plenty of capable men in my hire who can ensure that Slidell is delivered the rest of the way back to Judge Parker's jail."

"Then why don't you send these 'capable men' to get Slidell? Why send me?"

"Because it's one thing to deliver a trussed-up prisoner from Kansas to Fort Smith. It's another thing to capture him in the first place. That requires a cunning, a skill, a ruthlessness—and especially a motivation—that my men don't possess. You, though—you're a different story altogether. I know enough about you to feel sure that you can do the job. And you already want to get him."

"I don't want to bring Slidell back alive. I want to kill him."

"Oh, but that won't do at all, Joe. You bring Slidell back to me alive, or else."

"Or else what?"

"Else your friend Will Ax never leaves this house alive. You see, Cherokee Joe? That's the special motivation you'll have. Caul Slidell, delivered safe to my hands, or your friend as dead as last January."

Christmas puffed his cigar again and smiled.

Chapter 7

Joe Wolfkiller rode through the cold Kansas air on a fine black mount provided by Christmas. His guns, too—a Winchester saddle rifle and a Colt Peacemaker—were of highest quality and out of Christmas' private arms stock.

Joe had accepted Christmas' bargain because he saw no other option save sacrificing Will Ax's life. He suspected there was far more to this bizarre setup than he had been told. Christmas' story didn't ring true. Why would a man who was an associate and supporter of the staunchest law and order judge in the American territories set up such an illegal machinery as this just to bring in a criminal as a friendly favor for the court? Christmas was taking a risk by holding Will Ax hostage. Indians had few enough rights, but even they could not be kidnapped and held hostage under threat of death.

Joe's curiosity was high about the whole business. Overwhelming even that curiosity, however, was a rising feeling of desperation. It had been one thing to set off to kill Caul Slidell, which could be done from a distance with a bullet. It was a far different thing to be charged with bringing Slidell in alive within five weeks, the deadline set by Jim Christmas. How could he hope to do it?

Joe's route out of the Wichita area roughly followed the Arkansas River and the route of the Missouri Pacific Railroad that extended down from its junction with the Rock Island and Santa Fe lines at the town of Hutchinson. Joe's horse was a fast traveler and served him well, and by nightfall he was near the common line dividing Sedgwick and Reno counties.

He slept later than he had planned the following morning, for the journey had tired him, and his black slipped its hobbles and wandered off, requiring him to hunt it down. He set off as quickly as he found it but already had lost three hours. Crossing the county line, he continued along the Arkansas River toward Hutchinson.

It was nearly dusk when he spotted a wagon parked by the roadside. Even in the waning light, this wagon was hard to miss. It had paneled sides and a high seat and somewhat resembled a circus wagon except for its plain white paint and slightly smaller size. On the panels were black letters that became legible as Joe drew closer: *PATRICK ST. PATRICK —QUALITY PORTRAITS MADE CHEAP.*

Joe was initially wary of the wagon, for even chance encounters with strangers had to be considered dangerous in his circumstances. He figured to pass the wagon by, but as he came closer, a man wearing a white suit, white shirt, and white tie came around the back waving his arms and stepped out into the road.

"Thank God above someone's come my way!" the man said in an Irish accent. "I'm having a devil of a time here, a devil of a time."

Joe might have kept riding except that the man was right in his way. An enticing aroma of cooking stew had reached his nostrils, giving him further motive to pause. There was a small cookfire burning a few yards off the road behind the wagon, a black kettle bubbling nicely with a coffeepot beside it.

"What's wrong?" Joe asked.

The man's expression of pleasure changed subtly for a moment, which told Joe he had just been recognized as an Indian. If the realization made much difference to the white-suited fellow, he didn't show it, for a moment later his expression was as before. He set up a busy chatter. "What's wrong, you ask? I'll tell you, sir, I'm on three wheels, that's what. Rolling right along, and there goes the hub, loose as a goose, so off I hop to try to fix it. But fixing a wagon wheel is a thing that I now know this Irish picture taker was not put into this world to do, for here now I sit with the wheel off and me not able to get it back on, and the jack's stuck tight besides. You look the sort who could put things right for me, if you will. Bless me, but I suppose I'd have sat here all night if you hadn't come."

Joe looked at the sky. "You might as well sit here all night anyway. It's late to start traveling again."

St. Patrick glanced around at the darkening land and lifted his arched brows. "Well, you're right about that. Too bad. I'd hoped to reach Hutchinson while the corpse was still fresh."

That comment intrigued Joe, but not nearly as much as the smell of the stew. "I'll fix your wheel for a bowl of that in the pot," he said.

"Why, if that's not a bargain, I've never run across one. Hop down there, friend, and see what you can do with that jack. The name's Pat St. Patrick."

Joe's mind scrambled for an alias. The best he could come up with was the one Tom Pease had given him the night of the shooting in the Indian Territory.

"My name is Henry Feather," Joe said.

"Good to meet you, Mr. Feather, good to meet you."

The wagon was easy enough to put right, and Joe had it

done before it was fully dark. Then St. Patrick dished out stew in big crockery bowls, accompanied by mugs of coffee. Joe couldn't recall a better meal in months.

While they ate, St. Patrick talked incessantly, first about Ireland, then about his entry into the photographic business during the Civil War when he cut his professional teeth taking pictures of dead bodies on smoking battlefields. "I daresay that's what got me going in my specialty. Corpse photographs, I mean. Dead papas and mamas, and grandpas and newborns and such. Shutter off a clean close portrait, print it all up nice and neat, and stick it in a gilded frame, and you've got your dead relative in eternal repose right on the mantlepiece. That's what I do, and make a pretty penny at it. And then there's the outlaws. That's what I like best. Portraits of dead outlaws sell like bakery bread, they do. Especially when the bullet holes show."

Joe took a sip of his coffee and looked out across the plains, wondering if St. Patrick would talk all night. He was on the verge of rising to ride off to camp somewhere ahead when St. Patrick said something that made him decide to stay.

"Speaking of dead outlaws, Mr. Feather, it's to make a portrait of such a one that's got me in such a rush to get to Hutchinson. I got it from a firsthand witness this very morning that Caul Slidell himself has been gunned down by one of his own men just north of Hutchinson. I'm eager to make a picture of him before they get him planted."

Nothing in Joe Wolfkiller's impenetrable veneer changed to indicate the violent reaction St. Patrick's pronouncement generated. "Caul Slidell? You sure it was Slidell?"

"Well, the man who informed me of it said he saw it all happen himself, and he swore it to be Slidell. I intend to be the man who gets the last portrait of that scoundrel." St. Patrick cocked his head and looked at Joe's face by firelight. "Speaking of portraits, Mr. Feather, I'd like to ask if you'd consider letting me make one of you—all for free, of course, in thanks for fixing my wagon and for the evening's company. I find you an intriguing man; quite an imposing face and presence you have. Do I detect, uh, a certain Indian bloodline?"

"I'm who I am. Bloodlines don't matter."

St. Patrick waved his hand. "Oh, please take no offense, for none was intended. Anything I say is intended only in the highest and most complimentary sense. Now, about that portrait..."

"I have no use for a portrait."

St. Patrick looked disappointed. He poured himself another cup of coffee and started talking again, this time about childhood memories of Ireland—boyish explorations in places with names that meant nothing to Joe: Tralee Bay, Castle Gregory, Blennerville, Dingle, Listowell.

Joe shut it all out, his mind filled with questions about the reported death of Slidell. He hoped it was not true. If Slidell was already dead, Joe had lost both his chance at personal vengeance and his means of saving Will Ax. He brooded over the matter for a long time, then looked up and interrupted St. Patrick in midsentence. "If I let you make my picture, will you let me ride with you to Hutchinson to see this body?" he asked. Joe was not content with thirdhand word of Slidell's death. He wanted to see for himself.

St. Patrick, obviously surprised, grinned broadly. "Indeed, Mr. Feather, and thank you, sir. Thank you indeed."

Will Ax put down his volume of *Pilgrim's Progress* and took a deep breath. He had just reread one of his favorite portions —Christian's battle with Apollyon—but even that had failed to overcome the deep depression that had gripped him.

Why he was being held in this third-story room he did not know. Nor did he know what had become of Joe Wolfkiller. He feared for his young companion. Even now Joe might be in chains and heading for Parker's court in Arkansas.

Will Ax rose from his chair and walked stiffly over to the single narrow window. He looked out the dusty glass and over the weathered top of a roof that peaked at an impossibly steep angle. He had stared at that roof scores of times since being locked in here, trying to ascertain if he could hope to make it across to the lightning rod and clamber down without falling and breaking his neck. Several times he had almost tried; each time he had backed out. He was too old and feeble to do such a boyish thing, especially since the *ulunsuti* was gone. Its absence seemed to siphon much of his strength and will to try.

Given his unwillingness to attempt the roof route, the only alternative Will Ax had been able to think of was an old formula taught him by an uncle who swore that its words would allow him to take the form of a *tlayku,* a jaybird, and fly out of troublesome situations such as this. Will had chanted the long memorized formula perfectly (he had noticed lately that for some reason it was easier to recall things he had learned long ago than things he had learned recently), but when he looked at his arms, they were still arms and not wings. After the first surge of disappointment he had decided that maybe he really was in the form of a jay but that to his eyes alone he looked the same. To test the theory, he called through the locked door until the man named Miller, who seemed to be some sort of employee or crony of the mysterious Jim Christmas, came grumbling up the stairs.

Miller opened the door and stuck in his head. "What is it now, old man?"

"Tell me, Mr. Miller, do I look like a man or a bird to you?"

Miller had sworn fiercely, threatened a beating if bothered with such stupidity again, then slammed and relocked the door. Will Ax had felt really dejected then, for he knew the old formula had not worked.

As much as he despised admitting it, it seemed that in the past few years a lot of old things, including the most venerable ancient formulas and even his precious *ulunsuti* stone, didn't work as they were supposed to. For that matter, Will Ax himself didn't work nearly as well as he had. His mind was slow, his body slower. Sometimes it hurt just to move; sometimes it hurt in a deeper way even to think.

Will Ax stood at the window looking out over that sharp roof peak at Christmas's backyard and the dirt road beyond it. He felt unwanted doubts trying to break out of the mental prison cells in which he had locked them for fear of facing them. The truth was, despite all his talk of being a magician, he had never really been able to achieve anything with his formulas that he could say wouldn't have happened anyway. Even his revered *ulunsuti* stone had never told him anything he could be sure was secret knowledge and not just some intuition or good guess. Back in his younger days, when the *ulunsuti* had reflected the light much more brightly than it did now, had been regularly "fed" with blood and correctly kept in a cave instead of a pocket, he had felt greater confidence in it. Perhaps his loss of confidence reflected a real change in the crystal—or a change in himself.

The more he thought about such things, the more Will Ax felt sad and forsaken. "I think I'm sinking in the Slough of Despond," he said aloud, making another reference to the "Pilgrim's Progress" allegory. He had made an instant mental shift from magician to Methodist, and without the slightest jolt. The process of jumping between two worldviews had become so practiced for Will Ax that he didn't notice anymore when he was doing it. He had discovered that contradictions weren't all that hard to live with if you put your mind to it—or more accurately, declined to let yourself think about it. Sometimes whole hordes of incompatible propositions would sit side by side in his mind, as comfortable with each other as old friends sharing pipes and memories.

Something on the road caught Will Ax's eye. A boy, walking slowly along and looking at Jim Christmas's house. He interested Will Ax. The lad was obviously a full-blood Indian. Will Ax's seasoned eye could tell that at this distance, even though the boy was dressed and trimmed up like a white youth. The old man proudly noted that at least his physical eyesight hadn't dulled along with its mystical counterpart. Just then the boy looked directly up at Will Ax's window, and Will waved at him.

Will Ax had figured the window would be too dusty and dark to allow the boy to see him and was surprised when the youth waved back. A burst of inspiration struck Will Ax, and he began a beckoning wave, trying to signal for the boy to climb up to him. The boy stopped walking and looked at Will Ax with a doubtful expression that slowly became fearful. He turned and darted away.

Will Ax was disappointed. He went to the bed and lay down. The day passed, and about seven o'clock Miller came up with a tray of food, grumbling about being forced to play "house slave to a wormy old redskin." Will Ax, assuming a stereotypical dime novel talking style, told Miller that "red man heap pleased to have such good white slave," and Miller slapped him across the left cheek. The blow smarted, but Will Ax didn't much care. It had been worth it to insult Miller.

Miller took away Will Ax's plates before he had a chance to eat his fill and left the old man locked in the dark. Will Ax again lay down, wondering why he was held here, and slowly drifted off to sleep.

A scratching noise awakened him. It was very dark in the room now, obviously quite late. He sat up, looked around, and saw nothing. Perhaps it had been a mouse in the wall. The noise came again, and this time he was able to trace it. The window. He looked over, bleary-eyed from sleep, and thought with amazement that he saw a jay scratching the other side of the glass. He blinked and realized he had been wrong: It was not a jay but a small hand, the hand of a boy. And then he saw the face too, peering in, and recognized it as that of the Indian boy he had seen earlier.

Will Ax rose and went to the window. As quietly as possible, he opened it. "Come in, *tlayku,*" he said. "Come in."

The boy thrust a leg through the window and entered. For several moments he looked up at Will Ax in undisguised awe. "Hello, Grandfather," he said in a whisper. He threw his arms around Will Ax and hugged him tight.

Chapter 8

"My name is Will Ax, the old man said haltingly, taken aback by the surprising affection with which the boy hugged him. The lad was about twelve years old. "And who are you, young *tlayku?*"

"My name is Timothy," the boy said softly. "Why do you call me—whatever that name was?"

"Tlayku. 'Jay' in my language. I call you that because you must have become able to fly like a jay to reach me across this high roof."

"I didn't fly. I climbed. I'm a good climber, Grandfather."

"Now I have a question for you, Timothy. Why do you call me Grandfather?"

"Because you are so much like my grandfather—my real grandfather. He was a Creek."

"He is dead?"

"Yes. When I saw you through the window today, I thought Grandfather had come back to this world. At first I was scared. . . but I had to come back to see." The young boy saddened. "But I can see you are not really my grandfather."

"No. I am just an old Cherokee conjurer who is a prisoner in this room."

"A prisoner? Why?"

"I don't know, Timothy. I am held here by a man named Jim Christmas."

"Yes. This is his house. He is a rich man and, my father says, a bad one. He got rich from the railroad and from buying and selling land. And he has cheated people, and that has made him richer. He makes friends of other people who have money and power and keeps them from knowing he's bad. That's what my father says."

"Your father, he is a Creek?"

"No. My Creek parents are dead. I've been with my white parents for six years. They are good to me... even though they'll thrash me if they find out I came here."

Will Ax smiled sadly. Timothy's situation made him think again of his lost daughter.

"May I still call you Grandfather, even if you are not really my grandfather?" the boy asked.

"Yes. It would make me proud. But while we talk here, we must keep our voices very low."

"Grandfather, if you are a Cherokee conjurer, why haven't you escaped?"

"Because, I'm afraid, I'm not a very good conjurer anymore. I'm old and not much good at anything except sleeping and making smoking pipes. And now that my *ulunsuti* stone is gone, it's even worse than before."

"What is an *ulunsuti* stone?"

Will Ax walked back over to the side of his bed and sat down. He lighted the single lamp beside his bed. By its light he got his first good look at Timothy, a small-framed but handsome boy.

"An *ulunsuti* stone is a powerful crystal, taken from the forehead of a fearsome beast called a Uktena. It is the greatest talisman a man can possess. For years it was mine, but now it belongs to a white man. Since it's gone, I—"

Will Ax cut off abruptly. Inspiration had struck him. He leaned forward. "Timothy, do you think you could enter another house as easily as you entered this one?"

"Yes."

"And as quietly?"

"Yes!"

Will Ax smiled. "Then you can do Grandfather a great favor and take back his *ulunsuti* for him."

"Where is it?"

"In a house belonging to a doctor who gives out bad-tasting medicine and doesn't much like Indians."

"Dr. Lansford."

"Yes, I believe that is his name."

"I know his house. I can get inside easy. Your stone is there?"

"Yes, and if you return it to me, I believe it would tell me how to escape this place."

Joe Wolfkiller stood like a statue in the morning light, staring out toward the horizon with a chiseled stone expression until St. Patrick made his exposure and told him he could move. The halfbreed let out a breath and relaxed.

St. Patrick was in high spirits. "Very good, Mr. Feather! That should be excellent, just excellent."

Wordlessly, Joe turned away and headed off to saddle his horse. He cared nothing for the portrait; only to remain in St. Patrick's good graces had he agreed to have it made. Now he was eager to get on to Hutchinson and find out the truth about the report of Caul Slidell's death.

St. Patrick, who had been so anxious to reach Hutchinson the previous day, today was far too unhurried to suit Joe. St. Patrick dawdled as he put away his camera and devoted most of his energy to talking. "Gone are the old days of wet plates and rushing to develop them before the emulsion dries up," he said as he packed his gear. "Dry plates, Mr. Feather! Wonderful things. They take much of the rush out of this business. Thank God for bright sunshine and Eastman's Instantaneous! That's my motto."

When Joe's impatience was about to lead him to begin riding toward Hutchinson alone, St. Patrick at last finished loading his darkroom wagon. They set off, wheels creaking and squeaking, St. Patrick singing an old number about Galway Bay and "that little Irish girl of mine in the land of emerald green."

Once they reached Hutchinson, they had no difficulty finding the whereabouts of the corpse reputed to be Caul Slidell's. A gang of excited boys, accompanied by an even larger number of mongrel dogs, met St. Patrick's wagon at the edge of town, having noted the writing on the sideboards.

"You come to take pictures of Caul Slidell, huh?"

"We'll take you there—just follow us." "You're going to show the holes in him, ain't you? I seen 'em, we all seen 'em —his chest looks like the top of a pepper box. It was a shotgun that killed him, you know!"

Joe felt exposed and out of place in Hutchinson, this white man's town in white man's country. He received some open stares from the boys who were steering St. Patrick through the streets. He hoped the people here would take him to be St. Patrick's assistant or employee and that the local law would not be looking too hard at the moment for Cherokee Joe.

The corpse was on ice in a storehouse located between a cafe and a wagon shop. The cafe owner seemed to be the recognized keeper of the body, for it was to his door that the crowd of boys ran.

The owner came out, wiping his hands on his apron. He beamed when he saw that a photographer had arrived. "Yes sir, I'd be proud for you to take a picture of our good Mr. Slidell," the man said after St. Patrick made his request. The fellow's name was Tarsus Castle, and he had a bald head and a nose that looked as if it had been mashed flat and pasted down. "And if you would, I'd like one with me standing right beside him. Something to keep for the grandchildren to have someday, you know."

"Indeed, indeed," said St. Patrick.

Joe stood to the side near the front of the growing crowd trying to appear inconspicuous but feeling very noticeable. Three men went into the storage house and came out with a blanket-wrapped body, now quite stiff. As soon as the cadaver was out the door, the mood of the crowd changed, dampering from vociferous excitement to hungry eagerness to see the gruesome body. Most of the people here had surely seen it earlier, Joe figured, but no one seemed less than eager to take a second look.

The body was on its back and bound to a wide board. After the knots were untied and the wrapping blanket loosened, Joe swallowed tensely and waited for the corpse to be unveiled, hoping it wouldn't be Slidell.

Tarsus Castle was about to pull the blanket away when four men on horseback came riding around the corner, generating enough ruckus and aura of importance to draw attention. Joe had a bad feeling about the new arrivals; they had the smell of law about them. He pulled his hat a little lower over his eyes and made sure his long coat was draped fully over his gunbelt. He leaned so the pistol butt wouldn't make a visible bulge.

The lead rider dismounted lightly and walked through a gap in the crowd to Tarsus Castle and the body. His companions followed. St. Patrick, meanwhile, was just finishing setting up his camera directly in front of the body.

"Well, hello there, Sheriff," Castle said.

Sheriff! Joe looked down at his boots, letting the brim of his hat intercede between him and the peace officer.

"Hello, Tarsus. This must be the body in question?"

"Yes, sir. We iced him to keep him fresh until you could get back to see him. Just getting ready to get a picture made when you rode in." He waved over at St. Patrick.

"Yes, yes," said the sheriff. "Well, let's see him."

The crowd surged forward a little as Tarsus Castle pulled away the blanket. A ripple and murmur stirred through the group as they saw the whitish dead face, going blue around the mouth, the eyes half opened and glazed. The sheriff leaned over and looked closely at the dead face.

"Looks like Slidell to me," he said.

"That's him, all right," one of the deputies commented.

"He raved right up until the end about the robbery at the train station down in Guthrie," Castle said. "He lay right in my own house raving about it. Died right in my own bedroom." It was evident that Castle considered it a great honor to have played final host to an outlaw. "It was one of his own men that shot him. Left him for dead. I figured it was my duty to tend him until he passed."

"You're a good man, Tarsus," someone in the crowd said.

The sheriff turned to his deputies. "We'll make official notification, then: Caul Slidell was shot just outside Hutchinson and is officially verified as dead as of this date and time, etcetera and so on. You know the process."

Joe Wolfkiller was in turmoil. He had looked at the corpse and like all the others had at first thought it to be Slidell, but a moment's further examination had shown that to be wrong. This blue-faced dead man was Ed Wiltflower, one of Slidell's hellriders. Wiltflower had always borne a resemblance to Slidell and sometimes had been confused with him in life. Now the same thing was happening in death.

Joe assessed the two possible results of the confusion. One was positive, one negative. The positive was that the real Slidell, once he learned he was now thought dead, would let down his guard and be more susceptible to capture. That could give Joe an edge he needed.

Then there was the negative. Word would surely reach Jim Christmas that Slidell was reported dead, and that would be disastrous for Will Ax. Will was useful to Christmas only as a means of keeping Joe on his leash until Slidell was brought in. If Christmas heard that Slidell was dead, he would have no more use for Joe and therefore no reason to keep Will Ax any longer. Maybe Christmas would set Will free, but Joe doubted it. Most likely he would put a bullet through the old man's brain and dump him out on the plains for the birds and scavengers.

Joe couldn't risk that happening. So despite the danger, he stepped forward.

"Sheriff."

The lawman turned around, frowning at the swarthy young stranger.

"That dead man... that's not Caul Slidell."

The sheriffs eyes were droopy and soft, roofed by brows that slanted up toward the crest of his forehead at nearly a forty-five degree angle. They tilted even more as he scanned Joe Wolfkiller up and down. Joe bristled under his gaze, feeling the rising fury that so often came when white eyes trailed over him like that.

"Who are you, redskin?"

Joe ignored the question. "That isn't Slidell," he reasserted. "I've seen this man before. His name is Ed Wiltflower."

"Wiltflower!" The sheriff looked around at his deputies and snorted. "What kind of name is Wiltflower?"

"That's his name," Joe said flatly.

The sheriff put a thick finger on Joe's chest. "Look here,

Injun, don't waste my time. I know what Slidell looks like. That's him on the board. Now, I suggest to you that you ride south down to the Nations where your kind belongs."

As Joe looked into the meaty face, anger flared in him like coals in a drafty oven. Such anger never went away for Joe; it only burned hotter or cooler, depending upon who or what had fanned it most recently. With wrenching effort, the halfbreed managed to restrain himself. He turned and walked off to the side, pulse pounding in his temples.

St. Patrick took his pictures, several of them, some of the corpse alone, others of the sheriff by its side, others including the proud Tarsus Castle.

Joe didn't watch. He stood alone, feeling he had failed. The body of Ed Wiltflower was being officially accepted as that of Caul Slidell. Telegraph wires would quickly carry the news across the Midwest. Jim Christmas would hear, and then...

Joe felt deeply depressed. Will Ax, crazy as he was, had been a good man to ride with. And it seemed awfully sad that he would die with his quest unfulfilled, his lost daughter never found.

Joe sat glumly on the back doorstep of Castle's cafe eating a bowl of beans with corn bread as he mused over the peculiar twists of the last few days.

St. Patrick, whose generosity was responsible for Joe's current meal, came around the cafe s back corner. He was bright and bubbly as ever. "Ah, there you are, Mr. Feather! Oh, what a day it's been, what a day! Excellent photographs they were, and sure to bring a good price. These I'll sell to the eastern papers, no question. But tell me, what were you saying to the sheriff about Slidell's body? I couldn't hear."

"I told him it wasn't Slidell," Joe said.

"Wasn't Slidell!" St. Patrick's face fell. "But it has to be Slidell—everyone said so."

"Everyone was wrong."

"How can you be sure? I would think a sheriff would know a wanted outlaw if he looked him in the face.

Speaking of wanted outlaws, do you know what I overheard just now? I heard a man say the sheriff is all in a mad fury, declaring that Cherokee Joe is in town. Apparently he saw him on the street earlier and realized who he was when he went back to his desk and looked through his *wanted* posters."

Joe's now-empty bowl of beans slid from his lap to the ground. He was looking not at St. Patrick but at an upper window of the adjacent storehouse. His eyes narrowed. He had seen something there—a subtle motion, a shifting of the light...

"The sheriff has men out looking for Cherokee Joe right now. If he really is in town, I'm hoping they catch him. It would be a fine accomplishment indeed to add a portrait of Cherokee Joe to my portfolio."

Joe stood. "You already have," he said. Then he put his hand on St. Patrick's head and pushed him straight back. The photographer yelped once in surprise, then yelped again when a shot rang from the upper window of the storage building. A slug slammed into the wooden porch just where Joe had been seated a moment earlier. St. Patrick realized after sitting up that the halfbreed's pushing him back had put him well out of the line of fire.

Joe dived to the side as the next shot came. It was one of the deputies firing. He was a nervous and inaccurate rifleman, and a treacherous and cowardly one, firing from hiding as he was.

St. Patrick stood and backed up against the cafe wall, palms flat and eyes wide. He watched as the man he had known as Henry Feather yanked back the tail of his coat and drew out a well-oiled Colt Peacemaker in one smooth motion. The pistol cracked, and the man behind the window above screeched and disappeared into the storehouse.

"By the saints!" the Irish portrait maker said. "You really are Cherokee Joe!"

Around the corner behind Joe came another man, carrying a scattergun. Joe wheeled and fired just as the newcomer blasted off a shot. The effort did him no good, for the entire load of buckshot missed Joe and ripped a hole in the white-painted back wall of Castle's cafe. St. Patrick, standing near the point of impact, yelled and took off at a run. Meanwhile, Joe's shot took the shotgunner in the shoulder and made him drop his weapon. The man gripped his wound; blood came between his fingers. He staggered back and out of sight.

The back door of the cafe swung open, and Tarsus Castle appeared, an old cap-and-ball Colt in his left hand. "What's going on here?" he bellowed.

Joe swung his pistol toward him. "Back inside!" he ordered.

Castle went pale, glanced down at the old pistol he held, tossed it aside as if it had suddenly gone hot in his hand, and ran back inside.

Joe darted behind the big storage building, hoping to find a back way to circle to his horse, tethered to a hitchrail on the street a few buildings down. A man appeared before him, coming from the end of an alley. Joe fired. The man clutched his midsection and fell to his knees—the sheriff himself. He wavered and pitched forward. Joe had no chance to see if he was dead, for he heard others running up the alleys on both sides of the building. Lacking any other option, he ducked into the rear door of the storage house.

Inside, Ed Wiltflower's corpse still lay on ice in a big wooden box on two sawhorses. Joe leaped it, heading for the stairs. The toe of his boot caught the corner of the box and tipped it over. The blue-faced cadaver fell out, ice chunks sliding across the floor. Joe ran up the stairs.

He had forgotten the gunman who had fired down at him from the window of this building—forgotten, that is, until he saw him again.

He was lying in the corner bleeding from a wound on his neck. He stared at Joe in utter fear, his face white. "Don't kill me!" he pleaded. "Don't kill me, please!"

Joe kicked the gun out of the deputy's limp hand. It clattered across the floor and struck the wall. "Why shouldn't I kill you?" he said. "You tried to murder me from hiding."

The wounded man had no answer. His eyes went big and bright, and then he fainted, sinking into darkness and no doubt expecting never to reemerge. Joe saw now that the man's neck wound was hardly more than a bloody scratch and felt contempt for the fellow.

Joe scanned the room for a way out. He hoped for a ladder to the roof, a walkway across to an adjacent building, any escape route. But there was none. And now he heard men entering the room below him, exclaiming as they found the overturned box and the body on the floor. "Upstairs!" one shouted. "He's upstairs!" Their feet pounded loudly on the steps.

Chapter 9

When he traveled to Guthrie in the Indian Territory a few weeks later to photograph the first land run and make a property claim for himself on the side, Pat St. Patrick would talk expansively and proudly of how he watched Cherokee Joe make his incredible escape from Hutchinson, Kansas. He would keep talking of it for the rest of his life, which he mostly spent in the little Guthrie photographic studio he established. As he talked, he would show off the photograph that made him famous: Cherokee Joe himself, long coat draped to hide his gun as he posed stiffly on a roadside, staring into the Kansas morning sunlight.

Some years later, St. Patrick would print his recollection of Cherokee Joe's flight for life. The story, first printed privately in Guthrie and then in a newspaper in Wichita, would be published by other newspapers and finally across the nation.

The story would tell of his chance meeting with "Henry Feather" on the road to Hutchinson and the young man's aid in fixing the wagon. "Though I did not know my new companion, I could tell even then the young man had in him a dark secretiveness, a secretiveness as dark as his swarthy skin," St. Patrick wrote, giving himself credit for a foresight he had not possessed. "I suspected him at once of being an Indian in northward flight from the Nations for some trouble or another that had come his way, though never in my most lurid imaginings did I then consider that this might be the feared Cherokee Joe Wolfkiller, whose infamy even at that moment was spreading like a fire across the plains because of his dramatic gunning down of peace officers on the plains of the Nations."

Such verbosity would be skipped over by many readers, who would scan directly to the most exciting part—St. Patrick's description of Cherokee Joe's escape from the upper level of the storage house where he was finally cornered.

St. Patrick: "There I stood on that earthen street, shaken to my heart, nay, my soul, by the violence I had witnessed. I knew that my former companion was now trapped in the upper floor of that building, for I had seen a half dozen armed men converge upon it and enter. I waited in grim expectation for the gunshot that would mark the end of Cherokee Joe's life, and as was my anticipation, a shot rang out, muffled by the walls of the building. No sooner had I lowered my head to voice a quick prayer for the heathen's soul than did the single front and upper window of the storage house explode outward, and through it came the form of the man I had assumed had just been killed.

"It was, indeed, Cherokee Joe, very much alive, with pistol in hand and long coat trailing in high dramatic fashion behind his slender form. Onto the roof of the porch of his former prison he had leaped. He darted to his right, then upon seemingly changing his mind, left again, discharging his Colt pistol back through the shattered window as he passed. That shot, I was later informed, sadly took the life of an innocent man, named B. N. Smith, who had joined the peace officers in their pursuit of the fearsome halfbreed.

"From the porch roof Cherokee Joe made a leap most impressive, flying through the air a remarkable distance to the slightly lower porch roof on a building adjacent. From this perch, clearly, he intended to make his descent to the ground and race to his nearby horse, but the sudden appearance below of another armed man intent upon his capture forced him to remain where he was. He moved down the roof approximately ten feet and then climbed to the rooftop, dropping over the high false front that then hid him from my sight for the span of fifteen seconds.

"He emerged next on the ground, holding before him a young woman around whose neck his arm was tightly crooked. He had taken his hostage, I later learned, from the back door of a dress shop—the poor maiden had stepped out to see what was causing all the commotion. As he advanced toward his horse, he alternately held his pistol to her head and waved it generally at all his observers, ordering all the while that he be allowed to escape or the unfortunate young woman would pay with her life. In this manner he reached his horse. He was forced to release the girl in order to mount, and she ran quickly to the relative safety of the other side of the street. A great explosion of gunfire immediately erupted from the pursuers who were now emerging again onto the street, but Cherokee Joe escaped the borders of the town without harm, a feat later attributed by one local preacher to a miracle of devils. Whatever its nature, the escape had the effect, so common in cases of this sort, of making Cherokee Joe something of a dashing and heroic figure in the eyes of many, including those old and intelligent enough to know better."

Including, had he been honest enough to say it, Pat St. Patrick, who for the rest of his life did more than any other man to keep the legend of Cherokee Joe alive and thriving.

When the night came again to Will Ax, so also came the Creek boy named Timothy. The old Cherokee, who had been seated on his bed anxiously waiting, helped him to enter.

"Timothy, did you—"

"It was easy, Grandfather," Timothy said as he held out his small brown hand. "I waited until Dr. Lansford was in his office downstairs and climbed up his trellis to the window. I had to break the glass to reach the lock, but no one heard me, and no one saw me. The crystal was on the table beside his bed."

Will Ax took the little pouch from the boy's hand, opened it, took out the *ulunsuti* stone, and cupped it in his palm. He closed his eyes and squeezed his treasure lovingly, then opened them and touched the boy's shoulder. "You have made me complete again, Timothy. Now I will find the way to escape this place."

"When you do, will you come and visit me?"

"If I can, I will. If I can't, you can know that I am always grateful to you and will see you when we both are in the Celestial City." Will Ax turned his head suddenly. "Go now —I hear someone coming."

Scarcely had Timothy slipped out the window when the door rattled and opened. Miller thrust in his head. "Who you talking to up here, old man?"

"To myself. I have been giving myself wise counsel, telling myself I should be more grateful to my fine hosts for the hospitality they have shown an old Indian."

"Well, do your wise counseling during the daytime— else maybe we won't be such good hosts anymore."

"Thank you, friend Miller. Your counsel is even wiser than my own."

The lamp in Miller's hand sent flickering light into the room; some of it glinted with surprising brilliance on the *ulunsuti* stone in Will Ax's hand.

"What's that you got there?" Miller asked, stepping in.

Will Ax knew that to hide the *ulunsuti* would only ensure it being taken from him, so he held it out for Miller to see. "It is only a piece of quartz stone," he said. "Just a pretty rock."

Miller was suspicious. "Let me see that. I never seen a quartz flash that bright."

Will Ax did not let his dismay show as he laid the *ulunsuti* stone in Miller's hand. The ugly little man held it up and examined it in the lamplight. In his fingers it did not seem the bright thing it had been in Will Ax's hand; it glinted dully like any piece of quartz.

"Huh," Miller said grumpily, thrusting the stone back at Will Ax. "Thought you was keeping something from me there, old man. Thought you had a diamond or some such."

He turned and left the room. Will Ax took a deep breath. He put the crystal back into its hide wrapping and put the package under his pillow, then went to the dark window and looked out. "May your pilgrimage be safe and all your quests successful, Timothy," he whispered.

He climbed into his bed. When he slept, his dreams were peaceful and full of renewed confidence.

The rattle and squeak of an approaching wagon awakened Will Ax early the next morning. He got out of bed and went to the window. A large freight wagon pulled by a team of mules had rumbled up to the front door. Jim Christmas emerged and talked to the driver, who then pulled the wagon around the far side of the house out of Will's sight.

The aging Cherokee stretched and yawned, and noted happily to himself that he felt stronger and younger today than he had in a long time. He took the *ulunsuti* from beneath his pillow and examined it again. "Today we will escape," he said to it.

Miller later brought up Will Ax's breakfast—toasted bread and eggs on a heavy china plate. "Tell me, friend Miller, does Mr. Christmas own you like I own my piece of quartz?" Will Ax asked. He knew the question would anger Miller, but he felt feisty today.

Miller swore at him and left, slamming the door hard. When he returned for the plate, Will Ax was standing where the door would hide him when it opened. Miller thrust his head in. Will Ax came around and smashed the china plate down on his skull. Miller fell unconscious.

Will Ax beamed. He dragged Miller farther into the room and rifled his pockets. He found a small amount of cash, some twist tobacco, and a loaded pocket pistol. Putting the items into his coat, he stepped across the prone form. "Thank you for all your kindness," he said to Miller.

Miller groaned and started to stir. Will Ax picked up half the china plate and knocked him cold once more.

Will Ax slipped into the hallway and crept along as quietly as he could. He heard movement, and thinking someone was about to mount the stairs, ducked into the next room, another bedroom. He heard voices from below. Near the fireplace a ventilation grate was cut through the floor to allow heat from the iron stove below to rise to the upper level.

Will Ax went to the grate and looked down. Jim Christmas stood, coffee cup in hand, talking to the man who had driven the freight wagon. Will Ax heard that the wagon was loaded with plow parts and other farming equipment picked up from a warehouse in Wichita. Christmas, he gathered, had sold the items to a merchant some miles to the north and was delivering them by wagon because of some foul up at the railroad freight yard.

Such talk was of no interest to Will Ax, but he lingered

anyway, trying to figure out the layout of the house from what he could see and remember. It appeared he would have to make it past the door of the room Christmas was in if he was to find an exit. Could he do it without being seen?

He was about to try when the conversation below took a new angle that caught his attention and stopped him. The man with Christmas asked, "What you intend to do about Slidell, Jim?"

"Slidell is being dealt with," Christmas said. "And you'd never guess how."

"The truth is, I know a little about it already," the man said. "Miller told me you somehow got Cherokee Joe himself to go after him."

"He told you that, huh? Miller talks too much. But that's right. The halfbreed turned up out in the shed, hiding out from a storm with an old Indian codger. I tell you, it was a gift from Providence. Now I have the old Indian locked upstairs—a hostage, you know, to make sure Cherokee Joe brings Slidell back. I'll set things square with Caul Slidell as soon as I get my hands around his double-crossing neck. Kind of funny how it worked out because Cherokee Joe was already going after Slidell for murdering his father. That's another bone I've got to pick with Slidell. He had no reason to clutter up our carefully planned robbery with the murder of those Indians."

"I ain't worried about no lousy dead Indians," said the other man. "I worry about getting our cut of those jewels back from Slidell."

"Well get them back, never fear. I'll carve them out of his hide if it comes to that."

"You really think Cherokee Joe will bring him back?"

"I do. He seems very attached to that old red coon upstairs. He won't let harm come to him."

Will Ax smiled. He was touched to hear of Joe's devotion. At the same time he felt a mounting sense of alarm.

Now he understood why he had been kept a prisoner and what had happened to Joe Wolfkiller.

"Is Slidell still up beyond Great Bend?" the other man asked.

"As far as I know, yes. That's where I sent the halfbreed."

"Well, if there's any who can haul in Slidell, it'd be the likes of Cherokee Joe. I hear he's a fierce one."

"He's just another angry Indian who happens to be a little angrier than most," Christmas said. "When he comes back, I'll take delivery of Slidell, put a quick slug through Cherokee Joe's skull, and ship his corpse off to Parker for a present." He chuckled.

The men left the room. Will Ax followed the sound of their voices farther back into the house. Now was the moment for escape, now before they came back, before Miller regained consciousness in the next room. He headed down the stairs as lightly as he could. He was tense but unusually alert and confident. He was on top of his situation again. He had his *ulunsuti,* his *Pilgrim's Progress,* and a gun. Nothing could stop him now.

He made it out of the house and headed for the road. He peered around a corner of the house and saw the loaded wagon. He crept around it, and then a side door of the house opened. The voice of Jim Christmas wafted over. Will Ax panicked and looked wildly for a place to hide.

The wagon pulled out a couple of minutes later. Christmas said goodbye to the driver and wished him luck on his delivery, then wondered aloud where Miller had gone for so long. The other said he didn't know and didn't much care because he thought Miller was an irritating little squat anyway.

The wagon creaked off. Hidden among the crates and plow parts, beneath the tarpaulin spread across it all, Will Ax grinned. He thought it funny and ironic that Christmas' cargo wagon had turned into his vehicle of escape.

Will Ax was eager to get back to his quest to find his daughter, but for now he would have to lay that aside to take up a more pressing matter. He had to find Joe Wolfkiller and tell him he had escaped, that Jim Christmas no longer was a threat to either of them. He did not know how he would find Joe...unless the crystal could help him.

He pulled the *ulunsuti* from his pocket and by the sunlight seeping in around the edge of the tarpaulin looked deeply into its crystalline facets. This time, he hoped intensely, the stone would not keep silent. This time it could not, or he might never find Joe Wolfkiller.

The wagon jolted along, heading northwest across the rolling land.

CHAPTER 10

Joe Wolfkiller slipped the smoking pistol back into its holster and looked sadly at the horse he had just shot to death. There had been no choice; the horse had broken a front leg so thoroughly that the fractured bone protruded through the flesh. An unseen hole had caused the accident, which had tumbled Joe to the earth so hard the breath had been knocked out of him for several moments.

Now he was on foot, the worst situation for a man fleeing the law on the plains. There was no question that he would be pursued; the shootout in Hutchinson had been a horrific one. If Cherokee Joe had coveted fame as an outlaw, he had certainly found it.

It couldn't have come at a more inconvenient time.

He took his rifle from the saddle and began walking. It was a terrible feeling to be bound to a speed no greater than he could walk or run. And to be captured would be certain death, either on the spot or on the gallows.

He walked a long time until he was tired and sweating, despite the cool temperature. A sound caught his ear, coming over the hump of land ahead: the whistle of a train running northwest on the Atchison, Topeka, and Santa Fe rails.

Joe stopped for a moment thinking, then with a new burst of hope took off at a trot up the rise.

Will Ax's old bones were getting sore from the jolting the wagon was giving him. The driver had also taken to singing, and that was equally rough on Will's ears. Furthermore, the *ulunsuti* was being stubborn again and would not reveal anything about the whereabouts of Joe Wolfkiller no matter how intently Will Ax looked into it.

Will Ax had long ago come to think of his crystal as a personality (one much like himself) and at the moment was peeved at it. The ungrateful *ulunsuti* was simply being ornery, like a foul-tempered old goat, refusing to help when needed the most. Will finally tucked the crystal away in his pocket with disgust. As time passed and he thought about it more, he began to feel differently. Maybe the *ulunsuti* wasn't unwilling to help. Maybe it was just too weak.

A feeling of irresponsibility descended upon Will Ax. He knew he had not taken care of the *ulunsuti* as he should. A man as versed in the old lore as he had no excuse for not following the rules. An *ulunsuti* required a rubbing with the blood of a small game animal at least every seven days and the blood of some larger animal about twice a year. And its home should be a hidden cave, not the pocket of a tattered old Union coat. Will Ax felt chagrined. The *ulunsuti's* lack of responsiveness was probably his fault.

He realized he was fortunate that the *ulunsuti* had let him get away with such carelessness. According to the old stories, an *ulunsuti* improperly cared for changed to a flame by night and took the blood of its mishandler or one of his kin to replace what had been denied it. Yet no such revenge had befallen Will Ax, and since he had no kin left, it couldn't have befallen anyone else either. He was lucky.

A frightening thought suddenly came. He was wrong to think he had no remaining kin. He had kin in the daughter he was even now seeking, so long gone from him that he often failed to remember her as his own flesh. What if the stone had taken its revenge upon her, wherever she was? Will's heart beat faster, harder. His mouth began to go dry.

He reached into his pocket, pulled out the crystal again, and unwrapped it. "I am sorry I've neglected you," he whispered. "I will do better and feed you with blood as soon as I can." He began to fold the pouch around the crystal again, then stopped. "But I will tell you, talisman: If I find harm has come to my daughter because of you, I will smash you to pieces with a hammer."

He put the crystal away, wondering if he had been prudent to threaten it. He set his jaw. Prudent or not, he was glad he had done it. Sometimes the Methodist side of him made him antagonistic toward the conjurer side.

His thoughts were interrupted when the wagon gave a huge heave that threw Will Ax bodily off the wagon bed. The tailgate fell, and a crate beside him slid out from beneath the tarpaulin and crashed onto the ground. Will Ax barely retained his perch in the wagon.

He huddled down under the tarpaulin as he heard the driver curse and pull the wagon to a halt. In a moment he would be discovered, and there was no way to escape it.

Upon topping the rise, Joe Wolfkiller was surprised and pleased to see the train he had heard pull to a full stop below. He quickly saw why: Smoke was pouring out around one of the wheels of a freight car. The engineer and crew were spilling out of the engine cab and running back toward the smoking wheel, a brakeman coming around the other end of the train to join them.

Joe grinned. The train would be stopped for some time as the trainmen repacked the bearings in the overheated wheel journal. If Joe was lucky, he might be able to find a way to slip into one of the freight cars while they were distracted.

He made a wide circle around the train for fifteen minutes; he wanted to approach from the rear to minimize the angles from which he could be seen. The full attention of the crew would be on the repairs, he figured. His biggest problem would be finding a way inside a freight car. He reached the train near its end on the side opposite the area under repair, then stopped, looking up hopelessly at the big closed doors. Even if they weren't locked, he doubted he could open one without attracting the attention of someone on the crew.

He was startled when one of the doors on the next car down slid open as if of its own accord. Joe threw himself up against the side of the train and watched as a man came flying from the open door to sprawl on the ground. The trainman who had just booted him out stuck out his head. Joe caught a warning not to try to freeload on the railroad again. The trainman watched the man stomp off to begin his long and lonely walk to the nearest town, miles away, then pulled his head back inside—and did not close the door.

Joe could hardly believe his good fortune. He crept to the open car and looked inside. The door on the opposite side was also cracked open. The trainman had apparently heard movement inside the car after the stop and entered from the opposite side to investigate. He had now left the same way he had come and was talking and laughing with his fellow crew members at the repair site, describing how he had tossed off the freeloader.

Joe climbed in quietly and looked around the jumble of

crates, boxes, and shapeless tarpaulin-draped freight items. He clambered onto some of the crates and headed toward the back corner. A space between two crates provided just enough room for him to sit down.

Only now did he have time to reflect on what had happened back in Hutchinson. How many men had he killed or wounded? He didn't know; he remembered the entire incident only as a disturbing blur of running, shooting, and fearing. Mostly fearing... but not as much as before.

It had been a little easier this time for Cherokee Joe to kill.

But only a little easier. As he sat waiting for the train to move, the fear came back and brought new ones with it. What if a posse overtook the stalled train and searched it? What if he found the law waiting for him wherever this train finally stopped? He was out of his home area now, away from the familiar plains of the Territory. This was Kansas, white men's country, crisscrossed by railroads and full of towns, farms, and people among whom he stood out like a cinder in a snow pile.

Joe jerked his head up and gasped through his teeth when he heard one of the big sliding doors slam shut and latch. The meager light in the freight car diminished by half. The other door slammed moments later, and it became as dark as late dusk. Joe closed his eyes, feeling a little safer behind hiding walls.

The train chugged and lurched and began moving again, picking up speed. The multi-branched Atchison, Topeka, and Santa Fe track ran a long way, passing through Larned, Kinsley, Dodge City, Cimarron, and many other towns. But first it passed through Great Bend, and that was as far as Joe needed to go, for it was near Great Bend that Caul Slidell and his hellriders were said to be holed up.

Knowledge of the task before him was daunting. Now it was even more complicated than before, for every telegraph wire was probably already singing with news of the terrible fight in Hutchinson. Alerts would be out. How could he hope to search down Caul Slidell when every law dog in Kansas was on his tail? It astounded Joe when he realized that his reputation might overshadow that of Slidell at the moment. He had gunned down men in the Territory and in Hutchinson. Some had been officers of the court.

It came to Cherokee Joe that men who did the things he had done usually lived short lives, and the thought gnarled his stomach. Despite the many times he had told himself that he did not fear death and would rather die young, rebellious, and vengeful, it had all been hypothetical talk. Now it was likely. Maybe a certainty.

Joe pulled out the little knife he always kept in a sheath inside his left boot, removed his hat, and hacked off his hair by the handfuls. He was desperate to change his appearance, to do anything to increase his chances of survival.

When he was through, he put the knife back in his pocket and his hat back on his head. He closed his eyes and noted that his head was pounding. The train rumbled along mesmerizingly. He slept and dreamed of Parker's gibbet and Maledon's noose.

Will Ax came out of the back of the wagon with a scream worthy of a panther. The driver, who had just tossed back the tarpaulin so he could put the fallen crate back in place, screamed just as impressively and fell back on his rump, staring up in abject fright. Will Ax reached into the big pocket in his coat and brought out his heavy volume of *Pilgrim's Progress.* He raised it and pounded it as hard as he could on the driver's head three times in succession, then hammered a fourth blow square across his face. The driver's eyes rolled up, and he fell back, blood pouring from his broken nose.

Will Ax smiled and glanced up at the sky. "Thank you, Mr. Bunyan," he said. "Your book has again been a benefit to me."

The driver carried a Remington pistol, and Will Ax took it. The gunbelt was too big to fit Will's thin waist, so he draped it over one shoulder like a Mexican bandolier. Now he had not only the little derringer he had taken from Miller but a large side arm as well. He stood proudly, feeling that with such armament he cut a fine and invincible figure.

The sight of the blood on the unconscious driver's face gave Will Ax an idea. He pulled the *ulunsuti* from his pocket, unwrapped it, and dabbled a good amount of blood on it. "I don't know if white man's blood will serve in place of an animal's, but it seems a good trade to me," he said to the crystal. "I hope this will make you strong again and take away any anger you have against me."

Will Ax pulled off the tarpaulin and spread it over the unconscious man. "I don't want you to get too cold sleeping on the ground," he said. "Such a thing isn't healthy. I have nothing against you, and you did give me a fine wagon ride." He climbed onto the wagon seat, pulled it forward a little, and began scooting the wagon's contents toward the back and onto the ground. It was hard work for an old man and left him winded, but when he was done, the wagon was lighter and fit for faster travel.

"Tell Mr. Christmas I'm sorry I stole his wagon, and Mr. Miller that I am sorry I broke his china plate," Will Ax said to the senseless figure. Then he climbed onto the driver's seat again and set off.

Cherokee Joe awakened suddenly and opened his eyes. He did not know for a moment where he was or why he was in gray semidarkness and in motion. His head cleared slowly, and he remembered that he was on the train. Out of instinct, he reached to check his guns.

And found them gone.

Joe stood, amazed and horrified. His guns couldn't be missing—his pistol had been in his belt, his rifle in his hand.

Then he knew he was not alone. He lifted his eyes. A man sat on a crate across from and slightly above him, a big fellow, white, scruffy-bearded, and very familiar. In his possession were Joe's rifle and pistol.

"Hello, Joe," he said.

"Hello, Hambone." Grogginess and tension had Joe feeling as if he were in the midst of a none-too-pleasant dream. "What are you doing here?"

"I was just getting ready to ask you the same thing," said Hambone Coltrane.

"I'm running from the law," Joe said. "I killed some men in the Territory and some more in Hutchinson."

"Hutchinson! Dang, Joe, you been busy! I'd heard about them deputies down in the Territory—everybody's heard about that by now—but I hadn't heard nothing about Hutchinson. When'd you do that one?"

Joe's sense of time was scrambled, so it took a few moments for him to remember. "This morning... if this is still today."

Hambone laughed. "Listen at you! You sound drunk, Joe."

"I'm not drunk." Joe rubbed his head. "What are you doing here? How'd you get on this train?"

"I got on pretty much the same way you did, and for pretty much the same reason. Me and an old boy name of Billy Spratlock got ourself into trouble down at Shadrah Camp's post. Billy and me went over for a little liquor, and I seen that old mule I give you back in the lot. I got to pining for it and wound up trying to steal it back, and it didn't quite work out. To make a long story short, I stuck a knife into Camp's shoulder, and me and Billy rode off on a couple of Camp's horses. That's when we decided it might be good to hitch us a train ride up into Kansas for a while, till things settled down a bit, you know. We slid ourselves into this here freight car, but dang if one of them railroad men didn't find Billy and toss him off back yonder. I was better hid, and he didn't find me. I heard you climb in, Joe, though I didn't know it was you till I crawled out and saw you sleeping here."

"Now you know," Joe said. "Give me my guns back, Hambone."

"No can do, Joe, no can do. You're my pris'ner, I'm sorry to tell you."

Joe glared at Coltrane in disbelief.

"It's just that I figure you're worth a whole lot, Joe. Not only in money but to help get me out of what trouble I'm in too." He flashed an apologetic smile. "I'm right sorry—you know how it is. Hey, you had any food?"

"Not since this morning."

"You're in luck, then. I got a big old hunk of corn bread I'll be happy to share with you."

The corn bread was dry and made Joe even thirstier than he already was. Still, he ate it to the last crumb. Coltrane munched his more slowly and with his free hand kept the pistol aimed at Joe's chest.

"You can't do this to me, Hambone," Joe said. "They'll hang me."

"Like I said, Joe, I'm sorry. By the way, what happened to your hair?"

"I cut it off."

"Did you now! Trying to change your looks, huh?"

"That's right."

Hambone Coltrane took another bite of corn bread. He chewed it slowly—and stopped suddenly. "What'd you cut that hair with, anyway?"

"With this." Joe came up as swift as a cat, lunged forward with the boot knife in his right hand, and cut a big slash across the hand of Hambone Coltrane. The big man yelped, jumped up, and dropped the pistol.

Chapter 11

Joe had the pistol in his hand an instant after it had thunked to the floor of the freight car. He expected Coltrane to swing around and grab for the rifle he had laid on a box behind him, but the porcine fellow lurched forward, grabbing at his throat. His eyes grew wide and wet, and he seemed to be trying to talk, though no sound came out.

Joe sheathed his knife, reached up behind Coltrane and took the rifle. "That dry corn bread's bad for choking a man," he said.

Hambone Coltrane stood, his fat legs bowed to either side and his hands at his throat. Joe holstered his pistol as he watched the big man choke. Serves him right, Joe thought. If he strangles on his own corn bread, it will be one of those rare cases of justice in an unjust world.

Then Coltrane fell to his knees. His watering eyes looked up pleadingly at Joe, and the halfbreed sighed. "All right, Hambone, all right." He turned the rifle butt forward and jammed the buttplate hard into Coltrane's diaphragm.

A sodden crust of corn bread came flying out of

Coltrane's mouth. The big man sucked in the most welcome breath of his life as he sank to the floor.

"First time I ever whipped a man in a fight by choking him on corn bread. I should have let you strangle," Joe muttered as he stepped past Coltrane and made his way through the piles of cargo toward the center of the car.

He opened one of the doors a couple of feet and looked out. Nothing in the passing landscape gave him any hint of where he was. He wondered how long he should remain on the train. It seemed likely that by now news of what had happened in Hutchinson had been wired to every town and station along every rail line. The law would probably be on the alert for him wherever he went. He couldn't afford to be caught in a railroad car. And this car wasn't a pleasant place to be anymore with Hambone Coltrane along. Joe decided to jump, but first he pulled his head back in to make sure Coltrane was still in his place and prepare himself for what would be a rough tumble to the ground.

Coltrane was right behind him. He had crept up silently. A big fist swung out and pounded Joe's jaw. Joe was knocked out the open door. Instinctively he dropped his rifle and grabbed for a handhold to keep from falling out. Coltrane kicked the rifle away and chortled.

Joe let go with one hand and reached for his pistol. Coltrane, his face red, managed to grip the wrist of Joe's gun hand. Coltrane was as strong as he was big, and Joe could not level the pistol to fire. He was trapped in a deadly position, his entire body leaning back out of the speeding freight car, the toes of his boots barely retaining a hold on the edge of the floor.

"I'm still going to take you in, Joe!" Coltrane said through his gritted mossy teeth. "Give me that pistol or I'll snap your arm!"

Joe's entire arm was racked with pain as Coltrane began to twist it. The clinging fingers of his other hand began to slip from the edge of the door, which was beginning to slide away from him, making him even more unbalanced. His gun hand became weak; the gun fell, landing half in and half out of the car.

Coltrane reached down and grabbed it with his free hand, retaining his hold on Joe's arm. In the process he unwittingly wrenched Joe's arm even further, and the pain was more than Joe could take.

He let go of the car and fell straight back with an involuntary yell. For a moment Coltrane kept his grip, and Joe dangled in the air by his wrenched arm. Then he fell.

He couldn't have found a poorer place to drop. Beside the track lay the badly broken skeleton of a dog that had come to the end of its days under a train weeks before. Joe landed right atop it, and a sharp upthrusting shard of bone gashed his left arm painfully. He rolled down the embankment and lay gasping in the dirt and gravel.

Twisting his head, he watched the train pass, Coltrane's head sticking out of the car. He watched Joe until the train made a curve and his line of sight was cut off. Joe swore and stood, gripping his bleeding arm. A broken piece of dog bone was sticking out of it. He pulled it out with a shudder and dug into the back pocket of his denim pants for a bandanna, which he pressed tightly around his cut.

"Next time, Hambone... next time I let you choke!" Joe yelled at the disappearing train.

He sat down and collected his thoughts. He had wanted to leave the train, but not at the cost of a painful and infection-prone injury and not without his weapons. All he had now was his little boot knife. And he didn't even know where he was.

The sun was in the western half of the sky. Joe wondered if by dark he could find a place to sleep and steal some food and a horse. He had his doubts. Luck seemed to have left him the moment he awoke and saw Hambone Coltrane's ugly face.

Pressing the bandanna tighter, Joe staunched the flow of blood from the gash in his arm. His hat lay on the ground beside him. He picked it up, plopped it onto his raggedly shorn head, and began trudging along the side of the tracks.

Will Ax was nearly in despair by the time his commandeered wagon rolled into sight of Hutchinson the next morning. After stopping for the night along the road, he had consulted the *ulunsuti,* and from it he had gained no intuitions. The crystal felt heavy and cold and dead in his hand.

It had been a mistake, he decided, to bathe it in the blood of a white man. How could he have been so foolish?

He might have rendered the *ulunsuti* useless forever by exposing it to so alien a substance. "I've killed you, old friend, I've killed you," Will mourned. "Now I have nothing to give to my daughter before I die."

Will Ax was so hungry that he knew he would have to go into Hutchinson and see if he could find any white folks friendly enough to give some food to an aging Indian. After the team had eaten more grain, the Cherokee climbed on the wagon again and rolled into town.

He found the place in a state of excitement. He had expected to receive many curious and cold looks when he entered town—white folks usually acted that way toward Indians—but he had not expected the hostility he detected in every stare aimed his way. He pulled up the wagon in front of a cafe and climbed down stiffly.

He knew better than to go to the front door, so circled around to the back. Three men were there in a line with their backs toward him. One of them wore an apron. The others were nondescript, typical plains townsmen. All were standing stiff and straight as telegraph poles.

A fourth man was in front of them, behind a camera. When Will Ax came into view behind the men, the man lifted his head and glowered at him. "You're in the way, old fellow," Pat St. Patrick said. There was nothing unfriendly in his tone.

"I'm very sorry," Will Ax muttered. He backed up. St. Patrick took the picture and nodded at the men. They relaxed and broke line.

The one in the apron turned to Will Ax. "What are you doing here?" he asked. It was Tarsus Castle, the cafe owner.

"I came hoping to find someone willing to give a hungry Methodist some food," Will Ax said, trying to look very sad. White people, he had learned during his years of begging gifts from the cattlemen who trailed through the Indian Nations, often saw sad looking Indians in a romanticized and tragic light that made them more generous.

"Methodist, huh?" Castle chuckled and looked at the others. "Hear that? This one's a Methodist." Castle's grin faded when he looked back at Will Ax. "You'll have to pardon me if I don't act too nice toward your kind today.

The last redskin we had in this town sure wasn't no Methodist. He left us with some new widows, one of them the sheriffs wife."

Will Ax didn't understand but sought no clarification. Overly inquisitive Indians were not popular among whites. "I'll go somewhere else," he said.

"That's the best idea you'll ever have, old man," Castle replied. He turned to St. Patrick. "You'll make sure I get a copy of that?"

"Indeed."

Castle gave Will Ax one more sour look and disappeared into his cafe through the back door. The other two subjects strode away through the alley up to the street.

Will Ax turned to follow, but St. Patrick said, "Wait, old fellow. Talk to me a minute."

Will Ax turned. "If you want."

"What kind of Indian are you?"

"Cherokee." He added proudly, "I'm a conjurer."

"You don't say! You look like you could stand to conjure up some food at the moment."

Will Ax's stomach answered with a well-timed growl.

"I'll make a bargain with you, Mr...."

"Ax." Will Ax liked the ring of "mister." He seldom was granted such dignities.

"Mr. Ax. I'll buy you something to eat if you'll allow me to make your portrait."

"My portrait?" Will Ax's ego rose to a new height. "Yes. Thank you, sir."

"Pat's the name. Call me Pat."

St. Patrick went into Castle's cafe and emerged with a tray piled with food—hot eggs, biscuits, coffee, bacon, bread soaked in molasses. Will Ax sat on the back doorstep eating, wondering if Bunyan's Celestial City could boast a feast to match this one.

Meanwhile, St. Patrick went about setting up the camera for a new shot. "This has been a busy little stretch for me, Mr. Ax," St. Patrick said as he worked. "That spot you're sitting on was last occupied by another Indian who turned this town upside down."

"What happened?"

"A one-man massacre, that's what. Cherokee Joe himself —and he rode into town at my side, and me not knowing who he was."

Will Ax was frozen. A biscuit hovered between plate and mouth. "Cherokee Joe? You are sure?"

"Took his portrait myself." He reached into a leather valise on the ground beside the camera stand and pulled out a picture, which he handed to the Indian.

Will Ax stared at the stern black-and-white depiction of Joe Wolfkiller. "Where is this man now?" he asked.

"On the run, unless somebody's caught him. He took off toward the northwest. If he keeps going and fighting like he did here, they may never bring him in—not alive, at least. He fought through a big gunfight that started right where we are now and ended up with him riding out of town like lightning in a saddle. Hah! Since then, I've shot ten, twelve pictures of people back here, near that hole in the wall beside you there. That came from a shotgun blast fired at Cherokee Joe. Folks like to be able to show that they were where something big and bad happened, you know. They love that sort of thing—and it's surely good for my business, I can tell you!"

St. Patrick told the story of Joe Wolfkiller's escape, embellishing it hardly at all, for the true version of the tale was so astonishing, it did not require it. Will Ax continued to eat, but his mind was no longer on his meal. At last he set the tray aside and thanked St. Patrick for his generosity.

"You can thank me by walking right over here and standing... yes, right there. Good! Now hold still, tilt your head a bit. Give me that look you did before—no smile, no smile. Look sad and noble. Good, good..."

St. Patrick made the photograph and smiled. "That will be a fine one, Mr. Ax. But I want another if you don't mind." He rubbed his chin. "Do you have anything that marks you as a conjurer? Something you could show in the picture?"

Will Ax produced the *ulunsuti.* "This is my divining crystal," he said. "It tells me things I need to know. I thought it had grown useless, but now I believe it just found a new way of talking to me." Before catching himself, Will Ax was about to speculate aloud that the stone, having been bathed in the blood of one white man, had obviously chosen to give its information through the mouth of another white man, St. Patrick.

St. Patrick took another picture of Will Ax, this time with the crystal held before him at chest level. He was so pleased with the view that he decided to take yet another shot. This required him to return to his wagon for a new plate. When St. Patrick returned, Will Ax had gone. He had vanished in a manner appropriately mysterious for an avowed Indian conjurer.

Later, when St. Patrick developed his portraits of Will Ax, he found himself surprised again. The first portrait was excellent, sharp and focused. The second portrait was equally good, except for the middle portion where the *ulunsuti* had been. There, instead of the dull crystal St. Patrick had seen when the plate was exposed, was a brilliant starburst of light, as if the crystal had caught some stray shaft of sunlight and sent it flashing back to the camera fifty times brighter than before. It was a most remarkable phenomenon, even though it did ruin a good photograph.

Will Ax's hunger upon reaching Hutchinson had been minor compared to the agonizing gnawing in the gut of Joe Wolfkiller when he finally reached the town of Great Bend the next day. The town, which stood where the Arkansas River arched down toward the southwest, had broad streets and neat buildings. Joe was weary and empty, and his injured arm throbbed. All the ordeals that he had suffered over the past days were beginning to wear badly on him. He wondered where he could find food.

The day had warmed, but Joe still felt chilled and huddled inside his coat. He hoped the arm was not already infected. Maybe he could locate some whiskey and disinfect it, though he doubted that would do much good after so much time.

Despite the hunger that drove him on, Joe at last realized it was rest or drop. He was at the southwest border of the town. The sky was growing cloudy, and Joe figured it would rain within the hour. The thought of being drenched brought a new chill. He sank down on his haunches and looked despairingly around. A barn stood on the edge of a nearby small farm. Joe rose and wearily made for it. A good sleep in the loft might revitalize him and give his arm a chance to begin healing. He found the barn empty and climbed to the loft. Old heaps of hay were piled all around. He lay down on one heap and pulled more hay up around him. He dozed off, warm externally but still cold inside.

When he woke up, his hunger burned like acid in his gut. He sat up and felt dizzy. His arm was swollen beneath his coat, and he was afraid to look at it. He silently cursed Hambone Coltrane.

Through the open double doors of the barn Joe heard the noise of a door opening and closing at the nearby house. He crept to the wall and peered out through a hexagonal ventilation window. An old woman in a long housedress, apron, and bonnet had come outside and was feeding scraps and bones to a fat dog. The dog ate the scraps quickly and lay down to begin lazily gnawing one of the bones.

Joe watched until the woman reentered the house. He climbed down from the loft and went to the barn door. He peered around it until he was satisfied there was no one to see him. The dog had put its head down to sleep, several bones on the ground beside it. Joe swallowed nervously, then advanced.

Being this hungry, it wasn't hard for him to ignore the indignity of coveting a dog's meal of raw and meaty bones. He advanced through the barnyard, his eyes flickering between the canine and the house, until he reached the picket fence. He lifted his leg and stepped over. The dog stirred, and Joe froze. A few moments later he pulled the other leg over and sneaked right up beside the dog. His hand crept down toward the pile of bones, beef bones with quite a bit of ragged raw meat clinging to them.

The dog sensed Joe's presence and awoke suddenly, leaping up, barking and howling. Joe grabbed a handful of bones and turned to run back toward the fence. He heard the door of the house open as he tried to jump the fence. Any other time it would have been an easy hurdle for him, but today he was so weak that he didn't make it. His boots caught on the pickets and tripped him up. He dropped the bones and caught himself on the ground with both hands, jarring his wounded arm so badly that he groaned. The dog came at him, leaping up and biting at his right boot, which was lodged between two pickets, leaving his foot still inside the fence.

"Don't move!" a tremulous voice ordered. Joe looked back through the fence and saw the old woman on the porch, a shotgun leveled on him. "If you move, I'll have to shoot!" she ordered.

The dog calmed a little now that the woman was there. It backed away and stood with its hackles up, snarling at Joe.

"I want to get up," Joe said.

The woman advanced to the edge of the porch, still holding her shotgun. She was shaking. "You may get up," she said. "But do it slowly."

Joe freed his boot from the fence and stood. He was shaking too, not from fear but weakness and hunger.

"What are you doing creeping around my house?" the old woman asked.

"I was hungry," Joe said. "I came to take the bones you gave the dog."

The old woman blinked. Her expression softened. After

a few moments she lowered the shotgun. "You poor man," she said. "Are you that hungry?"

"Yes."

Another pause. "All right, then. Come inside. I'll not send away a man hungry enough to steal the bones from a dog."

Joe thought of running. The old woman came down from the porch, took the dog by its rope collar, and held it. "Come on," she said. "I won't let the dog bother you."

Joe hesitated, then nodded. He climbed over the fence again and walked wearily, dizzily, toward the house.

Chapter 12

Joe Wolfkiller was no philosopher, but he could not help marveling at how peculiar life was. One moment a man can be a renegade on the run, empty, wounded, and the next seated at a table in the homey surroundings of an aging white widow's house, eating roast beef, potatoes, and apple pie from a fancy plate. The old woman, who identified herself as Mrs. Alabama Fleck, widow of the late Stansfield Fleck, Esquire, of Indiana, hovered around the table with a nice little smile, obviously enjoying her task of rescuing the perishing. She kept Joe's coffee cup full and urged plate after plate of food upon him. He refused none of it.

"It's not often I entertain a guest, and never have I had one so obviously in need of a good meal," she said. "I notice, young fellow, that your arm is hurt. Perhaps you should let me call in Dr. Davies and—"

"No!" Joe said a little too sternly. The widow looked a bit taken aback. Joe calmed his tone. "No thank you, I mean. My arm will be fine."

"Whatever you wish, young fellow. Do you mind telling me your name?"

"Henry Feather."

"Feather! Oh, I knew some Feathers back home in Indiana. Gilbert Feather and Audrey—wonderful people. They had the sweetest little baby and named her Downy. Downy Feather—a name that just floats in the air, don't you think? Might you be kin to the Gilbert Feathers, Henry?"

"I don't think so," Joe replied around a mouthful of pie.

"Oh, I guess not. Am I right that you are Indian?"

Joe started to tell her he was only half Indian, then changed his mind. He surely didn't need Alabama Fleck telling people she had given help to a wandering half-breed, not with the law looking for the halfbreed Cherokee Joe right now. "I'm Cherokee," Joe replied, then wished he had said Choctaw or Creek to steer her even further from the truth.

"Cherokee. Such a lyrical word, *Cherokee.* My son Stanley once had a Cherokee friend. Poor Stanley's gone now, died at Chickamauga during the war. My other son, Jerard, lives in Illinois and has a wife and three children. Then there's my only daughter, Marie, who is in Kentucky at the—"

"May I have some more coffee?"

"Oh yes, oh yes indeed." She bustled to the stove and brought back the pot whose contents Joe had already almost drained.

After she had refilled Joe's cup, Alabama Fleck looked at him seriously and asked, "How did you come to be in so bad a way, Mr. Feather?"

Joe wasn't sure how to answer. He had never been good at coming up with lies off the cuff. "I fell from a train miles up the track," he said, giving her the truth without the details.

"How terrible! I'm sure your companions must be worried about you."

"I was traveling alone."

"I see." She returned the pot to the stove. "Mr. Feather,

please don't take offense to this, but your fall from the train left you rather dirty. Let me heat some water for you, and you can bathe in the back room."

"Thank you," Joe said. "That would be good." He sipped his coffee and tried to adjust to the feeling of appreciating a white person. He had somewhat liked Pat St. Patrick, but for Alabama Fleck he was developing a deeper affection. He wasn't used to such gentle cordiality.

The bath was soothing and healing. Joe sat languidly in the warm water, half dozing. He felt good—or as close to good as he could given his throbbing arm. The wound was beginning to putrify. He washed it gently and bound it with a clean rag he found in a cabinet, then dressed in some oversized clothing Alabama Fleck had left in the room for him while she washed out his clothes. Stansfield Fleck had been a sizable man. When Joe was dressed, he paused by the mirror and used a pair of scissors to clip his hair neatly. Dressed in white man's clothing, groomed and washed, he felt like a completely different person than Cherokee Joe. He hoped he looked completely different too.

When he emerged, his old clothing was drying on a rack near Alabama Fleck's fireplace. She was in the kitchen, putting Joe's dirty dishes into a sink full of soapy water.

"I can't pay you for your help," Joe said.

"Why, I didn't expect you to," she answered. "I'm just trying to give you the kind of help I would want in a time of trouble. Do unto others, you know."

Joe didn't know and didn't ask. "Let me wash those dishes lor you," he said.

"Why, thank you, Mr. Feather. You truly are kind."

Joe's arm hurt as he scrubbed the plates. He felt relatively safe here in this house, but inwardly he was still chilled and feeling sick. He hoped his arm wouldn't worsen, for he could not afford to linger here long. There was still the law on his trail, and Caul Slidell to be found.

As he finished the dishes, Joe wondered what to do with Slidell once he found him. It was likely Jim Christmas had learned of Slidell's wrongly reported death by now. If so, Will Ax was probably dead. Joe felt sad. He had come to love that crazy, contradictory old Indian with his big book and divining stone and feet planted in two worlds.

In light of all the uncertainties Joe could think of only one thing to do: Find Slidell and return him to Christmas's house as promised, on the feeble possibility that Will Ax was still alive. If he found Will Ax gone or dead, he would let Christmas experience Cherokee Joe's law of blood firsthand.

Joe had planned to leave Alabama Flecks house as soon as the dishes were clean. But an offer of a warm bed in a spare room proved impossible to decline. As the evening advanced, Joe felt more and more sick, which he hid from the widow. If he showed his illness, she would fetch that doctor she had talked about, and Joe might wind up identified and jailed.

The next morning, he slept late and ate a big breakfast. The night's rest had done him good, though he was still sick. Only one thing had marred his sleep—the Uktena. Though the dream had made him fearful, in the morning light he found it strangely hope-inspiring. The previous times he had dreamed it, he had been close to Will Ax and his *ulunsuti*. Maybe the fact that he had dreamed it again was an indication that Will was still alive. Joe didn't believe much in such mystical things as portents and dreams, but there seemed nothing wrong with hoping.

Joe was about to leave Alabama Fleck's when a fire in the chimney changed his plans. The old widow had been building up the blaze when a big rush of fire raced up the coated chimney and began gushing smoke back into the room. Joe rushed to the fire with the coffeepot and used the dregs to extinguish the logs. With much effort and at the expense of scorched fingers, he closed the flue and let the fire above burn itself out.

"Thank the good Lord you were here," Alabama Fleck said. "Likely as not, I would have burned the house down otherwise."

"That chimney needs a cleaning," Joe said.

"I know. I've been meaning to do it, but it's hard for me to do, and I hate to impose on others."

Joe nodded. "I'll do it for you," he said. "Then I have to go."

Heights normally didn't bother Joe, but normally he wasn't sick and dizzy as he was today. He climbed up a ladder to the roof with the chimney brush and perched for a long time on the roof peak getting accustomed to the height. A cold wind blasted against him so hard, it threatened to topple him and made him feel sicker. *I'm as crazy as Will Ax ever was to be up here,* Joe thought. *If I don't break my neck, somebody will see me and fetch the law.*

Nevertheless, he went on with the job. It was actually a pleasure to help Alabama Fleck, who was a full-fledged novelty to Joe Wolfkiller. He had never dreamed people as kind as she really existed; he thought they were nothing but creations of the storybooks forced upon Indian children in the Territory schools, stories designed to make Indians feel they were doing something praiseworthy turning the other cheek every time a hand slapped them. Usually, Joe had noticed, the hand was white.

Up on the widow's roof. Joe had a good view of Great Bend and the plains all around. He looked northward. Somewhere out there, supposedly, was Caul Slidell. How could he hope to find him in so vast a region? The prospect seemed hopeless.

Fighting off a new burst of dizziness, Joe ran the long brush down the chimney again and scraped more black soot off the masonry. He saw something moving down a road that led from the northwest. A wagon, piled with furniture, followed by a carriage. The two vehicles drew closer. At length Joe realized they were approaching an empty two-story house not far from the widow's place.

A white man descended from the loaded wagon when it reached the house and walked back to meet the carriage as it pulled to a stop, a white boy in his teens driving. Its other passengers were two women, one middle-aged and white, the other about Joe's age and obviously Indian. Joe stopped working as she descended. He had never seen so beautiful a young woman.

What was an Indian girl doing with a white family? She was nicely dressed and seemed to be part of the family. He guessed she had been adopted and raised by them, as Will Ax had said his daughter had been.

Then a stunning thought: Could this be Will's daughter? The vehicles had come from the northwest, the direction of Hays City. It was at least possible that this was the very family Will sought. Joe mulled it over, then decided such a thing would be too coincidental.

He watched the women enter the house as the man and boy began unloading the wagon. They were moving into the empty house. Joe waited for the girl to reemerge, but she never did. He finished his work, feeling worse than ever now, and tossed the chimney brush to the ground. His arm hurt badly. He clambered down the roof toward the ladder, and a burst of dizziness washed over him. He needed to get down, fast. The ladder seemed a long way off, though it was only a yard away. Joe reached for it, felt himself waver—and then he fell. The ground rose up to meet him with crushing impact. He groaned, rolled over, and passed out.

When he awoke, he was back in the bed in the widow's spare room. His arm was bound up in new bandages, and he was undressed, buried in covers and propped up on three plush pillows. A white man with mounds of snowy hair was standing beside his bed looking down at him, holding a leather bag like a doctor's valise. Joe swore beneath his breath. Alabama Fleck had gone and done it. She had fetched the blasted doctor.

Joe sat up. "I'm leaving," he said. "Got to leave."

The doctor pushed him back down. Joe was so weak, it was like pushing down a sack of fluff. "You're not going anywhere until you get that arm healed and some strength back, young fellow. If you had let that wound go uncleaned much longer, you'd have lost the arm."

Joe closed his eyes. When he opened them again, the doctor and Alabama Fleck were on the other side of the room talking.

"Just who is he?" the doctor asked.

"His name is Henry Feather. I saw he was sickly when he came, though I didn't know he was this sick."

"An infection will run a man down fast. He's likely gotten worse since he arrived. Tell me, Alabama, you're sure his name is Feather?"

"Well, yes."

"I have a reason for asking. Have you ever heard of an outlaw halfbreed named Wolfkiller? They call him Cherokee Joe most of the time."

"I've heard of him."

"I'm wondering if this man might be one and the same."

Alabama Fleck paused only a moment. "No. I assure you he's not. I've known Henry since he was just a boy. Henry was raised by my dear friends, the Gilbert Feathers of Indiana."

The doctor sounded concerned. "Alabama, you wouldn't be selling me a bill of goods, would you?"

"Dr. Davies, don't you know me by now? You think I'd do that?"

"The answer to both is yes."

"I'm surprised at you."

"You're too goodhearted, Alabama. I don't doubt you'd take in a stray outlaw, just like you took in that stray dog last year."

"Henry would be very upset to be called an outlaw, Dr. Davies. And his family would be scandalized."

"All right, Alabama. I'm taking your word for it... but you be careful, hear?"

He gave the widow some instructions on caring for her patient and said he would return the next day to check his progress. When he was gone, Alabama Fleck came to Joe's bedside. "So you were awake?" she asked.

"Yes."

"Then you know why I have to ask you: Are you this Cherokee Joe that Dr. Davies talked about?"

Joe shook his head. "My name is Henry Feather."

She looked at him a long time. Joe wondered if she believed him. Finally she nodded. "If you say you're Henry Feather, you're Henry Feather. That's that."

Joe had a question that couldn't be held back: "Why did you lie to that doctor about knowing me?"

Alabama Fleck pointed toward the wall across from the bed. Joe looked and saw an aging portrait of a stern-looking man with a bald head and fierce eyes. "That was Stansfield Fleck, my late husband," she said. "He was not only a good lawyer but a good man, and not afraid to think and believe differently than those around him. He despised slavery and before the war helped many slaves to freedom at great risk to himself. He also despised the evils done to the Indians of this nation. He was good to every Indian he met, tried to help them, to treat them like they were fellow human beings and not just, well, Indians. You know what I mean."

"I do. Very well."

"Since Stansfield passed on, I've tried to live by the same standard he set. That's why I took you in yesterday and why I lied to Dr. Davies. I want to help you, Henry... if Henry you really are."

She left Joe alone and went to begin cooking. He lay in bed staring at the portrait of Stansfield Fleck. He had heard of white men like Fleck, men who really believed an Indian deserved the same rights and privileges of anyone else. Heard of them, but never met one. Too bad the kind was so scarce.

He closed his eyes and slept until Alabama Fleck awakened him for supper, and after that he slept again for the rest of the night.

Chapter 13

Joe was in the most peculiar circumstance of his life. This was no time for him to be laid up in bed, not with the law after him, not with Caul Slidell out there waiting to be found. And that doctor gave Joe the willies with his silence and the suspicious way he looked at him during his calls. Nevertheless, Joe was too weak to ride out just yet, and the truth was he was enjoying the unusual pleasure of a warm bed and a woman who cared for him as lovingly as if he were her own son. Alabama Fleck was giving Joe a new perspective on the white race.

After only two days, Joe's arm was much better, and his illness was substantially gone. The main problem was that the illness had taken his strength. Never before had Joe required so much sleep. Most of his life he had risen before the sun; now he slept until mid-morning. And sleeping away the morning was what Joe was doing when an empty freight wagon rolled into town trailing a small army of boys tossing taunts and occasional stones at the skinny old Indian on the driver's perch.

Alabama Fleck was sweeping her porch when the parade rolled by. Her eyes widened with surprise. Another Indian arriving in Great Bend! First Henry Feather (or whoever he really was) then that pretty adopted daughter of the new family down the street, and now this old white-haired man in a big wagon. It was remarkable.

Will Ax, meanwhile, was having a devil of a time with his young harassers. They were irritating, drew attention to him that he did not want, and were endangering themselves, for just as he was not a very good Methodist or a very good conjurer, he was not a very good wagon driver. He turned onto a side street, nearly running over one boy in the process, and pulled to a stop. As gravel pelted him in the side of the head, he reached into his coat and produced the *ulunsuti* with a great flourish. He raised it above his head, enclosed in his fist. The Remington pistol he had stolen from the wagon's original driver swung menacingly in the gunbelt draped over his shoulder.

"In my hand is a powerful crystal that kills white boys who look on it!" he said. "Leave, or I will open my hand and make you see it!"

The boys, surprised by the old man's dramatic style, backed away. "You're a lyin'," one said.

Will Ax growled and lifted his fist higher. The boys turned and scrambled away. One tossed a stone back at him and missed by ten feet.

Will Ax grinned and reached toward his pocket to put away the *ulunsuti*. As he did, a ray of sunlight glinted brightly off the stone. The old man examined his crystal. Today it glistened more brightly than it had in a long time. The sight excited him, and he peered into the shining crystal, hoping it could tell him something about Joe Wolfkiller or maybe his daughter.

He received no message from it. He sighed and put away the shining crystal. The *ulunsuti* was still stubborn, still leaving him on his own.

On his own. Well, that would simply have to be good

enough. Will Ax looked around at the town. It was all new and strange to him, but at the same time there was something in the atmosphere here that roused a sense of excitement in him, a sense of being close to something or someone of significance. Joe Wolfkiller, maybe. He might be on the next street or around the next corner.

Someone did come around the corner just then. It definitely wasn't Joe. It was a white woman, the tallest and most rotund Will Ax had ever seen. She wore a blue dress the size of a revival tent and carried a blue-barreled shotgun that was almost as long as Will Ax was tall. At her feet were two of the boys who had harassed Will as he came into town. The two were look-alikes, tow-headed and ruddy-cheeked. One pointed up at Will. "That's him, Aunt Pru."

The shotgun leveled down. To Will Ax, the muzzle holes looked as big as twin cannon.

"You threatened my nephews, you foul old coot. Get down from that wagon right now and hand over that gunbelt!"

Will Ax wasn't inclined to disobey. He stood before his rotund captor like a scraggly pine in the shadow of a great oak. Aunt Pru took the gunbelt and handed it to the first boy, who seemed pleased and surprised by the move.

"He pulled something out of his pocket and said it would kill us, Aunt Pru," the second boy said.

"Time for you and me to take a walk, you black-bottomed heathen," the woman said. "I want you to tell the good men down at the jail why you came into our town threatening children."

Will Ax shook his head sadly. Why, he wondered, did the unseen forces that shape a man's destiny determine it was so vital that he meet Aunt Pru today when he had such important things to do? Couldn't this have waited until some more convenient time?

Good questions, but Will Ax expected no answers. There

was one good thing balancing the bad: Jails served food—usually good food, and hot.

"I am ready, Aunt Pru," he said, lifting his hands.

They marched off down the street—boys, woman, shotgun, and Indian, making a most interesting processional.

The door opened, and Alabama Fleck came in bearing another trayful of food for Henry Feather. Joe sat up and grinned slightly with closed lips, the closest thing to a full smile he ever gave to anyone. It was obvious that Alabama Fleck was enjoying having someone to dote over; likely she had not been able to do anything like this since her children had left home.

"I hope you like fried chicken," she said. "There's fresh bread and some of those pole beans you enjoy so much. Gravy's in the boat, and there's a good slab of butter to put some flesh onto you. So many of you Indians are just too lean to be healthy. This is the kind of supper you need."

Joe began smearing butter on one of the three thick slices of bread on his tray. No wonder so many white men got fat; Joe was already a few pounds heavier than when he came. As he bit into the bread, Joe wondered if the white men's diet also contributed to their tendency to lose their hair, a characteristic that had intrigued Indians since their first contacts with whites.

"Speaking of lean Indians, you should have seen the old Indian man who rode into town today," said Alabama.

"Old Indian man?"

"Yes." Alabama Fleck was heading over to dust off the portrait of her husband, as she did at least twice daily. She kept her entire house spotless, that portrait the most spotless of all. "He was riding in a big old empty freight wagon and had the whitest hair I've ever seen. He wasn't any bigger around than a telegraph pole. There was the biggest gaggle of boys teasing him all the way into town. Terrible, how boys can be."

Joe was frowning thoughtfully, staring into his coffee cup. Could it be? No... Will Ax was surely still imprisoned or killed by Jim Christmas as useless baggage. "Where did this old man go?" he asked.

"To jail, from what I heard down at the store. Apparently he threatened the boys with some sort of stone. Prudence Flatt hustled him off at the end of a shotgun. Prudence is prone to overdo things when it comes to those foul little nephews of hers."

"Threatened them with a stone.. ."

"Yes. He would have thrown it at them, I suppose. Humph! I wish he had. They were throwing enough stones of their own at him and calling him indecent names. There's some mothers in this town who could stand to keep a closer eye on their sons, let me tell you. In any case, the poor man is in jail, and everybody is calling him Eagle-eye. He gave his name to the town marshal as Eye of the Eagle or something like that. Henry—you're not eating! Is something wrong with your food?"

"No," he said. "It's good. Very good."

Alabama Fleck smiled. "Eat it all, every bite. You're looking so much stronger since you've been eating good. I'll be back for the plates later. And in the morning, my best hotcakes, topped with jelly. I'll fatten you up yet, Henry Feather!"

Joe Wolfkiller moved through the dark house on bare feet, making no noise. He carried his boots in his right hand and wore his coat and hat. The gentle snores of Alabama Fleck wafted through the house as he went to her writing desk, took paper and pencil, and in his crude blocky letters wrote her a note of thanks and a promise of repayment for the money he had taken from the little tin cashbox she kept hidden behind a loose stone in her downstairs mantlepiece. Joe had secretly observed her getting money from the box the day before. It made him feel bad to take it, but he could think of no alternative. He had to have some way to buy food and weapons—and maybe to bail out Will Ax if Will Ax it really was down in the local jail. He wished he had been able to steal the widow's shotgun too, but she kept that in the corner of her bedroom, between her bed and the wall. Joe had not felt he could risk waking her by trying to take it.

He felt almost certain that it was Will Ax in that jail. If Will had managed to escape or had been freed for some reason, there was one less worry hanging over him. He could get on with his original quest to kill Caul Slidell and not have to concern himself with Jim Christmas's "bargain" anymore.

One thing Joe tried hard not to think about—the danger of what he was about to do. For Cherokee Joe to walk right into a domicile of the law was quite risky, especially since a broad alert was surely out for him by now. All he had going for him was his chopped off hair, slightly more filled-out look, and false name of Henry Feather. One thing he was sure he would not have any longer would be the support of Alabama Fleck. She would probably hate him when she discovered he had stolen from her.

Joe left his note and gave a final look around Alabama's house. This place had become familiar and homey to him. Leaving it gave him a sadness strange to one whose feelings seldom broke out of a range bounded on one end by bitterness and on the other by fury.

He left the house and went out to the street. It was a cool, clear night, Great Bend a dark cluster of houses and commercial buildings lining broad dirt streets. Joe walked across town, a moving shadow in the alleys and beneath the eaves. It was as if all the world were asleep except for Joe Wolfkiller. Joe liked the feeling.

At length he found the jail and noted a light burning in the front office. Tight nervousness began to creep up his spine. Someone was in there, awake. He could hear a male voice humming a tune. He walked up to the jail and peered into the window.

A young man sat in a chair tilted against the wall, his feet crossed on the desk. He seemed too young to be a marshal. Joe pegged him as a deputy holding the dull job of tending the jail at night. There was nothing interesting at all about the young man, nothing but the object he was holding up before his face and examining carefully.

The *ulunsuti.* Now Joe knew. It really was Will Ax who was locked away somewhere in there under the name Eagle-eye.

The way Joe saw it, he had two recourses. He could knock, enter politely, and present some of the widow's money to bail out Will Ax. Or he could enter, be not so polite, and take Will out by force. The deputy was just a kid, scrawny and so boyish, he was still freckled. Joe decided to play the situation as it went along. Surely he could get the better of the runty jailer one way or another.

Peering through the window, Joe kept his eye on the deputy as he knocked on the locked door. The young fellow almost fell out of his chair in surprise, obviously not used to night callers. Joe watched through the window as the young jailer put the *ulunsuti* into his pocket, took a small pistol from a desk drawer, and came to the door. He cracked it open a foot and looked out at Joe suspiciously. "What do you want?" For so young a deputy, the voice was deep.

"I've come to bail out the old man you have locked up here."

"Bail out? I don't know that I can do that. Don't rightly know how—that's always been the marshal's job."

"Let me visit him, then."

A long pause. "You an Injun?"

"No."

"You sure do look like one."

"Not me. I hate Injuns. I think the one you got locked up might have stole something from me. Let me in, and I'll see if it's the same one."

"If he stole from you, why do you want him bailed out?"

Joe saw that his lies were crossing each other. To the devil with it, then. He forced the door back, knocking the deputy on his rump. Joe was on him in a moment, wrenching the pistol from his hand. The *ulunsuti* fell from the deputy's pocket and skittered across the floor to the corner. Joe pounded his fist into the deputy's face—once, twice, thrice. The young fellow grunted with the first blow, gasped with the second, passed out with the third. Joe rose and pulled the ring of keys from his belt.

Will Ax was awake, having heard all the ruckus in the office. He rose from his bunk and went to the door, which like the walls and low ceiling of his cell was made of flat bars of iron crossed and bolted together. The door to the office opened, and Will Ax was amazed when Joe Wolfkiller stepped through.

"Hello, old man," Joe said. "Gotten yourself into trouble again, I see."

"Joe, how did..."

"We can talk about it later. I got to get you out of here. I'll have to find which key—"

A fearsome figure suddenly appeared behind Joe, the deputy, hair mussed and face soaked with blood from his nose. In his hands was a sawed-off shotgun, the muzzle of which he thrust against Joe's spine.

Though young, the deputy could cuss almost as impressively as he could revive from a beating. He peppered Joe with every foul name he could muster, which was plenty, then began putting them together in unique combinations. Joe could do nothing but lift his hands and take it, the deputy angry enough that the slightest sign of resistance might prompt him to blast the heart out of Joe's chest.

When the cussing was done, the deputy shoved Joe toward the cell adjacent to Will's. The two cells shared a crossed-bar wall. He forced Joe inside, made him put his hands flat on the wall, and searched him quickly but well. He took the knife from Joe's boot and Alabama Fleck's money from his pocket, then locked him up.

Once Joe was safely caged, the deputy cussed him again for a full minute until his fury was drained. Still bleeding from the nose, he sagged back against the wall. "Don't know who you are, mister, but you'll sure as devil's hell pay for what you done," he said. "Reckon I showed you it ain't smart to pick on this boy, huh?"

He slammed the door behind him and returned to the office. Joe went to the bunk in his cell and sat down onto it, putting his face in his hands. Right now it wouldn't have taken much to make him cry, and he hadn't cried since childhood.

"Cheer up, Joe," Will Ax said. "Everything will be all right."

"You are a fool, old man," Joe muttered.

"No, no—everything really will be all right. I've gotten it back again. See?"

Joe looked up. Will Ax was holding the *ulunsuti* up beside his grinning face. "The deputy kicked it into the cell when he came in. It was a miracle! Pretty wonderful, eh?"

"Yeah," Joe muttered, lying down. His mental eye was inspecting an image of himself on Judge Parker's big gallows. "Wonderful."

Chapter 14

It took Will Ax the rest of the night to dig information out of Joe Wolfkiller, who was far too depressed and angry to want to talk. For the first hour Joe remained mostly silent, softly rubbing his still-healing arm. But by the time the sun was rising, he had told Will what had happened since they parted in the little office room of Jim Christmas' house. Will told his own tale, almost as remarkable as Joe's.

Will Ax was disturbed by Joe's description of the violent encounter at Hutchinson, and forced to face up to the dark and deadly side of his young companion. He wondered if it was right for him to be traveling with, much less giving aid to, so violent a fellow. "Listen to me, Joe," said Will Ax. "This life you live is not a life. It is a road to the grave if you don't get off of it. Death travels the same route you take, and if you do not get off it, you will be overtaken."

"It's too late," Joe said flatly. "I've already killed. I've already run. If the law gets me, it's the noose."

"The law does have you," Will Ax reminded Joe.

"Not for long. I'll find a way out. I'll kill Caul Slidell, and then if I die, I die. It won't matter then."

It required no divining stone for Will Ax to feel the aura

of deep, dangerous despair surrounding Joe Wolfkiller. Will weighed his next words carefully. "Joe, maybe you should let Slidell go."

Joe turned on his bunk, staring in disbelief at Will Ax. What Will had said sounded as absurd to Joe as if he had suggested he cut off his own head.

"Listen to me, Joe. It is the law of blood you follow that has brought all this evil to you. For every evil thing that comes, you seek to balance it with more evil. That is like trying to empty a bucket by pouring even more water into it, or putting out a fire by fanning its flames brighter. You must learn another way."

"There is no other way."

"There is. It is simply to forget, to put aside. To forgive. I have lived a long time. I have had to forgive many things in my life."

Joe laughed derisively. "You have read too much in your white man's book, Will Ax. It's made you more a fool than ever. The old ways you claim to follow say every wrong must be avenged."

"The world is changing, Joe. Maybe some of the old ways no longer work when the world becomes different."

Joe was surprised to hear that from Will Ax, whom he had perceived as clinging to old ideas and old traditions far more fiercely than anyone else he had known. But he was in no mood for a philosophical discussion today. His biting reply was, "You're not only a poor Methodist and a poor conjurer. You're also a poor Cherokee. You're old and weak. You bend under every wind. Joe Wolfkiller does not bend, ever."

He knew from the look on Will Ax's face that the words had stung. The older man turned away. "Sometimes," he said, "those who will not bend find they can only break."

"I do not break," Joe said haughtily. "I break others."

Will Ax could think only that Joe, locked away in a tiny

cell, hardly looked like a man who could break anyone. He felt a wave of fear for the destiny of his violent young companion.

The deputy who brought breakfast to the cells was a big man, at least five inches over six feet with a head the size of a late-summer melon and a look that hinted a melon might be smarter. He wore a dirty yellow shirt with a badge stuck on upside down. He shoved the plates to the prisoners without a word, then stared at Joe for almost a minute. "What's your name, redskin?"

Joe didn't answer. He began gnawing one of the overbaked biscuits from his dirty tin plate.

"You deaf, boy? Answer me!"

"I'm Henry Feather."

"Well, Henry Feather, you've bit off a mouthful of trouble, doing what you did. Is this coot your kin or something?"

"I have nothing to say to you."

"All right, suit yourself. Don't matter to me—I'm just holding down the fort. Henry Feather, huh? I'll sign you in on the book. Herman, he was so tore up last night, he didn't even put your name down. His nose was the size of a baked potato when I come in this morning." The man chuckled.

When he was gone, Joe asked Will Ax if the man was town marshal.

"No, I don't think so. He is a chief of some sort."

"Chief?"

"Yes. Chief Deputy. That is his name. He told me. Town Marshal is gone somewhere, he said, and won't be back for several days."

Joe saw no purpose in pointing out to Will Ax that he was confusing titles and names. He gnawed his biscuit, then devoured the three runny eggs that composed the rest of breakfast. The coffee was so thin, it was like dirty water.

"How long will they keep us locked up?" Will Ax asked.

"Chief Deputy told me yesterday that I would probably be free by breakfast."

"It's my fault," Joe replied. "Now that I tried to break you out, they'll probably keep both of us until the marshal gets back."

They talked some more, Will Ax doing most of it. When Will made reference to the daughter he sought, Joe suddenly remembered the arrival of the family with the young Indian lady and told Will Ax of it.

The old Cherokee's face became bright with excitement. "It's her, my little Gatunlati!" he said. "I have felt she was near since I came to this town."

"You don't know it's her," Joe said, but Will Ax didn't seem to listen. He produced his *ulunsuti* and began looking into it.

"I wish you'd put that rock away," Joe said. "It aggravates me to see you staring into it all the time. What's it saying to you now, old babbler? Does it say when I'll hang?"

"It says only that it wishes you would shut up and quit bothering its keeper so much."

Joe spent the morning waiting for the chief deputy to return and inform him that he had identified him as Cherokee Joe, but that never happened. Joe began to develop a cautious optimism. The chief deputy did not seem a very bright fellow, and with the marshal gone, it was just possible that he would never make the connection between the widely sought Cherokee Joe and the sullen Henry Feather in his cell. Perhaps he would eventually just let his prisoners go. As far as Joe knew, there were yet no official charges lodged against him for the previous night's incident and no talk of courts and judges.

The weather changed as the morning passed. The wind

rose, but the day warmed until even the enclosed little cells gave up their chill. The chief deputy opened the office windows and cracked the door to the cellblock, letting the breeze seep in. Will Ax thanked him profusely and told him he was a fine and decent man. Joe could see that Will Ax hoped to flatter his way out of jail.

Joe was dozing later when Will Ax's urgent whisper roused him. "Listen!" said the old man.

Voices caught in mid-conversation came from the front office. One was the chief deputy's. The other, a smooth talker's, was also familiar, though Joe could not immediately place it.

The chief deputy: "If you're a U.S. marshal, why ain't I heard of you, Mr. Crenshaw?"

"I don't know, Mr. Johnson. But my credentials should speak for themselves."

There was a shuffling of papers. "Well," said the deputy, "it looks square to me. But like I say, you can't talk to Marshal Drenmore because he ain't here."

"That's too bad. Maybe you'll be in a position to help me. You look to be a capable fellow."

"Well, I reckon I do all right."

"Can I give you information that needs to be held in confidence?"

"Why, sure you can!" The chief deputy didn't try to hide his eagerness.

"All right. I'm on special assignment." The voice lowered. "I've been sent to locate and arrest Caul Slidell."

Right then, Joe recognized what Will Ax already had: The deputy's visitor was Jim Christmas.

The chief deputy laughed. "I would have figured you federals would be more up on the news than that. Don't you know that Caul Slidell was gunned down by one of his own men just days ago down about Hutchinson?"

"I know that's the official report, yes."

"Well, then! How you aiming to arrest a man that's already dead, Mr. Crenshaw? You going to dig him up and put chains on him?" The deputy guffawed at his own joke.

"I saw a photograph taken of the body purported to be that of Slidell," said Christmas. "It's the suspicion of my superiors—and my own firm conviction—that the dead man was actually one of Slidell's confederates, named Wiltflower. The two have been mistaken for each other before."

The deputy sounded confused now. "Well, who shot this Wiltflower, then?"

"I don't know yet. Perhaps Slidell himself."

"Why would he do that?"

"For any number of possible reasons. Maybe just an argument. Maybe to lead people to believe, just as they have, that it was Slidell who died. The man had just completed a major robbery at the railroad station in Guthrie, Indian Territory. Old European jewels, purchased by a New York buyer from a wealthy importer in Corpus Christi and in transit by rail by way of San Antonio. It's suspected, on the basis of evidence I cannot divulge at the moment, that Slidell was to divide the jewels with some other co-conspirator in the scheme but that he then absconded with all the spoils himself. I believe the shooting of Wiltflower was a deliberate effort by Slidell to throw the law—and perhaps his cheated partner—off his trail by in effect giving the false impression that Slidell was dead."

Christmas had spoken quickly and authoritatively, and seemed to have lost and intimidated the chief deputy, whose answer was a vague "Uh-huh." Joe Wolfkiller was not so dense. Now he understood why Christmas had been so determined to take Slidell alive. Slidell had cheated him, and he wanted the chance to torture the whereabouts of the stolen jewels out of him.

"So, Mr. Johnson, the purpose of my visit here is to ask you if you have any information about the whereabouts of

Caul Slidell. You're aware, I'm sure, that the general belief is he is in this county."

"I've heard that, yeah."

"Tell me, then. I'll keep the information in the proper confidence. We certainly don't want average citizens taking out after Slidell and his stolen jewels on their own."

"That ain't likely to happen," the deputy replied. "There ain't nobody around here eager to meet up with Caul Slidell. Folks figure that if he'll leave them alone, they'll leave him alone."

"Does that include the local law?"

"This is just the town marshal's office. As long as Slidell stays out of town, he's not our worry."

Christmas let out a long disdainful sigh through his nostrils. "That's a pitiful attitude for peace officers to have, if I may say so."

The chief deputy took on an offended tone. "We're just doing our job, and that's all."

"I question whether ignoring a murderer and train robber can accurately be called 'doing your job.' But let that lie. Let's put aside our official status a moment. Man to man, can you give me any information, no matter how second- or third-hand, about Slidell's whereabouts?"

A long pause followed. "I don't know nothing official, but I've heard the marshal say where he thinks Slidell might be. I'll tell you this, Mr. Crenshaw, I don't much like you talking down to me like you have, but since you're federal, I'll help you out. I'll draw you a map. Can't say you'll find Slidell when you get there, but it's where I'd look if I was you."

Joe heard the scratch of a pencil on paper. He looked over at Will Ax and could tell that the old man, as dim as his mental lights seemed to be sometimes, had understood the situation as well as he.

"There you go, Mr. Crenshaw," the deputy said after a

few moments. "And good luck to you, especially if you're going after Slidell alone."

"I'm not alone," Christmas said. "See those riders outside? That's my posse."

"It'll take one devil of a posse to get the best of Slidell's hellriders."

"Good day, Mr. Johnson, and thank you for your help."

"So long, Mr. Crenshaw."

The front door opened and closed. Joe and Will Ax heard the deputy give a long low whistle of easing tension.

The door opened again.

"Why, howdy do, Mrs. Fleck."

Joe and Will Ax exchanged looks of surprise.

"Hello, Mr. Johnson." It was indeed the voice of Alabama Fleck. "I hear you have in custody a young friend of mine. I've come to ask if you'll release him into my care."

"Young friend? You mean the redskin?"

"Unless you've got more than one, I'm sure it's him."

"Fact is, I do have more than one, but only one who's young. The other's old. The young one—says his name's Feather—busted in here last night and gave Herman no end of holy hell—pardon me, holy Hades—trying to bust the old one out. I'm keeping them both penned until Marshall Drenmore gets back."

"Oh, my! Is Herman all right?"

"Busted nose. Looked like a baked potato jammed onto his face when I come in this morning."

"How terrible! I'm surprised Henry would do such a thing."

"Henry... yeah, that's his name, all right. Henry Feather."

"Oh, Mr. Johnson, I beg you, please let Henry go. He's an old family friend, and I'm sure he didn't mean any harm. He may have been drinking—the Feather men all have had a certain problem with their liquor, sorry to say."

"Pardon me for saying it, Mrs. Fleck, but this bird sure

don't look the type to be no old family friend of somebody like you."

"You can't always judge by appearances, Mr. Johnson. Henry has had a hard life. Please, please let him go in my care. I'll keep him out of trouble."

Joe was amazed by what he was hearing. Why would Alabama Fleck come and plead for mercy for him after he had run out on her hospitality and even taken money from her?

"Well... I don't know..."

"I'm sure Marshall Drenmore would approve. What charge have you placed against Henry?"

"Ain't really got around to that yet. Waiting on the marshal, you know."

"Oh, dear—the marshal surely won't be happy that you've held an old friend of mine in jail without an official charge!"

The deputy was silent a moment. "You think so?"

"You know Marshal Drenmore—by the book, fair and square. I'm no expert on law, but you do remember, don't you, that the late Mr. Fleck was a licensed attorney? I clearly recall him saying that a jailer can't hold a prisoner without a charge and expect to get away with it. Why, one time he made absolute hay defending a prisoner in a situation like this. The poor jailer lost his job and had to pay a huge fine besides."

Joe grinned. It sounded like Alabama Fleck was pulling a substantial bluff on the dim-witted chief deputy. Why she was doing it was the mystery.

"You telling me straight, Mrs. Fleck?"

"Mr. Johnson! Are you implying I would lie to you?"

"No, no! I'm just thinking, just kind of afraid that. . . Listen, if I turn him over to you and wipe his name off the book here, you think he'd be willing to let bygones be bygones? Shoot fire, he can even take the old coot with him if he wants. I was half thinking about letting all this go anyway. Ain't no reason to give Marshal Drenmore one more thing to worry about."

Will Ax smiled at Joe. "I think I like this Mrs. Fleck," he whispered.

"I believe Henry will be willing to forgive and forget," Alabama Fleck said. "And certainly I'll say nothing of this. But what about Herman?"

"Herman'll keep his mouth shut if he knows what's good for him," said the deputy. "As far as I'm telling it, he busted his nose going out the door and made up the Injun story to cover up for being clumsy."

Joe heard the rattle of keys and the fast clumping of the deputy's boots on the floor as he headed back to the cells.

"Yes indeed," said Will Ax. "I do believe I like this Mrs. Fleck."

Chapter 15

It was the first time in his life that Joe Wolfkiller had not been able to endure the gaze of another person—and to make it all the more agonizing, this was a woman, a white woman, who had him so humbled. Alabama Fleck's eyes upon him made him feel a shame he had no idea how to handle.

She drove him and Will Ax out of town in her carriage, a fancy rockaway that had been her husband's. She kept the curtains drawn. If it had been anyone but Alabama Fleck, Joe would have figured the curtains were drawn to hide the embarrassment of fraternization with Indians. In Alabama Fleck's case, he knew it was to keep him from being seen for his own sake, not hers. She was still protecting him, as she had before.

Joe wasn't sure why Will Ax had come along. He had opted to leave his commandeered wagon abandoned in Great Bend. Joe did not yet know what his plans were.

Alabama Fleck stopped the rockaway outside town. A horse, wearing an old but good saddle, was tied to the back of the carriage. Joe didn't need to ask for whom it was intended. She was giving it to him. "Henry, I don't know who you are, where you come from, or what you've done, and I don't want to know," she said. "God only knows what it is I see in you and why I feel this need to protect you, but feel it I do."

She turned to Will Ax. "Sir, I don't know you or what your relationship is to Henry. Nevertheless, I wish you well. I'm sorry I didn't bring you a horse as well, but when I went to the jail, I didn't realize I would be walking out with more than one man. If you're together, you will have to share the horse until you can buy another." She shifted over to Joe again, handing him a leather pouch. "Here. There's money in there, from my bank account. Enough to see you through until you. .. well, until you get wherever it is you're going."

"I have to know why you're doing this," Joe said. He was looking sheepishly at his feet.

"If I knew, I would tell you. I don't fully understand it myself... but I think that maybe you're my second chance, my chance to make up for—" her voice broke, and now it was her turn to drop her gaze, "to make up for what my husband did."

"I don't understand."

"I lied to you about Stansfield, Henry. I told you he was a man of open mind and sympathy for Indians. He wasn't. Years ago, back in Indiana, Stansfield allowed a young Indian man to be lynched for horse theft. The poor man was innocent. It was Stansfield's nephew by his first marriage who had stolen the horse, and Stansfield knew it. He steered the vigilantes in the wrong direction, told them it was the Indian, our own stableman, who did it. Stansfield carried the guilt of that to his grave. Maybe it's what finally killed him. I never knew of it until the hour before he died. He confessed it to me, poured it out on me like scalding water. I still can feel the burn of it... ." She shuddered. "I vowed that day that if ever I had the opportunity to help someone like that poor stableman, so help me, I would do it. I remember that sad young man's face so clearly—sometimes see it in my sleep. He was much like you, Henry."

She paused, wiping away her tears on a silk handkerchief she dug out of her cuff. "I don't know that what I've done is right. I've lied to the law. I've set free a man who may be guilty of things that would horrify me. I don't know, and I don't want you to tell me. All I want to remember is that I gave a second chance to a young Indian named Henry Feather. Whatever you might have done, Henry, whoever you might really be, I hope you will take this chance I've given you and make good with it. You've seen many bad things in your life—I can see it in your eyes. I want the satisfaction of knowing that I've let you see at least one good thing." She leaned forward and kissed Joe's cheek. "Good-bye, Henry Feather. God go with you. If I've done wrong today, may God forgive me."

She turned away and went back to the carriage. Will Ax had already freed the horse and was holding its reins. He and Joe watched as Alabama Fleck climbed into the seat and drove away.

For a minute or so the two men remained silent, alone on the flatlands outside town.

"She was right, Joe. It is best she doesn't know who you are and what you've done," said Will Ax. "I wish I myself didn't know what you've done."

Joe wheeled to face him. "Are you my judge now, old man? If you think I'm so bad a man, why don't you just get away from me?"

"I've been asking myself that question. I think maybe it's because you need somebody to take care of you. Besides, it was you who came to me in the jail, not me to you."

"Yes, but you came to Great Bend to find me. You didn't have to do that."

"Yes I did. I couldn't let you ride under Caul Slidell's gun still thinking I was a prisoner of Jim Christmas. I couldn't have you shot down trying to protect me when I no longer needed protection."

Joe looked back toward town, watching Alabama Fleck's rockaway disappear.

"What will you do now?" Will Ax asked.

"What I planned from the beginning. I'll go and avenge my father by killing Caul Slidell. Now I'll have to find him before Jim Christmas does."

Will Ax nodded sadly. "That's what I thought you would say."

"And what about you?" Joe asked.

"I'm going back to town. I'm going to find this Indian girl and see if she is my little Gatunlati."

"And if she isn't?"

"She will be."

"The *ulunsuti* has told you, eh?"

"No. This time it's just me who tells me. I can feel that Gatunlati is close. Soon I'll have given her my treasure and can go on to the Celestial City in peace."

"You talk like you want to die, Will Ax."

"No, Joe Wolfkiller, it's you who wants to die. Else you wouldn't do the things you do."

Parting with Will Ax was more difficult for Joe than he had anticipated. With Will Ax perched behind him on Alabama Fleck's horse, he rode back as close to town as he felt he safely could. His heart was heavy, which he found inexplicable. He should be happy. He was free, had escaped identification in the jail, and had a horse, courtesy of Alabama Fleck. Furthermore, Will Ax had given him the Remington pistol he had taken from the original driver of Jim Christmas' freight wagon. The weapon had been returned to Will when he was freed from jail. Now Joe could continue his quest for Caul Slidell unimpeded.

The strange thing was, he wasn't sure he wanted to. Joe was growing weary of this violent journey. He had killed men and found no glory in the killing. It was the strangest thing. He didn't want to be Cherokee Joe anymore. He wanted only to be Joe Wolfkiller, unknown, unsought, living the quiet life of a normal man. Too late for that. He had already set his course. He could not undo what had been done.

Will Ax climbed down from the saddle and stood looking up at Joe. There were tears in his eyes as the wind stirred his stiff white hair. He looked very small and frail. He reached inside his coat and pulled out his leather-bound book. Handing it up, he said, "For you. I am finished with it now."

Joe reached down and took the volume. He started to say something but could not find his voice, so he merely nodded.

"Maybe we will see each other again, Joe, if ever you can find your way out of the City of Destruction. If we don't, I'm glad to have ridden with you."

Joe cleared away the knot in his throat. He slipped the book into his coat pocket. "I hope you find your daughter, old man."

"I'll find her," said Will Ax. "Very soon now I'll be with her."

Joe watched him walk away toward Great Bend, then turned the horse and rode slowly away.

It was night, but the wind still blew warm across the flatlands. Will Ax stood beneath a squatty tree and stared across the street at a tall house that spilled light from its big windows. This was the house that Joe had described to him, the house where the Indian girl lived.

The old man's heart was beating fast. Now that he felt so close to the end of his quest, he found he was not nearly as courageous as he had thought he would be. How could he approach a young lady who had never known him and tell her he just might be her true father? And how could he prove that he was, even to himself, much less to her?

No answers to those questions appeared. Will Ax scratched his chin, shuffled his feet, and felt more nervous than ever. Another walk was what he needed. Another slow trek through Great Bend to calm his nerves.

A shadow passed across an upper window in the house. A curtain pulled to the side, and a young woman looked out. She was silhouetted in the light, so Will Ax could not see her features, but he knew it was she. "Gatunlati," he whispered. "My baby girl." The girl moved away from the window, and he saw her no more.

Yes, another walk was definitely in order. He began trekking along slowly, his hands deep in his pockets, his white hair wisping out on both sides. A couple of men rode by, and one of them spat a dollop of tobacco juice toward him, barely missing. The men laughed coarsely and made a comment about "lousy redskins, dirtying the streets," then passed on by. Will Ax paid them no heed.

As he passed a livery stable, the big door swung open. Will looked inside and saw the commandeered freight wagon he had abandoned. Beside it stood Jim Christmas, Miller, and a gaggle of others. Will's eyes swept to the man who had opened the door. It was the wagon driver he had pounded senseless out on the road north of Wichita. The old Indian backstepped into a dark alley. He could hear Christmas's voice.

"That's the wagon, sure enough," Christmas said. "Reckon that old redskin drove it all the way here?"

"Sure appears so," another man said. "Or maybe somebody took it from him. It was sitting parked on the street when we found it."

The wagon driver returned to Christmas' side. Christmas looked at him with displeasure. "I can't believe you let that skinny old heathen steal my wagon."

"I told you how that happened, Jim. I swear it must have been an anvil he hit me with."

"Hell, forget it. What's done is done. Come on—let's all go find us a little relaxation," said Christmas.

Will Ax watched them stride out of the livery and to the left, relieved they had not seen him but glad he had seen them, for it reminded him that he had to be careful as long as Christmas remained in town. He hoped Joe would not encounter Christmas during his quest for Slidell. Christmas would certainly kill Joe if he had the opportunity.

Will continued his walk but made sure he stayed in the darkest areas. His thoughts returned to the big house and the girl inside it. Part of him felt ready to return and knock on the door, but a bigger part of him was still too scared. He kept walking until finally he had circled back near the house again. Then he stood as before, looking up at the bright windows.

"Well, old man—you going in or not?"

The voice came from behind. Will Ax wheeled. His eyes widened as Joe Wolfkiller stepped forward. "Joe— you have killed Slidell already?"

"No. I still have that ahead of me. I thought about my quest after I left you today.. . and I thought about yours. Yours seemed more important. So I came back." Joe nodded toward the house. "She's in there."

"I know. I saw her at the window."

"Then why haven't you gone to meet her?"

Will Ax looked sheepish, then put on a smile. "I'll go, soon. But first let's celebrate your return, Joe. Let me take you to a saloon."

"I can't risk going into a saloon."

"Oh... you're right. I can, though."

"Lead the way, old man."

Together they walked toward a well-lighted tavern on the far side of town. Joe was glad he had come back to Will Ax, though coming back made little sense. Sensible or not, he wanted to know if the girl in the house really was Will's daughter, wanted to see the old man's happiness at reuniting with her if she was. Joe's was a quest of death, Will's a quest of life that roused in Joe an aching longing for something that he could not explain or identify. Ironically, Joe Wolfkiller, the halfbreed who had so long been enamored of living on the edge of death, was now becoming enamored of life.

Outside the tavern Joe gave Will Ax money and drew back into the alley beside it to await his return. As he waited, he fiddled with the Remington pistol, adjusting to the feel of it and wishing he also had a good rifle or shotgun. A handgun had too many limitations. Maybe in the morning he could get Will Ax to buy a rifle for him as he was buying the bottle right now.

Time passed, and still Will Ax did not return. Joe turned the Remington's cylinder, listening to the clicking whir of the oiled mechanism. He unloaded the pistol and took a few practice pulls on the trigger, determining its action and sensitivity. He reloaded the pistol and holstered it. Still no Will.

Growing impatient, Joe walked around the back of the saloon and over to the far side. There was a window there, wide and hinged on the top so it could be left open in the rain. Closed tonight, it provided a clear view into the saloon. The window was located behind the long bar and gave Joe an angle of view roughly equivalent to the barkeep's. What it showed him was startling.

Will Ax was being held against the bar by Jim Christmas. Christmas had a big cruel grin on his face as he pushed the tip of a knife against Will Ax's throat. His men stood around, laughing and enjoying the treat of seeing their superior terrorize the Indian who had escaped him and stolen his wagon. Others in the saloon were also enjoying the show. Two or three seemed disturbed by it, but no one was lifting a hand to stop it.

Joe's fury roused like a sleeping lion and roared. Jim Christmas would not get away with this. Joe was just about to head around the front door when Christmas pulled out his pistol and whipped Will Ax hard across the side of the face. Will Ax slid down. He would have collapsed completely had he not been wedged between Christmas and the bar.

That did it. Joe's anger flared beyond his control. He backed up and ran toward the window, thinking as he leaped that Christmas was about to get the surprise of his life. The leap was made with the instinctive grace of a cat springing upon a bird. Joe's uplifted knees shattered the window and his entire body launched through, landing him directly behind the bar. One spring, and he was atop it.

Will Ax, badly stunned by Christmas' blow, looked up. "Joe..."

Christmas, meanwhile, had staggered back, his eyes big. Will Ax slid to the floor. Christmas's men fell back, too amazed to react to the fearsome halfbreed with anything more than stares.

Christmas looked into Joe's eyes and saw a dead glitter in them that made him winter-cold to the soul. "Cherokee Joe!" he said with awe and alarm. "That's Cherokee Joe!"

Then Christmas reached under his jacket for the pocket pistol he kept hidden there. He hardly had it cleared when Joe's Remington spoke. The first bullet struck Christmas in his ribs, driving him back.

Grunting, he hunched down and fired a random shot that passed into the floor. Christmas' men, loyal only to his dollars, backed away and gave no assistance. Christmas swore, lurched forward, and lifted his pistol again.

This time Joe shot him through the heart. As he died, Jim Christmas fired one final blast, the jolt of the shot flipping the pistol from his weakening hand. The slug missed Joe by several feet.

It did not miss Will Ax. The old Indian had pushed himself up at the wrong moment, and the slug caught him in the side.

Joe yelled, "No!" He leaped down from the bar and came to Will Ax's side.

"Joe... he's killed me, Joe."

Tears in his eyes, Joe scooped up the crumpled form of his friend and carried him out the front door. Joe's horse was tethered nearby, and he heaved Will Ax onto it, then slid into the saddle, gave a yell, and rode off, no one daring to stop him.

Chapter 16

Rebecca Pullette darted across the street just in time to avoid being knocked down by three riders who galloped too fast around the corner. The pretty young Cherokee lady paused beneath a windmill well pump and collected herself before continuing on toward her house. That had been close. She had not even heard them coming. Her heart thumped in excitement over the near accident.

She wondered who the riders were. They wore big hats and long coats, and there were about a dozen others just like them in town. They had arrived by train the day before on a special car with closed shades, their horses riding in locked boxcars. Folks who had watched the special train unload talked about the several crates of rifles and ammunition that composed the only cargo besides men and horses.

All Rebecca knew about the mysterious newcomers was that they were federal men who had come for some reason having to do with the railroad. Rebecca did not know what the reason was; young women were seldom told of such masculine matters and in the Pullette house were expected not to ask.

Keeping a more careful eye now, Rebecca continued

down the street and around another corner. From here she could see her house, the big impressive place that seemed like a palace to her in comparison with the much smaller house the Pullettes had occupied in Hays City. Ross Pullette, Rebecca's adoptive father, had worked hard during the early lean times in Hays City, and it had paid off. Through over-frugal living he had managed to save enough to buy into a promising hardware and feed business here in Great Bend, and through some additional dealing and bargaining had obtained their new house at an excellent price. The move to Great Bend just a few days back had been a time of joy for all the Pullettes.

Yet for Rebecca a vague and ominous feeling had accompanied the joy. Since Great Bend came into her view as she rode in on the carriage seat, she had felt tense, expecting the unexpected. Her feelings mystified her, and she tried to explain them away as simple nerves, but that was not convincing. That first sight of Great Bend filled her with the conviction that something was coming her way, something significant and unusual.

Already half of that expectation had been fulfilled. Plenty of unusual things had come along in her brief time in Great Bend. First there was the sight of that slender young Indian chimney sweep atop a nearby house the day the Pullettes moved into their own. Why he struck her as unusual Rebecca had not yet figured out. Then there was that second Indian, the old man who stood across the street in the darkness watching her window. He had frightened her and also intrigued her.

Unusual things had come not only to Rebecca but to all of the town. First there was that terrible gunfight at the tavern. According to what she had overheard, it had involved a young halfbreed outlaw people called Cherokee Joe and a stranger who had come to town claiming to be a federal marshal but now was thought to be a powerful Wichita businessman named Christmas. According to what Ross Pullette had said at last night's dinner table, the law was trying to finalize his identification even now. Whoever he was, he was thoroughly dead, and before he had been gunned down, he had publicly called his assailant Cherokee Joe.

Then, as if all that wasn't enough, the posse of riders had showed up on the train and had been galloping hell-for-leather all around town ever since, flashing rifles and pistols and stirring a crazy quilt of contradictory rumors, most of them tied to Cherokee Joe. Rebecca had heard several theories about them so far but had no idea which if any was true.

As she continued into her yard, she glanced at the house where she had seen the Indian chimney sweep that first day. Could he have been Cherokee Joe? That possibility had suggested itself as soon as she heard of the fatal shooting in the tavern. And that old man outside her house—might he have been the old Indian who reportedly was being protected by Cherokee Joe in that gunfight? Rebecca wondered, thinking she would never answer those questions.

She found out more at that night's supper table. Ross Pullette was in an unusually talkative mood. He had been in town all day and had picked up the latest information about the Cherokee Joe incident, the man who had been shot, and the riders who now circulated throughout the town.

"Despite what you might have heard, those riders didn't come to Great Bend looking for this Cherokee Joe fellow," he said. "I've got good information. They're a specially formed federal posse come to find and capture Caul Slidell, the outlaw. You've all heard of him, surely. This Slidell pulled off a robbery at a train station down in the Indian Nations and came riding up this way. Supposedly he hides out in this county from time to time. Well, the railroad was plenty riled about the robbery, which involved the murder of some Indians, sorry to say. The railroad barons pulled all their strings in Washington to get something done about Slidell. Next thing you know, there's a federal posse put together. That's who those riders are."

"So why are they still in town?" asked Jimmy Pullette, Rebecca's adoptive younger brother.

"Complications, from what I hear. It seems this fellow Cherokee Joe shot down was named Jim Christmas. I've heard of him—wealthy and powerful gent down about Wichita. Had ties to the railroad. And listen to this: There's federal suspicion that he was backing Slidell in that train station robbery and that Slidell cheated him out of his share of the loot. Furthermore, one of the Indians who was killed during the robbery was Cherokee Joe's father. Amazing, huh? All these things are fitting together, and the federal marshals leading the posse are trying to make sense of it all. Add to that a rumor that the local law actually had Cherokee Joe in jail before the shooting and then turned him loose without identifying him, and you can see how confusing it all gets. It's really slowed up that posse. Funny part is, the local deputy who supposedly turned Cherokee Joe loose is trying to weasel out by blaming the whole thing on that old widow up the street." Ross Pullette chuckled.

"The one in the big house you can see from the yard?" Rebecca asked.

"That's the one."

"Oh!" She took another bite as she mulled the realization that it was at that very house she had seen the Indian chimney sweep. Now it seemed even more likely it had been Cherokee Joe.

"Seems to me the posse ought to go after Cherokee Joe before they worry about Slidell," Jimmy Pullette commented. "I was told today that he's killed peace officers in the Indian Territory and down in Hutchinson too."

"So he has," Ross Pullette replied. "But I doubt this posse will concentrate much on Cherokee Joe. The only reason it officially exists is to deal with Slidell. The railroad cares a lot more about him than some short-lived triggerman like Cherokee Joe."

"Short-lived? You mean he's dead?" Rebecca's adoptive mother asked.

"Not yet," Ross Pullette replied around a mouthful of beef. "But he will be. Men like that don't live long. Like my father always said, if a bullet doesn't lay a bad man low, a noose will lift him high.'"

"If he killed that man because he was tormenting an old Indian, then maybe Cherokee Joe isn't so bad," Rebecca said.

"Rebecca!" her mother responded. "How can you talk so? He's a killer! A murderer!"

Rebecca flushed. "I'm sorry," she muttered. "It was just a thought."

"And hardly a good one," her mother muttered.

"Let it go, Mother," Ross Pullette said. "Pass those potatoes, will you?"

Rebecca said nothing more during the rest of the meal. Her ears burned in embarrassment at the comment she had made. She had surprised herself as much as her mother by her sentiment. She didn't mean it, not really. Cherokee Joe surely was very bad if he really had killed men of the law. Still, the story she had heard was that no one else had stepped in to help the poor old Indian being tormented by that Christmas fellow. If Cherokee Joe was bad, at least he was also willing to protect the downtrodden.

Rebecca finished her meal, said she didn't feel well, and excused herself to her bedroom to turn in early. Once beneath her covers, she found she could not sleep. She kept thinking about all the excitement in town, about all the talk and drama, about Cherokee Joe and the old man he had protected.

The clock ticked on the wall. Outside, horsemen passed, the restless posse members sweeping through town again. When they were gone, there came a lull, and the howling of a dog somewhere outside town sounded lonely and a little scary. Rebecca Pullette pulled up the covers, shivered, and went to sleep.

She awoke without knowing why, staring up toward the high ceiling. Sleep had been fitful all night. She had dreamed about Cherokee Joe, seeing him in the form of that Indian chimney sweep atop the widow's house. When she sat up now, she thought she was dreaming still.

Silhouetted in her window, which gave onto the roof of the porch, was the form of a man, a slender man, and young, clad in a long coat, denim pants, and a flat-brimmed hat. Rebecca Pullette drew back in fear. The window behind the man was open, the curtains blowing in the breeze that stirred through. He had come in across the porch roof.

"Don't be afraid," he said in a whisper. "You have nothing to fear from me."

"Who are you?"

"That isn't important. I've come to take you to your father."

"My father is downstairs. If he finds you here, he'll shoot you."

"It's your real father I mean. Your Indian father."

Rebecca drew in her breath. Her Indian father! She had no memory of the man, knew nothing about him except what little her adoptive parents had told her. She had often wondered if he still lived, and what he was like.

"My real father. . ."

"Yes. Or so he is convinced. His name is Will Ax."

Rebecca knew she should scream, but she didn't. What she was hearing was too intriguing. Fascination was beginning to overwhelm fear, and this despite her rising suspicion that the young intruder was Cherokee Joe himself and the old man he was calling her father was the same one he had protected in the tavern.

"But how can I know what you're saying is true?" she asked.

"You can't. But you've got to believe it is, like Will Ax does. Come on. There isn't much time, and it's not safe for me here. Don't be afraid of me. I promise you on the blood of our fathers that I'll let no harm come to you."

"Are you Cherokee Joe?"

A pause. "That's what the white men call me. My name is Joe Wolfkiller."

Rebecca looked around the room. It was the room of an American white girl, domestic, familiar, tame. The dark figure of Cherokee Joe was out of place here... and suddenly, she felt out of place too. The wind blowing in through the window, the slender man before her, the prospect of a meeting with a father she could not remember— these things awakened a deep wild impulse in her. She could not remain in this house tonight. Tonight she belonged out there on the open land with Cherokee Joe. This was what that sense of something significant coming her way was all about. The feeling was overwhelming now, but not ominous as before.

"I'll come with you," she said. She rose, her nightgown like a white shroud around her, and went to her wardrobe for her clothing.

Cherokee Joe turned away as she dressed, looking out the window in a posture as tense and fragile as a catgut string. "He is badly wounded," Joe said. "He was shot."

"Will he live?"

Joe answered only after a pause. "No. I don't believe he will." Rebecca watched him lift his hand and touch his face, still turned away from her, and realized with surprise that the feared outlaw Cherokee Joe had just wiped away a tear. "I wanted to find him a doctor, but he wouldn't let me leave him. Now it is too late for doctors."

Ten minutes later, Rebecca Pullette was riding behind Joe Wolfkiller, feeling a great sense of unreality. As they rode, he told her more fully the story of Will Ax and his quest.

Rebecca's arms were around Cherokee Joe's waist, and her cheek rested against the back of his shoulder. The wind whipped her hair. She knew she was foolish for being here. It did not matter. She had done what she wanted to do, and this would be a night she would not forget for the rest of her life.

Will Ax's eyes blinked as warm drops fell upon his face. He looked up at the crude leaky roof of boards above him and hoped the rain would not be so heavy that water would fill the little gully in which he was lying. A gully was no place for a wounded man to rest, but he did not fault Joe Wolfkiller for placing him here. There was no other good place to hide on the flatlands.

It was terribly dark. Will Ax felt alone.

The boards that so poorly sheltered him had been put in place by Joe Wolfkiller, who had found them scattered about the ruin of an old shack foundation nearby. Joe had built the crude ground-level shelter over the gully and then tended Will's wound as best he could. Upon seeing the bloody hole, Joe had looked grim and declared that he would return to Great Bend for the doctor. No, Will had told him. If you return, you'll die, and I'll be left out here alone. I don't want to be left alone. If you stay with me, I will live. The *ulunsuti* has told me.

So Joe had stayed, and Will had waited for his miraculous healing. It had not come, and now Will knew it would not. He was too sick to get better, no matter what the *ulunsuti* said. He was going to die. The thought bothered him some, though not as much as the feeling of aloneness overwhelming him now. "Joe?" He said the name as loudly as he could and was surprised to find his voice nothing more than a weak, grating whisper. "Where are you, Joe?"

No answer came. Joe had abandoned him. Will closed his eyes, and tears mixed with the rain on his face. He had not thought Joe would leave him to die alone.

A suspicion came, making Will open his eyes again. Might Joe have gone back to Great Bend to get a doctor, despite Will's urging to the contrary? He hoped not. No doctor would come with an outlaw killer onto the plains in the middle of the night just to tend a dying old Indian. Joe would only be endangering himself needlessly.

The rain passed over, and no more drops fell on Will's face. He dug his hand into his pocket, held the *ulunsuti* in his fist, and slept again. When he awakened, he no longer felt alone. Yellow light flickered on the underside of the low board shelter. Will was confused.

"Old man, I see you're still alive," a familiar voice said from the end of the shelter.

"Joe... I thought you had left me."

"Only for a while. I had to go fetch someone to you."

"If you've brought a doctor, it's too late. Death is in my heart, Joe."

"Tell it to wait long enough for you to meet who I brought."

Joe Wolfkiller lifted the boards above Will Ax and laid them aside. The old man watched Joe, too weak to lift his head, and wondered whom he had brought and why he felt such a mounting excitement. Then before him was a face, feminine and dark, beautiful in the flickering light of the little fire Joe had built farther down the gully, the first fire he had dared to make since fleeing Great Bend.

"Gatunlati?"

Rebecca Pullette smiled and knelt beside the old man. "Yes, Father. I've come to you."

"Gatunlati!" said Will Ax, and as weak as he was, he managed to lift his arms and put them around Rebecca. She lowered herself to let him hold her.

For several minutes after that they talked. Joe stood off to the side by the fire, watching, his slender form dangerously exposed. He did not care. The only thing that seemed worth caring about at the moment was happening a few yards away where Will Ax was at last fulfilling his final quest.

Rebecca Pullette watched silently as Joe Wolfkiller pulled Will Ax's old Union coat up over the old man's unmoving chest, upon which now lay the Bunyan volume, and then over his face.

Joe patted the dead man's shoulder, stood, and looked at Rebecca. His eyes were red and damp, and this time he did not try to hide his emotions. "Thank you," Joe said. "You made him happy in his last hour."

"He said strange things at the end," Rebecca said. "He spoke one moment of joining the spirits of his fathers and the next of crossing a river and going to some great city, and of Jesus and the cross. He talked like. . ."

"Like a man living in two worlds," Joe replied. "That's the way Will Ax lived, and it's the way he died."

"He really believed I am his daughter," Rebecca said.

"Maybe you are."

"No. I know very little about my father, but one thing I do know—he had only one arm. He lost the other during a battle in the big war."

Joe nodded, thinking it would have been better not to know what Rebecca had just told him. "I suppose it doesn't matter. To him, you were Gatunlati. You were real."

"He gave me this ... he called it his treasure." Rebecca held up the *ulunsuti.*

The sun was rising over the horizon, and some of its light struck the crystal. Joe was surprised to see that it did not cast back the light as it had other times he had seen it. It was dark and dead. Its light had faded with the life of its keeper.

"I don't understand what it is," Rebecca said.

"Once it was an *ulunsuti,* the most powerful of the Cherokee divining crystals," Joe replied. "Now I think it is just a stone like any other." He looked down at the still body at his feet. "Or maybe it was always just a stone. Maybe it just reflected the spirit of Will Ax, like its surface reflected the sun. I don't know much about such things."

Rebecca held the *ulunsuti* close to her, cupping it in her hands. "I will always treasure it," she said.

"Yes. You should," Joe said. "Now we have to ride. I'll take you as close to town as I can safely go. It's time for you to go home."

Chapter 17

Joe, weary and dirty, sat beside the newly covered grave he had scraped out with a board and filled with the body of Will Ax. The effort might have been wasted, for the grave was shallow and could easily be dug up by burrowing animals. Nevertheless, the burial seemed important to Joe. He could not let his friend's corpse lie on the open plains like that of some dead dog.

Deep loneliness settled over Joe as he sat looking at the grave. Not until now did he realize how much he had come to love Will Ax. He hoped Will had found his way to the Celestial City he talked about so much.

He stood and stretched his tired muscles. On the ground nearby lay a rabbit he had snared. Joe scrounged around in the scrubby brush for fuel to roast a late breakfast. As he skinned the rabbit and roasted it on a stick, Joe thought about Rebecca Pullette. On the way back to Great Bend he had asked her why she had come with him to see Will Ax when a single question—whether Will had one arm or two—would have let her know he was not really her father.

Rebecca had not given a very clear answer. It came to

this: She had come because she had wanted to. Because it seemed right. Because, despite her raising, she remained Cherokee in heart and heritage. Whether Joe could understand that she did not know.

"I do understand," Joe replied.

Rebecca told him of events in town since the shooting, including the arrival of the posse searching for Caul Slidell. Joe asked when they would ride out, but Rebecca didn't know.

He left her within walking distance of Great Bend. She would find trouble at home, she speculated aloud, for by now surely they knew she was missing. She didn't care. She was glad she had met Will Ax, glad she had met Cherokee Joe.

Joe watched her walk away and thought how it might have been had he known her under other circumstances— if he had been simply Joe Wolfkiller and not Cherokee Joe, outlaw.

The rabbit was hardly enough to fill Joe's empty stomach, but it would have to suffice. He stood, wiped his hands, and went to Will's grave a final time. He looked down upon it thoughtfully, reached into his coat pocket, and pulled out Will's leather-bound book.

"You may as well keep it, old man," he said. "I doubt I'll find any bright cities at the end of my road." He tossed the volume onto the grave, mounted, and rode away.

An hour later he halted at the base of a low slope. On the other side he heard the noise of many horses. Dismounting, he slipped to the top and peered over. A band of horsemen in long coats were riding north. Their route indicated they had come from Great Bend.

This had to be the posse Rebecca had told him about, setting off at last to find Caul Slidell. Caul Slidell— the killer of Joe's father, the man Joe had vowed to kill.

Joe went back to his horse, mounted, and after several minutes rode to the top of the rise. The horsemen were faint specks in the distance. Joe watched them until they were nearly out of sight, then turned his mount to ride in the opposite direction. He got only a few yards before he turned again and eyed the receding riders. Swearing at himself, Joe fell in behind, following their trail.

The cluster of buildings where Caul Slidell and his hellriders made their occasional camp had once been a ranch, but had been abandoned four years ago. Its former occupants could hardly have imagined that their spread would become the scene of the sort of violence taking place today.

Caul Slidell, bleeding from a shallow leg wound, grimaced and bobbed up to send another slug from his Winchester speeding toward the hiding place of one of the long-coated gunmen who had descended upon the hideout an hour before. Slidell was inside what had once been a stable, fighting out of the loft along with three of his hellriders. Within Slidell's view three other hellriders lay dead in the clearings between buildings. So far, he had seen only one of the attackers killed. His men, badly surprised by the assault, were taking the worst of it.

Who were these long-coated gunmen? Some sort of lawmen maybe, or perhaps private guns hired by the railroad —or by Jim Christmas, curse his soul. Whoever they were, they were the first to take on Caul Slidell's hellriders in their home base. No one, law or otherwise, had dared try anything like this before.

Slidell lifted his rifle and took another shot at one of the gunmen. He missed. Swearing, he levered in another bullet. Yeah, it was Jim Christmas behind this, sure as the devil. Jim Christmas, mad because Slidell had gotten the best of him.

Maybe it had been a mistake to cheat Jim Christmas out of his cut of the stolen jewels. Maybe the mistake had been to deal with Christmas in the first place. Slidell had had a gut feeling it would turn bad. The whole thing had taken on a sour taste ever since he had shot down Ed Wiltflower back around Hutchinson.

Still, he couldn't regret it all. The haul at the Guthrie train station had been the richest of his career. Already he had used a contact, set up, ironically, by Jim Christmas, to convert the jewels to cash before Christmas could get word out to abort the transaction. Part of the cash Slidell had divided among his hellriders. His own cut, the largest, was safely stashed where only he could find it. He had been only an hour from going to fetch it and disappear for a few months when the attack had come.

One of the attackers darted across a clearing, hurdling one of the dead bodies. Slidell fired another ineffective shot. The gunman dropped and rolled, coming up behind the stone wall of a well, raising his rifle and firing. One of the men fighting beside Slidell jerked and pitched backward, blood pooling around him. The slug had entered his skull and killed him instantly.

"We can't whip 'em, Caul!" one of his remaining gunmen declared. "Them fellows, they're trained fighters—you can tell. I seen a federal badge on one of 'em. We'll have to give it up."

Slidell barked an order to keep shooting, then headed around to the other side of the loft. Peering out, he saw nothing encouraging on the other side. Two more dead men, both hellriders, and another, seemingly wounded. Slidell swore.

Behind him, the gunman who had talked surrender yelled and fell back, a bullet through the chest. He died looking accusingly at Slidell.

The outlaw swore again, stood, and leaped out of the

loft. Pausing at the door of the barn, he fired another shot at one of the attackers and was gratified to see the man fall. He didn't get up. Slidell took a quick look around, drew in a breath, and ran across the clearing toward an adjacent building.

He drew no fire. Apparently no one had noticed his flight. Inside the building he paused to reload his Winchester with the last of the cartridges in his pocket. He was beginning to see that the hellrider in the loft had been right: This was one battle he and his men could not win. Used to law that turned its eyes the other way, they hadn't been prepared for this kind of onslaught.

He had to find a way to get away from here, to get his treasure and run. Capture would mean death on the gallows, especially since he had murdered those Indians, including Sam Wolfkiller, before witnesses at the train station. A stupid move that had been, made under the influence of that wild, impulsive urge that always seized him in the midst of committing an armed crime. He didn't regret the killings, only the trouble they could mean for him.

Slidell went to another window and looked out. There was one of the attackers, crouched behind a pile of logs. Slidell grinned as he took aim and laughed as he fired. The man took the slug in the side, tried to run away, then fell.

Slidell worked his rifle lever and laughed again, for tethered near the man he had just killed was a saddled horse. Slidell opened the door and made a run for the horse. His move was poorly timed. Around the corner came two more attackers. He wheeled, firing off a shot from hip level, and drove them back. He vaulted into the saddle from behind, jerked the tethers loose, and took off at a run.

One of the gunmen behind him stepped out, aimed carefully, and took a shot. Slidell cried out as a slug ripped through his shoulder. Blood poured down, front and back.

Slidell bent low in the saddle and rode as hard as he could, hoping he could make it away before he passed out.

At least he had his money.

Slidell, grunting with exertion and pain, pulled the dirty sack from the metal box in which it had been buried. He was in a rugged rocky area, two miles from the embattled ranch site. No one but he knew of this little rocky enclave, his own private stash for stolen money, goods, guns. He grinned as he plopped the money sack down before him. He dug into the metal box and removed a smaller bag containing the few stolen jewels he had not turned into cash. These he dropped into his pocket. Closing the box, he slid it back into its little cavern in the rocks and placed stones over the opening.

Exhaustion overwhelmed him, and pain rumbled through his shoulder. Slidell longed to lie down, even on these rocks, and sleep. Couldn't do it, though. Had to go on. At least he had his money. He slung the money bag over the saddle horn, mounted, and rode.

An hour later he jerked spasmodically in the saddle. He had gone to sleep and almost fallen. Turning, fighting the pain and weakness raging through him, he looked behind. Someone was back there, following him. He could sense a presence upon that wide landscape.

He felt cold and noted a north wind blowing. Eyes scanning upward, he saw a dense black cloud rolling across the sky like a coat of thick paint. The spring wind rode on its mantle. Between powerful gusts he felt the stickiness of humidity in the air, moisture driven all the way from the Gulf of Mexico far to the south. Thunder rumbled like a growling belly somewhere inside the dark cloud.

Slidell felt the wind, tasted the air, studied the squall line forming in the sky. He was a man of the flatlands and knew this sort of weather and what if often led to. The thought brought fear. He remembered a time in his boyhood when he had watched a house in his native Kentucky explode with his grandfather still inside. They had found him a day later, hanging ten feet off the ground, impaled on a sharp branch like a ham on a meat hook. He had been sucked into the sky and stuck on the tree when the swirling demon that had grabbed him finally tired of making him its toy. Ever since then, Caul Slidell had suffered a deep fear of tornadoes.

He pushed on, heart pounding like a hammer, his blood a dry crust on his shirt and coat. The wind continued to rise. He could feel the coming storm as he could feel the unseen presence behind him. He stopped and turned again, looking for his follower. The day was darkening. "That you, Jim Christmas?" he yelled. "Come on, damn your eyes, show yourself!"

No response but a peal of thunder.

A mile due north, Slidell recalled, was an old shack. If he pushed hard, maybe he could make it there before the storm hit and before Jim Christmas, if Christmas it was, caught up with him. He feared Jim Christmas even more than the cyclone.

Halfway to the shack he felt the presence again, more strongly, and twisted in the saddle. This time he saw him, starkly outlined against the purple-black sky. It wasn't Jim Christmas. For a moment that brought relief—then he looked more closely at the rider and felt a shudder of fear.

Cherokee Joe. He knew him even from this distance. The same Cherokee Joe who had ridden with him a time or two in the past and whom he had come to despise because he sensed him the better man. The same Cherokee Joe he had tried to frame for attempted murder back in the Indian Nations and the same Cherokee Joe whose father he had gunned down for the fun of it at the Guthrie railroad station.

Slidell's heart bolted to his throat. Panicking, he wheeled the horse and pushed hard toward the shack. The thunder pealed like cannon fire, and rain began, mixed with hail. Slidell didn't have to look back to know Cherokee Joe was matching his pace. He felt him like a hot breath on his neck. Through the storm he rode, battered by rain and hail. He hardly noticed the pain in his shoulder now; he felt too much fear to feel anything else.

There. The shack. Slidell spurred the horse as hard as he could. Then the horse's leg found a hole, and the animal fell. Slidell pitched forward.

When he sat up, he knew that time had passed. He had been stunned by the fall. His eyes swept the land, looking for the horse. It had galloped off. On the ground lay the money bag. It was empty, the last of the bills blowing out of it and sailing off into the wind. Slidell watched it a few moments and heard someone laughing aloud. He recognized the laugh a moment later: his own.

He stood. His shoulder was bleeding again. The wind was so strong, it threatened to blow him over. He heard a roaring that rose suddenly, like a train about to come over the rise. Wheeling, he saw a black cyclone descend and etch a scar across the land, the shack that had been his goal in its path. It exploded before his eyes as if a bomb had been set off inside. Slidell screamed and threw himself into a ravine, clung to the brush in it, and heard himself laughing again. Death had come to claim him the same way it had claimed his grandfather, and he had cheated it, cheated it because of a fall from a horse.

He passed out again, and when he awoke, the cyclone was past. The wind had declined significantly, and the clouds were not as thick. The raindrops were just drops again, not bullets.

He sat up, groaning, then looked up and saw Cherokee Joe staring down at him. A peculiar gurgling sound rose from his throat. He dug for his gun and found the holster empty. Cherokee Joe lifted his hand. Slidell's pistol dangled from his forefinger.

"You killed my father, Caul Slidell," said Cherokee Joe.

"Joe, I didn't mean to do it, I swear, and it wasn't me—it was Wiltflower."

Cherokee Joe shook his head. "It was you, Slidell. Confess it!"

Slidell had no will to defy the halfbreed. Weakly he nodded.

Joe Wolfkiller flipped the pistol in his hand and aimed it at Slidell's head. The outlaw began to cry. He squeezed his eyes closed.

Click.

The hammer had clacked into an empty cylinder. God help me, Slidell thought, he's going to toy with me before he kills me. Going to toy with me like that Kentucky twister toyed with my grandfather.

The cylinder turned with a clean metallic whir.

Click.

Slidell sank to the ground, putting his hands over his face. Another whir.

Click.

"Please, Joe, please," he pleaded. "If you're going to kill me, then kill me!"

Click.

"Please, Joe. Don't play this game with me. Don't make me wait for—"

Click.

A long pause followed. Slidell knew the time had come. Cherokee Joe had reached the last shot. This time the sound of the turning cylinder was not a whir but a slow ratcheting.

Cherokee Joe spoke. "The first five were for the sake of a crazy old Indian named Will Ax who told me that those who won't bend will break, and that sometimes a man has to let himself forget, and that maybe the old ways of revenge are dead. And they were for the sake of an old widow woman in Great Bend who gave me a second chance and told me to make good of it—and for a Cherokee girl who wouldn't turn her back on her own kind, even though she could have."

Joe squatted by the ravine and aimed the pistol carefully at Slidell's head. "But this last one—this is for the sake of Sam Wolfkiller, but mostly for the sake of Cherokee Joe."

Slidell couldn't keep his eyes closed for some reason. He found himself compelled to stare into the grim face above him and the hole of the pistol muzzle only two feet from his face.

"Joe, please. I'll make it worth your while if you won't—"

Click.

Empty. The last one was empty too. Slidell put his hands to his face and sobbed.

Joe Wolfkiller stood and holstered the pistol. "Me and you, Slidell, we've got something in common. There's nothing but the noose ahead for both of us. It may come sooner, or it may come later, but it will come. Men like you and me live short lives. That's all right. That's how it ought to be. We haven't earned the right to anything better.

"I've lived close to death these last days, and I've lived close to life. Now I know which is best, even though the knowing's come too late to count for much. The time I have left before they finally catch me will be short, but I'll have the satisfaction of knowing that one time, just one time, Cherokee Joe knew what it was like to forgive someone who wronged him."

Joe Wolfkiller turned and walked away through the rain. Slidell, his voice tight, stood. He gripped his wounded shoulder. "Cherokee Joe!" he called.

Joe turned.

"Why?"

Cherokee Joe looked him in the eye. "Because Will Ax was right. The old ways are past," he said. "The law of blood has faded. The *ulunsuti* no longer shines."

He turned again and strode away, long strides across the sodden, storm-ravaged land until Caul Slidell was alone.

Afterword

Cherokee Joe was written under the inspiration of two events. The first was a drive from Wichita to Oklahoma City on a pleasant day in the summer of 1990, during which the impulse to write a story set in that beautiful portion of the Midwest became overwhelming. The second was reading in James Mooney's classic collections, "Myths of the Cherokee," and "Sacred Formulas of the Cherokees."

Among the subjects Mooney explored was the legendary Uktena, a large, serpentine creature said to haunt hidden pools in the mysterious mountains of western North Carolina, particularly the gorge of Nantahala. The dragon-like Uktena was said to have a brilliant crystal crest on its brow. This, the *ulunsuti,* was the rarest and most desirable of Cherokee divining stones, and was believed to give much power to its possessor. Mooney recorded that one *ulunsuti* was said to remain in possession of the Eastern Cherokees as late as 1890, but was kept hidden in a cave by a hunter who staunchly refused to desecrate and likely ruin the crystal by allowing any white man to look at it.

Several references to legends of the Uktena and the *ulunsuti* exist in early sources, including the recollections of

Henry Timberlake and James Adair, both of whom lived and traveled among the Native Americans of the Southeast in the 18th century. Examination of this and other lore of the period is a rewarding effort highly recommended to interested readers, who may wish to compare the Cherokee stories with the similar legends of dragons and great serpents that abound across the globe.

One unrelated and final note is in order: The towns of Hutchinson and Great Bend, Kansas, are, of course, well-known actual locales. In *Cherokee Joe,* however, these towns are given a substantially fictional treatment. No characters presented in association with them (whether townsmen or local law enforcement officials) are intended to depict or represent any actual figures out of the histories of those communities.

Cameron Judd
July 15, 1991

Jerusalem Camp

Chapter 1

He came to the mountains as the snow fell, and the clip of his big bay's hooves marked off the changing of the seasons. Later, the people of Jerusalem Camp would recall his time among them as the Killing Winter. The man himself they would recall only by the single name he gave them, for he never gave another, and when at last he rode out again with a new season at his heels, he rode out for good.

He climbed the Sierras with a bullet crease in his leg and the two armed riders who had put it there close behind him. He pushed the bay along canyon flanks, beneath granite cliffs, and up washes lined with tamarack and sugar pine. Gray clouds spat snow that piled thickly on the ground and hampered the bay. The rider looked back frequently, and bent low, perhaps from pain, perhaps just to make himself less conspicuous.

He slowed when he reached a snow-encrusted stand of pine that was so closely bunched his horse could barely push through. When at last it did and then ascended a slope, the rider looked back and saw his pursuers already coming through the stand. Too close. He spurred his horse, but the weary animal, sides heaving and nostrils spewing steam, could go no faster.

On a jumble of talus at the base of a black escarpment, the bay stepped into a hole and pitched, whinnying, to the left. As the rider fell painfully on rock shards, he heard the snap of the horse's left foreleg.

He rose and wiped blood from his shattered lip onto his sleeve. He glanced once into the tormented eyes of his fallen horse and vainly wished he had the time and spare ammunition to end the beast's suffering.

In the cold air a shot from behind him made a flat, slapping sound that echoed off the escarpment. He struggled forward, came to a ravine, and leapt into it. He pulled icy air into his lungs; it burned like cold fire.

He looked at his wounded leg: still bleeding. At least it didn't hurt. The strain and the cold had numbed him so he did not feel it, the snow beneath his thin boot soles, or the slice of the wind through his canvas trousers.

He scrambled along the ravine, but his progress was too slow. So, gritting his teeth, he rolled up out of it on his back and belly. He stood and was surprised to see four men before him. Strangers, armed. They had just emerged from a scraggly forest of pine a hundred feet ahead.

Another shot sounded behind him; the bullet zipped over his head. One of the strangers ahead raised a rifle and fired back. The lone man was caught in the middle.

He dropped back into the ravine, his face digging into the snow. He heard more gunfire back and forth, then suddenly it stopped. For several seconds, the Sierras were utterly silent. The man cautiously stood and peered over the edge of the ravine. The four from the forest approached, rifles smoking. He glanced behind; his pursuers were gone.

He smiled as the four men reached him, and said, "I'm obliged—" but one of the men drew back his rifle, brought down the butt, and knocked him cold.

The four men gathered around the edge of the ravine and looked at his still form, silent as their breath made white fog in the mountain air and fear they dared not reveal tasted like bile in their throats.

Jared learned of the capture from Jimmy Essler, a boy who lived several houses up from his forge. The gap-toothed boy was very excited and lisped it out to the blacksmith like this: "Mither Cable, they got a man caught and down at Mither Rupert and Mither Rupert ith ready to hang him!"

"What? Hang who?"

"The man! They caught the man!"

Jared saw that he would gain no understanding from Jimmy, so he hurriedly dusted off his hands, doffed his leather smith's apron, and slipped on his coat. The smithy was hot, but outside the snow churned down in a near-blizzard and the twilight air was biting cold.

Jimmy came out at Jared's heels and passed him at a dead run through the contorted field of white. The flakes fell so thickly that before Jimmy was twenty feet ahead Jared lost sight of him.

Rupert's was a store in one way of looking at it, and a saloon and gambling house in another. Loren Rupert was dedicated to keeping vice alive in Jerusalem Camp, a purpose that had set him firmly against Jared Cable's preacher father ever since Rupert had drifted up from the American River camps years ago. Now that Jared had accepted the mostly symbolic job of town marshal, he suspected that he was replacing his aging father as Rupert's chief object of wrath.

Rupert's door tended to jam, then pop open loudly, so when Jared entered he got the full attention of every man inside. It was a solemn gathering: Rupert and four no-goods who hung around his place. Jimmy Essler was there, too, having scrambled in ahead of Jared. Jared smelled the familiar mix of hot coffee, wood smoke, chalk dust, and whiskey that permeated the building.

Rupert, his gray and black hair slick with bay rum, said with thick, smiling sarcasm, "Well, look here, boys. It's the marshal."

"Hello, Loren," Jared said. He looked down at Jimmy, whose red hair was growing damp as the snow flecked on it melted in the heat of Rupert's pine-fed stove. "Boy, you'd best get on before your ma worries."

"Aw, c'mon, Mither Cable," the boy complained. "Any-time anything geth tharted I get thent off."

"Get on," Jared repeated.

The boy's face darkened, but immediately brightened. "I know what I'll do," he said. He opened the door and vanished as before into the white swirl.

Jared said, "The boy mentioned something about a man, and a hanging—"

Clyde Ingersoll, whose bulbous nose might have been red from cold but more likely from something else, said, "This ain't your business, Cable."

"You got a man here or not?" Jared demanded. Rupert gave an almost mischievous grin. "We do."

"Where?"

Rupert thumbed toward a storage room behind him.

Jared entered. The rider lay on the bare floor. He had been unconscious, but was starting to rouse.

"Who is he?" Jared asked.

"How should I know?" Rupert said. "We caught him coming in toward town with two men shooting at him. We took it they might be shooting at us, too, and shot back. He's the one we're after—that I'll wager."

"Now how do you know that?"

"Who else could he be?"

Jared shook his head. "You never fail to astound me,

Rupert. Not a shred of evidence and you're ready to string up a man just because he rode through at the wrong time." Jared paused when he saw the blood on the man's trousers. "You've shot him!"

"He was shot before we ever seen him," Rupert said defensively. "It's just a crease. And nobody's said nothing about stringing him up. That was just the boy talking."

"I'll bet."

Jared briefly searched the man's pockets, looking for identification. He found nothing, but he noted a leather string around the man's neck, extending below his shirt. Jared pulled it out. On it hung an oval brass medallion, worn nearly smooth so its image of a tree and a river was now only scarcely visible.

"What's that?" Rupert asked. Jared shook his head.

Behind them the bulky door popped open again and Logan Hull entered. Doc Hull, the townsfolk called him, though his medical credentials didn't strictly justify it. He had worked in field hospitals during the war with Mexico—an effective school of medicine, but one that issued no diplomas or shingles to swing above doors.

Doc Hull walked into the back room and knelt beside the supine man, whose eyes fluttered open a second later. The others regrouped around him. The man looked around the room, resting his gaze for a moment on each face. Doc said, "Easy, my friend. I'm a doctor. Let me check you."

"How'd you hear about this, Doc?" Jared asked.

"Jimmy Essler just now told me. I sent him home."

Hull prodded the furrowed bullet wound. The man winced.

"Sorry, son," Doc said. "I'm just checking on—"

With speed that surprised them all, the man burst upward. He pushed back Hull, who fell on his rump. A fast swing brought down Ingersoll, and the follow-through hammered Rupert's jaw with a sound like a cracking walnut.

The store owner staggered, flailed out for a handhold, and grabbed the hot pipe of his wood-stove. He screeched, let go, and fell atop Ingersoll.

Rupert's other cronies yelled and leapt away. Wild-eyed, the stranger brought back his fist and charged at Jared.

The man was fast, but Jared, spurred by surprise, was faster. He rolled up a fist big as a muskmelon and drove it bullet-straight into the stranger's mouth. The man's legs went soft, and he fell to his knees, teetered for a second with his arms limp at his sides, then pitched facedown onto the floor, once again out cold.

———

Two men stood shivering in the snow-whipped mountain wilderness. One said, "We're lost. Sooner we admit it and get to town, the better."

"A group from that town shot at us, Joe. It wouldn't be sensible."

"Is it sensible to freeze to death?"

The other had no answer. All about them snow blotted the horizon, making every direction the same. Finally, the one named Joe said what both had been unwillingly thinking: "We'll be like the Donner party if we don't get to shelter. Maybe we should go back to the cabin with Frank."

Mansell looked around at the deathly white. His horse stamped and pawed in the snow. "Forget about Frank," he said. "We'd never find the way there anyway. We'll try for the town. It lies yonder."

The other frowned. "I thought it was that way—"

"Yonder," Mansell said emphatically. But he wasn't as sure as he sounded.

They plunged forward, leading their mounts, stepping high in the rising drifts. The effort was three times harder than it would have been on bare ground, and their hearts hammered at their ribs. Joe screwed his hat low in a vain effort to shield ears so cold he couldn't even tell without feeling for them that they were still there. As they moved, terribly slowly, the day waned. Night slid over the sky like thick gray paint.

"We're going to die out here," Joe said.

"Shut up."

After fifteen minutes, neither could tell how far they had gone, nor if they had traveled straight or merely circled. Nor in which direction lay Jerusalem Camp. They plodded on as the snow piled to their knees.

At last they reached a clearing, now just a wide expanse of drifting snow. Without trees to filter and divert it, the snow had piled deeper here. It reached to the middle of their thighs; walking through it was like wading in half-frozen molasses.

Halfway across, they stopped. They had seen someone. A gray man who so blended with the murky, motile background that only with concentration could they distinguish his silhouette against it. He carried a Henry repeater and wore a heavy fur cloak that was colorless in the gloom.

Mansell felt a warm burst of relief. "Hello!" he called. He waved his arm above his head. "Can you help us!"

The figure stood unmoving, as silent as the snow that nearly hid him.

"Hello!" Mansell called again. "How far are we from Jerusalem Camp?"

There was a long silence. Then a deep voice said, "Near."

"Praise be. Which way?"

Another long pause, then, "You pilgrims lost?"

Some fast-rising instinct kept Mansell from answering. But his partner said, "Yes. Bad lost. Which way?"

The figure edged forward two steps. They could see his outline a bit more clearly now, but the dashing flakes blurred the details of his face. Only his wind-whipped beard, long and gray, was clearly visible. "Bad place for men to be lost," he said.

"Which way to Jerusalem Camp?" repeated Mansell, fighting a peculiar urge to back away.

The man waved to his right. "Beyond that rise."

"Thank you." They pulled their horses southward a few yards. Joe stopped and turned. The Gray Man remained as before.

"Are you going there, too?"

He didn't answer or move.

Mansell said, "You could freeze out here."

"I won't freeze. I can warm myself any moment in the fires of hell."

Mansell, amazed at the singular comment, wondered if the man was insane. But it was nearly dark; urgency compelled him to move. He and Joe struggled to the rise and looked across in the remaining feeble light. They saw no town. Nothing but wild, snowbound wilderness fading into gray nonentity.

"What the..." Mansell muttered. He turned. The Gray Man had followed them, but remained several yards behind. "Are you sure this is the way?"

"You will reach the town," the man said. "That I promise."

"But there's nothing there."

"I will send you to the town. I know it well. It is only just now beginning to know me."

Mansell looked at the sky. It was the color of slate and growing darker. A burst of panic constricted his throat.

"Who are you?"

The old man smiled and came toward him. "Who are you?" Mansell demanded again, backing away, cold hands vainly fumbling for his weapons as the old man, still smiling, bore down upon them with the Henry upraised.

Chapter 2

Ceaselessly the snow fell from clouds that blocked the stars and moon and made the night black as a cavern. As the people of Jerusalem Camp huddled by their fires, sheets of white covered the mountain passes. Heaps of snow piled thickly on evergreen branches, making them strain, then break. Massive limbs crashed earthward, across narrow paths and wagon roads that would accommodate no travelers from now until spring. High on the notch-shaped pass that was the only route out of the basin in which Jerusalem Camp lay, the snow lay especially deep, as it did there every winter, blocking the trail and turning the pass into a natural trap where avalanches were easily triggered.

The stranger slid for the second time into sluggish awareness. He lay in semidarkness, hurting all over. Tough rope bound his wrists and ankles. He was cold and very confused.

I had to tie you up, what with how you went at us before," a voice said. "My name's Jared Cable. I'm a blacksmith. Town marshal, too." The speaker's face came into focus. Smiling but stern, it was the face of a strong man. One the stranger had seen when he had come to the first time.

The tied man strained at his bonds. "Cut these ropes."

"I can't. I don't blame you for flying off like you did, the way Rupert and his gang knocked you out. But until I know you're going to stay calm, I can't cut you loose."

"Why am I being treated like a criminal?"

"Because there's been two murders in this valley this past week. First in its history. Everybody's scared. Maybe that didn't give nobody the right to jump you, but jump you they did. And I might as well ask you, why were those riders gunning after you?"

"I owe you no explanations."

"No. But if you don't talk, you'll spend the rest of the winter tied in that bed."

The stranger exhaled slowly, frowning. Finally he said, "They were trying to rob me, I think. Followed me in from the foothills. You going to cut me loose now?"

"I might. What brought you to Jerusalem Camp?"

"My business, not yours."

"What's your name?"

"Not your business either."

Jared scratched his day-old beard. "All right. Suit yourself." He turned toward the door.

"You're leaving me like this?"

"You ain't cooperating, friend."

The prisoner glared bitterly at him. Finally he said, "I came here just to be coming. No reason. That's the truth. My name's Tellico."

"Tellico who?"

"Tellico's sufficient."

"So, Tellico's sufficient, you rode in to the mountains at the front end of a blizzard—for no reason?"

"That's right. Now cut these ropes and I'll ride out again."

"I'm afraid you won't," Jared said. "This town is snowed in. Funny thing about the lay of our land: The valley's like a bottle, with the pass being the spout. Once snow corks it, you don't get out again." Jared produced a knife and began sawing at Tellico's ropes.

"What's this about murder?"

"Two so far. Man name of Davison and his boy, both out in the mountains when it happened. You picked a bad time to ride in to Jerusalem Camp."

Tellico stood with difficulty, rubbing his wrists. He went to a window and threw back the burlap curtain. Snow pelted the pane, flakes frozen so hard they rattled the glass. He laughed ironically. "Snowed in, in a murder town."

"That's the size of it," Jared said.

Tellico turned and gave Jared his best chance yet to view him. His hair was sandy, slightly long and rather unruly. His eyes were an intense green. His skin was ruddy and fair, though a heavy undergrowth of whiskers somewhat darkened his cheeks. He was slender but far from frail, and seemed tense as a fiddle string.

His shirt was blue, his trousers made of heavy, slightly greasy canvas, his boots well-worn and devoid of ornamentation. When they had captured him he had been wearing a gun belt with a Remington tucked into it. Rupert had taken it, but Jared had re-confiscated it from him.

"Am I a prisoner?" Tellico asked.

"Only of snow and circumstances. I've got no reason to hold you, as long as you keep yourself out of trouble."

"All right."

"What are you going to do with yourself? You got any means of support?"

The question, strangely, made Tellico laugh. "I've been asking myself that very question for some time now," he said. "But I'll survive. If I get hungry I can hunt."

"You're taking being trapped here mighty well. Especially given the circumstances. There are those who won't think it a coincidence that you came in at the same time two people got murdered."

"I'll be careful."

"I won't lie to you, Tellico. I'll be watching you myself. I find you a believable man, somehow. But I can't believe any man rides into a wilderness like this, at a time like this, for no reason."

From the perspective of the hawks that circled above the white mountains, Jerusalem Camp was a nondescript, smoke-belching scattering of lumber squeezed between the granite mountainsides. It lay high above the foothills that were the more typical domain of California gold grubbers.

If it was an unusual town, that was appropriate for it was populated by unusual people.

Three decades before, thousands of forty-niners had swarmed into California, panning the streams—and building flumes and races where there were no streams—erecting towns of canvas and wood along the rivers and tributaries, then quickly abandoning them when the gold ran out.

Amid this explosion of foothills activity a rumor arose: A gold-lined lake, people said, was hidden somewhere high in the mountains. Chunks of wealth just lying there to be picked up. An incredible story, but widely believed. So men scoured the mountains, looking for the lake and never finding it. But gold they did find here and there, and at those places they established camps. Jerusalem Camp was among them.

The Jerusalem Camp strike wasn't huge, but proved steady, so the camp lasted when many others did not, although it was an isolated settlement. It was seldom visited, except by the freighters who hauled in supplies enough to last the town through its isolated winters, and by occasional hunters and mountaineers.

On the edge of Jerusalem Camp stood a church. It was much more finely crafted than any of the town's other structures, with a steeple, bell, and arched double doorways made of oak slabs and hung with brass. Except for miners' crude shacks, it was the first building in the camp.

That was fitting, for the men who had founded the church—the elders, people called them—also had founded the town. They had led the men of their congregation from Indiana across to the Sierras to establish a mountain Utopia where civil, church, and work life would merge into one blissful existence. They named it New Jerusalem, but the name was quickly corrupted to Jerusalem Camp. That, to the dismay of the elders, proved symbolic of certain other corruptions to come.

But not at once. For a year and three months Jerusalem Camp remained a religious community of labor under the control of the church. The saloons, whorehouses, bear-and-bull pits, and gambling halls that dominated other camps did not arise here. Jerusalem Camp's sanctified atmosphere was inhospitable to vice, choking it like a brine-doused weed.

Proud of their new town, a selected delegation of churchmen at last traveled east to fetch the families left behind. But when they arrived back in their utopia it had changed. That was chiefly because of Loren Rupert, who had come by way of the American River with a gambling wheel, several cases of whiskey, and a gaggle of decidedly unregenerate friends. All the opposition of the town's founding elders, led by the Reverend Isaiah Cable, could not drive him away. Jerusalem Camp lost its innocence. The church's exclusivity of influence was gone. The Reverend Isaiah Cable stood before his congregation and declared that now he knew firsthand what it was to see Eden fall. Then he leaned across his pulpit and cried. In the congregation his young son, Jared, newly arrived from Indiana, cried too. He had never seen his father weep, and it scared him.

It surprised no one that Loren Rupert and Isaiah Cable became foes. Isaiah preached against Rupert, and prayed from the pulpit for the damnation of his trade and the salvation of his soul. Rupert ridiculed him in return, and so it went on for years. Eventually, the people accepted the antagonism as a fixture of Jerusalem Camp, like its muddy, haphazard streets. Eventually, for lack of other options, the saints and sinners learned to live together, both sides reluctant and suspicious, but each affecting the other more than they would admit.

Jimmy Essler became suddenly and totally awake. His heart pounded rapidly; he felt a tingle of cognition that made him rise from his bed and slip to the window. Cold air poured in around the loose panes of glass, upon which snow piled in upward-slanting triangles against the crossbars.

The boy squinted through the darkness.

Nothing but deep night and swirling flakes. But he listened and heard the faint whinny of a horse.

Silently he darted through the little house, his footfalls softened by heavy woolen socks. His father snored in an adjacent room as Jimmy's mother stirred beside him, then settled again into the warmth of the rustling bed tick. Jimmy went to the front door and flung it open.

Snow spiraled into the house and stung his face. He diverted it from his eyes, with a hand laid knuckles-first against his forehead, and looked across the street. There was little light, but enough. Since the murders, some lamps in Jerusalem Camp were kept burning all night.

Jimmy looked at one of the lighted windows, and something dark passed across it.

His eyes grew wide and he became frightened. He closed the door. In a far corner of the house a mouse scratched for crumbs. The wind sang around the eaves and sent another blast of cold under the door.

His mother came to her bedroom door. "Jimmy?"

The boy looked at her. "Ith happened again, Ma."

"What are you talking about? Why are you out of bed?"

"Ith happened again. There'th dead men out there."

The woman stood silent a moment.

"Witt," she called to her husband. His snores became sputters, then he was awake. "Jimmy says there's dead men outside."

Witt Essler rose and dressed. He took his rifle and went out.

In the center of the street stood two horses, shuddering in the cold. Two men sat astride them, straight and still, and despite the cold they did not shiver, and no steaming breath escaped them.

Witt raised his rifle and immediately wondered why he did so, for these men could be a threat to no one.

Whoever had lashed them to the horses had done a good job of it, even bothering to set poles to hold them erect. The right hands of both corpses were tied to their chests, making them appear to be vainly feeling for their own heartbeats. The right thumbs of both men were gone. Cut off just like those of the two Davisons when they were murdered.

Witt turned his face to the sky and shouted as loud as he could.

Chapter 3

Jared stood in the doorway of his smithy and watched the populace of Jerusalem Camp pass on the street. These were people he had known all his life, but they were afraid and their fear made them like strangers.

Two bodies strapped on boards leaned against the wall, awaiting an investigation by Doc Hull. From the expressions on their faces, these men had been very scared when they died. Fear was everywhere Jared looked.

He shivered. The wind stung his face like a slapping hand. The stock of his shotgun was cold and unfamiliar in his grip. He wasn't accustomed to carrying a firearm in town. Being the law in Jerusalem Camp wasn't supposed to have been a serious enterprise—or so the town fathers said when they hired him. That they had named a town marshal at all had been mostly for propriety's sake. A proper town had to have a marshal, they reasoned, even if few people broke the even fewer laws.

"But I don't want to be a town marshal," he had protested when Doc Hull told him of the decision. "I don't know nothing about the law business."

"Nothing to know," Doc had said. "You wear a badge if

you want, and make sure Loren Rupert and his friends don't get too rowdy, and that's about it."

"What if something really bad happens?" Jared had asked.

Doc had laughed. "Nothing really bad ever happens in Jerusalem Camp."

The snow had diminished in the early morning, and now only sparse flakes danced on the brunt of the breeze to settle on the previous accumulation. Jared shifted his chilled frame within his heavy leather coat.

The people watched him subtly as they passed, flashing sidewise glances. Most remained silent. A handful actually approached the door, wanting to gawk at the bodies. Jared shook his head and waved them away.

At last Doc Hull came down the street, slightly bent as usual and puffing white steam through his whiskers. To his displeasure, Jared saw Rupert and Ingersoll approaching behind Doc with a handful of others. Jared scowled. Hang the human race; why do folks treat death like some kind of show?

"Howdy, Doc," Jared said sullenly, eyeing the others. "Come on inside."

Rupert started to walk inside as well. "Hold on," Jared said. "This ain't a circus."

Doc said, "Let them in, Jared. What's the difference?" So Jared shrugged and let them pass.

Doc knelt, winced arthritically, and studied the bodies. He pulled back the shirts and exposed the ugly bullet holes in their pale chests. He touched the stiffened hands and ran his fingers over the half-frozen red places where thumbs had been hacked away.

"Heaven help us," he said lowly.

Rupert grunted disdainfully. "The help we need is a dozen armed men scouring these mountains—or maybe scouring the town would be enough."

Jared turned to him. "What do you mean by that?"

"That maybe we got our killer right here in town. Already caught."

"If you're speaking of Tellico, he was in town when these two were carried in. He couldn't have done it."

"He could have slipped out of town and come back in."

"That's unlikely, as beat-up as he was."

"Were you with him all the time?"

"No."

"Well, then! He could've done it."

Doc interrupted. "Jared, there was a note of some sort?"

Jared nodded. "Pinned to one of the dead men. It was smeared, hard to read." He dug in his pocket and produced a crumpled wad of paper, which he handed to the doctor.

Doc spread it and squinted at the smudged writing on it.

"What's it say?" Rupert asked.

Doc handed the paper back to Jared. "Vengeance," he said.

"Vengeance for what?"

"It doesn't say," Doc responded. He studied the empty spaces where thumbs had been.

No one came to the burial except Isaiah Cable, Jared, Doc, and the stable keeper, Lee Weller. It was interesting, Jared observed, that folks so taken with gawking at the pair when they were laid out in the smithy, now were so indifferent as the snowy earth swallowed the bodies.

Lee was there because it was his job. Along with keeping up the town stable, doing simple carpentry, and cleaning here and there, he customarily dug and filled the graves of Jerusalem Camp. Lee was lanky and longhaired, nearly forty years old, but people still called him boy and always would, for his mental development had stopped in adolescence.

With his father dead now for a decade and his mother likewise gone for seven years, Lee lived under the general care of the town as a whole. He survived satisfactorily, residing in a Spartan but snug room built onto the side of the stable. The townsfolk liked him and kept him busy in small-change tasks, though Rupert and Ingersoll made him the butt of pranks when times got dull.

Today, Lee's usual smile was absent, for he was cold. He shivered in the wind, hugging his shovel as if it could warm him. Digging the two graves had generated a sweat that now felt like ice on his forehead.

"...and receive unto your mercy these two souls, unknown to us but known to you, and this we pray in the name of Jesus Christ, amen."

Jared ran through the prayer rapidly. The snow fell so fast the blanket-wrapped bodies in the holes now wore white shrouds and soon would be hidden altogether if Lee didn't quickly get some dirt on them. Doc muttered an amen and Jared nodded at Lee. The gangly fellow fell to at the dirt pile, his shovel making a steady *chunk-chunk-chunk* as he labored.

Jared scanned the mountains all around them—vast masses of rock and dirt covered with evergreens and smothered in snow. Somewhere out there, he was sure, was the killer of these two men and also of John and Clark Davison. A grim and icy wasteland those mountains were now, not a place one would expect any man to winter. But if he weren't out there, he could only be in the town itself. Jared didn't like to think about that. He thought again of what Rupert had said about Tellico.

Doc pulled his coat more tightly around his thin body. "I'm heading home before this wind does me in. I feel it in every joint."

"I'll be on shortly myself," Jared said. "I got some thinking to do first."

Doc shuffled down the hill, leaving long furrowed tracks

in the snow. Lee, warmed from exertion, was smiling again. He worked with characteristic enthusiasm, moving quickly, eagerly, and with no apparent awareness of the morbidity of his job. His manner reminded Jared of a wiry pup, always eager and cheerfully energetic.

"Never have buried two men at once before, Mr. Jared," Lee said, puffing. "I buried Mizz Jane and her little baby when they died, but I never buried two whole grown-up men at the same time."

"You might be burying more soon," Jared said, mostly to himself. Lee straightened and looked mildly bewildered.

"Is more people going to die, Mr. Jared?"

Jared attempted a reassuring smile. "Maybe not, Lee. Not if I can help it."

"Who killed these men, Mr. Jared?"

Jared shook his head. Then movement at the base of the hill caught his eye. It was Tellico, ascending. The man's lean body moved in an easy flow, only a slight limp giving evidence of his bullet-furrowed leg.

Tellico wore no hat and his hair waved in the cold wind. The steam of his breath immediately scattered into nothingness in the breeze.

"Doc would fuss at you for being out on that leg so quick," Jared said when Tellico reached the graveside.

"I never listen to doctors," Tellico responded, looking at the graves. "Doctor's no good but to put a man in one of these holes while he's still young."

Lee finished his job and grinned heartily at the others, then took his shovel on down the hill.

"Where did you first meet these two, Tellico?" Jared asked.

"In San Francisco. Somehow the story got started that I was carrying money. They followed me for days."

Jared smelled a lie. He faced Tellico more squarely. His eyes flashed like cold glass. "I want to know who you really are, and why you happened to show up in this town just when you did. And why two men who tried to kill you suddenly turn up murdered. Keeping secrets isn't going to help you. It could cause you to end up dead yourself."

"Is that a threat?"

"Of course not. Just a fact. Men like Rupert and Ingersoll aren't as restrained as me. They've got no respect for law, and if they get suspicious enough of you nothing will stop them from doing what they think they have to do."

"In that case, I'll be ready to protect myself," Tellico said.

Then he thrust his hands deep into his coat pockets. He shivered. "I forgot my hat," he said, and strode down the hill toward Jerusalem Camp.

Jared saw him next about one o'clock when he came down from his borrowed shack to Jared's house. Jared watched him through the window as he sat down for his midday meal. Tellico wore his hat now, and his limp was a little more evident. He strode to the door and knocked. Jared rose from the table and answered.

Tellico took off his hat as the door swung open. "Good day, Marshal," he said. "I'd like to talk to you."

Jared waved him in. "Glad to hear it. Come in and share the meal. Bread and soup is all, but it's hot."

"Obliged."

Anna Cable had not met Tellico until now, though she had heard of him from Jared, and knew he was living in the shack up the hill behind them. She wasn't pleased that Jared had invited Tellico to use their old house, and had told him so, for she was frightened like the rest of the townsfolk and distrusted strangers. She couldn't quite understand why Jared had done it—but then, she never had understood Jared and his impulses.

She greeted Tellico politely if coolly, and Jared introduced his son, Michael, to the newcomer. Michael said hello and stared openly at the visitor.

Tellico looked hungry, but waited with politely restrained impatience as Jared muttered a short prayer. Tellico fell to on the bread like a starved man. He slurped the soup with enthusiasm. Jared and Anna exchanged glances, Jared fighting back a little smile. Michael continued his full-bore stare, to which, Jared noted, Tellico seemed oblivious.

When he was sated, Tellico leaned back in his chair. His eyes swept the three faces before him, and suddenly he was embarrassed. He lowered his gaze to his plate.

"Beg your pardon, ma'am," he said. "It's been quite some time since I sat at a real table, and longer than that since I sat at one with victuals made by such a cook as yourself."

"I'm glad you enjoyed the meal, Mr. Tellico," Anna said. "Did you get enough?"

"I'm satisfied, thank you."

"You will have some pie? Cold, I'm afraid, but sweet."

"Dried apple," added Jared.

Tellico smiled again. "I'd be pleased, Mrs. Cable. I'm not a man to turn down dried apple pie in any circumstance less serious than running for my life."

At that Michael piped in. "Have you done that a lot, Mr. Tellico?"

"Beg pardon?"

"Run for your life. Like from the two who were chasing you with guns."

Jared frowned. "Michael..."

"It's all right," Tellico said. "No, Michael. I've not had much experience with that."

"I heard Mr. Rupert knocked you on the head."

"That's enough, Michael," Jared said. "Go eat your pie in the kitchen."

Chagrined, the boy left the room. Jared apologized to Tellico for Michael's inquisitiveness.

"I don't mind it," Tellico said. "Young folk have an advantage over us older ones—no secrets, no deception. Just honest questions and honest statements."

Peculiar talk, coming from a walking secret like yourself, Jared thought. Tellico continued, "I hope you don't mind my coming. I wasn't looking for a meal, but for a job."

Jared frowned. "A job?"

"Yes. I..." Anna came into the room, and he cut off. She put slabs of thick, golden-brown pie before the men, and steaming crockery mugs of coffee. The pie swam in cream.

"You're a fortunate man to have such a cook for your bride, Marshal," Tellico said as Anna reentered the kitchen. He said it in just the right way, Jared noticed, while Anna was departing but still within earshot, where she could absorb the compliment without having to put on a responding mask of humility.

"Thank you," Jared said on her behalf. "You were saying..."

"Yes. I want to talk to you about a job. If I'm to occupy your dwelling yonder, I owe you something in return. I think I can help you."

"Help me do what?"

"Find the killer stalking this town," Tellico said.

Chapter 4

Jared put down his mug of coffee. "Just how do you propose to help me?"

"Well, how do you plan to find the killer? Whatever your plan, I'll help you carry it out."

Jared smiled ironically. "Maybe I was hoping you would have a plan in mind. Because, frankly, I don't."

"Then let's work together and see if we can come up with one."

Jared took a sip of coffee and thought it over. It was a most remarkable request, made by a man who was, if anything, the closest thing Jared had to a suspect. Was this an attempt by Tellico to cover his own tracks? Maybe, but Jared couldn't really believe Tellico was the killer. It would have required superhuman speed for him to slip away from town, find his two pursuers in the mountains at night, kill them, prop their bodies on their horses, then steer the corpse-bearing horses back into town. Besides, Tellico just didn't strike Jared as a murderous type, and Jared's intuitions about people seldom failed him.

Jared balanced his fears, suspicions, and instincts. "Room and board for you in return—is that what you ask?"

"Yes."

Anna always told Jared he was impulsive. Well, he thought, I'll just live up to that. He nodded. "All right. I'm probably a fool, but let's try it.'

Tellico smiled and extended his hand.

Outside, the light grew brighter as the clouds thinned substantially for the first time since the storm had set in. By the time Jared and Tellico had finished their pie and coffee, little strips of blue sky showed through here and there, and the wind diminished.

From the window of the little room where he had sat since early morning, Reverend Isaiah Cable watched the brightening day and gave thanks. His thick, ancient Bible lay across his lap, opened to the Psalms. All morning he had been reading and praying, asking God for a sign of hope, something he could share with the people of his congregation in this time of fear.

"Yea, though I walk through the valley of the shadow," he said to the increasingly blue sky. He smiled, and nodded firmly, shut the Bible, and stood. The old widower still wore the woolen nightshirt he had slept in, and his thin white hair had not been combed all morning. He walked to the mirror and examined his reflection. I'm an old man, he thought. When did I become so old? He looked at himself awhile, then combed back his hair, smoothed his beard, and put on the same dark, heavy woolen clothes he had worn for the past fifteen winters.

Outside, a handful of Jerusalem Camp's men were shoveling pathways through the snow in the street. It was a job they had done for years, and they did it well and quickly, so that when Isaiah was through with his dressing, already a long furrow was cut from his doorway almost to the church.

God bless Witt, he always cleared that way first. It was a kindness that Isaiah always appreciated. Seeing Witt up ahead, now almost to the church door as his shovel sent big bites of snow flying, Isaiah hurried, his coattails dusting the edges of the narrow furrow path on both sides.

"Brother Witt, you never fail to bless your old pastor!"

Witt turned, face ruddy with exertion. "Preacher, you spooked me, coming up behind so unexpected!" He grinned. "Then, it might be that I've been a bit jumpy since Jimmy found the dead men."

The preacher shuddered inwardly, his hard-gained good spirits lessening a bit. "Yes," he said. "A hard thing for the boy, no doubt."

"Harder on us grown-ups, I think," Witt said. "Jimmy doesn't understand much what's happening. He thinks it's all rather exciting, I'm afraid."

"Typical boyish feeling."

Witt became very serious. "Preacher, does Jared have any idea who is doing this, or why?"

"I haven't talked to him. But I believe we will see the moving of an almighty hand soon, Brother Witt. God reveals those who do evil."

Witt said nothing, but it was obvious Isaiah's words had given no reassurance. Seeing that, the preacher felt his own confidence slide away to nothing.

"I believe I can wade the snow the rest of the way," he said. "Thank you, my friend, for clearing my path."

"My pleasure, Preacher. When you come out you'll find it clear up to the door."

Isaiah stepped through the snow up to the church, his black coat flapping down, his thin legs rising and falling, making him resemble a crow wading through a deep puddle.

Lee Weller finished a lunch of cold biscuits with a piece of ham Anna Cable had given him the day before. He wiped crumbs from his mouth onto his sleeve, then went to a wooden box in the corner of his room. Glancing out the window to make sure nobody was looking in, he opened the box and began removing its contents—an old shirt, a torn pair of trousers, pieces of harness, a broken knife—refuse he guarded like treasure.

He lifted out a piece of pine plank that formed a false bottom to the box. From beneath it he pulled a tattered old catalog with pages corn-yellow and brittle. Excitedly he flipped it open, and it fell automatically to the portion he was seeking: several pages of etchings of plump women in various types of underwear. His own secret paper harem.

He sat on his bunk and flipped the pages, back and forth, studying the stiffly posed figures. Then something moved outside his window and he tossed the catalog to the floor, kicked it beneath the bunk, and hid it behind his feet.

Preacher Cable had passed. Walking to the church along the pathway Witt was shoveling. Lee felt a surge of shame; the preacher had not seen what he was doing, but what if he had? Lee had sat through many sermons by Preacher Cable, searing diatribes, eloquent and impassioned condemnations of sin and sinful man that sometimes made Lee wake up in the night feeling hellfire lapping at his feet. If Preacher Cable saw him now, looking lustfully at etchings of women without dresses, it would be almost as bad as if God himself saw him. He wondered if God had eyes like Preacher Cable, the kind that could look warmly at you and make you feel happy and good, or glare at you and open hell beneath your heels.

Lee picked up the catalog, disgusted with himself. I ought to throw it away, he thought, and never think of it again. He balanced the catalog in his hand and options in his mind; then he crept back to his wooden box and sheepishly hid the book away, ashamed he didn't have the moral strength to part with it.

Several minutes later, out in the stable as he cleaned a rear stall, Lee looked up and saw a lone figure at the place where the mountain timber reached the clearing beyond the edge of town. An old man, it appeared, standing so still he might have been carved from wood. He was leaning on a rifle, looking toward the town. Intrigued, the stable keeper watched the figure for a long time, then raised his arm and waved. The old man turned and vanished into the trees.

"So the town was built around the church?" Tellico asked.

"It was," Jared said. "There are four men who are the pillars of Jerusalem Camp, and all of them are churchmen. One is my father, who you'll meet soon—Isaiah Cable, the preacher. Then there's Logan Hull—Doc Hull—one of the church elders. He's the old fellow who examined you. Another is Claude Gregory, another church elder. He ran a dry goods store up until a year ago when he sold it out. He and Matty still live above it. Then there was Jubal Wallen, the last of the four. He's been dead now about a dozen years, and he's buried out behind the church.

"Those four were the founders of this town, and they've kept it going through the years. They put a lot of themselves into it, and when it was first starting they put a lot of their own money in too, until the gold started coming in regularly."

"Your pa must be quite a man," Tellico said.

"He is indeed. I'm mighty fond of him, and proud." Jared paused, thoughtful. "It's hard to see him get old, you know."

"How's he reacting to the murders?"

Jared shook his head. "I haven't talked to him about it.

Maybe I'm worried it's more than he can handle. Pa always takes it on himself to be the comforter during hard times. But how do you give comfort for murder?"

Tellico drew a slim cigar from his pocket, walked to the fire, and lit the tobacco with a flaming stick. "This killer—could we track him?"

"Maybe," Jared said. "It depends on the weather and the snow. And on him killing again, which I hope to God he doesn't."

Tellico said, "I'd like to see him caught."

"This not being your town, what's your interest?" Jared asked.

Tellico shrugged. "I'm here for the winter. Guess that makes this my town for now."

"Reckon so. But there's likely to be trouble for you here."

"Rupert and Ingersoll?"

"Right. They'll be suspicious of you until there's proof you're not the killer yourself. Others, too."

"And what do you think, Marshal? You still suspicious of me?"

"No. I suppose not."

"Obliged you trust me."

"Maybe sometimes I trust too many people too much."

Isaiah leaned on the heavily varnished pulpit and looked across the rows of empty pine benches in the church house. The shutters were closed, so sunlight entered the sanctuary in slanting yellow lines between the panels, revealing floating dust and smoke that leaked from the woodstove in the center of the room. Isaiah had built a small fire in it, not enough to really warm the place, but enough to take the edge off the chill. He never built large fires when he came to practice his sermons, which seemed to generate heat on their own.

The sermon he practiced today would be perhaps the most important one since the time, as a much younger preacher in Indiana, he told his congregation of a vision he had: a town high in the mountains to which men would be drawn. The congregation had listened to him then, and responded. Now it was just as important that they listen to him again, and that he give them something worth listening to.

He stood erect and cast his practiced stare over the benches, mentally painting in the familiar faces that would be there come Sunday, each person in his habitual spot. "My brethren," he intoned, "we are passing through the valley of the shadow of death. It is a dark valley, a grim valley. But one well-trodden by the people of God since Abraham left Ur. In that valley, says the psalmist, I will fear no evil, for thou..."

The door at the back of the church opened and a man stepped in. About the preacher's age, he was heavy-set, wide-jowled, and very pale. This was Claude Gregory, church elder and close friend of the preacher. Yet he looked so changed and so shaken that for a half-moment Isaiah didn't recognize him. The door shut behind Claude, and in the gloom of the shuttered church house the portly man simply stood there.

"What is it, Claude? You look as if—"

"The thumbs, Isaiah. One thumb cut off each one."

"I know about the thumbs, Claude."

"Then do you see what it means? A cut-off thumb..."

Isaiah frowned, thinking, the room silent except for the hissing of the fire. Suddenly he leaned weakly across the pulpit.

"No," he murmured.

"It has to be, Isaiah. What else could it be? Who else?"

"But he's dead. It's impossible."

Claude sat down heavily on one of the pews. It squeaked beneath him.

"You're right. It is impossible. But the thumbs..."

Isaiah spoke with a strained voice. "Let's say nothing of this to anyone."

"Yes. Of course." Claude rose and wearily stepped out the door into the pathway that Witt had shoveled for the preacher.

Chapter 5

Tellico, Jared could tell, was not accustomed to snowshoes. He stomped clumsily along as they traveled the deeply piled hillside toward a little house that stood outside Jerusalem Camp.

"Is this where they died?" Tellico asked as they drew near.

"No. They were hunting out in the mountains. When they didn't come back, Molly—that's John Davison's missus—came into town to get help to find them. Find them they did—a quarter-mile from home, both shot and their thumbs cut off. There was a note with them, but it was wet and the letters had run together so you couldn't read it. Probably said the same thing as the last one."

"So the Davison lady's left alone now."

"Not entirely," Jared said. "She's got one son, Geoffrey, about seven, eight years old. Think what it must be like for him, trying to understand that his pa and his big brother have been slaughtered like pigs."

The house they approached was typical Jerusalem Camp architecture: rectangular, with three windows on the front and one door. Chimneys stood on both ends of the house, marking two fireplaces—one for cooking, one for heating the sleeping quarters on the far end.

They approached the door, Jared deliberately making a lot of noise so their arrival wouldn't surprise the jumpy widow inside. Since the murders, Molly's unmarried brother, Horace Bailer, had been caring for her. But Horace had a fondness for liquor and spent a lot of time hanging around Rupert's. His horse was gone even now, along with the sledge he used for winter travel. Jared figured Horace right about now was leaning over Rupert's woodstove, warming his hands with the fire and his belly with some cheap whiskey.

Jared rapped on the door, identified himself, and asked for entrance. A moment later the latch moved and rattled and the door creaked open. A woman whose face was forty and eyes were ninety wearily beckoned them in. They doffed their snowshoes and entered.

"Good day, Molly. Horace around?"

"He's in town. Took Geoffrey with him. " The woman's voice was a tired slur, devoid of inflection. Jared felt a burst of anger at Horace. He's probably got that boy down there at Rupert's with him while he's getting drunk.

"I'm going to talk to him, tell him you need him here." Jared paused. "Have you heard there were two more killed, same way as John and Clark?"

Horribly, the woman chuckled. "You don't say."

"This time it was two strangers. By the way, Molly, this is Mr. Tellico. He's a new partner of mine, a deputy."

The woman didn't react to the introduction. She plodded to a chair by the window and sat down, resting her elbow on the sill and her chin in her hand, staring out at the snow.

"Molly, we came to check on you and talk to you some about what happened. I know it's not easy, but—"

"I don't care no more. I'll talk if you want."

"Thank you, Molly. Mostly I just want you to think back over the past weeks, even months. Did John ever have trouble with anybody, make any enemies? Anybody ever threaten him?"

Molly, still staring out the window, shook her head.

"Did he seem nervous or scared any time before he was killed?"

Same reaction.

"Did he have any hint at all that something was going to happen?"

She suddenly sat straighter, lowered her hand, and looked at Jared. "John didn't have no hint, and neither did Clark. But Geoffrey did."

"Geoffrey?"

"Yes. I only just now remembered it: He knew something was about to happen. For a month he was upset, hardly sleeping, and when he did he had dreams. Bad ones, and they always involved his father."

"Dreams." Jared had hoped for something more substantial to work with than a child's nightmares.

"Yes. His father falling off a cliff—that was one— and his father being mauled by a bear. And other things that weren't so specific, just frightening to a boy. Moving shadows, a face at his window at night, that kind of thing." She mused for a moment. "Funny I should think of it only now. Geoffrey knew. You ever heard of folks just knowing when something's about to happen?"

"I have indeed," Tellico said thoughtfully.

Jared said, "Thank you, Molly. If you think of anything else, let me know. Send Horace down after me."

The woman, momentarily re-spirited while speaking, now grew old and tired once more. She collapsed into her chair, resuming the same pose as before, watching the winter landscape beyond the window.

When they were going, Tellico paused at the door.

"Mrs. Davison, the face that Geoffrey saw at the window in his dreams... what kind of face was it?"

"Didn't say."

They started back over the hill toward town. "Why did you ask that?" Jared said.

"No reason. Just crossed my mind."

Jared said, "Let's knock on some doors. I think it's time for a meeting of the people."

Silent, hidden among the rocks and shadows, the Gray Man watched the town. Watched its rising smoke, the movements of its people, its huddled livestock feeding in pens. He watched boys gathering fuel from woodpiles—working in groups of two or three, rather than singly as before—dogs scampering at their feet. He also saw two men moving from door to door, knocking and speaking briefly to those who answered. They were barely visible in the distance, often hidden altogether. He did not know them or what they were doing, but he guessed it had to do with him and hated them as he hated the entire town.

Heavily dressed in furs, wearing a thick capote over his body and a Balmoral bonnet on his long-unshorn head, he did not feel the cold. His big, oiled boots kept the chill from his feet. He knew mountain life well; survival was no problem. He could move as silently as a cougar and vanish like a ghost.

Through an alleyway between two buildings the Gray Man saw the pair go to another door, knock, and talk to the person who answered. He squinted. This was the same pair, he believed, whom he earlier had watched visiting the house of the first ones he had killed. That house... still someone living there.

So far he had taken only four victims; it was time for

another. It really didn't matter who—and that house might provide the best opportunity, for it was relatively remote and hidden from the view of most of the town. Yes. The house would yield him yet another victim. The Gray Man slipped back into the forest.

Ingersoll pushed open Rupert's sticking door, making it pop and shudder on its hinges. Rupert stood inside, gently rubbing the jaw that Tellico's elbow had pounded earlier; it had been visibly bruised and only now was beginning to look better.

"Loren, you going?" Ingersoll asked.

"Yeah. Yeah, I'm going," Rupert responded. "If the good saints don't mind me dirtying their meetinghouse, that is."

"C'mon, then."

Together the men walked down one of the shoveled-out pathways toward the church down the street. Subsequent snows had partially filled the walkways; keeping them clear would require repeated shoveling until spring. And if the winter brought snows up to thirteen or fourteen feet, as it often did, no amount of shoveling would suffice. Winters like that kept people locked in their homes, free to move about outside only on webbed snowshoes or homemade skis, which the old-timers also called snowshoes.

The street was relatively crowded with people moving single file through the walkways toward the church. Somebody pulled the bell rope, sending rich, purple tones reverberating against the mountains. The lines of people converged at the church door and entered with the solemnity of mourners gathering for a funeral.

Rupert and Ingersoll were among the last in, and finding no seats, leaned against the back wall with a score of others. They looked across the rows of people to Jared, who sat in a chair beside the pulpit, Tellico off in a corner behind him. Tellico looked vaguely nervous and out of place, obviously conscious that he was being scrutinized by the people. Near him was Isaiah Cable, noticeably pale and looking old. Rupert had not seen his old sparring partner for more than a week, and Isaiah's wan, unhealthy countenance was very noticeable to him.

Ingersoll nudged Rupert and subtly pointed at Tellico. "There he is, Loren. Old thumb-chopper himself."

"Yeah. And have you heard—our good marshal's hired him for deputy, to help him solve the killings!"

Ingersoll hadn't heard, but before he could express his surprise Jared stood and walked to the pulpit. He put his hands flat on its sloping top and leaned against it in the universal pose of the uncomfortable public speaker.

"Neighbors, I thank you for coming here," he said. "I'm sorry to put this disturbance in your day, but you know what we're here to talk about."

"When you going to catch him, Jared?" somebody at the front demanded. "There's never been a murder in this town before, and now we've got four of em!"

"Well, Claymore, I know that. We all know that. What we don't know is who it is or why he's doing it. It's my opinion that it's somebody outside the town. That's the only way the last two could have been killed. They had never been in town at all."

"Why were they chasing your deputy, Jared?" Claymore Smith asked. "And who is he?"

Every eye turned to Tellico, who looked back across the crowd, unflinching but reading hostility and fear in almost every face.

"This is Mr. Tellico," Jared answered. "He's a man I trust. The two who chased him were apparently thinking to rob him. It's my opinion they had the bad luck to run across the killer in the mountains right after that."

Rupert crossed his arms and cocked his left foot across his right, resting it on its boot toe. "Did you call us here to tell us your opinions, Marshal, or do you have some facts for this town?" he said. Then he smiled, enjoying Jared's obvious discomfiture, making Jared hate him for it.

"If you mean do I have the answers, then no, I don't," Jared said. "But I do have something to say: We've got to assume the killings will continue. So anybody—everybody—is in danger. And our lives are going to change from now until this is resolved."

"Meaning what?"

"Meaning we're going to start guarding this town just as carefully as our forefathers guarded their stockades a century ago," Jared said. "Especially at night. We're going to organize us a guard militia—not a fool vigilante gang like you had, Loren—but a group of guards who'll watch the town in pairs through the night. I want mounted guards beating a path all the way around town all night. That's the first thing.

"Second, we're all going to start keeping our eyes open. Looking out for our neighbors. Checking on the folks next door. Keeping the women and children in the company of at least one man all the time. Keeping ourselves sober and our guns loaded. Keeping guns by our beds. Using our common sense.

"There's a killer loose. We don't know who he is, where he is, or when he will kill again. It's my fortune, like it or not, to be the one chosen to provide whatever protection I can. But I can't do it without the help of everybody. Can I count on you? Will you work with me to protect this town?"

Boots scuffed against the plank floor in accompaniment to a murmur of whispers. A woman with a quaking voice said, "Are you saying my children are in danger?"

"Yes, Cora. Yours, mine, everybody's. And you, too."

The woman began to cry; beside her, her young daughter

looked up at her. The child's lip began to quiver and then she too was in tears.

"You're upsetting the women and the young'uns, Jared!" a man said. "Shouldn't this have been talked out in private among the men?"

"The women and children have got to be just as aware of this as the men. And to tell you the truth, I didn't want to leave the women unguarded while we jawed it over."

The crowd thought about that. "You really do believe we're in danger?" the man asked.

"Don't you?" Jared responded.

The man paused, then nodded.

"Thank you. Now what about the rest of you?" Jared raised his right hand and held it high.

All about the room hands rose, until at last even Rupert and Ingersoll joined in.

Suddenly the church doors burst open. The people turned; Horace Bailer stood in the middle of the double doorway. Geoffrey Davison clung to Horace's leg, trembling and crying.

In Horace's arms was Molly Davison. She was bloodied and dead, and her right thumb was missing. Men shouted, women and children screamed, and then the church broke into pandemonium.

Jared closed his eyes and lowered his head for a moment. Then he turned to Tellico and said, "Well, Tellico. It appears you have been exonerated."

Chapter 6

Coal-oil torches flared in the wind but made little impact on the snow-driven darkness. The band of armed men led by Jared winced against the hard flakes that battered their faces and made them numb. Tellico came to Jared and shouted through the blizzard, "It's no use. We lost the tracks. Got to get back."

Jared gave one desperate look around, fought back the frustration that gnarled his stomach, then reluctantly nodded. He turned to the others, who looked like dark ghosts through the bullet-fast snowfall. "Head back!" he shouted, half his volume lost to the wind.

No one argued. The men turned and trudged back toward the town, walking slightly bowlegged in their snowshoes, as if straddling a crack in the ground. Far below, flickering pinpoints of light marked the town. The thought of warmth and firelight drove them on.

Jared mentally cursed the blizzard, which had blasted through only moments after Horace Bailer had appeared with the corpse of Molly Davison. Despite the snow Jared and his quickly formed posse had hurried to Molly's cabin and followed what tracks they could find until the blizzard at last obliterated them.

The returning group entered the west end of the town, stepping over drifts, walking in the rapidly filling remnants of the shoveled pathways. Jared went to his smithy, and several of the others followed.

Inside he built a fire in the forge and blew it hot with the bellows. The men gathered around, extending hands to the blaze, letting heat and orange light play across their frosty faces. They had the look of soldiers the night before battle, or sailors who have seen signs of a hurricane in the eastern sky. There were none who doubted the danger anymore.

"I want to get to my family," Witt Essler said, breaking the silence. "Come get your folks when you're ready, Jared."

Jared, who had left his wife and son with Deb and Jimmy Essler at the Essler house, said, "I'll be on in a few minutes, Witt. Thanks for your help out there."

Others departed too, heading for homes and families, facing a night of lying awake listening for noises in the dark.

At last only Jared and Tellico remained. Despite the roaring fire, Jared was still shivering. Eventually he walked to the window and threw back a sackcloth curtain that once was nearly white but now was charcoal gray with the residue of a thousand smoky fires. He looked at the dark street beyond through the well-frosted windowpane.

"I'm going to get my family and head home," Jared said. "Come stay in our house tonight if you'd feel safer."

"Thank you, but I'll be outside tonight."

Jared realized what, in the excitement of the search, all but Tellico had forgotten. "You're going to guard the town?" Jared asked. Tellico nodded.

"You can't do it alone."

"Sean McFee said he would help me."

"I appreciate you both, then," Jared said. "Most of the

men tonight have enough to think about just watching their own families. Tomorrow night we'll set up guard shifts."

"Glad I can help," Tellico said, and Jared could tell he meant it.

Jared left Tellico at the forge and walked through the darkness toward Witt's house.

Doc Hull heard Jared pass his combined medical office and undertaking parlor. But he kept his attention on the remains of Molly Davison stretched before him on the stained cadaver table. A blanket covered her torso, hiding ugly knife slashes and stab wounds. Doc had examined the corpse carefully; Molly had died a brutal death, killed by someone with powerful arms and a large, very sharp blade. In his time Doc had seen too many corpses to easily become squeamish, but this one bothered him—not because of its gore, but because of who it was and the atrociousness of her murder.

He lifted the blanket and looked again at the wounds. Why? And who? Was the motive somehow related to the Davison family, which now had lost three members to the same killer? But if so, why had the two strangers also been killed? They had nothing to do with the Davisons.

Doc let the blanket fall as he turned away. The right hand of the body flopped out from beneath it and dangled. The place where the thumb had been was raw and red and ugly. Doc reached down and lifted the arm to tuck it beneath the blanket again, but suddenly he stopped.

He stood frozen in place, holding the stiffened wrist while staring at the empty thumb socket. He pushed the hand beneath the blanket, walked away to a corner chair, and sank into it, breathing rapidly, mulling a suspicion too terrible to consider.

Michael and Anna Cable smiled at Jared when he entered the Essler house. Anna appeared close to tears. Michael ran to his father and Jared slipped a burly arm around the boy's shoulders. "Son," he said, "let's go home."

Witt was sipping a cup of coffee. He raised it and said, "Fresh. Want some before you go?"

"I thank you," Jared said. "I am a mite chilled."

Witt disappeared into the kitchen and returned with a mug of coffee that he handed to Jared. At Witt's heel was Jimmy, beaming his gappy grin as if oblivious to the tense adults around him. Deb Essler followed her son, her face like that of a bereaved woman.

Anna smiled tensely at her hostess. "Deb, thank you for your hospitality. I've felt much safer with Michael and me being here with you."

Jared and Witt stood sipping and talking quietly for a few minutes. Finally Jared drained off the last half of his coffee at one swallow. "Thank you, Witt. Deb, you make a good cup. We'll go on now."

Deb took Jared's empty cup, but dropped it. "Damn!" she exclaimed.

Witt, never before having heard his wife curse, gaped at her in amazement. "Deb!"

Her chin quivered, then tears came. She turned on Witt like a lioness.

"What? You never heard your wife talk like that before? Well, listen again: Damn! Damn it all! There! I've said it and it feels good. I'm sick of living with this tension and not letting it out! Damn!"

Jimmy's eyes were big in his face like twin full moons. He grinned. "Thay it again, Ma!" he urged. "Thay the bad word!"

Witt grew angry. "Deb, you're not fit to be in the presence of decent company. What's gotten into you?"

"Let's go," Jared uncomfortably mumbled to his family.

Then to Witt, "It's a tense time for everybody. We take no offense that—"

"Oh, you take no offense?" Deb said mockingly. "Your preacher's-son ears don't take offense to a fool woman's babbling? Then hear some more from her: When are you going to do something about these killings, Marshal?" The last word dripped sarcasm. "Who's next to die? Me? My son? My husband? What are you going to do?"

Jared's face went red. "I'm doing what I can, Deb."

"And a lot of good it did Molly! You left her alone in that cabin to be slaughtered like a cow! Who's next?"

Jared swallowed, with much effort holding in a sudden surge of anger. Witt stepped between Deb and Jared.

"Get to the bedroom, Deb. Now!"

Crying, she turned and stalked back through the house. A door slammed, and the sound of muffled sobs followed.

"I'm sorry, Jared," Witt said.

"It's all right, Witt." He swallowed. "Maybe she's right. I didn't do Molly any good. I did leave her alone."

Witt shook his head. "You left her alone, Tellico left her alone, her brother left her alone, she left herself alone. Nobody—you, me, her family—protected her. If you want to toss out blame, then toss it out to everyone. Just don't take it all yourself."

"Thanks, Witt. I wish that made me feel better."

"None of us is going to feel better until this killer is caught, Jared."

"Yeah. Good night, Witt."

The open door cast a beacon of yellow across the snow. The storm had diminished to flurries. The Cables stepped into it and the door closed behind them, cutting off both the light and what Jimmy was saying to his father: "Ma thaid the D word, Pa. Just like Mither Rupert. . ."

Any other time Jared would have laughed. Not tonight.

In silence the family returned to their house. Jared built

up the fire, put Michael to bed, and checked the bars on the doors and shutters. He brewed coffee in the pot that hung on a hinged arm in the fireplace. Anna went into their room and came out in the blue calico gown Jared had given her for Christmas a year before. She had a heavy shawl over her shoulders, and Jared could see she had been crying in secret.

Jared swallowed some of the coffee, swirled the remainder in the bottom of his cup, then suddenly tossed it into the fire. The hiss made Anna jump.

"Why, Anna? Why am I the one everybody expects to catch this—this whoever-he-is, wherever-he-is killer? I'm a blacksmith, blast it! I'll not take the blame for not being a proper marshal when I never asked for the lousy job in the first place! Pretty soon everybody in town will be blaming me, just like Deb did."

He waited for Anna to speak, but she didn't. Her silence was grim. He wheeled toward her.

"You blame me too?"

She looked surprised and hurt. "Of course not! I just don't know what you want me to tell you."

Jared leaned against the mantelpiece, forcing himself to calm down. "I want you to tell me that if I go to bed and sleep long enough, it all will go away and everything will be all right again."

"Maybe it will."

Jared shook his head. "No. I wish it would. But it won't."

He paced about the room. Anna returned to the bedroom. A few minutes later Jared lifted his head with a start. "Pa!" he said. "I got to see to Pa!"

He couldn't believe he hadn't thought of it before. Isaiah, down there alone, and him up here feeling sorry for himself. Not only a poor marshal, but an even worse son.

He had just started back to get Anna and Michael when a knock on the front door startled him. He went to the fireplace, slid his shotgun off the mantel hooks, then carefully opened the door.

It was Tellico. Dusted with snow, he carried the rifle Jared had loaned him. Beside him stood Isaiah, huddled in his coat, two blankets and a bag in his arms.

Tellico said, "I thought you'd want him with you tonight. You'd have thought of it yourself if you didn't have so much on your shoulders." He touched his hat. "I'll see you in the morning."

He trudged off, his snowshoes shuffling as he vanished in the night. He didn't seem so clumsy on them now.

Jared and his father talked for a time, but Isaiah seemed reluctant to say much, and soon went to bed in the spare room. Jared went to the window and opened the shutter. He sought Tellico's form there in the darkness, and finally made it out. Tellico stood on a rise a hundred yards away, where he had a good view of the town. A sudden break in the attenuated clouds let moonlight stream through. Tellico, with his rifle cradled in the crook of his arm, suddenly seemed otherworldly and magnificent as he watched over the cluster of snowy rooftops and smoking chimneys below.

Jared was very tired. He closed the shutters and went to bed. He curled up close to Anna and listened to the snores of his father in the next room. He closed his eyes.

He didn't feel as edgy as before.

Tellico was out there. Tonight, at least, the town would be safe.

CHAPTER 7

The morning broke clear and pure. Jared, up early, watched the eastern sky grow pale and luminescent until suddenly the sun burst over the rocky summits and poured light into the enclosed valley of Jerusalem Camp. The morning lessened the hopelessness of the night before. Jared dressed, pulled on his boots, and ate a good breakfast, ready to begin the day.

He trudged up the hill on his snowshoes toward Tellico's shack. The sight of Tellico on the knoll during the night, rifle on his arm, had removed any remaining doubts about Tellico's character. Jared congratulated himself on his good instincts. He had sensed almost from the beginning that Tellico was a man he could trust, despite his aggravating secrecy about himself.

He reached Tellico's door and lifted his fist to knock. He noticed, though, that the door was not fully shut. He grew cautious. Quietly he pushed open the door.

"Tellico?" he said softly.

He heard soft snores from the bedroom and approached. It was Tellico, sleeping soundly. He apparently had merely failed to shut the door completely when he came in. Probably he had been exhausted from his sentry duty.

Jared turned to leave, not wanting to disturb a man who had so earned a good rest. But he noticed again the medallion that hung around Tellico's neck. He wondered why Tellico wore such an unusual ornament, and what it meant.

As Jared went back down the hill, he saw his father ahead of him, walking toward the church. Jared hurried, and by the time Isaiah was struggling to open the door against snow drifted upon it, Jared had caught up with him.

"Let me get that, Pa," he said, pulling open the door. "Dadgum snow can be heavy. You ought to be careful to—" He looked at his father's face and stopped, stunned. "Pa, are you all right?"

Isaiah looked at his son with an expression so grim and hopeless that it belied his words: "I'm fine. I've just got a sermon to prepare."

He entered and closed the door. Jared stood overwhelmed by the thought Isaiah's changed face had roused: My father is dying.

Jared saw Rupert on the porch of his store. Rupert waved him over. Bracing for the worst as he always did when dealing with Rupert, Jared trudged over.

"Come inside, Jared. It's plenty warm in here." Jared was surprised by the unusual friendliness of Rupert's tone, and that he had called him by name rather than his usual sarcastic "marshal" or "blacksmith."

Rupert gave Jared a chair by the stove and a cup of coffee. Then Rupert sat down across from him, leaned forward in his chair, and began talking intently, almost whispering.

"Jared, you and me and your pa have had our differences.

I'll never be a psalm-singer, and your pa won't ever warm to an old sin-seller like me. You neither, I'd guess. But the fact is, Jared, I've always liked you. No, don't give me that look—it's true. I've just always been expected by folks to fuss at you and your pa, and so I have.

"But now I want to help you. When I saw Horace at that church door with Molly in his arms it made me see what this town is up against. All of us. I want to bury the hatchet with you and help you find whoever is doing this."

Jared, amazed at what he was hearing, nodded. "Thank you, Loren. I need your help. I need every available man to take a shift at guard duty at night."

Rupert shook his head. "That's not what I mean. I want to go for help. Get the law, the real law. Don't take offense at that, but you know what I mean."

Jared nodded. "Yes, I do. But how can you get through the pass? You'll just get buried under an avalanche."

Rupert licked his lips. He drifted back in memory. "When I was a younger man I was mighty good on snowshoes. I won my share of races, you know."

Skis—or snowshoes, as some still called them—had opened the High Sierras to settlement. In the first days of the mountain towns, winter snowfall had driven the miners back down to the foothills to wait out the snow, but Scandinavians soon taught them the art of skiing. From then on the mountains remained populated even through the worst winters, when snow would pile to the rooftops and drifts would reach thirty or more feet.

Jared had heard that Rupert, in younger days, had been an excellent skier. But that was thirty years ago. What Rupert obviously was offering was infeasible at best, crazy at worst. But Jared was touched by Rupert's desire to help.

"Loren, I appreciate that offer more than you can know. But I can't accept it. Too dangerous. Besides, what can anybody from the outside do that we can't? We can search the valley better than anybody, and guard ourselves better than outside law."

Jared said it as diplomatically as he could, but Rupert was offended. He seemed to withdraw into himself.

"Maybe you're right," he said. "Just a fool idea from an old man."

"Don't put words in my mouth, Loren. I really do appreciate your offer."

After Jared left, Rupert sat by his stove, lost in thought. Finally he got up and went to a rear storage room and found two long, homemade skis and a thick wooden balance pole. He ran his hands over the smooth wood, then nodded resolutely.

"Got some preparing to do," he said aloud.

For the rest of the day he was busy, and when the next morning came, he was gone.

As Jerusalem Camp slept that night, two guards circled the town in opposite directions as Tellico rode the maze of snow-and-mud gulleys that comprised the streets. He was under no duty to ride guard tonight, but he had nothing better to do, and he couldn't sleep.

Typical of mountain mining communities, Jerusalem Camp had been built with no apparent design, so that what at one place looked like a good-running street would suddenly be blocked off by a building and the street would veer like a stream around a boulder. The main street was the only straight one in town, and the only reason for that was Isaiah's insistence. "It isn't fitting for the house of God to stand on a crooked way," he had said. "He makes the crooked ways straight, and this one shall be."

Tellico was pleased with the horse and rifle Jared had loaned him. Tellico had a good feeling about Jared. He was solid, unassuming, levelheaded. The kind of man who could weather a tough crisis despite his own feeling that he couldn't. That was part of his very strength. Tellico had known many men over the years who thought themselves weak when in fact they were strong, and others who thought themselves strong when really they were weak.

He had known both types in life and in death. Through his mind flashed memories he despised: bloody, mangled soldiers in tattered blue uniforms, crying in pain, not wanting to live but afraid to die. He remembered holding the clammy hands of such men, saying words into their faces that they didn't hear. He recalled the frustration that had brought, and what frustration had finally led him to do.

He halted his mount and looked around the town. "Jerusalem Camp, what am I doing here?" he asked aloud. Well, why not here? If not here, then somewhere else just as meaningless.

But maybe not. Nothing happens without design, he once had believed, maybe still did. If so, he wondered what design it was that had brought him to Jerusalem Camp, and what its result would be.

He spurred his mount and began slowly winding through the snowy streets again.

Chapter 8

Sunday morning, and Jared stood outside the church, dreading to enter. The body of Molly Davison lay inside in an open pine box, her pale hands carefully placed to cover the missing thumb. There would be no traditional Sunday morning sermon today; this would be a funeral service.

Jared looked up on the hillside; Lee Weller labored there, just now finishing his grave-digging. Unusual thing, for Lee seldom fell behind in his work. But even the simple-minded Lee had been sad and preoccupied since Molly's murder.

Anna came to the door. "It's about to start, Jared."

"All right."

Jared found a seat in the back. Though the church was filled with its usual attendants, there was no feeling of communion here tonight. The very air was oppressive. It was more like a gathering of prisoners than anything else.

He saw his father's face, and his heart dropped to the pit of his stomach. The aging preacher seemed a caricature, or an animated wax figure.

Isaiah stood behind the pulpit and looked over his

congregation. He spoke in a voice lacking its normal booming, sonorous timbre.

"Beloved people," he said. "We come to lay to rest the body of one we have loved. And to ask a question with no answer: Why?"

Jared heard a sniffle, then a muffled sob. It's starting already, he thought. I don't think I can stand a lot of crying and nose-blowing—especially with Pa looking half-dead like that.

". . . Evil has come upon us, unexplained, and taken the life of an innocent lady. Who can understand the strength of evil? Who can know either the ways of God or the ways of the wicked one? Who can..."

Jared rose and slipped out the door. Let the funeral go on without him. He had enough to put up with. Once outside, he breathed deeply and enjoyed the cold air against his face. Inside the church the stove belched near-hellish heat, the kind to dry a man's throat and turn his eyes to sand. The cold felt better.

Jared smelled tobacco smoke and heard a cough. In the alley between the church and the Smith & Wilson leather goods store stood Lee, puffing a big cigar, hacking and coughing.

"I didn't know you smoked, Lee."

"I don't. Not most the time. But they say it makes you feel better."

"If you're used to it. If you're not you just get sick."

"I want to feel better. I'm scared."

"Everybody's scared, Lee."

"The man's going to come kill me. I know he is." Lee seemed on the brink of tears.

"You don't know that."

"I do too know it. I'm bad and he's going to kill me."

Jared asked, "What do you mean, bad? You're a good man."

"But..." Lee looked down. The cigar trembled in his fingers. "I got bad pictures I look at sometimes."

Jared had to think that over to make sense of it. He smiled. "Lee, God bless your heart, you're probably the most guiltless man in Jerusalem Camp."

The words went right past the simpleminded man, who now leaned against the side of the church as the tobacco got to him. "But I'm bad, and he's going to kill me."

Suddenly the church door flew open; Witt thrust out his head.

"Jared, your father's collapsed."

Jared rushed inside. In the alley, Lee lost his fight with the cigar and emptied his stomach with great cramping heaves.

Doc Hull put his arm on Jared's shoulder.

"He's alive, but it's affected him. You'll see he won't talk as plainly, and that his right side is a little paralyzed. You'll notice it most in how his mouth droops. But there's no reason I can see he shouldn't recover quickly."

"What caused it, Doc?"

"Who can say? Age, health, anxiety. Just be grateful he's alive. It could have killed him."

On the bed Isaiah looked even more corpselike than before. His white hair bushed out from the back of his head around his ears. The right side of his mouth drooped.

"Pa, it's Jared."

The old man's heavy-lidded eyes shifted sideways. He looked at his son with a strange and wild glare.

"You're going to be all right. You're in my house, and we're going to take care of you."

The preacher did not try to talk. Jared reached across and patted his hand, but Isaiah didn't seem to notice.

After a few minutes he was asleep. Jared slipped out of the room. Anna waited in the kitchen.

"You need to resign as marshal," she said. "You can't deal

with protecting this town and with taking care of your father, too."

"I can't resign, Anna. Not now."

"It never should have been your problem to begin with. You only took the job because they asked you!"

"But that's the point. I took it."

Surprisingly to Jared, Anna grew angry. She spun on her heel and went back to their bedroom. The door slammed.

Jared shook his head and lifted his eyes. "Oh, God, help me now," he said. "If ever I needed it, it's now."

A few minutes later, Tellico appeared at his door. "Can you talk for a minute?"

Jared nodded and left the house. He and Tellico walked through the snow together. Tellico expressed his regrets about Isaiah, then dropped news that hit Jared like a boulder.

"Loren Rupert's gone," he said.

"What?"

"Gone. Not a trace of him. His store's locked, everything in its place. But he's gone."

Jared felt a surge of dread. "Another victim."

"I don't think so. Ingersoll said Rupert had been talking about trying to ski out for help."

"That's right...he said the same to me, in fact. But I never thought he'd really do it."

"He seems the kind to do what he wants," Tellico said.

"He does, at that. The old fool! He'll get himself killed."

"How can he get out? I thought the pass was impossible to get through."

"It is, without a whole heap of luck," Jared said.

Across the snowbound town, plumes of gray smoke rose from chimneys and wafted into the clouds. The two men watched.

Tellico seemed to be thinking. At last he said, "Do you

believe in fate, Marshal? Or providence or destiny or whatever you want to call it?"

"I suppose I do. Why do you ask?"

Tellico smiled and shrugged. "I don't know. Just thinking out loud."

Rupert wasn't sure, but he thought he had cracked a rib. It sure as the devil felt like it. He had rolled a long way over a drop he hadn't even noticed until it was too late to stop.

He gripped his side and grimaced in pain, struggling to breathe. Jared had been right; he was too old to have tried this. Too late now. He was at least three miles from Jerusalem Camp, one of his skis was gone, and he was hurting so badly he doubted he could make it on foot back to the town. He had his web snowshoes strapped to his back, but they would do him no good if he couldn't bear to stand.

But he couldn't lie here, either, and freeze to death in the snow. It wouldn't be long until dark and he had been here for an hour. He had to find shelter.

Straining, he reached around and pulled his pack from beneath him. He tugged it open and removed a spare shirt. He pushed upward, unsuccessfully tried to squelch a yell of pain, then sat panting, hurting with every heave of his lungs.

Got to go on. Can't stop.

With herculean effort, Rupert slid off his heavy coat. He wrapped the extra shirt around his middle and pulled it tight, binding up his damaged rib cage. Then, with great discomfort, he put on the coat again and donned the snowshoes.

He still had his balance pole, thank God. Dreading what faced him, he closed his eyes and tried to will away as much pain as possible. Finally, with teeth gritted, he began pulling himself to his feet, using the balance pole as a crutch.

At last he was firmly planted upright. His right knee throbbed with pain, and his ribs ached. Wincing, he began walking.

He looked about for any kind of shelter—a cave, a closely

bunched stand of pine, an overhanging outcrop. But he found nothing.

It was becoming colder. His ribs and knee hurt worse than before.

I'm still alive, he reminded himself. Got to hang on. Keep moving.

Time dwindled away. His mind drifted into limbo, and his feet moved along as if of their own accord. He lost all concept of distance.

Thus he had no idea how far or long he had traveled when he saw the cabin. He topped a modest slope, and there it sat below him, nestled by a little stream, belching smoke from its stick chimney.

Rupert was so grateful he cried.

He moved on down the slope. He made it to the door and everything began to grow unreal. His pain suddenly vanished; he became warm, content....

When he awoke, a face looked back at him. A man about thirty-five, with hard eyes and bright red hair that hung to his shoulders. Rupert was in a stupor. The thought crossed his mind that he might be dead, and this might be his personal angel. Or devil.

"Hello," he said, scratchy voiced. "My name's Rupert."

The red-haired man leaned close. "Ye got any money, old man?"

Chapter 9

Doc Hull slowly climbed the stairs to Claude and Matty Gregory's apartment above the dry goods store. At the top he paused for a minute to pant, and ponder the cruel things age does to a man. Then he knocked.

Matty answered. Usually jovial, today she was somber. The meager smile that did flit across her lips was pure formality and it showed. But she stood back and invited Doc inside politely enough.

The interior of the apartment smelled mustily of baked bread, closed windows, and moisture. A drab, sun-faded elegance permeated the place, perpetuated by Matty's constant dusting and sweeping. Neat but aging cloths circled with decorative hanging knots covered every table and stand, and pictures were everywhere: Jesus feeding the multitudes, Washington at Valley Forge, plump women in translucent clothing doing a pagan dance around a pole while mythological gods looked down from the clouds.

"Where's Claude?" Doc asked.

"Lying down." Matty's voice was weaker than usual. "He's done poorly these past days."

"I'll take a look at him."

"Well, Doc, to tell you the truth, Claude really doesn't want to see anybody."

"I think I know why. I've got to see him, Matty. There's no choice."

Claude didn't really seem ill, just depressed. He turned his face away from Doc and toward the papered wall. Doc stood beside Claude's bed until finally Claude had to look at him.

"I'd like to talk to him in private, Matty," Doc said.

"Well..."

"It's all right," Claude muttered. "Go on."

Matty reluctantly left the room. The door clicked behind her.

Doc smiled sadly at Claude. "Claude, we've got a problem."

"I don't know what you're talking about."

"I think you do. The chopped thumbs, Claude. What do they remind you of?"

Claude twisted his lip downward in a bitter scowl. He aimed it at Doc in silence.

"Isaiah collapsed, you know," Doc said. "I think he had figured it out too."

Claude said nothing of his encounter with Isaiah in the church.

"We can't pretend this is going to go away by itself, Claude."

Claude said, "If you're saying what I think you are, you're insane. That whole sorry event is thirty-five years dead and buried."

"Then why are you hiding away up here in your bedroom?"

Claude glared at Doc. "I'm feeling poorly. I'm an old man."

"We're all getting old, Claude."

Claude asked his next question hesitantly. "Are you going to say something about this to anyone?"

Doc thought it over. "It would be the honorable thing to do. If these deaths are even indirectly our fault..." He stopped for a moment. "But no. Not yet. Not until I'm sure."

"It can't be him, Doc. We saw him dead."

"We saw him shot and buried. Maybe not dead." Claude rolled over to face the wall again. Doc went out and spoke his good-bye to Matty.

"Don't come around upsetting him anymore," Matty said. "I don't like it."

"Neither do I," Doc replied. He left the apartment and walked stiffly down the stairs to the alley.

The face of the man with the red hair was masked in anger. Rupert's ears rang from the repeated backhand blows the man had laid on his jaws.

"Where did ye see Tellico?" the man demanded again.

Rupert had let the information slip bit by bit, against his own will through the persuasion of torture. Rupert had no devotion to Tellico and did not consider it his duty to protect him from this man who obviously wanted him so badly—but Rupert despised the notion of being forced to do anything.

"Go to the devil," Rupert muttered.

The red-haired man snarled; his brawny hand went up and down again, and Rupert had to struggle to retain consciousness.

Then the man stopped. He scrutinized his prisoner.

"All right, then," he said. "Old Frank Coop's a gentle man by nature, but ye ain't cooperating."

He pressed on Rupert's broken ribs. Rupert screamed and passed out.

When he struggled back to awareness, Coop's face was mere inches above his. "Where did ye see Tellico?" he asked once more.

Rupert could hold out no longer.

"In Jerusalem Camp. Jerusalem Camp."

The brows lowered. "Where's that?"

"Yonder way... three, four miles northwest." Rupert's voice was strained. He hurt so badly that the thought of being killed wasn't nearly as troubling as before.

"Four miles northwest," the man repeated. He stood straight and grinned.

"Help me," Rupert whispered.

But the man did not notice him. He began gathering supplies. When he was through, he put on his hat, extinguished the fire, and went to the door. He put on Rupert's webbed snowshoes.

He opened the door, turned, and drew his pistol. He aimed it at Rupert's head, squinting one eye. Then he lowered the weapon.

"No point in wasting a bullet when the cold will do the job just as good."

He thumbed down the hammer, holstered the rusty weapon, and walked out, leaving open the door. Through it blew cold air that stirred the ashes in the fireplace into a cloud of gray dust.

Tellico scanned the mountains as he walked up the slope toward the vacant cabin of Molly Davison. Horace Bailer had moved out after his sister's murder, turned the care of little Geoffrey over to another family, and taken refuge in liquor. He hardly showed himself about town, hiding away instead in a little rented room for which everyone knew he could not and would not pay. There Horace drank, starting early and ending late.

Tellico shifted his rifle and concentrated on his walking. If his time in Jerusalem Camp had taught him anything so far, it was that life in snowy mountains took a lot of endurance. A few strides in the snow and a man was nearly winded. That thought brought another: What kind of man must the killer be, living out in those wild mountains as he was? He must have had years of experience in the wilderness.

Tellico reached the Davison cabin and stopped to get his breath. He had come here on an impulse. Something Molly had said about Geoffrey's dreams of a face at his window had set him thinking.

He tried the cabin door, knowing it would be locked.

But it wasn't.

The latch moved in his hand and the door swung open. Cautiously, Tellico looked inside. Dusty rays slanted through the shadowed room. His eyes were drawn to the floor, where a brown crust showed the spot where Molly had died. He wrinkled his nose and averted his eyes.

Not a sound came from within the cabin. The place was ransacked, but Tellico did not know if it had happened at the time of the murder or later. Frowning, he quietly stepped inside.

For a long time he stood there listening and looking. Then he walked through the cabin, the floor creaking, his breathing tense and tight. At every corner he stopped, then moved around it quickly with his rifle ready. But he found no one there.

Within moments he had checked all the rooms but a small one in the back. The door was shut.

He approached it slowly, his rifle leveled at his hip, cocked and ready. A yard from it he froze; he heard a tapping noise, very faint, from the other side of the door.

Tellico's heart raced. His throat went tight and sand-dry. Steeling himself, he coiled his muscles, then drove forward, kicking open the door.

It burst back into an empty room. Tellico leapt inside, turning this way and that, almost firing when he saw a form before him and failed to realize for a moment that it was his own reflection in a full-length mirror. This was a bedroom. He looked in the wardrobe and beneath the bed. Nobody was here.

He stood, relieved. Then it hit him.

Tobacco smoke. The smell hung in the air. Somebody had been here only a few minutes before.

He went to the window, which was not quite shut. The unlatched shutters accounted for the tapping noise he had heard. Tellico raised the window, pushed open the shutters, and saw tracks in the snow.

Somebody on snowshoes. A light snow was falling, and the tracks were slowly filling, but they remained clear for the moment. He stared at them, suddenly wishing they were not there. He thought about turning away, pretending he had not seen them, and returning to town. Let Jared handle this job. After all, he was the appointed marshal, and Tellico was just a newcomer, here almost by chance....

No.

He had asked for this task, and he would see it through.

Tellico left through the front door and circled the house to where the tracks angled up the slope, cutting through the tamarack. Whoever had made the tracks had been careful to keep hidden behind the house. The tracks weren't too far apart; the man was not especially tall, nor was he heavy.

Tellico proceeded cautiously, though the amount of new snow in the tracks indicated his quarry was far ahead. Still, the farther Tellico got from town, the more vulnerable he felt.

The rise became more extreme and rocky. The path

narrowed. Eventually Tellico had to wind up a narrow gully extending up the mountain.

The sky grew more cloudy. Both the higher elevation and the rising wind made him cold, though the heat of exertion compensated somewhat for it. At last the pathway widened again and he came out into an area of barren rock.

Here the wind was incredibly strong. Over the years it had gnarled the trees so they looked like arthritic hands groping out from the mountainside. There were no tracks here.

Sweating, tired, with no sign to follow, Tellico paused on the windy rock face to gather his strength. Some minutes later he turned and began his trek downward.

Behind him moved a flash of gray and white. He whirled. Nothing. Perhaps it had been only a bird flitting over a gray boulder, or the wind-shaken branches of one of the stark trees.

Near the bottom of the mountain he stopped. Something lay in the snow. He hadn't noticed it on the way up, but it must have been there, judging from the amount of snow covering it.

It looked like a small book. He picked it up and dusted the snow from it. It was leather-bound, and inside was a portrait of a woman.

A chill shivered down his spine. This could have belonged only to the one he had tracked up the mountain.

Tellico tucked it into his pocket. Jared would want to see this. Occasionally he removed it and looked at it as he continued. Something about it teased at his mind, but he couldn't quite figure it out.

By now the sun was swollen at the rim of the western mountains, sliding down the sky. Tellico hurried, passing the Davison cabin and its window where little Geoffrey had seen a face that Tellico now was sure had been no dream at all.

His snowshoes kicking a white cloud, he entered the town and walked along its main street, grateful to be among buildings and people again.

Chapter 10

Louis Brooks was a strapping man nearing thirty, known throughout the camp as a fine marksman, a lucky placer miner, and a deacon of the Jerusalem Camp church who was sincere if not sophisticated. Tonight he rode counterclockwise around the random cluster of buildings that comprised the town, and pondered what a drab place it was. For him that was a novel revelation. Louis seldom ventured beyond his house after dark and usually saw Jerusalem Camp only by the more flattering light of day.

The butt of his well-oiled Spencer rifle rested against his thigh, the barrel pointed skyward. His circling, and the simultaneous clockwise circling of Sean McFee, had beaten into the snow a clear path that his horse followed without guidance.

Louis shifted his weight and smiled. He couldn't dare let anyone know it, but he was enjoying this. There was something exhilarating in riding guard; it fulfilled secret longings that Louis had coddled since childhood. He had missed military service, never encountered a hostile Indian, never seen an authentic outlaw or gunman, and because of his size and the peaceable nature of the people among whom he had been raised, had never even been called out to fight. It was very frustrating.

Louis had always longed to be heroic, but until now he had never had a chance.

Sean rounded the rear corner of the little book and confections store on the southwestern corner of town. His white stallion was almost invisible against the snow, making Sean appear to float like a ghost.

"Anything?" Sean asked as he passed.

"Nope."

"Good thing."

It was the same thing he had said every round, fifteen of them so far. Sean made something predictable out of everything he did.

After a while, Louis softly began whistling a nameless old folk tune and slumped in his saddle. This was too blamed easy. He knew that Jared and his newcomer deputy were convinced the town was in perpetual danger, but he was beginning to doubt it. The notion of a killer hidden in the mountains struck him as unlikely. He had his own suspicion: Horace Bailer. The old drunk probably had some personal grudge that he took out on his kin. As for the two murdered strangers, they probably were just a diversion from the obvious.

Here came Sean again. Louis rode past him. A few yards beyond, he halted his mount and turned.

Sean hadn't said his expected line.

"Sean?"

The white horse plodded on. Sean didn't turn.

Louis wheeled and went after him. He pulled up beside him. Sean stared straight ahead. He didn't blink.

"Sean, are you..." Louis's words choked off, for when he touched Sean's arm, the silent man slid slowly off his saddle into the snow. Sean's right thumb was gone.

Cold as he was, a sweat erupted on Louis's forehead. He backed away and opened his mouth to yell.

Something sharp touched his neck—just a slight sting, like a needle probe. But it took his voice. He reached to his throat and stared in disbelief at his hand when he pulled it away again, for it was drenched in brilliant blood.

Somebody had cut his throat.

He turned as weakness overcame him, and the last thing he saw was the gray figure and long knife that lanced forward like a sting. He fell from the saddle into the snow; the Gray Man loomed above and the knife came down again, again.

The Gray Man severed Louis's thumb and moved into the town, creeping silently into the alleyway between the millinery and the bank.

Horace Bailer turned the bottle upside down and shook its last drop onto his tongue. He licked the back of his teeth, wiped his mouth on his sleeve, and smashed the bottle against the iron stove. Fragments landed in a heap.

Horace paced around the room in a tight circle, shaking, wringing his hands before him and then clasping them behind. This was his routine since Molly's death —drinking and pacing.

Molly's death. His fault. He should never have left her alone.

He needed another bottle. But how to get one? All businesses were closed, Rupert was missing and his place locked tight, and besides, it wasn't safe for a man to go out on the streets with people so fearful.

But I got to have a bottle. Got to.

He went to the window and pulled back the curtain. He saw Red Pringle out there with his shotgun.

Small, wispy clouds scudded across the sky like roaches

on a pantry floor. They blocked the moon for one moment, let it shine through the next. Horace looked across the street just as the latest passing cloud unveiled the moon again and illuminated the false front of the Jerusalem Camp Gun Shop. That reminded him: Curly kept several bottles of good whiskey hidden away under a cabinet in there, slipping drinks from them when Isaiah and other church folk had their backs turned. And that back door of Curly's hadn't had a working lock in four years.

Got to have a drink. Curly won't care.

Red was gone now, somewhere on the other end of town. Horace was nervous about going out onto the street. But he could almost smell Curly's good whiskey. He went to the pile of dirty clothes in the corner and pulled out his coat, hat, and old boots.

The snow crunched beneath his feet, sucked at his boot soles with each step. He dug his hands into his pockets and trudged out into the main street, watching for Red. He hurried on as fast as snow and drunkenness would let him.

Sure enough, Curly still hadn't fixed the lock. The door swung open and Horace entered. He clicked the door shut and squinted into the darkness. Long rifles shone dimly in what little moonlight came in through the windows, pointing toward the ceiling in their neat oak racks along the walls. Powder casks and small kegs of solvent and gunstock finish sat at his feet. The shop smelled of oiled metal. Through the grate on Curly's stove Horace saw the remnants of the day's fire, a faint throbbing red beneath a blanket of ash.

He extended his hands to it, burning off the chill. Cozy place Curly kept here, still warm despite being closed for hours. Maybe Curly wouldn't mind if he curled up later in a corner and slept off the whiskey he would drink.

Whiskey. In which cabinet was it? He rummaged around, groping among dismantled firearms and strangely shaped gunsmithing tools until his hand touched cold glass. Smiling, he pulled out a half-full bottle of good rye. God bless you, Curly.

Fifteen minutes later Horace was in a near-stupor, wonderfully warm and content. He hugged the bottle like a lover, breathing slowly and deeply as he sat against the wall beneath the rear window. He raised the bottle and wrapped his lips around its mouth. As more liquor drained into his throat, something passed the window above him and cast a shadow across the floor beyond his feet.

Horace froze. The distorted shadow on the floor revealed a man was looking in the window. Horace watched with childlike fear, feeling like the shadow itself could see him. But the little part of his mind that remained lucid told him he was surely not seen, that his location directly below the window hid him. So he sat still, clutching his bottle, and tried not to breathe too loudly.

The shadow remained.

Frightening realizations came; he glanced about at the other windows, at the door that would not lock, and knew that if he couldn't be seen from the window above him, he certainly could be seen from the others if the silent watcher moved. Oh Lord, I'm a sinful man. I'll throw away the liquor if you'll keep me safe. Throw it away forever, Lord, or at least for a day.

The shadow vanished. For a moment Horace was relieved. Then he saw it again, this time outside the door.

He slid frantically across the floor, horribly scared, looking for cover. The latch clicked and the door moved slowly, gliding open on hinges lubricated with gun oil.

Horace pulled himself under a table as the open doorway silhouetted a man's form. The man reached down to loosen his snowshoes, then stepped in, heels clumping on the hardwood floor.

Horace tried not to whimper. From beneath the table he

watched the feet step across the floor and stop where the bottle of rye lay dropped, just now spilling the last of its contents onto the floorboards.

A hand descended and picked up the bottle. Then a voice: "Horace, you in here somewhere?"

Red. Thank God in heaven. Just old Red Pringle.

"I'm here, Red. I'm real sorry I busted in. I really am. I just needed a drink."

Red stooped and looked beneath the table. "Horace, I could've shot you."

"I know, Red. Thank you for not doing that, Red."

"Come on out and don't make noise. Something's wrong out there."

Horace grew just a bit more sober. "What do you mean?'

"I haven't seen Sean or Louis for quite a while. Maybe I've just missed them, us passing on opposite sides of buildings or something. But I think something's wrong."

Horace clambered out clumsily. "Don't talk so, Red. You scare me."

"You ought to be scared. When I saw you moving in this building I thought we had our man. I came in ready to shoot and almost did."

"I want to go back to my room."

"Come on. I'll take you."

They were almost out the door when they heard a sound from the front end of the store. A mouse scurrying across a newspaper, maybe, or a breeze cutting an unusual angle around the trim of the building. Whatever it was, it was enough to make Red stop cold and raise his shotgun.

"Leave it be, Red! Let's get out!" Horace said in a fearful whisper.

"Hush."

"Just let it be!"

"Shhhh!"

Red bent over as if stalking and gripped his shotgun

firmly. He crept toward the front of the store, peering about. Horace remained where he was until a big gust of wind rounded the building and shook the door in his face. He yelped and leapt back with remarkable grace, given his intoxication, and followed Red, preferring not to be alone.

"What is it, Red?"

"Keep quiet!"

"You see anything?"

"Blame it, Horace! Hush!"

Horace went no farther. He watched Red's slightly hunched form as he checked corners and probed beneath tables and behind partitions. At last Red turned, straightened, and shrugged.

"Just the wind, I suppose."

Horace wanted to tell him no, that it wasn't the wind, that a figure had emerged from the darkness behind him, but he couldn't even squeak, much less talk. He watched silently as Red stiffened and made a strange noise and dropped his shotgun. Red fell to his knees. He had been run through. Horace closed his eyes and thus heard but did not see the rest.

On Horace's gravestone, like Red's, they would put the words VICTIM OF MURDER. But for Horace that wouldn't be strictly accurate, for his heart already had stopped before the Gray Man with the long knife reached him.

When it was over and the bodies bore his identifying mark of mutilation, the Gray Man exited into the moonlight-mottled street, his blade flecking red onto the snow crust.

Chapter 11

Sleepless, Tellico lay on his bunk, his hands behind his head and his feet crossed. He looked unseeing at the low, shadowed ceiling. Images filled his mind.

A warm evening, dusky dark, with a drizzle of rain whispering on a canvas above. Thunder rumbled over leafless hills and gray lines angled down from the clouds to the gently rolling horizon.

A campfire struggled to burn in the clearing, and men in muddy boots, blue uniforms, and dark slickers moved about between the lines of canvas tents. Horses stirred about at a picket nearby, their smell pungent in the moist air.

Inside his tent a young chaplain knelt beside his cot and prayed. Oh God, give me an answer, for men die and I say words to them and feel unreal. Reopen my mind, Lord, to the understanding of your ways. Let me feel again the sense of your calling. Let me know the force that moves my life is you and the pattern of which I am a part is of your making.

Several nights now he had prayed like this, kneeling on the cold earth beneath his wet tent. But his answer had not yet come.

Since the war, everything had changed—including himself and the confidence he felt that God had called him to be a minister of the gospel. Upon joining the Union army at the outbreak of hostilities, he had at first done his job with righteous zealotry. The Southern rebellion appalled him. Atrocities committed against unionists in the border states disgusted him. He deplored slavery, and rejected its oft-heard scriptural justifications. He went into the war convinced not that God was on the side of the Union, but that the Union was on the side of God.

He still believed the Union was right, but now seldom thought about it. His broad view of the war had become obscured by the narrower view of its effect on individual humans. He had seen too many torn bodies, watched too many young men die to care much anymore about big causes and national concerns.

The chaplain didn't think he could bear to kneel by another field hospital cot upon which writhed some bloody-fingered, wrist-gripping boy who had never dreamed he would not be home within a month of signing on, but now would not go home at all.

He became aware of someone in the tent doorway. He looked up, peculiarly ashamed he had been caught with his head bowed. He stood. "Come in, Private."

His visitor was a slender, slightly wan young man. He ducked through the slitted opening and came inside. He slipped off his cap.

"Reverend, may I speak to you?'

"Of course. What's your name, son?"

"Cottier. Private Darius Cottier."

"Have a seat, Darius."

The young man perched himself atop a folding stool. The chaplain sat on the side of his cot.

"How can I help you?"

The young man looked at his own feet. "I'm going to die tomorrow."

"I beg your pardon?"

"I'm going to die tomorrow. I've known it for about a week now."

The chaplain searched for something to say. "Darius, there's not a man here who doesn't dream about dying."

"This is no dream. I can't explain it. I just know."

From his mental file the chaplain tried to pull the proper ministerial response. He did not find it. He felt awkward in his silence, and the younger man sensed it.

"Don't worry over it, sir. I didn't come for comfort. And I'm not planning to run away. I came because I want to leave this with you."

He reached into his pocket and produced a medallion, smoothly worn, slightly battered. He held it out to the chaplain.

The medallion lay cool and heavy in the chaplain's hand. Engraved on the slick metal was the image of a river and a tree. He closed his fingers over it.

"What is this?"

"It's a thing left me by somebody I never got the chance to know. I hold it sometimes, and think about how things might have been if... well, if things had been different."

The chaplain was confused. "Is this some sort of family token?"

"Yes, in a way. At least for me."

"Why did you bring it to me?"

"Because when I die tomorrow I don't want some reb pulling it off me and throwing it away." He paused uncomfortably. "But it's not only that—I just want you to have it, you in particular. Maybe it's because you're a man of God."

Man of God. The words hit the chaplain in the pit of his stomach.

The private looked more troubled and spoke more hesitantly now. "Reverend, why does a man choose to become evil?"

It was a strange question, another the chaplain did not know how to answer. But he tried. "We're fallen beings, Darius. Darkness and light together. Sometimes we choose the darkness."

"But why? Why would a man choose to murder another one, or steal..." Here he hesitated. "Or a father choose to desert his family and leave them nothing but a hell he created himself?"

The chaplain said, "I gather it's your family we're talking about here."

Darius Cottier nodded. For the next two hours he poured out the story of his life: desertion by his father even before his birth, the shame of bearing a family name ruined by the actions of a man he never even knew. Hearing it, the chaplain felt strangely humbled, ashamed of all the times he had complained about his lot, for young Cottier had seen much worse than he.

When he had told his story Darius and the chaplain prayed, Darius preparing himself for death. At length the young soldier rose, seeming now at peace. Outside the rain fell like hail, splattering the mud of the camp. The fire had surrendered to the downpour and now was just a steaming coal bed.

"God keep you, sir. We won't see each other again," Darius said.

The chaplain had the medallion in his palm. Darius looked at it and nodded. "I was right to give It to you. I think maybe there's a pattern to it all, even if we can't see it. Goodbye, sir." And he left.

That night the chaplain awakened to the crackle of thunder, wondering if he had merely dozed at his prayers and dreamed of the visit of Darius Cottier. But when he rolled in his cot the medallion lay on the trunk beside him.

The chaplain moved down a seemingly endless line of bodies covered with sheets soaked through with darkening blood. One by one he flipped them back, studying white faces, some with eyes tightly closed as if asleep, others with eyes wide open and scared, a few with no eyes at all.

These were old men and young, faces scarred and faces childlike. Some were freshly killed, others dead for days and horrible. Their stench was sickening; the chaplain held a handkerchief beneath his nose as he moved down the line.

Most were strangers, but several were men he had seen laughing and talking in the camps, or writing letters home or just sitting and staring as soldiers do before battle. A few were men who had sung and prayed in his services, or come to him in private for his counsel. *God, did I help them? I don't feel like I helped them.*

Then he turned another blanket and stopped. It was Darius Cottier. His face was white as bleached bone and unmarred, his lips and eyes closed.

The chaplain laid back the blanket and went out into the woods alone. That night he took a horse and rode away from camp.

Years now, yet the memory of Darius Cottier's dead face remained vivid. It haunted his thoughts, emerging at unlikely times, most often when he slept.

In the shack above Jerusalem Camp, Tellico rose and went to the stove. He opened the grate and added wood until flames rose and the room grew warm. He would get no sleep tonight, anyway; might as well have coffee.

He put the pot on to boil, went to the window, and looked out. No sign at the moment of the two who rode guard tonight; probably they were on the other side of town. He let the canvas curtain fall and turned away.

From the table he picked up the leather-bound portrait he had found in the snow. He hadn't yet shown it to Jared. Before he did he wanted to figure out what was so intriguing about it.

When the coffee was black and steaming he sat at his table and drank with slow sips, thinking back on the convoluted paths his life had followed since the night he had deserted.

He had never gone back to his home and congregation. He wrote a letter of resignation, then tore it up instead of sending it. Let them think he was dead.

He had ridden off with no aim in mind, crossing Missouri, meandering through many miles, months, and odd jobs, finally heading to Texas when the war was over.

He used his name at the beginning, but then one day someone asked him who he was and he gave a name he had once read on a map: Tellico. Why he did that he never figured out, but Tellico he remained from then on.

He worked as a hotel clerk, a line rider, a stage driver, even a barkeep. He slept in cheap rooms, bunk-houses, or beneath the stars.

Sometimes he would take out the medallion he now wore around his neck and look at it, thinking about the dead ivory face of Darius Cottier, and remembering the days God had been close and the pattern of life that Darius had mentioned had seemed apparent.

One night in a cheap hotel in Dallas, stirring on the feather-leaking, flapjack-flat mattress, he heard the door open and saw Darius Cottier enter. The young man, phantasmic and pale, seemed to float six inches above the floor, and he said: *Consider that there may yet be a pattern to it all.*

Tellico threw the medallion at him, and it clattered

against the wall and woke him up and he knew it all had been a dream.

He rode on soon after that, heading westward toward California as he followed a course that would inevitably lead to the snowbound Sierra town of Jerusalem Camp.

Chapter 12

Jared sat beside his father's sickbed, listening to his labored snoring, examining the lines of age marking his sallow face. He remembered when Isaiah's face had been young and strong; even now he could clearly picture his boyhood image of his father behind his pulpit, seeming ten feet tall as he boomed out the gospel like an angelic messenger. Jared had been in awe of his father throughout childhood; when Isaiah was in the pulpit he seemed to his young son like something between the earthly and the heavenly—flesh almost transformed to spirit. A magnificent but terrifying figure.

But he remembered as well the gentleness of that same face above him at night as he pulled the covers up beneath Jared's chin. And the short, beautiful prayer: "God, keep this son I love safe as he sleeps tonight."

Jared resettled himself for the hundredth time in the chair beside his father's bed. He drew tighter the blanket around his shoulders, his defense against the cold room.

"God," he whispered, "keep this father I love safe as he sleeps tonight."

He must have slept himself, for his next awareness was of

his own sudden movement—catching himself from falling out of the chair—and then of his father's eyes upon him.

Jared recovered his senses, then smiled. Since Isaiah s collapse Jared always forced himself to smile when his father looked at him, for Doc Hull said it was important to keep his spirits and hopes as high as possible.

"How you feeling, Pa?"

"Better, I think," Isaiah said. "Much better."

The words roused emotion in Jared, for though they were mangled by Isaiah's partly paralyzed mouth, they were the first Isaiah had spoken since his collapse.

Jared went to the bedside and put his arms around his father.

"I love you, Pa."

Isaiah smiled as best he could.

Ingersoll heard the noise outside his window. He thought at first it was Belle Montgomery's old red hound, digging in the woodpile for dead mice, but the more he listened the less likely that seemed. It sounded more like somebody moving around.

"Loren?" he whispered.

Then he realized it might be the killer. He reached to his bedside table and picked up his Smith & Wesson. He went to his window and peered out through the slats of the shutters.

For a while he saw nothing unusual, but as he was about to turn away a patch of darkness moved at the edge of the forest. His eye caught it, lost it, caught it again. It was a vague image, better seen from the corner of his eye than straight on. It moved, stopped, darted, stopped again....

A man. Ingersoll's breathing deepened, his hands began to sweat. "I got you, you murdering devil," he muttered. "It'll be Clyde Ingersoll who brings you down."

He put on his clothes in a clumsy rush and went to the door. He stopped, trying to calm himself. His heart pumped beneath his shirt like the bellows down at the smithy when Jared Cable was pumping the fire to its hottest. Common sense tried to take over: I'm not up to this; I'm not young anymore. The time I shot down two highwaymen outside San Francisco is long past. But common sense faded when he again heard the stirring outside. There was a chance for glory here.

Ingersoll opened his door as quietly as he could and went outside. He paused on his porch, looking left and right. His knees felt as gelatinous as tree gum.

He headed left around the house. He tried to keep to the shadows, to move without noise, but he did an oafish job of it. By the time he reached the back of the house, he knew he must have been detected.

The clearing and adjacent dark woodland were utterly still, a frozen scene of snow and evergreens. Ingersoll pointed his shaking weapon here and there from a tense gunfighter stance. Cold and tension made his neck hurt.

But there was nothing there.

Relieved but also disappointed, he lowered his pistol and turned back toward his house.

He heard the faintest hint of movement. He wheeled, training his pistol toward the edge of the forest from where the noise had come.

There... someone moving. He almost fired, but didn't. It might be Rupert.

"Loren?" he said. He immediately wished he hadn't. Here he stood, exposed, and now he was deliberately drawing attention to himself. He felt foolish.

He had two options: return to the house or try to determine who was out there. The first was the most inviting, but pride wouldn't let him take it. So nervously he stepped toward the woods.

There, up ahead. Ingersoll dropped to one knee and leveled his pistol, but then the form was gone. He rose, beginning to feel the thrill of the chase. Whoever it was, he was running away. Old Clyde Ingersoll had the best of him. He pushed on.

Two, three more times the same thing happened: He spotted the figure, leveled on it, then lost it. He swore each time.

The woods yielded to another clearing. To the right stood the boot store and two of the town's oldest cabins, one now a storage shed, the other a chicken coop. Here Ingersoll stopped, having lost view of his prey.

He saw movement between the cabins. The man was crouched, apparently, for he moved low to the snowy ground. Ingersoll smiled. Try to skulk away from me, will you!

He rolled up his strength like a fist and unfurled it in a spurt of loping bounds to the narrow alley between the log structures. His bulky form scarcely fit in the space. "Hold it!" he commanded. "Not a move!"

Belle Montgomery's red hound yelped and ran off, leaving Ingersoll to slowly deflate in private humiliation.

"A dog!" he murmured. "I just chased down a dog!"

Disgusted, ashamed, grateful that no one had been about to see him, he slid the pistol beneath his belt and turned to go home.

He saw a face only inches before his own. His heart nearly exploded. He staggered back, mouth open, and fell to his knees.

The man, teeth flashing, leaned over Ingersoll. His long red hair dangled about his face like the strings of a dirty mop.

"Why ye trailing me, old man?"

Ingersoll searched vainly for his voice.

"I'll slit your throat right here! Why ye after me?"

"I... I..."

The other, though, apparently didn't expect an answer. His train of thought already had jumped to a new track. He asked, "Ye got money, old man?"

"No. No. But here... you can have my pistol."

"I will at that." The red-haired man disarmed Ingersoll.

"Now listen to me, old man. Ye didn't see me, ye didn't hear me, ye don't know a thing about me. Ye been in your bed asleep all night. Savvy?"

Ingersoll frantically nodded.

"Tell me something—there a man name of Tellico about this town?"

Ingersoll nodded again.

"Where?"

"In the old cabin on the hill across on the other side of town."

The man grinned. "Ye done good, old man."

He put his foot on Ingersoll's chest and pushed him into the snow. "Word gets out about me and I'll squash the entrails out of ye like the mush out of a beetle. You savvy that?"

"I won't talk."

"I'd kill ye except they'd miss ye and start looking. That's the only thing between ye and eternity, old man."

"Don't kill me. I won't talk."

"That's right, ye won't. Now git."

Ingersoll stood, so scared he could hardly keep his balance. He flailed along, thrashing clumsily in his fear, until he reached his house. He entered and slammed shut the door, bolted it, then fell onto the floor, shaking.

The red-haired man checked Ingersoll's Smith & Wesson. A good pistol, and a bonus for him, a souvenir to mark the night.

He began circling the town, searching for the cabin where he would find Tellico. He did not see the gray figure who watched him from the darkness and then moved with no more noise than a whisper toward the flight of stairs leading to the second-level apartment of Claude and Matty Gregory above the dry goods store.

Tellico knew what he would find even before he rolled over the bodies of the dead sentinels. White faces with fearful expressions, thumbs chopped away from the right hands. Little warmth remained in the bodies. Whoever had done this could have been in town for some time now. He might have killed others already.

God, Tellico prayed, I've deserted you, but don't desert me. Especially not tonight.

He looked up to Jared's house. Should he rouse him? No. Not enough time. If Red Pringle still was walking guard in the middle of town he must be warned immediately.

Tellico loped as best the snow would let him down the slope toward Jerusalem Camp, wondering what kind of man it was who could surprise and kill two armed and mounted sentinels.

Jerusalem Camp was eerily beautiful here in the darkness. And eerily empty and still. Tellico entered the main street near the church, deliberately exposing himself so as not to surprise Red and risk getting shot. But as he moved through the town, he could not find Red.

Moments later he found Red's tracks in the snow, but that helped little, for Red had made many rounds and left tracks in all directions.

Tellico stood alone in the middle of town, trying to decide what to do.

Farther ahead a yellow spill of light moved across the snow. It came from Clyde Ingersoll's window; Ingersoll apparently was up and moving about inside with a lamp in his hand.

On impulse, Tellico headed to his door. Quietly, he knocked, then cupped his mouth against it and said, "Ingersoll—it's Tellico. Let me in!"

Ingersoll was a long time answering. When he did answer, the sight of him surprised Tellico: He was fully dressed, and the flickering kerosene flame from the smoking lamp in his hand illuminated the face of a man who apparently had been crying.

"Ingersoll, you all right?"

"God, Tellico, I'm glad you're alive. I was afraid I'd done you in.'

"What are you talking about?"

Ingersoll pulled Tellico inside and bolted the door behind him. He shook like he had a fever.

Within a few minutes he had spilled out his story. When Tellico heard the description of the red-haired man he frowned.

"I'm lucky he didn't spot me," Tellico said. "He would have dropped me where I stood."

"Who is he, Tellico?"

"An old acquaintance who couldn't have come at a worse time. His name's Frank Coop. Ingersoll, listen to me. There's more dead men out there. Louis Brooks and Sean McFee—throats cut and thumbs gone. And I can't find Red Pringle anywhere."

Ingersoll started to cry. Tellico seized his wrist.

"Pull yourself together, Ingersoll. This is no time for it. We've got to sound an alarm. The church bell— I should have thought of that before. You got a weapon?"

"That man got it off me." Ingersoll hesitated. "He... uh... had to fight me for it."

"You're lucky he didn't cave in your skull. You got nothing else?"

"An old shotgun..."

"Get it."

Ingersoll went with his lamp to a wardrobe on the west side of the house. It was hung with musty-smelling clothes. He pushed them aside and from behind pulled out an old percussion-cap double barrel.

He raised the lamp to examine the rusted weapon, and the window beside him imploded, curtains bucking in and shredding as three slugs ripped through, two immediately snuffing out Ingersoll's life, the third blowing apart the lamp and scattering flaming liquid onto the clothes in the wardrobe.

Chapter 13

A grating laugh pierced in through the shattered window. The voice of Frank Coop said, "I got ye, Tellico!"

Tellico had dropped to the floor when the shots were fired. Now he rolled toward the door. The wardrobe already was engulfed in fire. The burning clothes inside it spewed choking black smoke.

"Are ye dead, Tellico?" Coop bellowed. "Or do ye need some more attention?"

Tellico pushed himself upright and burst out the door, cutting to the right. He made for a nearby barn. From the corner of his eye he saw his foe come around Ingersoll's smoking house, and heard him swear in disappointment at seeing him alive. Red flashes and loud gunfire blasts ruptured the snowy stillness.

Jared had jerked awake in his chair at the sound of the first shots. "What the—" He rushed to the window and looked toward the town, but he saw nothing out of the ordinary, except lights flickering on in a score of windows as others reacted to the gunfire.

By the time Jared had hefted up his galluses and found

his coat, though, he saw something unusual: an orange glow on the far side of Jerusalem Camp.

He finished his rushed preparations. Anna appeared at the door, a white madonna in a gown of pale flannel. Michael nestled against her hip. "Jared—"

"I got to go, Anna. There were gunshots, and something's burning. I'll be careful."

She was saying something else as he went out the door, but Jared did not hear it. He did not want to, for fear it would overcome his resolve.

He trotted and slid down the hill, and encountered the dead bodies of the two sentinels, their horses still loitering nearby. For several seconds he stared at the corpses.

The orange glow steadily grew brighter, casting light against the tops of the conifer forest beyond it and silhouetting the row of buildings between the fire and Jared. The conflagration appeared to be at or near Ingersoll's house. Jared hurried, dreading what he would find.

In the meantime, at the far edge of town, Tellico ducked behind a rain barrel at the rear of a building. The water at the top of the barrel was frozen and piled with snow that overhung the rim like the head on a beer. Coop appeared at the end of an alley. Two slugs slammed through the rain barrel, making water spew but missing Tellico.

Tellico rose and snapped off a shot that plowed a furrow at Coop's feet. Then he ran. He stopped when he reached the other side of the gingerbreaded, brightly painted dress shop. He put his back against the wall, panting, and slid down until he sat on his heels.

He heard voices in the street—others coming now, roused by the gunfire and the blaze that now sent vast tongues of flame skyward.

Coop rounded the rear of the dress shop; Tellico whipped the muzzle of his rifle toward him and fired. Coop grimaced and cursed and jumped back minus a little notch of flesh from his arm. Tellico ran into the street.

"Hey! Hey you!" somebody shouted.

Tellico assumed the yell was directed at him, but it wasn't. Coop had emerged into the street and been seen. But the shout made Coop pivot and go back the way he had come.

The shouter was Witt Essler. Armed with a big shotgun, he ran haltingly after Coop like a man chasing a grizzly he isn't sure he really wants to catch. Something moved somewhere to Witt's right. Panicking, Witt spun right on his heel and sent buckshot patterning through the night.

Jared felt pellets fan his cheek.

"Witt! Hold your fire! It's me!" he shouted.

Witt almost dropped his shotgun. "God, Jared, I'm sorry..."

Gunsmith Curly Malone and a handful of other men appeared and converged in the middle of the street. Others rushed toward Ingersoll's burning house, scrambling for buckets, breaking the ice on rain barrels, and raising a babble of voices. Witt was shaking, still apologizing to Jared. Conversation for the next few moments came in a rush:

"Louis and Sean are dead," Jared said. "Has anybody seen Red Pringle?"

Witt said, "I didn't see Red. But I saw a red-haired man I never saw before taking after your deputy with a gun."

"After Tellico? Where is he?"

"I don't know. He headed yonder."

"What about the red-haired fellow?"

Witt pointed at the alley beside the dress shop.

Curly was looking at the fiery shell of Ingersoll's house. "Almighty God—is Clyde still in there?"

Suddenly, Witt pointed again at the alley and shouted a warning. Several shots popped. Jared felt like somebody had rammed a hot knife through the fleshy part of his upper arm.

He was hit with enough force to knock him down. The men scattered.

In the alley Tellico fired again at Frank Coop. During the confusion Tellico had recrossed the street and surprised Coop where he hid. Coop fired on him, Tellico fired back. The shot that had struck Jared was just a wild stray.

Tellico saw Jared fall and immediately forgot Coop, who took the chance to dart to the forest. Tellico came to Jared's side, picked him up by the left arm, and dragged him to the street. He gave Jared's bleeding shoulder a cursory inspection.

"Get Doc Hull," he ordered Witt.

"It's nothing," Jared protested. "Go after that man!" Then he fainted.

Tellico and Curly together hefted Jared to his feet, taking care not to stress the wound.

"Let's take him to my shop," Curly volunteered. "I've got some liquor hid in there we can clean the wound with."

Witt waved at Ingersoll's house, now thoroughly involved with the fire. "What about Clyde?"

"He's dead," Tellico said.

Claude Gregory looked into the snakeskin whiteness of a pitted face framed by a tangle of matted hair. The Gray Man drew back his lips and showed a row of broken yellow through a mustache that overhung his mouth.

"It's been many a year since I saw you last, Claude Gregory. Oh yes, I know you. And you know me, too."

"Please," Claude pleaded. "Do what you want to me, but let her go. She's done you no harm."

The Gray Man turned his yellow smile down upon the elderly woman struggling in his arms. "Indeed. Why should any man harm the loved one of another?"

"Damn you!" Claude whispered hoarsely. "Crawl back into hell and leave us alone!"

"It's hell indeed I came from, and soon enough I'll return. And I will have company."

Tears brimmed in Claude's eyes.

The old man looked at him with contempt. "You think you can move me with tears? Who saw *my* tears when I tore at dirt and rocks until my fingers were eaten away? Did you cry for me or for the son you took from me? Did you?"

Claude sobbed. "In the name of God, let my wife go!"

The Gray Man kept talking. "How many times have you lain awake at night, Claude Gregory, trying to forget what you did? I haven't forgotten."

"Please, let her go."

The Gray Man laughed. Matty struggled uselessly. The grime-caked face drew near to hers.

"Just how well do you know your husband, my dear? Has he ever told you about his little trip to Carolina thirty-five years ago?"

"Claude, make him let me go!"

Claude put his hands over his eyes.

"Perhaps I should tell you, if he hasn't. About this fine Christian gentleman who tried to cover his sin with shovels of dirt and years of silence. Do you want to tell her, Claude, or shall I?"

Claude suddenly grew angry and went at his tormentor.

The Gray Man flung Matty aside. Her head struck the corner of a cabinet and she collapsed. Claude wrapped his fingers around the old man's throat and began to squeeze. Suddenly he stopped. He staggered backward, blood streaming from a shallow stab wound above his stomach.

The Gray Man brought up his long knife again.

But then the noise of gunfire came up from the street below. The Gray Man went to the window and peered out.

Claude, fighting to keep his senses, tried with his hand to stanch the flow of his blood. The unsteady light of Ingersoll's flaming house detailed the angular profile of the old man at the window.

The man dropped the curtain and turned. Claude was crawling to his wife's still form. The Gray Man went to him and kicked him over. Claude lost consciousness.

The Gray Man knelt and stretched out Claude's right hand and brought out his knife again.

When he was done he spilled coal oil on the Gregorys' threadbare old couch. He removed the globe of a lamp and cranked the wick high. "For my son," he said, as he tossed the flaming lamp onto the couch.

He opened the door quietly, and with great stealth slipped back into the night, making for the forest.

Anna Cable heard the rattle of the latch and looked up in both anticipation and dread. The door swung open; Jared was there. His arm was bloodied and bandaged. "Don't fret, I'm all right," he said. "Just a scratch."

She went to him, put her arms around him, and kissed him.

"I've got coffee waiting for you, honey," she said. "Come in and sit down."

"Where's Michael?"

"Asleep in the chair beside Isaiah."

"Is Pa all right?"

"Sleeping, too. Here—sit." She put the coffee in his hand.

For several minutes Jared let the hot drink put life back into him and calm him.

"We saw him tonight, Anna."

"Saw who?"

"The killer. A red-haired fellow." He took another sip. "Tellico almost got him."

"Almost," Anna said, disappointed.

Jared smiled and touched her hand. "I love you. Couldn't make it without you."

"You don't have to."

Jared lowered his head. "It's hell down there, Anna. Five people are dead."

Anna gazed at him in horror. He continued. "Sean McFee. Louis Brooks. Red Pringle. Horace Bailer. Poor old Clyde Ingersoll. And Matty and Claude—he burned their place around them. We barely got them out, both of them unconscious. They may not make it yet. Claude had been stabbed. And his thumb..." Jared's eyes misted. "Clyde wasn't so lucky. There's nothing left of him at all. Horrible."

"How could one man kill five people?"

"Maybe he's more than a man. Maybe he's a demon."

"You have to get some sleep, honey."

"I can't. I'd just feel worse."

Anna hugged him. "I'll fix you something to eat." She went to the stove and stirred the fire.

Below, at the far edge of town, Tellico stood beside the black shell of Ingersoll's house. He sought out the place where Ingersoll had fallen. My fault he's dead. Coop was trying to kill me. My fault—and my responsibility to do something about it.

Chapter 14

Jared, trailed by a dozen men, picked his way up the steep incline of the snowy mountain. He was weary from his restless night, and his eyes blazed angrily.

Tellico should be here. But he wasn't. Not a trace of him. He had run out when things were at their worst.

Jared was ashamed he had trusted him so.

He couldn't dwell on that now. Had a job to do. An overwhelming sense of unreality hung over this whole amazing affair. Five dead in one night! And three well-armed when it happened. What kind of enemy did they face here?

Witt touched Jared's shoulder. The wind howled so loudly Witt had to shout at him.

"Wind's blown over all the tracks!"

Witt was right. They had been moving blindly ahead with little to guide them. The wind whipped the dry snow into shifting drifts, hiding real trails, creating false ones.

"So what do you suggest?" Jared yelled back through the bitter howling.

Witt shrugged. "Head back?"

"No. Keep moving. Maybe higher up we'll see something."

Witt looked skeptical, but Jared wouldn't stop. To him, just trying was better than sitting down there in that fear-ridden town, dreading the approach of another night.

So they continued up the slope. The wind screamed like a demon.

Elsewhere in the mountains, Tellico was as frustrated as Jared. He seriously pondered climbing up on some rock or deadfallen tree and yelling as loudly as he could for Frank Coop. He hated this impossible cat-and-mousing. Coop probably was three miles away from here by now. Coop was tenacious, certainly—that he had trailed Tellico as far as Jerusalem Camp proved that. But he wasn't foolish.

You've probably written me off by now, Frank Coop, but I've not written you off. You're trapped in this valley like the rest of us, whether you know it yet or not. I'll find you.

The defiant thoughts felt good but meant little unless he could find Coop quickly. Before dark he would have to return to Jerusalem Camp. At the moment the town needed every man.

Frank Coop. The very thought of the man took Tellico back to his first encounter with the red-haired devil.

That had been in Placerville. It was the end of an autumn day. Tellico rode in on his bay mare. He was hungry and very thirsty.

He saw a stark little outpost ahead, surrounded by a pine-pole fence and a pack of mangy strays. Several horses were tethered out front; from inside the light-spilling interior, loud laughter and shouts echoed out into the dusk. A saloon. He didn't think much of saloons, but he was thirsty enough to overlook that for the moment.

He tethered up beside the other horses and went to the

door. The clamor inside grew louder. He pushed open the door.

Unexpectedly, the saloon grew quiet as a funeral parlor. The dozen men inside turned to him with odd expressions on their faces.

Tellico stood stock-still in the doorway, wondering what he had walked into. Then from the midst of the group erupted the shrill cry of a woman: "Mother of God, help me!"

One of the men cocked his head and looked at Tellico like he was trying to peer through his insides. "Having us a little party, he said. "Kind of private."

"Where's the lady?" Tellico asked.

The man misinterpreted Tellico's intent, for he relaxed and grinned broadly. "If you're patient you'll get a turn too."

The group shifted, and what Tellico saw revolted him. A young Mexican lady cowered on the floor against the far wall, clinging to her torn clothing. Her lip bled and she looked pleadingly at Tellico.

Tellico felt like someone had just clubbed him in the gut.

The noise began anew as a big man with hair the color of fire moved toward the girl. His grizzly-paw hand swept down and roughly grasped her wrist.

"C'mon, honey. C'mon now," he said. "Old Frank Coop's nice to girls that are nice to him."

Tellico felt locked to the floor, but the floor seemed to be rocking. The girl looked at him again, imploring his help, but he remained still.

The red-haired man pulled her to her feet and wrapped his arms crushingly around her. His broad face went to hers, and he kissed her. His long red hair strung down over her cheeks.

The girl pushed him back and spat like she had ingested a roach.

Coop's smile died. He cursed, then brought up his hand and slapped her. The blow threw her against the wall, where she collapsed, stunned. Coop went toward her.

Tellico fired a shot through the ceiling. Again the place went quiet and every man turned to him. He was as surprised as any of them, for he had done it almost automatically.

"Put that away," somebody said. "Wait your turn like the rest."

Tellico waved the pistol across the group. "Against the wall, hands up," he said. "Ma'am, you come with me."

The girl ran to him, past him, out the door. "Mine's the bay mare," he called to her without looking away from the men. "Unhitch her and mount up. I'll be out directly."

"We'll swing you from a tree," somebody said. Another man slipped a hand beneath his coat. Tellico shot him through the knee.

"If anybody else moves, it's his judgment day," Tellico said. "When I get outside I'll be watching. So much as a face at the window and I'll put a hole through it."

Tellico backed away to the door. But suddenly the girl came back inside, and this time she had Tellico's saddle rifle.

"No!" Tellico shouted in tandem with the first blast.

Men screamed. One fell, then another. The shots continued, the girl yelling with every shot. It became a scene out of hell: men falling, blood on the floor, screams of agony and panic.

Somehow Tellico got her outside again, and on the horse. He freed and spooked the other mounts there, then mounted in front of her. The bay mare ran clumsily because of a loose shoe, but it ran well. When night came they were far from Placerville. The girl was asleep beneath Tellico's blanket and Tellico himself sat on the edge of a bluff hidden in brush, watching the road below where riders searched unrelentingly. One of them was Frank Coop.

Her name was Maria Alvarado, and in the light of morning Tellico saw eyes surprisingly different than those of the crying victim in the saloon. These were as cold as any he had ever seen before, and hard as marble.

She asked him who he was and why he had helped her, and he tried to explain. When he told her he had been a preacher, she laughed.

"You, senor, are a preacher? Well, for money I will make you a very happy preacher, no?"

Tellico merely looked at her.

She laughed again. "You are shocked at me? You sell holy words. I sell myself."

"Is that why you were in the saloon? It was not a rape?"

"Oh yes, it was rape. That happens sometimes to us. But I thought they would kill me this time. That is why I was afraid and angry. That is why I shot them."

Tellico turned away. God in heaven, what have I gotten into? Maria Alvarado had used his rifle—his rifle—to wound and probably kill several men. He himself had wounded one. There wasn't a court in the land that wouldn't hang him. He was at the least an accessory to murder.

They rode overland, through the mountains, and so escaped capture. Maria seemed to feel no remorse at what had happened, or any fear of its consequences. She offered herself to Tellico again and again, laughing when he spurned her. It was a tremendous joke to her until the final time, when he became angry and shoved her to the ground. She burst into tears and ran away.

The next night she stole his rifle and food and walked away. When Tellico found she was gone he was joyous. Let her have the rifle and the supplies; it was worth it to be rid of her. He was just glad she hadn't stolen the bay. She probably would have, if she could have done it without awakening him.

He rode to San Francisco and found a job cleaning and maintaining a store building with two attorneys' offices overhead. From one of the office windows, as he cleaned one night, he saw Coop ride in with two other men. They were so close he could hear their loud talk through the open window. Coop called one of them Mansell, the other Joe.

The next day he did not see them and hoped they were gone, but then word came back to him that they were asking around for someone of his description. Tellico thought about running, but pride and lack of resources wouldn't allow it. One night shortly after, he encountered Coop in the street. Coop reached first but Tellico somehow got off the first shot. Coop did not stay to battle; he turned and ran.

Tellico ran too, hiding elsewhere in the city. The next morning he sought out a church and attended the service, drinking in every hymn and word, stumbling to the altar when it was through and crying out a prayer. He walked out feeling better, cleaner.

But at dusk he saw Coop on the veranda of a brothel with a fat woman on his knee, so heavily painted she looked cadaverous. When Coop saw him he pushed the woman aside and came after him, shooting into the thickening darkness as Tellico ran. "I'm going to find ye and kill ye, Tellico," the bearded man shouted. "Hunt ye down like a varmint and skin ye alive."

Monday morning Tellico saddled the bay mare and rode out toward the Sierras, toward a little mining town called Jerusalem Camp. It was a place, he had once heard, where people worshiped God and a man could lose himself.

It did not take long to realize he was being followed. Frank Coop's threat, it appeared, was not idle. He and his partners really wanted him dead. Tellico had to outrun them.

So he had pushed on toward Jerusalem Camp as the first blizzard of winter blasted the Sierras.

Chapter 15

"Tellico."

The speaker was Coop, but Tellico hardly recognized his voice, for he had spoken softly and not in his usual harsh bellow. Tellico whirled to face Coop, who pointed a pistol at him from behind a boulder where he had been hiding.

"I could have picked ye off five minutes ago, but it's better to look ye in the face," Coop said. "And besides, I wanted to tell ye something."

Tellico asked, "How'd you find out my name?"

"That's just what I wanted to tell ye. The girl, she sang it out quick enough when we caught her. She won't sing no more." He smiled, letting the implication sink in. "Ye and her killed two of my oldest friends, Tellico, and in Frisco ye just made it worse. I ain't a man who forgets."

"I didn't kill anybody. I wounded one man."

"Ye killed, she killed, it don't matter. Ye did it together and I blame ye both."

Tellico wondered what Maria Alvarado had suffered at this man's hands before she died. He prayed for her soul.

"Drop your weapons, Tellico."

Rage boiled over. "No," Tellico said. Ignoring the risk, he swung down his rifle and fired off a shot, but the slug whined past Coop's head high into the mountain air. Coop fired his pistol. Tellico yelled at the impact of the bullet. It was like being pounded across the upper chest with a club. His feet kicked out and he fell on his back in the snow. The men were at the top of a steep slope, and Tellico rolled down it, staining the snow red as he went. Coops laugh became indistinct and more distant, muffled through a ringing in his ears.

Tellico slowly rose and examined himself. The bullet had entered low on his right shoulder. The wound hurt terribly, a pulsing kind of hurt that radiated out in waves from the bleeding hole.

He became dizzy and fell again, flopping across the top of a rounded boulder. Half conscious, he lazily slid down the other side, unable to stop himself, even when he saw there was nothing beyond the boulder but emptiness. He squeezed his eyes shut as he pitched into the air and fell about fifteen feet onto a huge, slanted rock face. He slid down it at a cross angle, and when he reached the bottom he was senseless.

His next awareness seemed to be a dream: He was dead, yet alive, too, and squeezed into a coffin far too small. It constricted his chest, squeezing tighter when he moved. It threatened to crack his ribs. Every breath came hard and painfully.

The dream gave way to reality, but reality was no improvement. He had reached the bottom of the sloping rock and was trapped firmly between it and a similar rock face that sloped down opposite it, forming a natural funnel. His own weight worked against him. He tried to move, but each time he only slid down a little farther. He had landed on his right side and his right arm dangled below him, touching nothing. He realized that he might not be at the true bottom of the funnel at all, that this tight hole might open into some dark Sierra cavern. He would never be found. His corpse would lie there, to rot and be eaten by worms and blind, crusty subterranean things. He could picture the foul, decaying thing that used to be himself, lost in ceaseless night.

He seized control of his mind at the last moment before panic. Think, Tellico. Don't give in. Figure out what you have to do and do it.

He evaluated his position. He could move a bit, though it hurt badly and seemed only to put him in more danger. His wounded shoulder ached horribly, but was wedged tightly against the rock and thus was not bleeding much. That was good, but that was about it.

He shifted his eyes to the left and looked up. The sloping rock face seemed endless; beyond its gentle camber the sky was an even gray. Much darker than before.

Night was coming. Tellico fought despair. His consciousness, mercifully, rolled away like a loose stone and so he did not have to watch daylight fade and darkness fall.

Where he was he did not know. He seemed to be floating in warm liquid, or hovering in the sky on a summer night. He felt no pain, just a strong sense of well-being. He opened his eyes.

He saw bursts of color spreading before him in no clear pattern. They moved and swirled, coming together to form images from his memory, lasting no longer than the faces one sees in the leaping flames on a hearth.

Tellico heard his own voice: Out of the depths have I cried unto thee, O Lord. Lord, hear my voice, let thine ears be attentive to the voice of my supplications.

Then something warm and furred brushed against his right hand and the dream became confused. When it happened again the dream vanished.

He opened his eyes as he felt a new stab of pain in his

wounded chest. Then, once again, a brushing, bristly something moving against the hand that dangled into the open space below the wedged rocks.

He curled his fingers, feeling helpless. Some beast down there—and any moment it would sink long teeth into his hand...

A happier realization came. If there was an animal moving down there, then there was a surface not far below. Hope arose. He squeezed his eyes closed. Out of the depths have I cried unto thee, O Lord...

He steeled himself and wrenched his body as powerfully as he could. He scraped between stones, yelled in pain, and fell hard against a smooth rock surface no more than five feet below.

Coop had long since given up on finding Tellico. He had seen him roll and fall out of view, but try though he did, he could not find him. Well, he must be dead. Couldn't have survived both a bullet and a fall like that. Job completed. Coop congratulated himself.

Now that night had come, Coop wished he was out of these mountains. It was mighty cold up here, and lonesome. Nothing to eat but a little hardtack. He wondered what had happened to Mansell and Joe. He hoped they had frozen to death, the lousy deserters. Mansell always had taken his poker too seriously. Losing a couple of games was no reason to split up their partnership and run out. He'd even taken Joe with him. And Coop sick and holed up in that deserted cabin.

He chewed his hardtack and huddled close to the small, smokeless fire he had built in a rock depression. It was barely enough to keep off the chill. He considered building a bigger one, but it could be that somebody from the town was still about in the mountains, unlikely though that seemed. Still, he had stirred up quite a ruckus in Jerusalem Camp. Watching the town after he escaped it the night before, it had appeared that more than one building had burned down. Probably spread from the fire in that house where he had shot at Tellico. Coop grinned, proud of himself.

He nodded and dozed until the fire burned low and the cold got to him. He blinked awake and rose with his blankets still around him to get more wood. He stopped, bewildered.

Across from him on the other side of the bed of embers he saw what appeared to be a mound of snow that, strangely, had not been there before. Maybe heat from the fire had melted loose some accumulation from a tree above. Yet now that he looked more closely it looked less like snow.

And it wasn't. It was a man wrapped in a gray-white fur cloak. He was looking down.

Coop danced back three steps in surprise.

"Who ye be? Why ye sneak into a man's camp?"

The man who was huddled beneath the fur cloak slowly lifted his head. Coop saw the glitter of two dark eyes. The man's form was hard to delineate in the darkness; he seemed part of the very mountain.

Coop spouted a threat, but with less bluster now that he had seen the unnerving eyes. "I ought to blow off your head, old man." He reached for his pistol and found the holster empty. The old man must have slipped out the pistol while he slept. He looked aghast at his tormentor, realizing that he was being toyed with like a mouse between a cat's paws.

Frank Coop screamed in tandem with the blast of the long Henry rifle whose muzzle suddenly prodded out from beneath the folds of the fur robe. The slug shot past him.

He turned and ran.

"I'm worn out," Witt Essler said to his wife. "Jared wouldn't give up the chase. We kept on long after we had lost all our sign."

Deb Essler gave him a terrible look. "Dead men in the streets. Thumbs sliced off corpses. Fires set to burn up old people. It's horrible. I can't understand why it's happening."

Witt didn't offer any answers. He was no philosopher and spent little time trying to figure out the whys of life. The whats were enough for him.

"I wonder what became of Tellico?" he said. "Jared thinks he cut out. Deserted after what happened last night."

"Good. I hope he has. This town has been a place of misery since he came. It's his fault," Deb said.

"Now Deb. You know he wasn't involved in the killing. It has to be that red-haired fellow I saw."

"And who did you say he was after? Tellico. Tellico may not be the killer, but he's the one who attracted him to Jerusalem Camp!"

Witt hadn't thought of it like that. His wife's words made some sense. Still, he wasn't ready to give up on Tellico.

"I don't believe Tellico cut out," he said. "I think he's out there in those mountains still looking for the killer."

"In the dark? No. He's gone. I hope he buries himself in an avalanche trying to go through the pass."

"Deb! You talk such terrible ways these days."

"These are terrible times. And this is a terrible town, Witt. I want to leave it in the spring. I don't want to live here anymore."

Witt patted her arm. "Honey, when we catch old Mister Red Hair you'll feel different."

"Pa?"

Witt and Deb jumped. They hadn't heard Jimmy slip into the room.

"The killer don't have red hair. Geoffrey Davithon thaw

him at hith window before he killed anybody, and he had a long gray beard. No red hair."

Witt briefly thought about it, then waved it off. "You boys ought not talk silly truck like that," Witt said. "Geoffrey's had enough trouble without making up spooks with gray hair."

"He didn't make it up, I thwear! Lee Weller, he theen him, too, looking at him from the edge of the woodth."

"Geoffrey Davison, Lee Weller...boy, you can't take the word of just anybody. I saw the man, and his hair was red as a woodpecker crest. And what are you doing up, anyway? You're supposed to be in bed."

"Can't thleep, Pa."

Witt smiled sympathetically. "Nobody's sleeping much these nights, son. Want to crawl in with us?"

Jimmy grinned, showing his gappy teeth. He climbed in between his mother and father, and was the only soul in Jerusalem Camp who felt utterly safe.

CHAPTER 16

Jared Cable came to his father's bedside.

"How you feeling, Pa?"

"A little stronger," the old preacher said in his twisted voice.

"I'm glad."

Isaiah said, "There's been more killed, I heard."

Jared's brows lowered. "Who's been talking to you? Michael?"

Isaiah nodded.

Jared glared. "I'll have a word with that boy, then. You weren't supposed to be told anything to worry you."

"Well, now I know. Tell me what happened."

Jared outlined what had occurred and who had died. Telling him about the near-murder of Claude and Matty was the hardest part. "The worst of it is he cut off Claude's thumb. He left Matty alone, thank God."

Isaiah closed his eyes.

Jared went on, "We went looking for the killer's trail but we had no luck. He's still out there."

The father and son sat quietly for a while. Finally Isaiah

said, "Jared, do you really understand that all men are sinners?"

Jared was puzzled. "Sure I do."

"I mean all men. Me included."

Jared nodded, wondering what his father was driving at.

"There are things a man does in his life—bad things he didn't want to do. Maybe he might think they're long forgotten, when they really aren't."

Jared was frightened by his father's seemingly directionless babbling. He wondered if the apoplexy had taken his mind.

Isaiah kept on. "Jared, it may be that soon you'll hear some things that you don't want to hear about me. All I want to know is that you'll love me just the same, and won't look down on me."

Now his voice began to rise and become choked with emotion. Isaiah gripped Jared's arm.

"You've got to understand, Jared, we didn't mean to do it. Nobody meant for it to happen. We were scared to death, that's all."

Jared could stand this no longer. He rose, pulling free from his father's clawing grip. The sallow hand fell back onto the sheets.

"You're getting all worked up and not making any sense. I don't know what you're talking about, and you don't either. You need to rest," Jared said.

Isaiah wiped his eyes. "We just didn't know what to do. We didn't mean for anything bad to happen."

"You're tired, Pa. Settle down. Sleep." He searched for something encouraging to say. "We'll have our killer caught soon enough. Witt Essler saw him—a fellow maybe close to forty. We'll catch up with him."

Isaiah appeared confused. "Forty?"

"Yes. You go on to sleep, now."

Jared walked out.

He closed the bedroom door gently. Alone, Isaiah looked to the ceiling and closed his eyes.

"Forty... then it isn't him after all," he said. A chuckle rose from deep within. "Praise Jehovah, it isn't him at all!"

Tellico could hardly breathe. The musky scent of fur and droppings hung thick in the atmosphere of this tight little cavern. He pushed up on his elbows and groaned. He had fallen directly on his wounded shoulder and blood flowed freely from it. It hurt like the devil.

He froze when he heard a growl nearby. In this black hole he could see nothing, but he had an immediate mental image of a dripping muzzle, cruel red eyes, a pink, hungry mouth....

"Easy, easy," he said. His hand slid back to his pocket and dug out a box of sulfur matches. "You don't want me, Ephraim. You'll break a tooth on me..."

He struck a match. It flared brightly for a moment before a burst of wind through the cave snuffed it. Tellico lowered his head in the darkness and sighed in relief.

Just a cub. More scared than he was.

He felt the wind again, and began crawling in the direction from which it blew.

The cub growled and squeaked and backed away, and Tellico made it out.

The night sky was half-covered with clouds; they lay like a gray beach against an ocean of velvet on which stars sailed. The moonlight delineated the serrated line of mountaintops against the backdrop of night. A vast and snowy desolation, wildly beautiful, but tonight seeming utterly alien and hostile.

Tellico found a recess, built a small fire, and let it burn to embers. He dug out a depression with his heel and kicked the coals into it, then covered them with dirt. He squatted Indian-style, with his legs circling the mound, and threw his coat around him like a robe to hold in the heat.

Lord, my shoulder hurts. Worse by the minute, and now I feel like I've got a fever. Let me make it until morning, and get me back to Jerusalem Camp.

He fell asleep and dreamed of the war and Darius Cottier.

How the old man had missed at that range Frank Coop didn't know, but he wasn't about to question providence. He had made it away with not a scratch. The bullet had whizzed past and he had turned on his heels and run.

When morning came, Coop struggled without his snowshoes through snow that reached his thighs. He came to the edge of the forest and waded into a snowfield, feeling very exposed. He continually looked over his shoulder, imagining he could feel the old man up there in the rocks, watching him, maybe drawing a bead on him.

Jerusalem Camp lay to the southeast. Coop pictured its warm houses, fireplaces, food... but Jerusalem Camp could never be an option for him. He pushed on.

He had in mind the deserted cabin in which he had been laid up sick when Mansell and Joe had deserted him—and where he similarly had deserted that battered-up old codger with the skis and busted ribs. The varmint would be dead by now, stinking up the place like a rat in a long-sprung trap. Oh well, maybe he would be frozen and not too rank. Coop could get rid of him, build a fire, snare a rabbit, and have a hot meal.

On the other side of the snowfield he found a ridge of rock from which the snow had blown clean. He climbed upon it and traveled much faster without leaving tracks. As the morning gave way to a cold noon, he reached and went through a familiar little pass. He saw the cabin.

Smoke poured from the chimney.

Amazed, he paused. That old fellow couldn't still be alive. Must be somebody else. A hunter, maybe... or the bearded fellow who had shot at him. No. Couldn't be. He couldn't have reached here that quickly.

Well, whoever it was would have to share that fire and whatever victuals he might have. Coop was almost frozen through, and he'd be hanged before he'd shiver outside when he could be warm by that hearth.

He crept as cautiously and covertly as his numb legs would allow him toward the cabin, wishing he were armed.

Tellico awakened feeling very ill. His wounded shoulder was swollen. When he stood he was dizzy and doubled over in dry heaves.

He realized he had to make it back to Jerusalem Camp soon or die. A fever would kill a man fast in the cold mountains. He forced himself to begin walking.

He either had to climb or circle the ridge to have any hope of reaching the town without getting lost. He was too weak to climb, so circle it would be.

He found a stout stick and used it like a crutch and balance pole. He wondered where Coop was, and if he was still looking for him.

Tellico felt too sick to care. He wondered if his wound was putrefying. He thought about looking at it, but decided against it. It would only make things worse.

He traveled through the morning and into the afternoon, stumbling along. His lack of snowshoes made progress difficult. He stopped for a few minutes to catch his breath, longing for rest....

Cold against his face woke him up. He had fainted and fallen prone in the show. Fear pulsed through him. He realized how dangerous his situation was.

He went on, even though he hardly had the strength to move.

The mountains and snow confused him. Too hurt and fevered to think, he wandered far off the course to Jerusalem Camp. He was unbearably cold.

Finally he saw a cabin ahead of him. It was occupied, for the chimney smoked and the window was a square of light. He descended to it, and collapsed at the door.

Someone moved inside. The door opened, and Loren Rupert looked down at him. Tellico figured he was dreaming. Dream or not, he crawled inside.

Tellico made it to the hearth and sank to the floor, bathing in heat. He let it drive the chill from him. He turned to Rupert, who was still there, looking too solid and tangible to be a hallucination.

Then he saw something on the floor. Frank Coop — dead. I'm seeing things after all, he thought blankly before he passed out.

Chapter 17

"It was amazing," Witt said to the men grouped around the woodstove. "There we were, just gone out to ride guard, when we saw them. Staggering in out of the woods. We almost shot them before we recognized them."

"Is it true Rupert was carrying Tellico?" asked a listener.

"Both carrying each other is more like it. Both in a bad way. Tellico's laid up in his cabin, still crazy with fever. Has a putrefied bullet wound. Rupert's doing better, and talking a mile a minute. I think he's right proud of being the one who did in the killer, even if it was an accident."

Witt outlined Rupert's story—how he had fallen and hurt himself, but had made it to a cabin where he found the red-haired man. The man had tortured him, asking for money and for information about Tellico's whereabouts, then had left him to die. But Rupert had found some canned food stashed in a cache beneath a floorboard, apparently there for years. He broke the rusty cans open with rocks, and on that food he had survived until the red-haired man unexpectedly showed up again, minus his weapons and the snowshoes he had stolen from Rupert. When he made a violent move toward Rupert, Rupert had picked up a heavy stick of firewood and swung at him. The move reinjured Rupert's ribs, but the red-haired man had fallen back and hit his head on the stone hearth, and from then on hadn't moved. Shortly afterward, Tellico also had appeared at the cabin door, in bad shape. Rupert, despite his own injuries, had nursed him as best he could and together they had made it back to Jerusalem Camp.

News of the death of the red-haired man brought elation to the town.

"But what I can't figure," Witt said, "is why this bird did what he did. It appears he was after Tellico— but why did he kill the Davisons, or Sean McFee, or any of them? And remember, the Davisons were killed before Tellico ever came to town. Some of it doesn't make sense. But one thing is clear: It was Tellico who drew the killer here. In a way that makes it his fault. I'll be anxious to hear what he has to say for himself once he's back on his feet."

Isaiah was much improved these past two days, and for that Jared was very grateful. The preacher was sitting up, talking, even walking about—and his speech was better. He also ate a lot more than before.

Jared attributed the improvement to the good news Rupert had brought back. The killer was dead; the threat was over.

For Jared it was a lifted burden. The only thing that bothered him was that the killer apparently was linked to Tellico. And Jared still did not understand Tellico's recent absence. Had he trailed the killer, or merely run away and encountered him by accident? Until Tellico was over his fever he would not know.

Jared pondered questions such as this as he carried his

father's midday meal to him on a steaming plate. He sat back and watched the old man satisfy his renewed appetite.

"Pa, what was that you said about the past and sin and all that?" Jared asked.

"Forget about it," Isaiah said. "It meant nothing."

Later, Jared headed up the hill toward Tellico's shack, where a couple of the town's men guarded him. Jared hadn't ordered it; the men of the town had taken the job on themselves. Jared found disturbing the amount of venom directed against Tellico now that he was perceived as being the one who had—at least indirectly—brought the Killing Winter to Jerusalem Camp.

"How is he?" Jared asked.

"Back among the living," one of them said. "His fever broke."

Tellico nodded a greeting when Jared entered.

"How you feeling?"

"Like I've been run over by a wagon." He rubbed his wounded shoulder. "I understand I've gone from deputy to prisoner again."

"Well, it seems pretty evident to folks that you attracted the killer to Jerusalem Camp."

Tellico scratched his thickening beard. "Frank Coop. He was after me, that I can't deny. He blamed me for the deaths of some friends, though it wasn't me who killed them. No need to go into all that, though. The important thing is that Frank Coop wasn't the killer."

"Not the killer? He shot Ingersoll, didn't he?"

"He did, thinking it was me, because I had gone inside Ingersoll's house just a few moments before. But he didn't kill any of the others."

Jared, eager like the rest of the town to believe the threat was past, did not like what he was hearing. "How can you be sure?"

"Because I know who the real killer is. Let me show you."

Tellico reached beneath his shirt and removed the medallion.

"I got this during the war," he said. "A young soldier named Darius Cottier gave it to me the night before he was killed. It was a memento of his father, who deserted his mother before Darius was born. That wasn't enough to keep the father's reputation from ruining the lives of Darius and his family, though. The boy told me all about it. Darius's father was a wicked man. Maybe insane, maybe just evil. He did some terrible things. There was talk that he had killed some people. There was an older Cottier son, too, who people said was almost as bad as the father. Darius never knew him, either.

"When Darius was old enough he became obsessed with finding his father. Strange though it sounds, the boy seemed to think that if he could only meet the man, that things could be made right, that they could be a real father and son. But he never did find him. Before Darius was killed he had some kind of premonition of what was about to happen. He brought me this medallion... and talked like somehow I was supposed to have it." He paused thoughtfully. "I wonder if he had a premonition of more than his death. I wonder if he somehow could foresee all of this..."

Jared said, "What are you trying to get at?"

Tellico looked him in the eye. "Darius Cottier never found his father. But we have."

Tellico picked up the leather-bound portrait from the bedside table.

"I went out to the Davison cabin alone, just looking around, and found signs somebody had been there shortly before. And I found this in the snow." He opened the case and showed the portrait to Jared.

"The woman bears a strong resemblance to Darius Cottier. I didn't notice that at first—but then I discovered this."

He held up the medallion and the portrait, and slid the medallion into a depression on the leather-bound case. It fit perfectly.

"Darius said the medallion was a token of his father, the only thing he had that had been his. And the medallion obviously came from this case. The killer wasn't Frank Coop. It was—is—Darius Cottier's father."

Jared pondered it, then rejected it. "That's insane, Tellico. I can't believe that."

"Remember what Martha Davison said when we talked to her—how little Geoffrey saw a face in his window before the first murders? Go ask Geoffrey if the face was young or old. Ask him if it was red-haired or gray. Go talk to Claude Gregory when he's able—ask him if it was a red-haired man who broke into his place and nearly killed him."

Jared took the medallion from Tellico. He fingered it. "All right," he said. "I'll ask. But if you're right..."

"The danger isn't over," Tellico completed for him.

"I hope to heaven you're wrong."

"I'm not."

Lee Weller, his head bowed, closed the door to Isaiah's bedroom and shuffled over to the bedside. There he stood wordless.

"Lee, what can I do for you?" Isaiah asked.

"I want to give you something," Lee said. Never raising his head, he handed his mail-order catalog to the preacher.

"What's this?"

"It has pictures in it. Of ladies," Lee mumbled. "I... look at them."

"Oh." Isaiah laid the catalog on his lap. "Why did you bring it to me?"

"Because it was all my fault, all the people getting killed. God made it happen because I looked so much at the pictures."

"Why do you think that?"

Lee seemed surprised at the question. "Because of you, Preacher Cable. The things you say in the church."

Isaiah was amazed. "But how have I made you think that God would actually cause murders because of such a little thing as you looking at this?"

"But you said there's no little sins, Preacher Cable. You said that, and that God punishes sin unless we confess it."

Isaiah thoughtfully repeated, "Unless we confess it."

"I never confessed about the pictures, Preacher Cable," the childlike Lee said. "I just kept on and kept on doing it." His lip trembled and tears came. "But I didn't think nobody would die because of it. I just didn't want to have to tell, that's all."

Isaiah looked at him with moistening eyes. "It wasn't your fault, Lee."

Lee mulled that over. "Really, Preacher Cable?"

"Really. Let that burden be gone from you. I know how heavy it can be." He hesitated as if unsure whether to say more, but then he continued. "For a while I thought the killing was my fault, Lee. I really did. You see, there are more men in this town than you with unconfessed sins."

But Lee wasn't listening now; he felt purged. "Thank you, Preacher Cable. I don't want to do wrong things, not really. But sometimes I do."

"The apostle Paul had the same difficulty, Lee. You are in good company."

When Lee was gone the old preacher thought about what had just transpired. Eventually he went to sleep, but after only a few minutes a hand touched him. He looked up.

"Hello, Isaiah," Doc Hull said. "I need to talk to you."

Isaiah wiped the sleep from his eyes.

"What is it, Logan?"

"This town thinks the killer is dead. He's not."

Isaiah was confused. "But Rupert said..."

"A man named Frank Coop died. But he wasn't the killer. Isaiah, the thing we were afraid of, the thing you and me and Claude have all been worrying about—it's true."

Isaiah grew pale. "How can you possibly think that?"

"I talked to Claude not an hour ago. It was no red-haired man who attacked Matty and him. It was... him. Claude recognized him."

Isaiah closed his eyes. "Does anybody else know?"

"I saw Jared going in to talk to Claude himself only a little while ago."

Tears brimmed in the preacher's eyes. "Why can't what's dead and gone stay that way?"

"Because it never was dead and gone at all. We only thought it was. We thought we could be silent and it would never find us out. It's almost funny, really. We seemed to think sin was restricted to the Ruperts and Ingersolls. But not us, not the holy men with the Bibles in our hands. And all the while it was eating us up inside, gnawing like vermin."

"I don't want to hear it."

"That's our problem, Isaiah—we never wanted to hear it. But now we have to hear it. And tell it."

"I couldn't bear that."

"We have no choice. People are dead because of something we did."

Isaiah suddenly became defiant. "No. I don't believe it. I

won't. The killer is dead, just as dead as that man we buried years ago."

"Claude recognized him, Isaiah."

"Claude's a fool."

Doc pondered his friend, then rose. "You're lying to yourself, Isaiah."

Rage surged within the preacher. "Damn you, Logan!" he shouted. "Damn your filthy soul!"

"That's right—it is filthy. As black as yours from carrying a secret for too many years."

As Doc left the room, Isaiah grasped at the nearest thing at hand and threw it after him. It was Lee's catalog, and it slammed against the wall and fell to the floor, opening to reveal plump etched women in etched undergarments.

Jared, fresh from a disturbing meeting with Claude Gregory, sat on a snowy step with his elbow on his knee and his forehead resting on the heel of his hand. Tellico had been right. It was no red-haired man who had attacked Claude and Matty. It had been an old man with a long gray beard. Claude had confessed it with surprising reluctance.

"Why didn't you say something, Claude!" Jared had exploded. "You've sat up here and let this town believe it is safe when all the time the real killer is still out there, alive!"

Claude had not answered. He just sat and rubbed the place where his thumb had been, while Matty ordered Jared out.

Now Jared faced the prospect of telling the town the thing it would least expect and least want.

Somebody approached. It was Doc Hull.

"Come to the church, Jared," Doc said. "I have a story to tell you. It will answer your questions."

Jared nodded, rose, and followed Doc to the church as fine new flakes of snow spat from the sky. He dreaded what he was about to hear, but knew he had to hear it.

In the church house Doc took a deep breath, closed his eyes for a moment, and began his story.

Chapter 18

The Western North Carolina Mountains, Autumn 1845

The storm came over the mountain like a rampaging beast, and the forest cowered before it, bending and trembling. The maples gave up the last of their leaves, leaving only the hardier beeches and oaks to cling to the twisted hulls of their dead summer foliage.

Through a massive thicket of laurel, five men ran from the coming rain. They laughed when the rain poured upon them long before they were near shelter.

In the lead ran Jubal Wallen, the most fleet despite his stocky build. He darted between the laurel tangles with his rifle muzzle-forward as if he were in a bayonet charge. At the top of the rise overlooking the hollow where the cabin stood he stopped and turned to the others coming up behind.

"Isaiah Cable, you're slower than your dullest sermon!" he shouted down at the lean, black-haired man who scrambled up toward him, grinning in the driving rain. "Not yet forty and you run like an old man!"

Isaiah came to Jubal's side, panting, and slapped Jubal's shoulder. "And you chatter like an old woman," he said.

Jubal laughed again, his ruddy face bright even on this murky afternoon. That was one of the things Isaiah loved about this man—brightness seemed to pour out of him, sparkling in his eyes and enriching his laughter.

Logan Hull reached them, followed a second later by Claude Gregory, whose soggy, shuck-colored hair hung around his face like an inverted bowl. The fifth man, Jubal's brother, Turner, owner of the cabin and long-time resident of these Carolina mountains, came up last. The others were his guests and he didn't think it proper to run ahead of them.

"Let's head in, gentlemen," he said. "We'll cook up some of Jubal's venison."

Jubal had drawn first blood on this hunting expedition three days before with a single well-placed shot, and he had not tired of bragging about it. They had been here four days now, greenhorn hunters following Turner along the winding valleys and the limestone slopes, killing a little game and scaring off a lot that Turner by himself would have easily brought down. But Turner hadn't become impatient. This was the first time he had seen his younger brother Jubal in six years, and he was happy.

They dried out beside the fire, listening to the venison sizzle in the pan. Then they ate like starved men and drank a gallon of coffee. Outside thunder rolled across the sky like a mythological god. When night came the cabin was a warm pocket of golden light on the dark expanse of the mountains.

When conversation had waned and the men were sated and content, Turner suddenly lifted his head as if listening. A moment later someone rapped on the door.

The man whom Turner let in was as rain soaked and rumpled as a stray dog, and smelling almost like one. He was a humped-over caricature of a man, with thick brows and a short, wide nose. He turned his intense eyes around the room, looking at the strangers with concern.

"Who this, Turner, who this?" he demanded in a squeaking voice.

"Relax, Doyle," Turner said. "This is my brother and some of his friends. You've heard me talk about Jubal."

"Jubal? Oh yeah. Jubal."

"Gentlemen, meet Doyle Honaker. Old friend of mine."

Nods were exchanged, then Doyle said, "Got some meat left, Turner?"

The man was even more fascinating when he ate. He put on a loud-slurping, greasy exhibition as he downed a fat-marbled slice of meat, seemingly without chewing, pulling the food down his throat like a snake eating a mouse. None but Turner had seen anything like it. It was all Jubal could do to keep from laughing.

When Doyle's meal was through, Turner asked, "What brings you down tonight?"

"I think our old hermit has kilt somebody," he said.

Isaiah firmly shook his head. "No man is pure evil," he said. "However bad this hermit might be, there's some trace of holiness buried within him."

Turner said, "You don't know this fellow like we do."

"You some kind of preacher or something?" Doyle Honaker asked.

"I am. I pastor a congregation in Indiana," Isaiah responded.

"You a good preacher?"

"I like to think so."

"Ain't nary such a thing. That's like dry water or an honest lawyer." Doyle dropped open his mouth and wheezed. It took Isaiah a moment to realize it was a laugh.

Isaiah smiled politely. "I'll accept the joke. But I still maintain this man cannot be as thoroughly perverse as you say. What's his name, anyway?"

"He's never told and nobody's never asked. He's a devil as far as I'm concerned," Doyle said.

Turner walked to the fireplace and knocked the ashes from his pipe. "Preacher, Doyle's not exaggerating. There's something bad wrong with that man. I run upon him once, and you know what he was doing? Pulling some fresh-hatched mockingbirds out of a nest and mashing them under his boot—a slow crush. Like to have made me sick. The man's sin on two legs, in my book."

"Do you really think he's killed someone?" Jubal asked.

At that, Turner lit his pipe and looked wryly at Doyle. "Don't take this wrong, Doyle, but it wasn't two weeks ago you swore you saw a two-headed bear." One of the others snickered; Doyle looked offended.

"I'm telling you, there's a dead man up there!" Doyle said. "Probably somebody gone looking for the old hermit's silver."

"Silver?" two of them said at once.

Turner blew a smoke ring. "There's a legend hereabouts about an old Indian silver mine somewhere in the mountains. I never gave it much credence, but a lot of folks believe the hermit knows where it is and has a lot of silver stashed away."

"Could it be true?"

"Could be, I suppose. There has been some silver found here and there."

"What are we going to do about the dead man?" Doyle said.

"Go up and check tomorrow, I reckon," Turner said.

When morning came, the rain had dwindled to a sluggish drizzle. Across the Carolina ridges fog rose from land to sky, drifting between the mountains like smoke. Turner, his four guests, and Doyle rode across the sodden land toward the mountain where the hermit lived —a man who in the minds of the four newcomers had become monstrous.

"Does he always live alone?" Isaiah asked.

"Not entirely. Off and on there's a young fellow with him a lot, a raggedy-looking devil they say is his son. He's full-grown and mean as the old man."

"Think the younger one will be there?" Jubal asked.

"I ain't seen him in a spell," Doyle said. "But you can't never tell—he comes and goes."

"Where'd the old fellow come from?"

"Nobody knows."

"How does he live? Does he ever spend any of that silver he's supposed to have?"

"Not to my knowledge," Turner said. "He hunts, fishes. That's about it."

The wind grew colder as they rode, and when they entered a narrow valley lined with mossy rocks, Isaiah felt a mood of oppression come upon him. This was a dark and somber place.

He wanted to turn back. But he said nothing of it out of pride. He glanced about at his companions. From their looks he suspected they felt similarly uneasy.

"Where'd you see the body, Doyle?" Turner asked. They had been riding silently for several minutes now, and Isaiah started as Turner's words unexpectedly broke the quiet.

"Up yonder beside the shack," Doyle said. "Sprawled out right in the open."

They dismounted as a group and tied the horses.

"Tie em loose in case we have to get back on fast," Turner advised, which did nothing to ease the fears of the others.

Turner parted some brambles with his hand to give them a view. Atop a hill they saw a dark and almost shapeless shack on a pine-covered hilltop. They watched it a long time. Nothing moved. There was no evidence of life about it.

"Maybe the old man really is dead," Doyle said.

"Let's go see," Turner said.

"Should we take our rifles?" Jubal asked.

"No. Me and Doyle will take our pistols. If he's still alive and sees strangers coming up armed it might spook him."

Turner took the lead, Doyle right behind him and the others trailing.

"Phew!" Claude said. "Something's dead, that's for sure!"

"Doyle, you were right," Turner said. He pointed. A body lay crumpled in the leaves beside the shack's door.

Wrinkling their noses against the smell, and dreading to see the body up close because they knew the birds would already have worked on it, the four future elders of the Jerusalem Camp church approached behind the two leaders. Turner stopped short.

"That ain't the hermit," he said. His voice dropped almost to a whisper. "That's just a boy."

Isaiah looked closely and saw he was right. A boy in his mid-teens. He was dead. There was a rifle-ball hole in his forehead.

"Is this his son?" Isaiah asked.

"No," Turner responded. "Looks familiar, but I can't place him."

The men gathered around the corpse. Claude turned away, making the sounds of barely stifled regurgitation.

"Why would he kill a boy?" Turner said. Suddenly he gave in to a burst of indignation. He drew the pistol he always carried and stomped over to the shack. He kicked open the door and went inside. A moment later he was out again. He holstered the pistol.

"Nobody here. Murdering old sot is gone."

"What are you doing at my place?" a voice from nearby said.

The group wheeled about as one. An incredibly dirty, bedraggled man with long hair and a longer beard stood beside a pine on a small rise to the east. He carried a rifle, but it was not leveled.

"This is my place. Get away."

Turner said, "The hell we will. Did you do this?" He gestured at the dead body.

The man shifted the rifle just a little. Turner's hand moved toward his pistol. Isaiah wished he had brought his rifle. "That was an accident," the man said.

"Sure it was. Why did you do it?"

"I didn't. The boy was out hunting with some others. One of 'em shot him and run off. My son's gone to tell this boy's folks what happened."

"You're a liar," Doyle cut in. "This boy's been dead at least two days. What did he do—wander too close to. your silver?"

The man on the rise made a strange gesture with his lips and shook his head. Then a lot of things happened very fast.

He lifted his muzzle-loader and shot Doyle through the heart. Turner shouted and drew his pistol, but the hermit drew a flintlock from his belt and shot him, too.

The others scattered, diving for cover, but Jubal made a guttural noise and ran to his fallen brother. He knelt, cried out, then picked up his brother's dropped pistol and shot the man on the hill. The ball hit him in the lower body. He grimaced, put his hands on his belly as if suffering a stomachache, and crumpled over.

Doyle was dead, but Turner wasn't. The bullet had torn a shallow path through his side without puncturing anything vital, and though the impact had stunned him, he came around quickly and did not seem in particularly bad shape.

Jubal sat against a tree, crying.

"What are we going to do?" Logan Hull asked.

"This is terrible," Isaiah said. "Terrible... I'm a minister of the gospel. I can't be associated with something like—"

"Shut up, both of you! Let me think," Turner said. At the same time, thunder pealed and the wind kicked up. It was a moist wind, riding the head of a new storm. A few moments later the first drops fell.

"Into the shack," Turner directed. "Somebody needs to patch me up a bit, anyway."

Isaiah glanced at Claude. Both men were shaking. Claude came near Isaiah. "I feel sick," he whispered.

"I can't be associated with this," Isaiah repeated. "It would ruin me. Ruin me."

They walked to the cabin. "Somebody bring in Doyle," Turner said. "Ain't right to let him get rained on."

Isaiah and Claude both swallowed with dry throats and turned to Doyle's body. The dead face was now very white. They did not want to touch him, but did.

When they came in from the rain, dragging Doyle's body in, they found Turner holding a candle and staring at handfuls of silver molded into crude oval slugs that looked almost like coins.

"So, it's true after all," Turner said very softly. "Look at it!"

"There must be hundreds, maybe thousands of dollars here," Claude said in a tone of awe. He picked up a double handful and let it clatter back to the tabletop.

For a long time the men were silent.

"What should we do with this?" Claude asked.

"The silver isn't ours," Logan Hull said.

"No? Then whose?" Claude suddenly had a greedy look. "The man shot at us. I say we got a right to keep it."

"The man has a son."

Turner nodded. "So he does. But he ain't here now, is he!"

Logan shook his head. "It isn't right. We owe it to the folks of whoever that dead boy is to tell what happened." He said the words, but they didn't matter now and he knew it. A decision had already been made among them, unspoken but fully known.

"You realize, Claude, that I can't be associated with this," Isaiah said. He was still shaking.

Lightning crackled in the west. Branches grappled skyward in the wind like the hands of old men. Jubal began patching Turner's wound.

It took a long time for the rain to stop, and a very long time to dig the hole, so when they were done it was nearly sunset. The mud-covered men dragged the bodies of the murdered boy and the hermit to the hole's edge. The rain began falling again, but this time it was gentle.

"I suppose we ought to say a prayer?" said Isaiah.

The suggestion fell among the men like deadweight; the idea of prayer in these circumstances was a travesty.

"Which one first?" asked Claude.

"Just dump them," Turner spat.

The boy's stiff body made a gruesome slapping sound against the mud at the bottom of the hole. It landed face-down. Brown water pooled around it. The back of the head was terrible where the ball had exited.

"I can't believe we're doing this," Logan murmured.

"Shut up," Claude said. "You're as much a part of it as the rest of us."

"You want the silver, that's all," Logan said, but Claude pretended not to hear.

They dragged the hermit's body over and threw it in, too. "We should have made the hole deeper," Jubal said.

Suddenly they sensed another presence; the awareness flew among them like a whispered message. Turning, they saw a slender young man standing near the spot where the hermit had fallen. He was mud-covered and wet, had olive-toned skin and jet-black hair. His beard was thin and straight.

"What did you do to my father?" the newcomer said.

"He had an accident," Turner responded, walking toward the fellow. "He cut himself and bled to death."

"You're lying." The young man backed away. He had no visible weapons.

"Come and take a look yourself," Turner said.

"No."

"Come on. You can trust me."

"No."

Turner drew his pistol and shot the youth through the head. Isaiah screamed. His cry echoed across the drenched mountains like the shot that preceded it.

They dumped the boy atop his father. Now even Logan knew there could be no turning back—this was clear-cut murder.

Claude took the shovel and began madly tossing muddy dirt atop the still forms. He packed it crudely around them with the blade of the shovel.

Jubal blanched. "God, Claude, slow down—you've sliced off the last one's thumb," he said.

Claude did not slow down.

When the burying was done they spread leaves over the grave to hide it. They took the silver from the shack, Doyle's body they put atop the table, and set the shack on fire. They took the silver back to Turner's cabin, silently.

Chapter 19

"Things were different from then on," Doc Hull said. "We never knew if anybody ever came asking about any of the dead ones. We kept part of the silver, and Turner Wallen kept some. But we never had the heart to spend much of it. Blood money, you know.

"We went back to Indiana, never telling a soul what had happened. But we could hardly look each other in the eye. When the Mexican War started, I volunteered. So did Claude. Isaiah kept on preaching, and Jubal just kept hoarding the silver. Too guilt-ridden and afraid to spend it, yet unwilling to let it go. It destroyed him before it was through."

Jared had been listening with his forehead resting in his hands, his elbows on his knees. Now he looked up. "Are you saying the rumors were true—Jubal killed himself?"

Doc nodded. "I passed it off as caused by his heart. We folded his hands in the coffin to cover the slash on his wrist. Another deception we 'elders' agreed to. It was guilt that made him do it, and fear."

"Fear of what?"

Doc's answer raised bumps on Jared's arms. "Of the

hermit. He dreamed of him. Funny, it doesn't seem so ridiculous now."

"What finally happened to the silver?"

Doc smiled sadly. "We used some of it to establish this town. God forgive us, we used part of that money to build this very church house."

Jared's heart was pounding hard. "I never would have dreamed Pa could do such a thing."

"Your pa's a good man. But a man he is, not a god."

Jared stood and paced. He craned back his neck, trying to ease the mounting tension in his muscles. "But if the hermit is dead, how can what's happening here relate to him?"

"We thought he was dead. Maybe he wasn't. He might have dug his way out of that grave—it was shallow enough, and the dirt was loose and muddy." Doc looked at the floor. "It must have been like digging out of hell."

"And all these years he's been looking and planning, trailing all of you..."

"Apparently so."

"What about the son? It might be him."

Doc shook his head. "There was no question he was dead. I examined him too closely to doubt it. His father I did not."

Jared asked, "You say you used part of the silver to begin the town. What happened to the rest?"

"When Jubal killed himself, your father and Claude and I decided to get rid of it. They gave it to me and told me to hide it where it would never be found. I'm the only one who knows today where it is."

Jared was silent a long time. "My own father. Preaching and leading a church. And all these years hiding a killing and a theft."

"Don't reject your father, Jared. He needs you."

Doc looked at him, his face sad. Jared went to the door, pausing to ask, "Whatever happened to Turner Wallen?"

"He vanished shortly after it all happened."

Jared felt a chill. "So he was the first."

"Yes."

"And now, thirty-five years later, it happens again. And all of Jerusalem Camp pays the price for the sin of its elders." Jared spoke thoughtfully. "The sins of the fathers are visited upon the sons."

He slammed the door as he left. Doc closed his eyes and took a deep breath.

Isaiah stirred on his bed, rolled over, and slowly awakened. Jared sat beside him, staring coldly, and immediately Isaiah knew the secret had been told.

"Logan told you?" he asked.

Jared nodded.

"I never wanted you to know."

"I don't understand, Pa. Hiding dead men, taking their silver, never telling even of the dead boy you found. Do you think his family ever knew what happened to him? They may still be out there somewhere, wondering."

"Don't, Jared. Don't you think I've gone through all that in my mind every day of my life? There's been hardly a night I haven't dreamed of that open grave, the dead bodies..."

"But one of them not really dead after all."

Isaiah shuddered. "Yes."

"It's your fault, Pa, you and the other elders. The Davisons, Red, Sean, Horace... paid for what you did. You've stood in that pulpit for thirty-five years since then, telling others to confess and repent of their sins and accept forgiveness. And you and Doc and Claude sitting there covering and nursing your own guilt...in a church house paid for with stolen silver."

Isaiah turned his back on Jared. His shoulders heaved. A

sudden burst of sorrow rose in Jared, but dissolved like smoke. A gulf too wide to cross lay between his father and himself.

There was a noise. Doc Hull stood in the doorway. Doc came to Jared and put his hand on his shoulder. Jared shrugged it off like it was foul.

"Leave Isaiah alone for now, Jared," Doc said. "He isn't in condition for this kind of confrontation. It could kill him."

Inwardly, Jared wanted to put his arms around his father, but felt frozen in his place.

"I've got to go," Jared said. "I've got to tell a town who thinks it is out of danger that it really isn't. And convince it that Frank Coop wasn't their killer after all. Don't worry, I won't tell your secret. I don't have the stomach to admit that my own father..." He faltered and stopped.

Jared rose and walked out the door, slamming it behind him. Anna waited in the front room, an inquisitive and slightly frightened expression on her face. Jared stalked past her, put on his coat and snowshoes in silence, and left.

In the bedroom Doc remained with Isaiah, who now had stopped crying and was staring at the ceiling.

"I've lost my son because of you," Isaiah said.

"Somebody else lost a son thirty-five years ago and we just hid it away," Doc responded.

"Get out of here, Logan."

Looking older and more stooped than ever, Doc Hull shuffled out of the room.

Jared looked across a crowd of expressionless faces. He sensed their disbelief even before it was voiced.

Bolivar Brooks, brother of the late Louis, stood with his hat in his hands. "Jared, I don't buy it. Frank Coop had to be the killer. Otherwise, we have to believe there were two murderers in one isolated mountain town in one winter. That's too much to swallow." Among the crowd Jared heard murmurs of agreement.

Bolivar continued, "Jerusalem Camp has lived peacefully for years until suddenly this Tellico shows up, refusing to tell who he is, pretending to be some kind of town guardian, and acting as if he were a help to you, Jared. I think maybe he fooled you, fooled us all. It's clear Coop came after Tellico. Tellico brought this... killing winter to Jerusalem Camp. Seems to me he's likely to be wanted by the law somewhere, with associations like he's got."

Jared said, "Frank Coop came after Tellico for personal reasons. It was strictly between the two of them. He had no motive to have done any of the murders."

"What about Clyde Ingersoll?" Once again the crowd murmured, more animated now.

"He saw Ingersoll moving on the other side of a window and probably thought it was Tellico."

Someone in the group said, "You're going to have to do better than that, Jared. If Coop wasn't the killer, who was?"

Jared faltered. He lacked the will to reveal his father's secret, and had pledged not to do so besides. He looked across the crowd, bewildered, feeling almost as guilty as the elders themselves, for now he was hiding the secret just like they.

Suddenly he noticed Claude Gregory at the rear. Jared's eye caught Claude's; Claude broke the gaze at once.

"Claude, tell them," Jared said. "Was the man who attacked you Frank Coop?"

Claude's eyes darted as every man turned to him. He looked like a trapped rabbit. "Well..." Jared saw the struggle going on within the man. "Yes. It was Coop."

Jared's legs almost went out from under him. "That's

not what you said when..." He stopped. It was useless. The battle was lost.

Bolivar said, "Jared, I'm sorry. I think you're telling what you think is the truth, but the strain has got to you. You need to relax for a while and forget what we've been through. All we need to do now is keep Tellico under guard and wait for spring. It's over now, Jared, and you've got to let it go."

"I'll let it go all right," Jared said. He reached beneath his vest and removed the homemade tin star the town council had given him. He plopped it on the pulpit in front of him. "I'm officially through as marshal of Jerusalem Camp. If you're not going to believe you're still in danger, then I've got no choice but to protect my family and leave the rest of you to yourselves. I can't guard all of you alone, and the one man who would be willing to help me you're treating like a prisoner.

"The real killer is still out there. He's an old man with an old grudge against some in this town." He met Claude's eye; the old man immediately looked away. "He'll be back. He's got a long-standing debt to pay off."

"Who's he got a grudge against?" Bolivar asked skeptically.

"Ask Claude," Jared said, descending the platform and walking down the center aisle to the church door. He turned before he left and said, "Be careful. I'm warning you. It isn't over yet."

When he was gone, Bolivar turned to Claude, whose face looked white as the snow outside. "What's he talking about, Claude?"

"I don't know. It was Frank Coop who attacked me. I swear it was. I swear."

In the night Isaiah lay in silence, still thinking about what had happened earlier in the evening.

Jared had returned from his town meeting at the church house and described what had happened there. Then he had put his arms around Isaiah and told him he loved him. And forgave him.

Isaiah cried the most purging cry of his life. It was as if an ancient wall of ice inside him started to melt. For the first time in thirty-five years, atoning for his silence began to seem more important than keeping his secret.

"It's up to me," he whispered to the ceiling. He rose and stood, a pale figure in a pale nightshirt.

He dressed as quietly as he could, putting on his old black coat and hat and Jared's snowshoes. He left the house with his Bible in hand.

The night was cold. Trudging down the hill, finding walking difficult because of his apoplexy and his long idleness, he nevertheless felt better than he had in months. His beloved church house loomed invitingly below. There he could think and pray and read his Bible, and God would send him the answer he needed. He would show him how to make it right.

Quietly he quoted, "Have mercy upon me, O God, according to thy loving kindness: according unto the multitude of thy tender mercies blot out my transgressions..."

Panting for breath, he continued toward the church.

Chapter 20

Lee Weller bolted awake with a cry. He had just dreamed of a face at his window. He sat up in his bunk and scrambled for a match, with which he lit the kerosene lamp on the upturned crate beside his bed. He pulled his knees to his chest and wrapped his arms around them.

Only a dream. But when he looked at his window he cried out again, for the face really was there.

An old man, with long gray hair and a heavy beard. The eyes were amazingly intense.

Lee leaped from his bed, knocking over the kerosene lamp as he did so. Burning oil poured across the floor.

He turned the lamp upright, pulled a blanket from his bunk, and beat out the pool of flames. When that was done he looked at the window again. The old man was gone.

His heart racing, Lee squatted to the floor, shaking.

That was the same man he had seen at the edge of the forest several days ago. The one he had tried to pretend was imaginary—at least since everybody had been talking about the killer being dead and the danger over.

But what if they were wrong like Jared said they were?

But I'm not smart, Lee reminded himself. Everybody says I don't think good, don't know much about nothing.

He sat on the floor beside the flickering lamp, afraid to move, wondering what he should do.

Shortly thereafter, Bolivar Brooks arose from his own bed in his house across town. Alone there—for his wife always wintered in San Francisco and had been gone since before the first snow—he had heard movement in his kitchen.

Clad only in long underwear, he carried his Remington gingerly, tiptoeing down the narrow hallway.

At the door to the kitchen he stopped, took a deep breath, then quickly stepped inside, saying, "Hold it right there!"

In the darkness he saw nothing. Then he made out a still form at the table. "Who are you?" he said, thumbing back the pistol's hammer. But the figure did not move.

He edged forward—still it sat motionless—and from a shelf Bolivar pulled a match. He struck it on the kitchen hearth and raised it as it flared.

What he had seen at the table was not a man. It was a big fur cloak, heaped between the edge of the table and the back of a chair so it looked in the dark like a human figure. Confused, Bolivar stared at the cloak until the match burned his fingers and he dropped it.

The room went dark and something darker moved in the corner behind him. He did not see it. It fell upon him and after that he saw nothing at all.

The Gray Man put on his cloak. He left the house and looked down the dark street. From behind the closed shutters of the church house a light shone. He quietly moved toward it.

Tellico helplessly examined the small window in the room, knowing he could never squeeze through it. Two guards remained in the main room, and the odds of convincing them that he had seen something important would be as likely as convincing them just to let him walk out.

But he had to get out, for he had seen Isaiah walking down toward the church—and later another figure had moved across the snow far below. A man, creeping around the church from the other side.

What could he do? Tellico's two guards were more than he could hope to overcome by himself. One of them was built like a bull and the other was edgy enough to be dangerous.

From the talk of the guards Tellico had gathered something of what had happened; the townsfolk had refused to believe Frank Coop wasn't the one responsible for all the killings, and Jared had resigned in disgust.

The light in Jared's house was out. Right now Jared probably was asleep inside; he must be, or else he would have detected his father leaving the house.

How to warn him? Tellico's mind probed his options. At last he went to the door of his room and listened. He heard rumbling snores; at least one guard was sleeping. He tried the door, but it was locked.

"Hey, friend!" he said through the door, careful not to speak too loudly. "Friend!"

He heard somebody approach the door, but—as he had hoped—the snoring continued in the background. Only one guard was awake.

"What do you want?" said a sleepy voice just beyond the door.

"I'm dying of thirst in here," Tellico said. "Bring me a drink of water."

Muttering, the man moved away. The snores continued.

Tellico steeled himself, waiting, and breathed a prayer.

———

Jared awakened at the first knock. He went to the door with his shotgun leveled before him.

"Tellico, how did you get..."

"No time, Jared. Listen, I saw your father leave the house; I think he went to the church. But I saw someone else moving down there, too."

The possible implications of that took a moment to register in Jared's drowsy mind. "Oh no," he said. He ran back to Isaiah's room—indeed it was empty—then into his own room, where he tossed off a brief, confusing explanation to his wife as he threw on his clothes. He checked his shotgun.

"Can't find my snowshoes. Pa must have taken them," he said to Tellico. He stepped out into the snow.

"How'd you get loose?" he asked as he waded through the thick accumulation.

"One was asleep. The other I knocked out and caught before he hit the floor. It wasn't easy."

They trekked quickly down toward the church.

The Gray Man smiled at Isaiah across the tip of his upraised long knife. Isaiah's face was a white mask, its expression of fear accented by his drooping, stroke-afflicted mouth.

"So, it is you," Isaiah said.

"Indeed," the Gray Man said. "Back from the grave of corpses, where a man hugs the dead body of his son and fights for breath. Have you ever breathed death, Preacher?" He spat out the final word like a mouthful of bad water. "Can you imagine what it is to dig yourself out of the earth itself and find your home just a smoldering ruin and all your wealth taken? That is what you did to me, you and your companions."

Isaiah withdrew until his back was against the pulpit. "It

was never our intention to hurt you—we didn't go there to wrong you."

"But wrong me you did, Isaiah Cable. Yes, I know your name. I know all about you, and about Claude Gregory and Logan Hull. Even the dead Jubal Wallen. I've made Claude pay already. Now your turn. Logan Hull will be last."

He thinks Claude died in the fire, Isaiah thought. For Claude's sake that was one misconception he would not correct. "How did you learn our names?" Isaiah asked.

"Turner Wallen was a talkative man with the right persuasion," the Gray Man said. "He died talking, talking. I would have found you more quickly if the war hadn't taken you away. I lost your trail for many, many years, but I never forgot you. Now my time is drawing near. I will not go to my grave without sending you, my old attackers—and as many of your people as I can—to their own. That I vow before heaven and before hell."

"I am a man of God. You mustn't harm me."

"Man of God?" The Gray Man shook his head. "I know you for what you are, Preacher. You are a child of Satan, just like me."

He advanced, still speaking. "It has taken me more than three decades to find you, but my life has been well occupied. I'm a bloodthirsty old devil, I am. Old and young, male and female... I've drained life from them all." He laughed. "Had you succeeded in killing me those years ago you would have saved many lives, Preacher."

Isaiah asked, "The boy we found dead outside your cabin —why did you kill him?"

The Gray Man's smile broadened. "There are pleasures some of us know that your tender preacher's ears would not care to hear about."

Isaiah felt a wave of disgust. "Turner Wallen was right. You are pure evil—and a madman."

"Without a doubt."

The door burst open, and the Gray Man wheeled.

"You leave my friend alone, Mister," Lee Weller said. "You get away from him."

Isaiah slid to his rump on the floor. "Lee, get away. He'll hurt you."

The Gray Man cocked his head, perceiving Lee's slowness of mind. He smiled. "Come to me, my friend. Let me show you my knife. Have you seen one like it?"

"You're bad. You hurt people. Get away from Preacher Cable."

"I don't hurt people, Lee. They hurt themselves. They do things to me that are wrong, and I make them pay."

"Get out, Lee!" Isaiah ordered.

The Gray Man clamped his teeth together and turned on Isaiah. He lunged at him, and the blade struck the preacher in the arm. Isaiah cried out.

Lee bellowed and leaped forward, closing his hands on the Gray Man's throat from behind. The old man almost fell beneath Lee's weight, but balanced himself and lunged upward with the knife. The blade sliced Lee's hand, but Lee wouldn't let go.

Under other circumstances there might have been something comical in the wild dance that went on for nearly a minute—the Gray Man lunging behind him with his knife, vainly trying to reach the determined man who clung to him like a fighting dog.

Suddenly two more were in the room—Jared and Tellico. Jared raised his shotgun and shouted something, but when Isaiah looked back again at Lee and the Gray Man, Lee had been knocked loose but immediately had been taken hostage, the long knife impressing the skin of his throat.

It was a standoff posed in silence: the preacher, collapsed helplessly at the foot of his pulpit; Lee endangered, his face full of fear; and Jared and Tellico in the open church door, unable to do anything.

"Move aside," the Gray Man said. "I'm leaving here—and if anyone follows me from the town, you'll find this man's head ten feet from his body." As if to make his point, he let the blade tip break Lee's skin; Lee yelped as a few drops of blood ran down the long knife.

Jared and Tellico stepped aside, and the Gray Man exited, taking Lee with him.

Chapter 21

The two men who had guarded Tellico came around the side of the church. The smaller one had a blood-crusted lip.

"Jared, Tellico got away. He hollered for me and..." He stopped, having seen Tellico there with Jared. "Hey, what are you—"

"Save it," Jared interrupted. "No time for that. The killer's been back, and Lee Weller's been taken hostage."

"Who's been back?"

"The killer, blast it!"

"But I thought Frank Coop—"

"You thought wrong."

The two newcomers exchanged confused glances. The bigger one, a veteran placer miner named Carlen Flatt, growled out, "You're dreaming, Jared."

"He's telling the truth." The voice was Isaiah's. He stood in the church door, and leaned against the frame. "The man almost killed me. Lee saved my life and was taken hostage for his trouble."

"We've got to go after him," Tellico said. "Should I ring the church bell?"

"No," Jared said. "Our friend in the mountains would hear it and might get spooked—and I don't like to think what he might do to Lee then."

Jared heard a noise and spun, leveling his shotgun. He lowered it again when Witt Essler came into view.

Witt was very white. "Bolivar's dead," he said. "Thumb cut off." He paused long enough to shudder visibly. "I couldn't sleep... I saw somebody leaving Bolivar's place, went over and checked. Bolivar was in the kitchen."

Jared turned to Carlen. "You believe I'm dreaming now?'

Carlen shook his head.

They separated briefly, each preparing himself for the mountains, putting on extra clothing, snowshoes, gathering arms and ammunition. Snow began to fall, quickly growing to a near-blizzard.

"No point in going with the snow like this, Jared," said one of the men when they gathered again, for the group had grown substantially as the town awakened and word spread.

"I'm going, point or not," Jared returned.

"But you're not healed up—"

"I'm going. That's Lee Weller he's got."

Nobody else argued. The wind rose so that the snow seemed not to be falling so much as blowing from west to east. The group set out.

They had barely reached the base of the mountain when it became evident that Tellico could not keep up. He remained somewhat weak from his recent sickness, and his gunshot shoulder ached in the cold. Jared turned to him. In the wind he had to shout. "Turn back, Tellico! We can't slow up for you."

Tellico argued, but Jared prevailed. Tellico turned back, disappointed, feeling helpless. In the driving wind he went back to town. The church still was open; he went inside.

Isaiah was there, Doc Hull beside him. Behind Tellico the sky began to change; morning coming on.

"I couldn't keep up," Tellico said. "Jared ran me off."

"Your return was a godsend," Isaiah said.

"What do you mean?"

Doc Hull came to Tellico and gently touched his wounded shoulder.

"Are you well enough to use a shovel?"

"A shovel? If I had to, I suppose."

"You do. We're going digging for silver."

The old man pushed Lee before him like a mule, prodding him with the knife and threatening him with the Henry.

"Get on, half-wit!" the Gray Man ordered, prodding Lee again. The snow was terrible here, blinding and cold against Lee's face. They were ascending a narrow wash between boulders hard as frozen iron. Lee was numb with cold and beginning to feel faint.

"I can't go on," he said. He sank to his knees.

The old man cursed and raised the blade. As it descended Lee dodged it, more out of luck than design. Blindly he punched at his captor; his fist sank deep into the fur cloak and the man grunted and fell.

Lee rose and ran upward, hoping for escape. On up the slope he slid on ice and fell back. He tumbled into the Gray Man and together they rolled like human snowballs several yards. Lee struck his head, and when he stood he had difficulty focusing his eyes. In his blurred vision he saw the Gray Man draw near, blood on his face, the knife up and ready to stab.

Lee lunged desperately to his left, plunging over a bluff and disappearing into the whiteness below.

Tellico, ignoring as best he could the pain of his shoulder, dug the shovel again and again into the dirt on the grave-pocked hillside overlooking Jerusalem Camp. The ground had been frozen about a foot down into the grave, but now he was in softer moist dirt, and the work was going faster. The cross atop the grave slid slowly to the right and fell, turning the etched name of Jubal Wallen to the snow-spitting clouds.

Tellico wondered why the devil he was doing this. Doc hadn't fully explained. At the moment Doc droned on in a steady monotone to Isaiah, who had no business on the hillside in his condition, but who had refused to go back home to his bed. Most of what he said meant nothing to Tellico.

"I knew that here it would never be found, Isaiah. And it seemed fitting, letting Jubal keep it with him—the thing that so obsessed his last years. The silver killed him, and the guilt. Like Judas Iscariot, you know."

The shovel hit wood. Tellico looked at the two old men beside the grave. Their faces were white and pasty.

He dug until the coffin's redwood top was finally uncovered. He paused. "Are you sure you want to do this?"

Isaiah looked uncertain. But Doc firmly nodded.

Tellico broke the lock on the coffin. He stepped out of the grave, caught the lid with the edge of the shovel, and slowly pulled it open.

What was revealed caused all of them to draw in their breath.

Decay had left only a gray skull where Jubal's head had rested. Bony hands lay folded together, leathery skin clinging to the knuckles. But the overall shape remained that of Jubal in life: a hefty man, barrel-chested.

Then it all began to change.

As snow and wind blew across the skull, it began to crack and crumble, seemingly blowing away. Then it collapsed, and a moment later the broad chest crumbled as well, the black frock coat falling flat. But not at the center of the chest cavity, where the coat draped the outline of a small box.

"Logan—you put it inside him!" Isaiah exclaimed.

"It was easy enough," Doc answered. "A quick incision on the slab, the strongbox slipped inside the chest. It struck me as appropriate, somehow."

"Just get it out and cover him back up," Isaiah said, turning away.

Jared lowered his shotgun and called the alert. "It's Lee! Hold your fire!"

Lee it was, stumbling down the hillside. Thirty feet from them he fell and rolled, almost burying himself in snow. Jared was the first at his side. He put a finger on Lee's neck. "Alive—but near froze. We have to get him back to town. Carlen, will you take him?"

"I might be needed up here, Jared."

"You're the only man big enough to carry him," Jared responded. Carlen thought about it a moment, then nodded.

"Good. Don't go slow—he might end up losing some toes if you do." Jared rubbed Lee's face. "Lee— you're all right now. We're getting you home."

Lee's eyelids fluttered. He flashed a weak smile. "Thank you, Mister Jared."

"Where is he?"

"Yonder...up the hill. I fell a long way. Into the snow."

"Do you know where he was going?"

"I think to High Ridge, Mister Jared."

"We'll get him, Lee."

With Lee supported on his broad shoulder, Carlen went back down the mountain toward town as the blizzard churned about them.

With Witt at his side, Jared led the group farther up the incline. The effort seemed almost futile, but Jared wasn't going to turn back. It was time for conclusion, for final encounter. No longer was it unwilling marshal facing unknown enemy. It was Jared Cable, going after a flesh-and-blood devil who had threatened his father.

He wished he could have known before now that the killer was making for High Ridge, for he knew a shortcut. But they were too far up this route to take another.

Up they climbed into the great circle of mountains around Jerusalem Camp. The steep escarpments were heavy with snow, piled in sagging heaps that could drop at the touch of the wind or the shifting of loose rocks.

Their difficult path wound around a mountain knob. The man they pursued left a trail that was remarkably clear; he seemed to be floundering along. It should have sounded a warning to Jared; their prey left too obvious a spoor.

When they were high and the air was thin, Witt suddenly stopped. "Jared..."

"What's wrong?"

"I'm not sure. I think—"

A tremendous rumble from above rendered him inaudible. Jared looked up in time to see what looked like the mountain itself bending down toward him. He shouted but could not hear himself. He saw men rushing back, others knocked into the air, at least two swallowed in a vast descending curtain of white. Then he himself was under, his breath driven from his lungs.

Tellico met Carlen and Lee like a man would meet two ghosts; their forms materialized slowly in the storm, and grew more substantial as they approached.

The silver remained in its box, and the box was slung inside a cloth pack strapped to Tellico's back.

"Where is Jared?" Tellico asked.

Carlen, looking back at him suspiciously, pointed in the direction from which he had come.

"Have they caught him yet?"

Carlen shook his head.

"Where are they heading?"

Carlen's glower remained. "I don't know why I should trust you," he said.

"Because I might be able to stop some people from getting killed," Tellico returned.

Carlen chewed his lip, but Lee answered without hesitation. "High Ridge."

"Is there a shorter way?"

Finally relenting, Carlen answered, "There is, but it's mighty dangerous. You walk the cliff line to the west and cut right up to the ridge. It's a fast way if you can survive it."

"How do I get there?"

Carlen seemed impatient but gave quick directions. Tellico thanked him and turned away. Carlen could see Tellico was weary and weak. He'll not make it, Carlen thought. Last we'll see of him.

"Come on, Lee," Carlen said. "Let's go put some coffee in your belly."

"And pie, Mr. Carlen?"

"And pie."

Jared came to, staring at luminescent gray clouds. A bearded face appeared above him.

"I've been through worse than what just happened to you, pilgrim," said the Gray Man. "I've known what it is to have the earth itself on top of me."

He was perched on a boulder. The wind tugged his beard.

Jared tried to talk; it took four tries before he could get his voice out.

"Where are the others?"

"Snow buried a couple. Another couple got swept over the bluff there. The survivors dug out who they could and left. But they never found you. Must have figured you for dead." The Gray Man made a pushing motion with his hand. "It was easy—one shove and the boulder dropped and set off the snow slide."

Jared stood with effort. He tried to lunge at the seated man, but his movements were slow and forced. He fell short and dropped on his face. The Gray Man laughed.

Jared rolled onto his back and slowly sat up again.

"I'm not sure why I pulled you out," the Gray Man said. "I think it was your face. You remind me of a preacher I first saw about thirty-five years ago at a certain burial back in Carolina. I'd make a wager you're his boy. Right?"

"Let me go."

He laughed. "Well, this is just prime! Old preacher-man gives me the slip but I wind up with his boy!"

"Don't kill me. I've got a wife and son."

The old man's expression became bitter. He said, "I had a family myself at one time. A wife, a daughter, a son. I held my son's body in my arms in a grave your pa and his psalm-singing friends put me in. Buried alive just like you were just now."

There came a sudden noise behind Jared. He turned. It was Tellico. He had just come up along the treacherous cliff line. Tellico was panting and pale.

"There was a second son, too, Mister Cottier. He died on a battlefield the day after I met him. His name was Darius."

The Gray Man turned his Henry on Tellico. Jared

expected him to shoot Tellico at once, but he didn't. "Who are you?" he asked.

"Call me Tellico. I knew Darius."

"I never knew no Darius."

"He was born after you left home. He fought for the Union in the war. Died for it—and you were on his mind the last night of his life, Mister Cottier."

Jared couldn't interpret Cottier's expression. "You're lying," Cottier said.

"No lie. He searched for you, Mister Cottier. Wanted more than anything to know the father he never saw."

Cottier's thick brows nettled. "You're a liar—I'll blast you to damnation right here!"

With amazing calm Tellico said, "You don't have the power to damn anyone but yourself. You don't really want to kill me. Put down the rifle and come with me. Let me tell you about your son. The last night he lived he talked to me, but in his mind I think maybe he was talking to you."

Cottier seemed very agitated. For a moment Jared thought the old man might actually surrender his weapon, for it was clear Tellico's words intrigued him. But suddenly he cursed and fired a shot. It barely missed Tellico, but Tellico hardly flinched. The sound echoed between the ridges. The mountain gave another grumble as if disturbed in its rest.

"I'm going to show you something, Mister Cottier," Tellico said. Slowly he lifted his hand to his neck and pulled out the medallion. He untied the cord and tossed the metal oval to Cottier. The old man stooped and picked it up. His eyes changed as he recognized it. Then Jared tossed over the leather-bound portrait.

"Where did you get..."

"From your son. He carried it because it had belonged to you." Tellico paused. "Darius knew you beat his mother, and he had heard all the rumors. But he never gave up on you. He believed you to be a better man than what people said."

Cottier closed his fist around the medallion.

"Something else for you too," Tellico said. He loosened the strongbox of silver, which he had strapped to him, and threw it to the old man's feet, where it fell open. Some of the silver spilled onto the snow.

"They tell me that's yours," Tellico said. "If it is, take it."

Suddenly the mountain rumbled again, then made a cracking noise followed by another rumble.

Tellico extended his hand to Jared, who lay below the narrow ledge on which Tellico stood. "Up!" he ordered. "Get away from there!"

Jared rose. Cottier ignored him. He was looking at the medallion in his hand. Jared reached up; Tellico took his hand and pulled him higher. Grimacing, Jared made it to his side. The mountain rumbled again. They backed away.

"Cottier!" Tellico shouted. "Get away from there!"

The Gray Man did not listen. He knelt beside his silver, picking up a handful of it.

"Cottier!"

But he remained where he was while high above him another cloud of white bulged off the mountainside. Tellico and Jared turned and ran, darting madly along the narrow cliff's edge, deafened by the terrible roar as a new avalanche came down on the old man named Cottier, burying him this time in a grave too deep ever to be escaped.

Tellico and Jared looked at the place where Cottier had been. The wind swirled around the peaks, bitter cold.

"Over at last," Jared said. "Why didn't you just shoot him and be done with it?"

Tellico shook his head. "I don't think I was supposed to kill him. I think I was supposed to salvage what humanity was left in him, if I could."

"You talk like this all was supposed to happen."

Tellico shrugged. "Who can say? Maybe it's like Darius Cottier said—things follow a pattern. It's done now, whatever."

Together they began the long descent to Jerusalem Camp, so battered and weak they could hardly move.

Chapter 22

Spring melted the snow and brought warmth to the Sierras. The meadows bloomed and the air became fresh and warm.

Tellico strode down the hill from his shack and knocked on the door of the Cable house. Anna answered and greeted him.

"Jared in?"

"He's on the hillside again."

Tellico shook his head. "Hard for him to let go. Do you think he'd mind if I joined him there?"

"I don't think he'd mind at all."

Tellico found him beside the new grave that bore the name Isaiah Cable. Jared was seated in a tailor's squat on the ground.

"Jared?"

"Howdy, Tellico."

Tellico squatted beside his friend. "What would Isaiah think of you sitting up here grieving over him day after day?"

"I'm not grieving. I'm saying good-bye."

"He's been dead a month now. It's time for you to make the break."

"That the preacher in you coming out again? What I'm talking about is different. I mean saying good-bye to this valley. The whole town."

Tellico lifted his brows. "That surprises me. I never figured you would leave."

"Maybe I won't. I haven't decided. It's just not the same as before.

"The people?"

"Yeah." Jared plucked a blade of new grass, stood, and began breaking the grass into little pieces as he paced. "He stood up there before them and confessed something the best of them would never reveal if they had been the guilty ones—and they just, well... you know how they reacted."

Tellico answered carefully. "They had lost friends and family to a killer who came here because of what Isaiah and the elders did."

Jared tossed down the last fragment of the grass blade. "Yeah. But when it's your own father it hurts mighty bad. I wonder if the response of the people was what killed him."

"Isaiah knew what the price might be when he told the story," Tellico said. "It took a lot of courage. More than Claude had."

Jared nodded. Claude Gregory and Matty had left the valley at the first touch of spring—old people with nowhere to go and no means of support, running from the shame of a thirty-five-year-old sin, told in detail from Isaiah's pulpit. And Claude forever to bear a reminder of that sin in the empty place where once a thumb had been.

"Look yonder—there goes Doc," Jared said. The old man was shuffling across the street toward his undertaking parlor. "I don't see how he does it, bearing the silence and the dark looks. I looked for him to move on, too, but I don't think he's going to."

"Doc's a strong man."

Jared looked at Tellico and smiled. "First time you laid eyes on him you knocked him on his butt."

Tellico chuckled. "Seems a long time ago now. But it's just a season back."

"A long season."

For weeks Tellico and Jared had talked at great length, Tellico revealing more about his own life, his fleeing from the war and the pulpit, and his conviction now growing that he should return to the latter.

"At your old home congregation?" Jared asked.

"Probably not. The man I was then has been too long dead in the eyes of those people. I'm Tellico now, and Tellico I'll stay."

Jared laughed. "A preacher with a false name?"

"Like I said, I'm Tellico now. Nothing false about it."

"You don't have to leave, you know. There's a vacant pulpit in the Jerusalem Camp church."

"That's not for me to fill. But somewhere out there in some little town or on the backside of a mountain there's a place where I'll belong. I think the Almighty will get some use out of me yet."

"So your destiny takes you full circle, right back where you started."

Tellico nodded. "It's like somebody once said to me: You've got to consider there may be a pattern to it all, even if we can't always see it."

Tellico rode out a day later with no good-byes and no glances back.

Jared never left Jerusalem Camp. Time went by and the wounds of the Killing Winter healed.

Witt Essler, who now limped on an avalanche-injured leg, made sure the story of Tellico became part of Jerusalem Camp's folklore. The story grew in the telling until finally Witt believed his own embellishments.

"He was on the run from the law," Witt would say. "He was a gunfighter—I knew it from the beginning. He had that look about him, that bearing and way of holding his hands."

Then he would tell how Tellico had fought the killer in the mountains hand-to-hand until an avalanche buried both of them and only Tellico emerged. On and on, more and more.

Jared corrected the growing myth at first, then gave up. It finally reached the point where his corrections would not have been believed anyway. People wanted to believe Tellico was a gunfighter, so they did.

"He was a preacher, nothing more, Jared told Anna. "Just a war-weary chaplain who ran away from the killing because he couldn't make sense of it all."

Anna slipped her arm around Jared's waist and hugged him. A hawk swooped down from High Ridge over the broad valley, drawing the attention of both.

"Think he'll ever come back?" Anna asked.

"No," Jared said. "But I'm sure glad he came when he did."

A Look at: Bitterroot and Caine's Trail

Two Full Length Western Novels

Spur Award Finalist Cameron Judd brings to life Simon Caine, a man on a mission who will stop at nothing to right the wrongs done to him, evading capture and death along the way as he leaves a trail of cold, hard justice in his wake.

For Simon Caine the War Between the States never ended. In *Bitterroot*, the notorious outlaw has hunted down and killed the former Union soldiers who murdered his family. Now, saved from a lynch mob by John Crosston, a man with a deadly secret, Caine is offered a chance at a fortune. He must lead Crosston into the heart of the Bitterroot Mountains in Montana Territory and to a showdown with a half-mad half-breed and a team of bounty hunters. If Caine survives, he will face his most difficult confrontation of all—with his own lust for vengeance, the deadliest enemy he has ever known.

In *Caine's Trail*, To Forgive And Forget Is Not An Option. When Union soldiers butchered his family, Simon Caine strapped on a gun. Now the government wants to string him up, a hired killer wants to bring him down, and Caine just wants to forget. But greater danger lies ahead—a renegade Confederate and his band of brutal outlaws has kidnapped Caine's nephew. And when Caine comes looking to get him back, gun trouble explodes with every step he takes.

"Judd is a fine action writer." — Publisher's Weekly

AVAILABLE NOW

About the Author

Cameron Judd is the author of more than fifty published novels of the American frontier, two of his works having been national finalists in the Spur Awards competition of the Western Writers of America. He has written under his own names and pen names including Judson Grey, Tobias Cole and Will Cade. A native and lifelong Tennessean, he has three adult children. He and his wife, Rhonda, share their Northeast Tennessee home with a cornbread-loving dog named Lola. He is a former award-winning newspaper journalist and editor.

CPSIA information can be obtained
at www.ICGtesting.com
Printed in the USA
BVHW032310270522
638376BV00015B/673

9 781639 775101